THE BOHEMIANS

THE
BOHEMIANS

A NOVEL

Jasmin Darznik

BALLANTINE BOOKS · NEW YORK

The Bohemians is a work of fiction. All incidents and dialogue, and all characters with the exception of some well-known historical figures, are products of the author's imagination and are not to be construed as real. Where real-life historical persons appear, the situations, incidents, and dialogues concerning those persons are entirely fictional and are not intended to depict actual events or to change the entirely fictional nature of the work. In all other respects, any resemblance to persons living or dead is entirely coincidental.

Copyright © 2021 by Jasmin Darznik

All rights reserved.

Published in the United States by Ballantine Books, an imprint of Random House, a division of Penguin Random House LLC, New York.

BALLANTINE and the HOUSE colophon are registered trademarks of Penguin Random House LLC.

LIBRARY OF CONGRESS CATALOGING-IN-PUBLICATION DATA
Names: Darznik, Jasmin, author.
Title: The bohemians: a novel / Jasmin Darznik.
Description: First edition. | New York: Ballantine Books, [2021] | Includes bibliographical references.
Identifiers: LCCN 2020026372 (print) | LCCN 2020026373 (ebook) | ISBN 9780593129425 (hardcover; acid-free paper) | ISBN 9780593129432 (ebook)
Subjects: LCSH: Lange, Dorothea—Fiction. | GSAFD: Biographical fiction.
Classification: LCC PS3604.A798 B64 2021 (print) | LCC PS3604.A798 (ebook) | DDC 813 / .6—dc23
LC record available at https:/ /lccn.loc.gov/2020026372
LC ebook record available at https:/ /lccn.loc.gov/2020026373

Printed in Canada on acid-free paper

randomhousebooks.com

9 8 7 6 5 4 3 2 1

First Edition

Book design by Jo Anne Metsch

For Rebecca Foust

"I think we conjure up and invent people, and then whoever happens to be there is the recipient of our imagination. A good deal of the attraction between people, I think, is based on the fact that one is able to absorb the creation."

—DOROTHEA LANGE,
The Making of a Documentary Photographer

"San Francisco isn't what it used to be. And it never was."

—WILL IRWIN tO HERB CAEN,
San Francisco Chronicle

THE BOHEMIANS

1.

There's a picture of us that ran in the paper in 1918. In it we're
standing side by side, me with my Graflex around my neck and
Caroline with a smile that dares you to look elsewhere. She's
wearing a tunic with long, bell-shaped sleeves and a thick satin
strap cinched at her waist. It's a kind of costume, and so is my
outfit: flowy crushed-velvet dress, stacks of silver bangles, a long
paisley scarf. We both have bobbed hair, except that mine's a mass
of dark-blond curls and hers is black and sleek. There's a glint in
Caroline's kohl-rimmed eyes, but it's a black-and-white picture,
so you can't see their color, which was the color of cut glass.

Whenever I saw this picture in the years that followed, I was
immediately transported back to our studio at 540 Sutter Street
in San Francisco—or 540, as we'd called it. As if it was still just
the two of us, Caroline and me, so lit up with hope and so at
home. We'd both gone so long thinking we had no place in the

world that we couldn't imagine belonging to anything but each other. By the time that picture was taken, the studio had become our home, the home we built through grit and sheer will. We worked eighteen-hour days, Monday to Saturday. Exhausted as we always were, we loved it, every minute of it, but if there was a time we loved more than any other, it was those nights when our friends streamed down from Monkey Block. Everybody brought everybody, and 540 filled with music and dancing and brilliant talk.

Within two years all that ended and I was on my own again.

After the scandal broke and Caroline disappeared, I'd see the whole story come into focus in a single frame. What happened. What I could never undo. I'd see Caroline sitting on the floor, knees pulled up to her chin, head bowed. I'd see her lifting her eyes and fixing me with a distant, unblinking gaze. I'd see the shadow on her cheek that would deepen to purple by morning.

If only I could have picked up my Graflex, flipped open the lens, and taken a picture, there would have been some kind of proof. But I couldn't do it. I loved her so much, and in that moment I couldn't bring myself to capture her pain. Still, the story was in every picture I took afterward, in the ones people talked about and remembered, but also in the ones that were hidden, destroyed, or forgotten. Especially those. It's the image that never varies or fades, even though I'm the only one who knows it's there.

To take a truly good picture you have to learn to see, not just look. I once said a camera can teach you that, but the truth is that sometimes it only gets in the way. The realization was born that night. This many years later, it takes me back to San Francisco, to a portrait studio at 540 Sutter Street, to a ravaged darkroom where one story ended and another one began.

The first and most important thing that happened to me when I got to San Francisco was that I learned what it felt like to be alone and penniless, to have no tie to the world but fear, hunger, and need. That's where it all started for me.

I set out in the spring of 1918. I was nearly twenty-three, eager and restless, with just-bobbed hair. I had all sorts of ideas of who and how and where I wanted to be. I'd scrimped for two years to save the hundred and forty-two dollars folded inside my wallet. Two years of hand-sewn dresses, borrowed books, lunch pails of leftover mackerel or canned beans on stale black bread, but I'd done it. I'd seen my last East Coast winter. Nothing could hold me there any longer.

I sailed from New Jersey in a steamer, traveled five days down to New Orleans in a third-class berth, then another twelve days across the country by train. I'd been saving up to go to Paris, but with the war on there was no chance of that. My plan now was to spend a few weeks in San Francisco, then head south to Mexico. The details fell off from there, but I figured I'd just keep going until my money ran out, and when there was no farther I could go, I'd work out what came next.

I carried my camera in a case that hung to my hips. There'd been little else to keep and even less I cared to hold on to. On my lap sat a battered leather valise I'd picked up in a thrift shop before leaving home. It held a half dozen rolls of fresh film, a pencil and sketchbook, a few days' change of clothes, a toiletry kit, and a secondhand copy of Edna St. Vincent Millay's *Renascence*.

The train was crowded and noisy; the food was terrible and cost too much. For days I was tired and hungry, my body was stiff from trying to sleep upright in my seat, and my bad leg had cramped up, but the moment the conductor lurched through the car calling, "Oakland Station! Next stop Oakland Station!" I sprang to my feet, belted my coat, and gathered my valise.

Someone propped open a window, and a breeze rushed through the cabin. There was a great deal of shuffling and maneuvering around me; people were crowding on one side of the train, craning their necks to catch sight of something outside.

At first I couldn't make out a thing, but then I edged my way closer to the window and stepped up onto my toes. The bay emerged, splendid and sparkling, the low angle of the sun catching it and setting it aglow. When I squinted hard, I could make out steamer tugs and fishing boats and beyond that a city skyline, clinging to the edge of the earth and struck gold by the afternoon sun.

San Francisco. *The Jewel City. Paris of the West.* A place where everything—absolutely anything—could happen, and probably was happening at this very moment. A place you could disappear into if you dared.

Here it was. Here *I* was.

I'd grown up close to the water, not far from the Hoboken shipyards, but nothing prepared me for that first glimpse of San Francisco in May 1918. Until that moment I didn't know everything around a city—sky, land, sea—could make it look so small. But even if San Francisco seemed smaller than I'd pictured, it was still a thing of beauty and wonder, what with the bay and deep-green hills encircling it. Also, it wasn't just beautiful; it was foreign to me in a way Manhattan had once been and wasn't anymore. No one here knew me, which meant I could be whoever I wanted to be.

When the view disappeared behind factories and rows of

clapboard houses, I cracked open my camera case and admired my Graflex, its sleek metal shine, its perfect polished lens. Arnold Genthe had given it to me a few months after I'd started working for him. It was my first camera and by far the best gift anyone had ever given me. "You have an eye, Dorothea," he'd told me. It always made me smile, remembering that day. Genthe's eyes dancing as he held the camera out to me. The moment when I took it in my hands, felt its exquisite weight, and understood it was mine.

The train jerked and tilted and stopped. I made my way down the aisle and out onto the platform, half-carried by the crowd. I hurried along as fast as I could, as fast as my limp let me. Soon I was in the streets, heading toward the docks with my bag thumping against my thigh and my heart slamming against my chest. I had on a split skirt that ended at my ankles, a tan mackintosh cinched tightly at my waist, and high-buttoned brown boots. The boots could've used a shine, but I was bent on catching the very next ferry out to San Francisco, so that would have to wait for now.

The whole business was over so fast. One minute the ferry was rocking softly, easing into the terminal, and the next minute it bumped hard against the piles, jostling the passengers and knocking us into one another. I stumbled and nearly fell, but then a hand grabbed my waist, its hold warm and firm.

"Careful there, miss," came a voice from behind me.

I twisted around. The man standing there was handsome and beautifully dressed, with a three-piece suit and a checkered bow tie, blue eyes, and blond hair slick with brilliantine. I felt myself staring. It was rare to see young men nowadays, particularly young men out of uniform. Somehow the war hadn't claimed him—or hadn't claimed him yet.

It took me a minute, but I came back to myself, straightening up and lifting my chin. When I thanked him, the man winked and gave me the richest smile in the world.

Well, hello, California, I thought, and felt my cheeks go warm.

Once we disembarked, there was no sign of that young man, but it hardly mattered, not with all the plans ticking through my head. Then, a few steps from the ferry building, I happened on a bakery. Through the window I saw a stack of doughnuts under a glass dome. My stomach gave a twist. The last real meal I'd eaten had been somewhere in Texas. It was only some minutes later, when I'd ordered two doughnuts and a cup of coffee, that I reached into my pocket and discovered that my wallet had disappeared. I reached inside the other pocket, the one where I always kept my watch, but it, too, was empty.

For one wild, dumbstruck moment I stood completely still, heart kicking against my chest, and then it came to me in a slow seep of understanding: That handsome and beautifully dressed man on the ferry was a thief. In what I'd always count as one of the genuine miracles of my life, I still had my camera, but as for my money, it was all—every dollar of it—gone.

Don't go. It isn't safe. Think of your crippled foot. Back in New Jersey I hadn't listened to the words—heard them, yes, but I refused to let them stop me—but now, standing in a bakery without so much as a quarter to pay for my food and the earth still trembling and swaying under me after so many days in motion, I heard nothing else.

I stood for a moment. Felt myself slump against the counter.

I couldn't seem to breathe. I felt faint. No matter how hard I tried, I couldn't shake the image of the man from the ferry. His rich smile and slicked-back hair.

"Miss, are you feeling all right?"

The girl behind the counter was looking at me quizzically. She repeated her question.

"Someone's stolen my money," I managed to say. "It's all I have. All I *had*. My whole savings . . ."

There was an awful quiet, and then the woman in the line behind me, a matronly lady all wrapped in furs, snapped open her purse and paid for my food.

By then a small knot of women had gathered around me.

"She'll need to find a job," one of them said.

"And a place to sleep."

This evaluation was made as if I was absent, which I suppose in those minutes I was.

"They're always looking for girls at the canneries in Sausalito," the girl behind the counter offered. "Doesn't pay much, but it's steady work."

A bag had been placed in my hands. Two doughnuts. In the other hand was a cup of coffee. I'd been staring into the cup, but at this mention of canneries I raised my eyes. I'd worked plenty of jobs but never in a factory.

"There's a boardinghouse for girls on Bush Street," one of the women was saying now. "The Elizabeth Inn. Can't cost but a dollar a week for a room."

A dollar a week was a dollar I didn't have.

All at once I felt the velvety softness of a fine leather glove brush against my hand. I turned to find that the lady in the fur cloak had opened her purse again and was pressing something into my empty hand. A one-dollar bill.

"The ferry to Sausalito runs on the hour," she said, peering at me kindly through round-rimmed spectacles. "If you hurry, you'll catch the next one."

My face burned with shame, but this wasn't the time for pride. I took the money, dredged up some semblance of a smile, and said a quick thank-you.

Outside in the street I caught a glimpse of my reflection in a plate-glass window. It was a sorry sight: a thin girl with mussed-up hair, battered bag, and creased mackintosh drooping over her shoulders and dragging nearly to her ankles.

My coffee had gone cold. The doughnuts were a long way from what they'd seemed in the bakery window. I stuffed them into my pocket anyway. For the next few minutes all I could think was it was no wonder I'd been offered a handout. I was pitiable. Pathetic. Newly arrived less than an hour ago and already a charity case.

It was already late in the day when I made my way back to the ferry building. I lingered outside for some time, gazing up at the clock tower; it read a quarter past four. The street ahead was wide and teeming with people coming and going and streetcars and horse-drawn carriages trundling by. Gulls and seabirds screeched and careened overhead. The cold air smelled of brackish water, fish, and tar. I'd expected California to be a paradise of sun and warmth, but it was colder here by far than it had been back in New York. The wind kept snatching at my hat and I had to use my free hand to hold it in place, all the while clutching my bag in the other. From a café came the sound of a lilting love song I'd heard played everywhere all spring. It filled me with a miserable sort of rage.

Think, Dorrie, I told myself, *you have to keep your head.*

I'd tucked the dollar into my stocking for safekeeping, sliding it all the way down to my ankle. It might get me a room in a boardinghouse, but how would I pay for supper? Or breakfast? In the morning I'd go looking for a proper job. Until then I needed money—and quick—but instead of looking for the ferry to Sausalito, I headed down Market Street.

"Seventy-five cents to wash the dishes and clean up for the day," said the man in the first place I went looking for work, a hash house on the corner of Market and Spear. There'd been no one behind the cash register when I walked in, but then, peering toward the back, I saw the outline of a man in the dark corridor that led to the kitchen. Tall and wiry, he wore a collarless shirt and a pair of pants lacquered with grime. He was balding on top, and his sideburns had gone long and ragged.

"All that work for seventy-five cents?"

He coughed and spat into the blackened rag he was holding, then fixed me with a hard glare. My need must have been obvious, because all he said was "You'd have to scrub and sweep the floors, too."

The man's face was grim as a boot, but I held his eyes—I wouldn't be intimidated. It would take hours to clean up that kitchen and we both knew it.

I cleared my throat, squared my shoulders, and told him I'd do it for a dollar, nothing less.

He didn't bother answering, only shrugged as if to say, *Take it or leave it.*

I left it. Back on the street, my mind flashed to the bakery near the ferry building, to the girl behind the counter calling out something about canneries in some place across the bay. It seemed worth a try. At the next street corner, I asked a policeman where I could catch a ferry to Sausalito, only to find out they'd stopped going in that direction for the day.

I tried my luck in a dress shop, but I didn't get work, not there or in the next place or the one after that.

"Fine, I'll do it for seventy-five cents," I said, trudging back into the hash house. It was now past six. I was thirsty. Not just thirsty—parched.

"Fifty cents," the man countered.

I swallowed hard, my face flaming. "But you said—"

"That was two hours ago. Day's almost over now." He palmed a hand over his bald head. "Fifty cents," he repeated. His voice was calm, dry, bored. "Times are tough, missy, as you must surely know."

It was filthy work. The water that ran from the spigot was brownish, and there wasn't a clean cloth in sight. The kitchen smelled of burnt toast, milk long ago gone rancid, and other ancient odors I couldn't and didn't want to place. I held my breath against the stink and did the best I could with the dishes heaped in the sink, scraping off the crusty plates with a knife and polishing the greasy cups with the edge of an apron I'd found bunched up in the back of a cupboard.

When I finished with that, I started in on the floor. Another hour, I told myself, and I'd be done. I'd take my measly fifty cents and tomorrow I'd find something else. I got onto my knees and began working a rag over the floor. After a while I threw a glance over my shoulder, and I saw the man—he hadn't told me his name or bothered to ask mine—watching me from a few feet away, his eyes glued to my backside. I glared at him, my blood rising, but he didn't budge or look away. Only leaned back, folded his arms across his chest, and gave me a leer.

I kept an eye on the clock, though the whole time I felt the weight of his eyes. Felt them as surely as if he were touching me. Every so often he'd shuffle off—in addition to cook and cashier, he served as the waiter of that dreary establishment. In those few moments, I managed to pry open a milk bottle and take a few swigs, but by this time in the day the customers had trickled away, and so he was free to linger in the kitchen and watch me work.

My fury took itself out on the dirt and disorder that surrounded me. Sweat beaded my forehead, pooled at my armpits, trickled down my back. He was still staring, but I wouldn't give him the satisfaction of looking his way.

He paid me with two grimy, nearly black quarters, making a show of placing them very slowly and one by one in my palm. They clung there as if they'd been seared onto my skin. I thrust them into my pocket and turned away without so much as a nod.

In a blink, he'd shoved up against me.

"Well, now," he said, and gripped my forearm to turn me toward him. His hand on my bare skin was meaty and damp. "Are you too good for it?" he said with a new kind of roughness that made me afraid.

I wrenched myself out of his grip. I had to get out of there—and fast.

Tears pricked at my eyes as I tore out of that place into the streets. It was night now, the moon a bright, sharp sliver. Gaslights glowed here and there, and people were out in droves. A horse-drawn cart clattered past, sending up arcs of dirty water and splashing my skirt. I wove between the pedestrians, shouldering my way through the crowd and once nearly bumping into a woman with a buggy. "Watch where you're going!" someone growled, but I didn't stop. I hurried along as quickly as I could, clutching my valise and camera to my chest with one hand and my sodden hem with the other, and I would have kept going, except that all at once pain thundered down my leg and bent me double.

I staggered toward the side of a building and leaned heavily against the wall. I knew I shouldn't have run like that. It made my leg hurt horribly. My limp was my one constant companion, as familiar to me as breath, but it'd been a long time since my foot had gone so heavy and numb.

I was sure people were staring, but when I at last caught my breath and lifted my eyes, I saw that they were streaming past me as if I were invisible. Not a head turned. No one stopped.

After some time, a streetcar came clanking from the right. I watched it approach. The travel, the hunger, the jolt to my nerves—I was spent. I needed to sit down. If I could just rest a bit, I'd feel better, I knew I would. Maybe I could even think up some kind of plan.

I crossed the street, dug a coin from my pocket, and stepped aboard.

Climbing the streets of San Francisco, with the tang of the bay and the wind against my damp skin and the hard wooden seat rattling under me, I was suddenly back in my grandmother's house in Hoboken, back in its ugliness and its darkness and its despair. The weight of it fell on me, crushing me against the seat. This was it, then. My dream of a fresh start—that was over now, gone, done, past. I'd made it clear across the country, three thousand miles from New Jersey to California, and now I couldn't even go back home if I wanted to.

Passengers climbed on and off; the streetcar strained up the hills and tore down them again and again; each turn and stop jostled me against a neighbor. I came close to breaking down, and I would have but there was no privacy at all, not with the passengers crowded so close, hemming me in on every side. My leg ached. My mouth was dry as paper. But still I didn't move. I didn't even raise my head to look out at the streets.

Then, just when it seemed we were going to go on forever, the streetcar came to a stop. "Lands End!" the conductor called out. I looked up, only to discover that San Francisco was gone. It was as if a switch had been thrown over the city. The sky that seemed so blue over the ferry building had disappeared, and the workaday world had also vanished. In its place stood windswept sand dunes and a fog so thick you could almost grab hold of it with your hands.

As I stepped from the streetcar and into the street, a gust of wind blew my skirt up and my gaze fell to my stunted right leg and my twisted foot. *Walk as straight as you can,* said a voice in my head. *People will look at you. You'll make them look at you if you limp.* It was my mother's voice, same as ever. I quickly smoothed my skirt, tugged it back over my knees, and pinched the collar of my coat closed. I'd spent more than half my life coaching away my limp, but all these years later, the fear and shame of it blazed through me. *You're over that,* I told myself, *you're long past it,* but the dark, slick, fogged-in streets brought it back—all of it.

It started as nothing—a sore throat, a light fever—and then one morning my legs disappeared.

It was the summer of 1902. I'd just turned seven. On the Fourth of July, my fever dipped slightly, and Mama let me sit outside to watch the parade while she straightened and scrubbed inside. I loved to sit on the front stoop of our house in Weehawken, elbows to knees, and watch people walk by, the ladies with their umbrellas and bustles, the men with their trilbies and walking sticks. There'd never been a time when I didn't long for the world beyond our house. I'd have given anything to join the stream of people in the street, but my world was bounded by the grocer to the east, the park to the west, and if I did go out it was only in the neighborhood and with my mother's hand clasped over mine. Always the same faces in the streets, and everywhere the sounds of German.

All at once I felt my thighs twitch, first the left one and then both of them. I pressed my hands against them to make it stop, but my legs kept jerking under my fingers. There was a great tingling all over my body, a burning that started at my chest and ran down to my toes. I called for my mother, but the noise from the street swallowed my cry. I stood up to go inside, but my head went hazy and my legs folded under me, and then there was a long, deafening silence, and after that everything went black.

When I came to, my legs were gone. Well, not exactly gone. They were still attached to my body, but there wasn't a trace of feeling in them, none.

Nothing my mother did or said could stop my screaming, but by the time a doctor came to the house I'd exhausted myself. My body had gone slack, and a haziness clung to my brain. Mama propped me up with my feet dangling over the side of the bed. The doctor tapped a small rubber mallet against my left knee. It didn't move. He tapped my other leg. Nothing.

"You need to take her to the hospital," I heard him say afterward. My mother had pulled the door closed, but it didn't latch, so I could see them in the hall, the doctor with his black bag and his round steel-rim spectacles and her with her arms folded over her chest, shoulders heaving with her sobs.

I woke the next morning in a room with pea-green walls and the biting stink of bleach. From the corner of my eye I glimpsed a woman in a mask and rubber gloves. As she came close, I saw she was holding a very long and very thick needle. When I screamed, she cupped a hand over my mouth. A second pair of hands flipped me on my side and held me down. In another few hours I'd be paralyzed, but when that needle plunged into my back, and then kept plunging, I bit my tongue bloody from the pain.

Polio. The spinal tap confirmed it. I'd never heard the word, and I didn't understand what it meant. The coming year would teach me that word, along with another one: "cripple."

But first this: My fever climbed to one hundred and four, lingered there for three days, then suddenly broke, and there was my mother's hovering, anguished face. My hair was pasted to my forehead, my lips were cracked and dry. I could talk, I could open my eyes, I could turn my head from side to side, but that was it. I was paralyzed from the shoulders down.

It took a year for me to get better, but for a long time no one thought I'd ever come out of it. I couldn't go into the street to play or even sit on the front stoop. I didn't want to anyway. For one thing, I had no hair—it'd all been shaved off in the hospital. It grew out slowly and in uneven clumps, and no matter how many times my mother rinsed it in vinegar to bring the brightness back, it stayed a dull, dark shade of blond. The rest of me was just as bad. My face had a hollow look and my ribs poked out from my chest; the doctor put me on a diet of fried liver and full-fatted milk, which I hated but was made to eat anyway.

Nothing was as awful as the brace I had to wear. The feeling in my legs had only just come back when a steel shank was strapped to my right leg and buckled to my pelvis, knee, and ankle. That brace weighed fifteen pounds and cut deep grooves into my flesh, slicing the skin. The pain of wearing it was relentless. Ferocious.

September came, but I didn't go back to school. Month after month I lay on a cot in the small parlor of our house, the room closest to the kitchen, staring up at the window, at a small square of sky. No one visited me at home, the whole year I was there. No friends from school, no relatives, no neighbors. They were all too scared I'd make them sick.

Unseen and unknown, I became flesh and sensation. I became a listener, a witness. I heard dogs barking in the neighborhood, bursts of birdsong, horses whinnying in the street, doors opening and closing, the kettle coming to a boil, the clock in the hall ticking and ticking and ticking.

My crippled foot was the place I lived, the way other people live in a house or a country—there was no world beyond it. My foot formed and deformed me, hid and humiliated me, guided and unmoored me. All those things, all at once. I had to wear diapers, and the few times I left the house—nearly always for doctors' visits—Mama pushed me in a special carriage that drew people's eyes and made them quicken their steps or cross the street. One day I watched from the window as she built a fire in the alley behind our house and fed my clothes and dolls and books to it one by one. For fear of contamination, everything I'd ever touched had to be thrown away or torched.

Turns out, it wasn't my body that'd disappeared. It was me.

I spent my first night in San Francisco on the streets.

I was the only passenger left. A last clatter of the streetcar and with no warning I was suddenly alone. Until I climbed out of the streetcar and into the fog, I'd felt rattled and miserable. Now I felt real fear. LANDS END DEPOT, read the sign above the station. The small clapboard building was shuttered and dark. I looked to the left and then to the right, but there was nothing to see. There were no shops or restaurants in this part of the city— was this even the city?—just a few scattered buildings, but after a while I could make out a light in the distance, and I set off in that direction.

It was a little, run-down place, as seedy as the roughest saloons on the backstreets of the Bowery. The windows were hazy with grime and salt spray, but after peering inside for a while I could see it was dim and empty except for a few men slumped over the bar.

I was standing by the door, considering whether to go in, when a man was dragged by the collar of his coat and hauled outside.

No, I couldn't go in there. Not at this hour, not as a woman alone. I ducked into the doorway, shivering as I watched the man, a sad bundle of bones, stagger into the dark and then disappear. I clung to my bag and surveyed my options. There were none. I was lost. There was no cover, no place to sit. I didn't know the names of the streets; with the fog so thick, I couldn't see street signs or even the streets themselves.

Just this afternoon I'd arrived on the train, looking out at a beautiful, unfamiliar city with all the hope in the world. The spell was broken now. I cursed myself for riding out all this way, for not paying attention, for letting myself get lost.

At the next corner the sharp stench of rotting flesh hit me— the remains of an animal. A large rat, or was it a dead cat? Or maybe it was my imagination, maybe I was seeing things, what with my nerves at a pitch and the silence so vast, so different from

New York or even Hoboken, where even deep into the night there was always the creak and clatter of streetcars, the beat of hooves against the cobblestones, the sound of people's voices.

I spun away and made off in the opposite direction. Eventually my feet led me toward the beach. The fog had enveloped the moon, and the sea was as dark as the sky, but the waves were beating hard against the shore, and I made my way forward by their sound. Sand leaked through my boots; clumps of sea grass scratched my legs. A gull winged past, keening wildly. I climbed through the head-high dunes until my legs went liquid and I fell.

Strange how the body remembers what we most wish to forget. The cold, wet sand sent me back to the night when three men in suits and bowler hats came to the door of our old house in Weehawken. I was twelve. My father had deserted us; after that night we'd move in with my grandmother in Hoboken and I'd never see him again. The three men marched my mother, my little brother, and me onto the sidewalk and then bolted the door with a heavy lock. In the street, Mama's eyes were wild with panic. I stood dressed in my nightgown and bare feet, my shoulders hunched against the cold, my steel brace digging into my thigh. We'd been evicted, and it all happened so fast that none of us had the chance to put on a coat.

I know this place, I thought then. *I've been here before.*

The long, low moan of the foghorns eventually gave way to the quieter sounds of the night. Here, at the lip of the ocean, there was nothing to hurry for anymore, no other place to get to. Riffling through my bag, I dug out a sweater and pair of pants and wrestled them on. After that I tucked my bag under my head, tightened my camera strap, and drew my coat about myself. And then, because I was too exhausted and too beaten down to do anything else, I closed my eyes and slept.

2.

Morning came. I woke up shivering on the beach with my foot still aching and a sharp belly-hunger tearing through me. I opened my eyes and stared up at the sky. It was early, but how early I couldn't have said. The sun was up, but if anything, the fog was thicker now, the sky milk-white. I pressed up on my elbows. Gazing about, I saw I'd landed in a country of jackrabbits and sand dunes. The sand had left scratches against my skin, and its dampness had seeped into my clothes. My hands were trembling and I felt faint. I'd never been so hungry in my life.

I stood and shook the sand from myself. The only answer to my troubles was to start thinking properly, and that meant I had to stop feeling so scared and sorry for myself.

All of a sudden I knew what I had to do.

My camera was the thing I most loved in the world, but it was also the only thing of value I owned. I had to sell it—there was no other choice.

A lone driver appeared. I flagged him down and he took me

as far as the Lands End station. From there I ventured downtown by streetcar, where I found a pawnshop and hocked my camera for forty dollars, five dollars less than what I wanted but as close to a fair sum as I was likely to get under the circumstances. I'd buy it back, I swore I would. Whatever it took, I'd find a job, rent a room, and buy back my Graflex. To remind myself of my promise, I kept the case and pulled it over my neck.

I'd bought some time—a few weeks' worth if I was careful with my money. After a breakfast of coffee and a single boiled egg that did nothing to ease my hunger, I drifted around for a while and considered what to do next. No use looking for a job until I got cleaned up. In the end I decided to take a cable car back to the ferry building. I'd get myself some lunch—a sandwich, maybe two—and then I'd go in search of the boardinghouse.

That's what was going through my head when I stepped onto a cable car and suddenly heard a voice say "half-breed." I snapped to attention. Just then it wasn't so much the word that struck me but the way it had been spat out. It rang in the air, sharp and clear. For a moment I thought I might have misunderstood, but a few people were averting their eyes as if what they'd heard hadn't registered, and that confirmed it.

I glanced around. Two women were staring at a spot just over my shoulder. I turned and saw a woman making her way through the car. Her hair was short, black, and sleek. From a distance she looked Oriental, but as she approached, I saw that her eyes made her something . . . well, different. They were bottle green.

"They're everywhere you go now!" I heard a woman say. I didn't have to strain to hear her, because she felt no need to whisper or to lower her voice. "Ten years ago you wouldn't have seen a single one in this part of the city, not a one. Now they think they have the run of the place!"

"Them and now their mongrels, too," came her companion's response.

I could tell by the young woman's face, all expression fading from it, that she'd heard at least part of what had been said. For just a moment she seemed to wince, but she soon composed herself, squaring her shoulders, thrusting her way into the cabin, and looking around for a seat.

The flash of hurt I'd caught in her eyes made me feel mutely, stupidly ashamed. I wanted to say something, but the only thing I could think to do was to lift my bag from the seat beside me to make space for her to sit. She answered with a slight nod, then sat down beside me, linking her hands in her lap and facing forward.

I tried not to stare, but faces, particularly strangers' faces, fascinated me. What they showed, how much they hid. After a few minutes, I stole a glance at her. Then another. Up close she was younger than she'd seemed at first, my age or maybe younger, with faint freckles across her nose and cheeks. She didn't look like anyone I'd ever seen. Still, something about her seemed familiar—I just couldn't put a finger on what it was.

Back when I was Arnold Genthe's apprentice, I'd spent hours studying his famous Chinatown portraits, the ones of men with their long braids and ladies in silk robes and bound feet. Genthe had ignited my mind and trained my eye, and those pictures were no small part of it.

That wasn't it. Couldn't be it. Except for the small jade ornament that hung by a black ribbon around her neck, the woman's clothes weren't just American but fully up-to-the-minute: a gray cloche hat and a narrow, plum-colored ankle-length skirt, which she wore with a matching jacket, belted at the waist, white blouse, and tall lace-up boots. Her feet in the smart boots were narrow and small, and when she sat down, her legs showed nearly to the knee. It was the sort of outfit a film star would wear—or a model in a magazine.

A painting by Modigliani, that's what it was. It took me a while, but at last I remembered whom, or rather what, she reminded me of: a portrait I'd once seen in a New York gallery, a sinewy, red-cheeked girl with knowing eyes. The woman sitting beside me had that same head-high grace.

She'd make a fine subject for a picture, I thought then: the pretty face, the dramatic hair, those extraordinary eyes. Still, for all my staring and wondering and thinking, it might have come to nothing, that encounter on the cable car, if it weren't for my camera case. If it weren't for that, I might've kept drifting. Instead, I found home.

When we reached the next stop, the woman turned toward me. Her eyes went to the case, and then, quite suddenly, she looked at me full in the face, green eyes alight.

"Are you a photographer?" she asked.

For some reason I'd expected her to sound foreign. She didn't. Actually, there wasn't a trace of an accent in her voice.

I drew myself up in my seat. "Yes," I said, and then, because I didn't know what else to say, I added, "Do you take pictures, too?"

This seemed to amuse her, and she smiled, revealing a magnificent set of dimples. Now that she'd turned toward me, I saw that her bangs were cut just a bit longer at the center, which accented her heart-shaped face.

"No," she said, "I'm not. I've got a friend who shoots pictures for the *Chronicle,* so I know a bit about taking pictures, but not very much." Her eyes went to my camera case again. "What sorts of things do you photograph?"

"People," I said. "I'm a portrait photographer."

"I see, and judging from your bag, I'd guess you've come a long way."

"New York," I said. This was a slight fib. I'd been born and raised in New Jersey, though it was true I'd worked in the city the last few years.

"Are you planning to stay in San Francisco?"

I felt my throat tighten. "I'm not—I mean, I wasn't but . . ." I looked down at my boots and my valise. For a few minutes I'd forgotten my troubles. I remembered them now. "I wonder if you could help me. I'm looking for Bush Street. There's a place for young women there, the—" I pursed my lips, trying to recall the name of the boardinghouse. I came up with nothing.

"The Elizabeth Inn?" she offered. When I nodded, her eyes seemed to harden ever so slightly. Whatever her association with the establishment, it wasn't pleasant. "Well," she said slowly, "if that's where you want to go, it's on my way. I can walk you there."

"You're sure that's not too much trouble?"

She looked at me evenly. "It's no trouble at all."

The cable car rattled up the hill and plunged down the next one. We both reached for the handrail and held tight, and then for a few minutes we were silent, watching the city scroll by in flashes of white and gray.

"What's your name?" she asked. She smiled, and again two deep dimples appeared in her cheeks.

I started to answer, then stopped. Until that moment I'd only ever been Dorothea Nutzhorn, but for some reason I answered with my mother's surname. "Dorothea Lange," I said. It felt right—strong and clear and somehow true. I smiled. "You can call me Dorrie for short."

"Dorrie," she echoed, tilting her head to give me a swift, assessing look. She seemed to conclude it suited me—or at least that it would do.

"I'm Caroline Lee," she said, and stuck out her hand.

Her name, like mine, was one part fiction, one part fact. I didn't know that yet, though, and I wouldn't for some time.

A sideways glance, an outright stare. If the sight of a self-possessed young woman of indeterminate race went unnoticed in some cities, San Francisco wasn't one of them. We'd be walking along, and suddenly I'd see some person following Caroline with a wondering gaze. Some people distanced themselves and gave her—and occasionally us—the sort of look the two women in the cable car had subjected her to earlier, the clamped lips and glittering, burning eyes. But there were other sorts of looks. Lots of them. Men's eyes latched on to her like magnets. I couldn't stop noticing it, and it made me embarrassed about my own gawking back on the cable car. But Caroline seemed to glide above all that surrounded her, separate and unfettered. She walked with long strides, as if the people we passed were invisible, she was free, and the street belonged to her.

Now, that was something to see.

I followed her as best I could, picking up my pace, determined to disguise the hitch in my walk and not fall behind. At first my stout, worn-out boots fell into step with her polished and heeled black boots. We didn't talk much—it was difficult to hear each other over the clatter of the streetcars and carriages—

but I learned a few things about her all the same. That it was her day off and so she'd been out visiting a friend, that she'd nearly walked home but wasn't it lucky for me she'd chosen to take the cable car instead?

I still had no idea where we were going, but I was glad to attach myself to someone who so clearly knew her way around. Market, Stockton, California—determined not to let myself get lost again, I made an effort to memorize the names of all the streets we passed. There was the smell of horse manure and rotten fruit, which reminded me of Manhattan, but all the buildings looked so new it seemed they'd sprung up overnight, which, though I didn't know it, they mostly had. The earthquake and fires of 1906 had left odd patterns in the streets; whole blocks were crammed with new buildings, but more than a few lots stood empty. Though no one seemed the least bit bothered by it, there was a sense, as you walked, of how recently it had happened, how awful it had been.

"Compared with New York," said Caroline now, "it must seem like a tiny place. Walk in any direction and you'll hit the water. You'll learn your way quick enough."

When we turned onto Montgomery Street, church bells rang out twelve times. A man was hawking something from a pushcart. As I came closer, I watched a small boy buy a cone of chocolate gelato. My stomach gave a twist. I wrenched my eyes away and hurried past with my head down. We passed a fiddler and tambourine player on one street corner and an old woman playing a harmonica on the next block. The streets were less crowded in this part of the city, rougher but also livelier and noisier, filled with arguments and laughter, bursts of music streaming from open windows. We passed a blacksmith shop and a tavern advertising ten-cent shots of whiskey. Down an alley, a woman sat on a stool outside an open doorway. She had a mouth as red as cherries, and her breasts spilled over the top of her half-buttoned stays.

It was getting harder to keep up with Caroline. Her eyes flickered as she saw me limping, but she didn't look away. "Would you like to rest a bit?" she asked when we stopped at a curb. The fierce, determined expression she'd worn as she walked through the streets had fallen away, giving way to a look of gentle concern.

All at once the whole story came tumbling out: the train, my stolen money, the man in the diner, the night on the sand dunes, my pawned camera. I even blurted out something about polio and my crippled leg. I was crying—something I never let myself do—and I didn't even bother wiping away my tears.

"So you don't know anyone here in San Francisco?" she asked when I finished speaking.

I shook my head.

"No family? Nobody who could come for you?"

Again, I shook my head.

"But you're a photographer, right? You know how to take pictures?"

"I am. I do."

All around us was the clamor of the city at noon, the calls of the street vendors and newspaper boys, the hustle of workers on their way to canteens and coffee shops, the odd bleat of a car horn. We were the only ones standing still.

"Listen," she said after a moment. "When was the last time you had a proper meal?"

"Last week," I said, though it came out more like a question than an answer.

"No wonder you look like you're ready to drop! Why don't you come have a bite to eat with me?"

I liked her. Liked her awfully. Her steadiness, her verve, her kindness. The scent of roasting coffee, cinnamon, and cloves drifted from a café, sharpening my hunger. But I didn't want to put her out, so I started stammering some excuse.

"Nonsense," she said. "You'll come to Coppa's with me, that's what you'll do. A plate of pasta will cost you ten cents there, and believe me, it's just about the best meal you can find in this city." She paused. "Besides, I know someone at Monkey Block who could maybe help you out."

"Monkey Block?" I asked. The strangeness of the name stopped me. "What's that?"

She grinned. "Oh, now, there's a question!" She reached for my hand and led me off the curb and into the street. "You'll just have to see for yourself, but if I had to guess, I'd say Monkey Block's exactly where you need to be."

And then I learned it was possible to float on solid ground.

When I saw the building at 628 Montgomery Street, I was dimly aware how far I'd wandered from the world I knew. This, I'd soon find out, was the Barbary Coast, the wild, wicked heart of the city, where three hundred saloons and dance halls were crammed into six blocks. Whether by design or oversight, no trouble had been taken to hide it from the neighboring streets, so that ordinary businesses, or seemingly ordinary businesses, stood shoulder to shoulder with dissolute, tawdry, and exotic ones. Montgomery Street was bristling with life. The particular building Caroline took me to—this "Monkey Block"—was surrounded on all sides by bars, restaurants, pool halls, and smoke shops, all of them doing what seemed a brisk business even though it was still early in the day. It was enough to make my eyes go wide, but what I couldn't see would've made my heart flip: I'd just stepped off the ground. I was floating now.

"It was the tallest building west of the Mississippi when it was built," said Caroline. "For the first fifty years it was full of bankers' and lawyers' offices. Very fancy, you know. All that's gone now, of course."

"Why? What happened?"

"After the earthquake, all that Gold Rush money flowed right down to Market Street. Rents in this part of town went down, way down, and now it's full to bursting with bohemians." She smiled. "The whole thing's floating on a raft of redwood trees."

"Floating? What do you mean?"

"Well, imagine all this was once water. The bay reached out for miles and miles. That's what it was here. Water, all of it, every inch." She paused. "Three hundred Chinese laborers worked, oh, let me see, six or eight months to dig the foundation and fill it in. People call it the 'Floating Fortress.' Think of it this way: It's just like a ship, except that there's more sludge than sea underneath it."

"Are you sure it's safe to go inside?"

She laughed. "It's safe enough to survive an earthquake and five massive fires, so if you mean will it sink or drift off into the ocean, then, yes, you're perfectly safe."

I threw another uneasy glance at the building, but already Caroline had put an arm around my shoulders and was propelling me toward it. Inside, she guided me down a long hallway, humming some tune I didn't recognize. The carpet was thick but faded, and gauzy light streamed from the lanterns on the walls. When we finally reached the end of the hallway, Caroline pushed open the door and together we stepped inside.

The aroma of Italian cooking was so potent and wonderful I felt I might faint. For a few seconds the only thing I could see was smoke and darkness, but as my eyes adjusted to the lack of light, I thought I saw the red walls shimmer. I was so hungry, I was seeing things. It took me a moment to get my bearings and find the source of the shimmering. With the silk-shaded lamps burning low and drapes drawn against the sun, it felt less like midday and more like midnight in here. I blinked, looked again. The walls were lined with crushed-velvet wallpaper of the deepest crimson, floor to ceiling, all the way around the room.

What had struck me most about San Francisco so far wasn't the newness of the place—that I'd expected—but the absence of the past. I saw now that whatever the city had once been wasn't completely gone. Stepping into Coppa's that first time, I had the sensation—and I never lost it, not in all the time that followed—that I'd plunged into the last century. If I just squinted, a woman in a bustle and a bonnet could easily slip into the picture.

"It's beautiful," I said, almost to myself.

"I've always thought so. People still talk about how grand it once was, but it's still something, isn't it?"

"Yes, it really is."

"Buon giorno!" a man called out as we made our way forward. This, I'd learn, was Mr. Giuseppe Coppa—Poppa Coppa to his adoring patrons. He wore a black silk vest and red cravat. He was short and thick-chested, with a square chin, heavy beard, and richly accented English.

He opened his arms to greet us.

"Dorrie, Poppa Coppa is the owner of this lovely spot."

He kissed us both in the Italian manner, first on the right cheek, then the left. That day I wasn't yet used to such a greeting, or the string of *bellas* that accompanied it, and I met it with awkward gestures and downcast eyes.

There was the sound of shattered glass, which made me jump, but it was followed by laughter. From the far end of the room, a Victrola played a raucous ragtime tune. The music mixed with talking and shouting, the clink of glasses on tables, and the scraping of chairs against the floor. It was a sort of saloon, and women didn't really go into saloons. It wasn't done. But there were almost as many women as there were men here.

"Sit, sit!" Mr. Coppa said, leading us to a table and drawing a chair back for Caroline and a second for me. The seats were red leather and faintly cracked with age.

Caroline unfastened her gloves, unpinned her hat, and then turned away to run a tube of lipstick over her mouth. I still didn't know where I was, but I knew where I'd been and where I couldn't go now that my money and my camera were gone, and so I set down my bag and shrugged off my coat.

"You're a regular here, then?"

She nodded happily. "I eat here at least once a day."

A waiter descended with a demijohn of wine. The last drink I'd had was a glass of cheap watered-down gin, and that was months ago, so the warmth of the wine hit me fast. I hadn't tasted alcohol in so long I couldn't remember what it was like—and then, suddenly, I could. It felt good, soft and soothing, and the tightness in me began to ease.

"Eat," said Caroline, nudging a plate of cheese and tomato slices toward me.

Tomatoes. Another revelation. I hadn't had them in so long,

since last summer or maybe longer. I watched her tear off a
piece of bread and dunk it in olive oil. She plunged it into her
mouth, drank some wine, and sighed luxuriously. I copied her.
The bread was delicious like that. I chased it down with a long
gulp of wine, took two more pieces of bread, and sandwiched a
tomato between them. I'd been hungry for days. Now I was eating too fast, and I couldn't stop. Soon my fingers were glistening
with oil and a lovely blurriness had settled over everything.

"Are you feeling better?" she asked after a few minutes.

"Yes. It helps to rest." I took another bite and added, "And to
eat."

"Good! Now tell me, who are you and what's your story?"

"Well, like I said, I'm a portrait photographer."

"That goes some way to explain the way you look so hard at
things! And how long have you been doing that?"

"Since before I held a camera."

She lifted her brows. "How's that possible?"

The few times I'd made this confession it had been met with
laughter or confusion, but Caroline was looking at me, waiting
for me to go on.

I tried to think how to explain it. Something I couldn't even
name had made me want to be more than what anyone thought
I could be, which was not much of anything. I was determined
to push past all that . . . smallness. And the way I wanted to do
it was with a camera.

"I just always knew that's what I wanted to do. I've never *not*
been sure I was a photographer, any more than you would not
be sure that you were yourself. Nothing else seemed worth
doing. Not to me." I cleared my throat and continued. "I learned
everything by watching Arnold Genthe, my first boss. He taught
me about taking pictures that show the truth of who people are.

I haven't wanted to do anything else since then. Not that anyone in New York would take a chance on me."

"That's why you left?"

I took a deep breath. "I worked hard—really hard—but it wasn't enough, and it never would be. Then last month the portrait studio where I worked shut down. The place had been sinking for a long time, but with the war on, no one seemed much interested in portraits. Clients drifted away, commissions ended. It wasn't that people weren't spending money anymore—oh, they were spending as much as ever, just not in ways that showed."

"And portraits show how much money you've got. That's the whole point of them, isn't it?"

"Yes," I said slowly, "I suppose that's right."

"What made you decide to come to California?"

"Well, I'd been saving up to go to Paris, but I couldn't do that with the war. Then I figured, why not go west? I've always wanted to see San Francisco. Genthe used to talk about it all the time. You see, he lived here before the earthquake." I took a sip of wine. "But there's another thing. Another reason I left New York."

"Go on."

I wasn't used to talking so much about my work, but it was bringing me back to myself. It made it easier somehow, having just met Caroline, and I realized I could say the thing I'd only ever told myself. "I want to open my own studio. Do something new, something good."

She smiled. "Then you will! It's your destiny!"

"You don't really believe in that sort of thing?"

"Oh yes," she said. Her voice was soft but earnest. "I most certainly do believe in that sort of thing."

She poured generously from the bottle into my glass. I took a long gulp of wine, savoring the sweet, tender heat on my tongue.

After a few minutes ticked past, Caroline swiveled around in her seat to catch a story at the next table. My attention wandered around the room. It was just past noon on a Thursday, and people were tossing back drinks and smoking as couples danced from one end of the room to the other. No one seemed to have anything to do except sit and dance and gossip. I was struck again by the presence of women and by the naturalness of it.

Is it always like this? I wanted to ask, but Caroline was now deep in conversation. And that was another thing: How was it that everyone at Coppa's seemed to know her? Already she'd introduced me to several of her friends—a Guatemalan sculptor, a skinny young journalist just back from the Far East, a graduate student of philosophy at UC Berkeley—every friend except Consuelo Kanaga, the one she kept insisting I most needed to meet. They'd wave at her, she'd wave back, and then they'd sidle up to the table to share some joke or story.

I couldn't keep up with all the talk, but I didn't mind; it gave me a chance to take it all in. I propped my chin on my fists and admired my surroundings. After the velvet walls, what most captivated me was the crystal chandelier that hung down into the middle of the room. It was enormous, about five feet wide, and the crystal pendants gave the place a soft, otherworldly glow.

"Gorgeous, isn't it?" Caroline asked when she caught me appraising the chandelier.

"Very." I turned to her and smiled. "I'm glad you insisted on bringing me here."

"You're about to feel a whole lot gladder," she said, and nodded toward the waiter who was approaching now with the main course.

It was a sumptuous spread: two heaping bowls of pasta, oysters bobbing in some garlicky broth, three different kinds of cheese, another generous length of sourdough bread. Caroline took up the serving fork and began piling food onto my plate. It was much more than I would have taken for myself, yet I didn't refuse any of it.

"It's all delicious, but this," she said, forking a huge helping of pasta onto my plate and then adding generous spoonfuls of Parmesan, "is Poppa's masterpiece."

"Do you live close by?" I asked between bites. I wanted to ask all sorts of questions, about what she did and why it was that everyone here knew her so well, but, then again, I didn't want to pry.

"Very close, actually. I live upstairs, on the third floor."

It hadn't occurred to me that a place with a red-velvet dining hall could also be a home. My confusion must have been obvious, because the next thing she said was "What is it?"

This time I said exactly what I was thinking. "I don't understand why you're being so kind to me. It's . . ." I fiddled with my fork. "I just can't understand."

She sat with this for a moment. "The thing is," she said, looking at me over the rim of her wineglass, "I think we've maybe got some things in common, you and I."

I blinked. "How so?"

"Well," she said slowly, "let's just say it seems we both know what it means to be alone in the world." She tilted her head back to drain her glass and then set it down. "You know that boardinghouse you're looking for? The Elizabeth Inn?" I nodded, and she continued. "I went there once, looking for a room to rent. I should've known better, but at the time it felt like my only choice. Well, the deaconess—that's the lady who runs it—wouldn't let me past the parlor."

There was no hiding my ignorance, because the next thing she said was "Don't tell me you don't know what I'm talking about?"

When I shook my head, she took a long, slow breath. "It's against the law for Chinese to live outside Chinatown. An old San Francisco tradition, you could say. 'No Orientals Allowed.' That means 'mongrels' and 'half-breeds,' too."

Here she paused and held my eyes—she'd heard every word back on the cable car and she wanted me to know it.

That stopped me. Not just what she'd said, but the anger with which she said it.

"I'm so sorry, I didn't realize—"

For a moment the air was taut between us, then she managed a faint smile. She had a way about her—I kept noticing it—of changing her tone or her posture and with that shifting the mood. She did it again now.

"There are far fewer Chinese women than men in San Francisco. They're not allowed into the country, you see. Only men can come, and only for work. The women who do wind up here don't usually leave Chinatown."

"Why not?"

"Choice? Circumstance? Of course, it doesn't help that no one outside Chinatown will rent them a place to live."

Had I seen any Chinese women besides Caroline? I didn't think so. Not in the shops or in the streets, and not here in Coppa's. Which, I now understood, explained, at least partly, why she caused a stir out in the streets.

"Long story short," she continued, "I grew up close to here. When I left home, Monkey Block was the only place outside Chinatown that would take me in. I landed in this place with nothing. Just a few weeks' rent, no job, no prospects. Not even the prospect of prospects. I was miserable. Everything here was so . . ." Her voice trailed off, and then she gestured around the room. "Well, it was just like this. Full of all sorts of people who don't belong anywhere else. I honestly didn't think I'd last a week."

"But you did last."

She grinned. "I did! I've been here three years. It's changed me, or maybe—" After a reflective sigh, she said, "Maybe it's made me more myself. Either way, I can't imagine living any-place else."

By then the plates had been cleared away and the wine was mostly gone. Someone had wound up the Victrola again, and a slow, quiet tune was playing. I couldn't remember the last time someone had spoken to me the way Caroline had, as though the only way to speak was openly.

"And what do you do?" I asked. "For work, I mean."

"What would you guess?"

"You're an actress."

She laughed. "An interesting guess, and true in a way." She gave the waiter a wave. "We'll have two espressos, please," she said, then turned back to me. "I've got a job at the White House."

"The White House?"

She laughed. "Oh, I forgot you've just gotten here! The White House is the biggest department store in town. They don't let Orientals work on the sales floor. That's another one of those San Francisco traditions. So it's ten-hour days in the storeroom, unpacking crates. That's part of it. Pressing and altering clothes, that's the other part. I was lucky, I guess, getting the job. Most department stores don't hire Chinese, not for any kind of work. The pay's lousy, so I model sometimes—there's always someone looking for a model around here. Also, I design and sew clothes. I sell them here and there."

She unhooked her jacket from the back of the chair and showed me the inside pocket. There was a monogram stitched there very neatly in ivory thread: C.L. It was beautiful work.

"You're very talented."

She thanked me, then draped the jacket back on the chair, tipped her head to the side, and looked at me steadily. "So, what's your plan, Dorrie?"

I shrugged. "I have no idea what to do now that I've lost my money. It feels . . ."

"Daunting?"

"Yes."

"I'm sure you'll figure it out, you'll see."

The waiter returned with two small cups, and I watched Caroline plunk a sugar cube into hers, then stir it with a tiny spoon. She stopped for a moment, biting her lip as she turned over some fresh thought.

"There's a party tomorrow night at a house on Pacific Heights. Actually, it's more like a show. A sort of . . . play. Anyway, my friend Consuelo's sure to be there, and I could introduce you two. Do say you'll come!"

"But—"

"But nothing! I'll walk you to that boardinghouse. The lady who runs it is awful, but the neighborhood's not bad and the rent's cheap. Get a decent night's sleep, and in the morning you'll be thinking well enough to realize the only possible answer is yes."

I hesitated. After my night on the beach and what had happened yesterday, I didn't know if I was up for it. But then I thought about a night in a boardinghouse, in a city where I knew no one, and suddenly I knew I didn't want to be alone.

"Okay," I said at last. "But only if you're sure I wouldn't be imposing."

She cut off my protest with a look of exasperation. "Come by my place at six." She extracted a creased cash register receipt from her purse, scribbled an address onto it, and handed the paper to me. "Third floor, number twenty-six. We'll go together."

When we'd drained the first coffee, and a second one, we made our way back out to the street. "I'm just wondering . . ." she asked.

"Yes?"

"Do you want to go back to New York, Dorrie?"

I considered this. "Even if I manage to get a job, it'll take me ages to save up for a train ticket."

"But if you did have the money? Would you go back home?"

"Home." The word conjured Mama's still-young forehead crisscrossed with worry; the slaps and punches that sprang from my grandmother's leathery, mottled hands; my own body clenched in a fierce, wordless rage. It was my grandmother eyeing my camera, her shrill voice asking, "You think you'll get anywhere with that?" It was the freezing studio above a saloon where I'd spent the last two years filing negatives and mixing chemicals by the gallon, changing the glass plates, making proofs, spotting photographs, retouching the plates, mounting pictures—always for some boss or another. It was life as a lowly photographer's assistant with blue ink-stained fingers whose chance to make her own pictures might come in ten years or twenty—or, more likely, never.

The list of things I was glad to say goodbye to was longer than I cared to count. Exhausted and tipsy as I was, I answered her straightaway. "No. I don't want to go back there."

She smiled. "So, Miss Dorothea Lange, there's another thing we have in common, you and I. We're never going back home, neither of us."

3.

By the time I paid for the room at the Elizabeth Inn and held a key in my hand, I could barely stand from exhaustion, and I fell into bed with my boots still on my feet. All night I heard voices from the hall and pacing in the room above, odd thumps and bangs against the walls, doors creaking open and slamming shut. I fell asleep only to snap awake to the room still dark. I climbed out of bed and pulled the chain hanging from the middle of the ceiling. Light seeped from a lone bulb. The room wasn't much bigger than a closet. Worse, it had a mean feeling to it, as if it wanted me gone.

I threw back the curtains. The paint around the windowsill was blistered and the panes had gone milky, but in the thin gaslight I could make out a brick wall across the way and, in the dark alley below, piles of rubbish.

I went back to sleep and woke again near dawn. It took me about a minute to unpack my bag and put away my things. My only treasure, apart from my camera, was a battered secondhand copy of *Renascence*. It had been my gospel, that book. I'd read it so many times the pages had worked loose from the binding. I sank onto the bed and thumbed through the pages, stopping at "First Fig."

> My candle burns at both ends. It will not last the night;
> But ah, my foes, and oh, my friends—It gives a lovely light!

Nothing had turned out as I'd planned or expected, but I was here now, in San Francisco, with a friend and a party to go to tonight. It seemed like no small miracle. I snapped the book shut, pulled on my boots, and ventured into the hallway. I was dying for a long, hot bath, but at the Elizabeth that was impossible. There was only one bathroom for the whole floor, with a heavy old door you had to shove closed, a small stained sink with an ash-colored cake of soap, and a notice taped to the wall above the mirror that read DOORS LOCKED AT 10 P.M. NO EXCEPTIONS.

The Elizabeth was full of rules. No smoking. No music. No female guests spending the night. No male guests for any length of time, ever. Still, the towels and bedding were clean, breakfast and supper were included with the price of the room, and, to my surprise, they served decent-enough food. Even though I had to wait an hour for the bathroom, I was glad for a chance to wash away the sand, sweat, and misery of yesterday. To my surprise and undying delight, the water from the tap was plenty hot. I stood over the sink and stripped to the waist. First I washed my hair, then I scrubbed my face and as much of my body as I could with a washcloth, wearing down the soap to a sliver, and I stopped only when someone starting banging, hard, at the door for her turn.

.   .   .

It wasn't easy to find Caroline's apartment in Monkey Block the first time. She'd written down the number and even some directions, but I kept getting lost. I walked along a broad tiled passageway and then turned left, through an oak door, and toward a curved staircase. The staircase was wide enough for five people to climb side by side, and two halls branched out from each landing, leading to a few dozen rooms.

I glanced into the open doors I passed. Some of the rooms were quite spare, others crowded with canvases or a jumble of books and papers. Down one hallway I passed a studio where a woman was standing before a half-finished sculpture of what looked to be a horse. I found myself in hallways that opened onto other hallways, room after room along long corridors. If one room had an easel, another had a dressmaker's dummy, and the third a grand piano. Despite the building's size, it had the feeling of a village or a settlement. There was a wildness to the place.

When I got to the third floor I paused. I looked this way and that, not knowing where to turn. I smelled turpentine, then the tang of tobacco. In one hallway I caught a glimpse of lovers huddled deep in the shadows. Opera streaming from a half-closed door, the scent of bacon frying—a rush and swelter of senses. Two men stood smoking cigars on the landing, and when they saw I was lost, they kindly pointed me in the right direction. I proceeded down a long narrow hallway, where a man in a silk dressing gown was smoking a pipe and reciting poetry. Here, at the end of the hallway, I finally found Caroline's door with a brass number twenty-six, very old and scratched.

I had to knock twice before she flung it open and flashed a smile. Her lips were painted the darkest red I'd ever seen, which set off the brilliant white of her teeth. "I knew you'd come!" she said, waving me into the apartment with a teacup in one hand and a cigarette in the other.

I loved the place on first sight. The sitting room was small and messy—books heaped up by the bed, clothes, hats, stockings, and shoes scattered everywhere—but also very cozy, with little bunches of flowers set out here and there and a fern-green velvet settee. A black-and-gold Singer sewing machine sat on a table alongside several spools of thread and little glass bowls filled with buttons. In the corner stood a dressmaker's model draped in fabric. The other room was Caroline's bedroom. Here the small dressing table was crowded with objects—a silver-backed brush, various glass jars and bottles of oils and perfumes, an uncapped tube of lipstick. In the corner stood a folding screen painted with pale-pink chrysanthemums.

She wanted everything to be beautiful and had a talent for making it so. I could see it straightaway, but that wasn't the half of it. The lithograph covered a crack in the wall, the lovely screen masked the spot where the wallpaper had curled away, and the tasseled brocade hid a bald spot on the sofa. Her apartment would only seem more, not less, beautiful when I knew its secrets.

"Come see my view," she said, and then showed me how, if you stood in a particular spot and craned your neck, you could see a sliver of water between the rooftops.

The thing that really struck me was the light—the room was alive with it.

"If I could find someplace like this, I'd never leave."

"Sounds like I'm lucky the Elizabeth wouldn't rent me a room."

"You are—very lucky, actually."

She frowned. "Is it really as awful as that?"

"Oh, it's fine for now."

She wrinkled her brow, then smiled. "Come," she said, "let's have some tea."

I settled on the sofa and she poured us each a cup. She'd set some chocolates on a plate and we each took one now. The tea was strong, and very good. The chocolates were perfection.

"Caroline, I meant to tell you soon as I saw you, but your dress is absolutely beautiful."

A spill of emerald-green satin nipped at the waist by a black satin sash, the dress made her green eyes all the greener, her hair darker and glossier. Her shoes were black patent leather, with straps across the front, and her only jewelry was the same jade necklace I'd seen yesterday.

"Why, thank you." She stood up and gave a quick twirl, which showed off its swing. "It's my own design."

I blinked. "You made that dress?"

She sat down and smoothed the skirt of her dress. "I make everything I wear."

"It's spectacular. . . ."

"Go on, please." Her eyes were shining.

"You're enormously talented."

"Thank you, Dorrie."

I was suddenly very conscious of my own outfit, a high-collared blouse tucked into a beigey-brown twill skirt at least two years out of style, as well as the run along the back of my stockings and my plain, unpainted face.

I stammered an apology for not having anything better to wear. I'd always loved beautiful clothes, but with all my scrimping and saving I couldn't afford anything that wasn't practical. I didn't own a party frock or jewelry or a pretty purse.

"I could lend you something if you want. Actually, I think I have the perfect thing!"

She popped another chocolate into her mouth, snuffed out her cigarette with a neat twist, and told me to follow her to the other room.

Flinging her wardrobe open, she rustled about a bit and then grabbed something from inside. She held out the garment and nodded toward the folding screen.

"I just finished this one the other day. It should fit, but you'll have to try it on to be sure."

I hesitated for a moment, then ducked behind the screen, where I shrugged off my skirt and blouse, then peeled off my cotton chemise because the bulkiness would ruin the dress. I pulled Caroline's dress over my head and smoothed it over my hips. The fabric felt cold against my skin.

Thankfully, the dress was long and covered my legs, but I had no idea how I looked until I stepped out from behind the screen and saw Caroline's smile.

"Go take a look," she said, gesturing to the mirror above her chest of drawers.

I was so used to seeing myself covered up, neck to ankle, in old, misshapen clothes that when I looked in the mirror, it took me a moment to recognize myself.

"Well?" she asked. "What do you think?"

I let my hands drop to my sides and looked at my reflection more closely. The dress was a low-necked cocktail gown, robin's egg blue. Voluptuous, rich, intoxicating. Silk—it had to be. The dress was a bit loose in the chest and I'd never worn anything like it, not by a mile. Not by ten miles. But it was very beautiful and, anyway, didn't I want a change? Wasn't that the point of leaving home in the first place?

"Caroline," I said, turning toward her. "This is magnificent! It looks like something Isadora Duncan would wear!"

"Well, that's high praise," she said happily.

"It's true," I insisted. "I could just see her in it!" I looked down at the skirt and slid my hands over the lovely fabric. "Are you sure you don't mind me borrowing it?"

"The only thing I'd mind is if you didn't like it."

"I absolutely love it," I said, and matched her smile with my own.

"Good! Now, turn around and I'll do you up."

Once that was done, she gave a tug at my neckline to make the material lie just so, smoothed the bodice, and flared the bottom. I stood very still as she made her adjustments.

"There, Dorrie. Now it really suits you. The color's perfect for your complexion and your eyes. Just lovely. From now on you'll wear any color you like, so long as it's blue." She looked me up and down, and then her eyes landed on my brown boots. "Say, what size shoe do you take?"

"A five, but—"

"We're the same size!" Scrabbling around in the closet, she produced a pair of low satin pumps in a nearly identical shade of blue to the dress.

"Try these on," she said, holding them out to me.

"Oh . . . I can't wear those. I mean, I'd really like to but—"

"Not to worry," she said brightly, returning the shoes to the closet. "The skirt's so long it won't matter a bit if you wear your boots. Gives it a bit of panache, actually. A little devil-may-care."

After a few more adjustments to the dress, she tapped a cigarette from a silver case and lit it. "Next time we're at Coppa's, remind me to ask Poppa a favor, would you?"

"What's that?"

"Why, serve you bigger plates of pasta, of course!"

That year every metropolitan city, from Paris to London, was caught in a fit of Orientalist fever called *Japonisme*. In San Francisco this fever fastened itself on to an entertainer known as the King of Bohemia. For the past month, he'd been thrilling crowds at a mansion he'd christened the House of Grand Passion, putting on a show that was giving the dancers and performers of the Barbary Coast a run for their money. To hear Caroline tell it, the whole city was buzzing about this gorgeous creature whose sudden appearance fed an insatiable appetite for the new, the exotic, and the strange.

How this squared with the city's treatment of its Chinese residents—if it squared at all—was something I couldn't understand. "He's *Japanese*, Dorrie," Caroline said by way of explanation. "They're the elegant Orientals," she said, and rolled her eyes. This only deepened my confusion, but I was beginning to see that certain evasions were necessary for getting on here. This, it seemed, was one.

The cable car took us most of the way, but we had to walk the last few blocks. When we reached the crest of the hill, we paused for a breath of air. We'd reached Pacific Heights, one of the city's most elegant addresses. The houses were tall and ornate, with wrought-iron gates and lush gardens in front. It looked like San Francisco's version of Park Avenue—if you could imagine Park Avenue edged up along the sea and set onto a twisted ribbon of hills.

The house Caroline led me toward seemed particularly beautiful, a temple of creamy white stucco against a faintly pink sky, its many leaded windows draped in thick flowering vines of purple wisteria and struck with the day's last light.

"Now," she said as we passed through the gate, "the rule is you must call him the King of Bohemia."

"But who'd call himself something as silly as that?"

"Hush," Caroline said, and we headed into the house, she in her gorgeous green satin dress and me in my borrowed blue silk one. She carried a little beaded bag in which she'd stashed her lipstick, lighter, and cigarette case. "You're about to experience the most perfectly exquisite nonsense." She slipped off her shawl, draped it over her arm, and sent a smile over her shoulder. "Don't spoil the fun."

Inside, the house was even bigger than it had appeared from the street. Also, the rooms and hallways were crammed with people. I'd been to a few parties in Greenwich Village, but this was something else—heady and glorious and more than a little terrifying.

I fiddled with the low-scoop collar of my dress, then ran a hand through my hair to smooth it.

"Stop looking so scared," Caroline said, throwing me a reassuring glance as we drifted through a foyer and then down a long hallway. "They're all friends—well, mostly, but what's a party without a few enemies?"

"You've got enemies?"

"Everyone has enemies, Dorrie. The thing is not to let them get under your skin."

"How do you manage that?"

She looked at me. "The only way anyone ever manages anything," she said. "Practice! Now, let's find that king."

As we pushed deeper into the house, the scent of tobacco mingled with the lush, overripe sweetness of tiger lilies. A sprightly violin concerto streamed from the back of the room, but it was drowned out by the many voices around us.

The whole place was so dimly lit and crowded it took a while to notice, but the house held no furniture. Masses of tall white candles had been placed along every mantel and ledge, but otherwise the rooms were bare. No rugs on the floors or paintings on the walls, no furniture at all except the odd tufted chair here and there.

This struck me as odd, at least until we reached a second, even larger parlor and I saw the view of the bay. The windows were flung open wide to the night, and there it was, silvered and shimmering under an enormous white disc of a moon. Once I saw that, I stopped noticing anything else.

"Oh, look! There he is," Caroline said, squeezing my hand. "Do you see the man with very black hair over there—the one in the tuxedo?"

I turned and glanced at him. "That's the King of Bohemia?"

"Indeed it is. Isn't he gorgeous?"

He was a slender Eurasian man with tawny skin and almost-awkward delicate features, dressed in a tuxedo and tails, with a deep-red rose for a boutonniere. He wore white gloves and spats buttoned over his shoes, and his hair was oiled and parted precisely down the middle.

Just then he was deep in conversation with a very tall woman in a purple dress. Her hat was as wide as a tea tray and bedecked with a whole aviary's worth of feathers, and she was holding two small dogs by the leash. When he saw us approaching, the man stepped forward and took Caroline's hand in both of his. The dogs lunged at us, yapping furiously. The woman in the feathered hat stole a pinched sideways look at Caroline before offering a sour little smile.

"Your Majesty," Caroline exclaimed, smiling but totally straight-faced. "May I introduce my friend Dorothea Lange?"

"*Enchanté,*" he said, giving a deep bow. A diamond sparkled on his pinkie. "Are you ready for a little ramble through the House of Grand Passion, ladies?" he asked, looking from Caroline to me and then back again. His voice was high and melodious, and it flew from a British accent to a Continental one in the space of one word to the next. "I very much hope you like theater, Mademoiselle Lange," he said once we'd exchanged greetings.

I was about to tell him I loved the theater, but a wave of people had come up behind us, and he was already in motion. One minute he'd been all gallant attention, and now he was swanning his way across the room toward the new arrivals.

"Onward!" said Caroline, taking my arm and steering me into the next room, a large wainscoted ballroom with an elevated balcony at one end. The frescoes on the ceilings mimicked a summer sky full of birds and cottony clouds, and along one wall was an enormous frieze decorated with reclining dreamy-eyed nymphs. A gramophone had been set up near the stage, and in this part of the mansion a lush aria from the last century—"I Dreamt I Dwelled in Marble Halls"—could be heard over the roar of voices.

As we walked, Caroline kept a running commentary on the scene, pointing out this poet and that dowager, who couldn't stand whom and on what account.

"Oh, there's Consuelo!" she said, interrupting herself and gesturing toward a woman who stood a few paces away.

"But she's a woman."

"What else would she be?"

"Isn't Consuelo a man's name?"

She laughed. "Is it? I suppose 'Consuela' would be the more usual thing, but there's nothing usual about Consuelo. Now, let's go say hello."

"The press's idea of covering the war is running puff pieces on every parade this town puts on," Consuelo Kanaga was saying to two men—one bald and one goateed—as we approached. A wreath of smoke encircled her head. "That and spewing out the same rot coming out of Washington every day."

Caroline put a hand on Consuelo's shoulder. "You're not threatening to quit working at the paper again, are you, Connie?"

She turned around. "As a matter of fact, I am," she said flatly, but the next moment her expression relaxed into a smile and she was pulling Caroline into an embrace.

She was a terribly attractive, dashing kind of girl. Her hair was reddish brown, cut just above her shoulders, and she'd clipped it back on one side while keeping the other side loose. She was smoking—no, savoring—a cigar.

"You do realize," said Caroline, "you've been saying that since the first week you started working there?"

Consuelo threw her head back, exhaled, and looked at Caroline. A smile lurked at the edge of her lips. "Isn't that all the more indication I'll do it?"

"And leave this city with nothing to read but puff pieces and rot?" Caroline shook her head. "I don't believe you'd do that, Connie!" Her eyes went to me. "Dorothea Lange, this is Consuelo Kanaga, San Francisco's own lady reporter and its finest writer."

There were introductions and brisk hellos all around. The goateed man gave my hand a particularly vigorous shake.

"Dorothea was Arnold Genthe's apprentice in New York," Caroline offered.

Consuelo raised an eyebrow. "That so?"

"For about a year, yes."

She pressed her lips together and took a longer look at me.

"I'm a great admirer of his portraits," she said. "Such . . ." She paused and studied the ceiling, as if searching the air for just the right word. She exhaled a lavish plume of smoke. "Humanity," she finally declared, pointing her cigar at me for emphasis. Even behind her round-rimmed spectacles, her hooded blue eyes were fierce and steady. "Why'd you leave New York, Dorothea?"

I was pulled up short by that unwavering gaze.

"She's just getting set up here in San Francisco," Caroline broke in when she saw me falter. "Which is why I wanted to introduce you two. Dorrie, on top of being the city's most absolutely brilliant journalist, Consuelo's a member of the California Camera Club." She placed her hand on Consuelo's forearm. "You wouldn't mind hosting her at your next meeting, would you, Connie?"

"Well, we could certainly do with a fresh pair of eyes around here." She turned to me. "The first thing you need to know about San Francisco, Dorothea, is that this city knows how to look away like no other place in the world."

"Isn't that the beauty of it?" said the goateed man.

"Oh yes," Consuelo quipped, "its ugliness, too."

"Stop scaring her, Kanaga," someone said. "She only just got here."

"Nonsense! She should know where she's landed. She should see it as it is. As well we all should and seemingly won't." She turned away from the others and back to me. "Anyway, Dorothea," she continued, "the club's meeting isn't until next month, but I'll mention your name to our members. In the meantime, I have an assignment coming up that might interest you."

It was unnerving, the way she stared straight into you, but I nodded and told her I'd be very pleased to join her.

"Now that we're all friends," the bald man called out, "would you please finish telling us your ideas about covering the war, Miss Kanaga?"

She drilled him with a look. "War means tanks and trenches," she threw back. "Death, death, and more death. You can't avoid the reality of all that just to keep selling newspapers and Liberty bonds. Men are dying by the thousands, and now there's this horrid new disease tearing through the training camps. Knocks a perfectly healthy young person down dead in a day."

"It seems to be a kind of plague," said the goateed man. "Something out of the Middle Ages."

"Or worse," Consuelo said soberly.

"They say it's the Germans who let it loose." This was the bald man. "Poisoned our water, most likely, though I've heard Bayer's been tainting the aspirin they sell in the States."

"You can't actually believe that!" Consuelo exclaimed.

"Why not? There's nothing the Huns aren't capable of. Anyway, it won't be long before the war is over."

"Like hell. That's what they told us last year," she said, her voice hardening. "And the year before that."

Consuelo turned then to the subject of a journalist's obligation during war, the need for absolute truth, and how we were becoming too tentative with our opinions at exactly the moment we should be bolder and more clear-sighted. There were a few interjections now and then, mostly from the bald-headed man, but she dispatched them easily, without hesitation or apology.

"What's her story?" I asked Caroline as soon as we were alone again.

"Well, the main thing is, Consuelo's got guts. She makes every other reporter at that paper she works for look like a cub.

William Hearst—that's the *Examiner*'s owner—is angling to hire
her. She's considering it, though I couldn't tell you why, except
they're both opposed to this horrific war."

"You're not for it, then, either. Not for the war."

"Have you seen the numbers of dead, Dorrie? Ten thousand
just this week."

The number hung in the air, and neither of us could say anything.

In the last months I'd read the news with increasing despair.
Firebombed villages, teenaged boys shot in ditches, rivers
choked with corpses poisoned by mustard gas—a collage of
gruesome images appeared in my mind's eye. Every month of
that year had been the worst month, more men gone, more
dead.

Caroline cleared her throat. "Consuelo's one of the people
actually doing something. Not to stop it—it's too late for that—
but she wants to make people see it for what it is." She paused
and glanced across the room at Consuelo, who was still holding
forth, waving her cigar as she talked. "She lives in a working-
man's hotel in North Beach with two dozen Portuguese fishermen. Can you even imagine?"

I couldn't—not at all. But, then again, until a few minutes
ago I couldn't have imagined someone like Consuelo Kanaga.
Where, I wondered, did all that courage come from?

"Don't let her fool you," Caroline went on. "She's tough and
opinionated and all that, but she's also the kindest, most helpful
person you could ever know. There's a story that when she was
growing up in Sausalito, she rowed out to Alcatraz by herself
one night. Apparently she felt so sorry for the inmates that she
got it in her head to rescue some of them. Think of it, a ten-

year-old girl rowing all that way alone in a dinghy. What a sight she must have been!"

"Did she really make it to Alcatraz?"

"She sure did, but the warden caught her and dragged her back home to her parents."

"Doesn't look like it did much to keep her in line."

"Exactly!" Caroline said, and we both laughed. "Nothing can shake that woman. Nothing I've ever seen, anyway. I can't tell you the number of times she's helped me out over the years. She's the one who helped get me my place at Monkey Block, you know."

By this time we'd come to the end of the gallery. Strings of lanterns crisscrossed the ceiling, which gave the room a lovely, warm glow.

"It's like a carnival in here."

"You have no idea," she said with a vague kind of smile. "Why don't you grab some seats while I get us something to drink?" She gestured to the far end of the room, to the several rows of high-back leather chairs. Pinned to the back of each chair was a red rose, great care having been taken to arrange it just so. "I'll be back in two shakes."

I made my way past the guests, catching bits of conversation as I went, memorizing a face here and there. I was beginning to feel at ease for the first time since arriving at the party. Of course, the dress helped. A lot. It was as if by wearing it I'd been given a share of Caroline's glamour and confidence.

There must have been two hundred or more people in the room, crowded shoulder to shoulder, society ladies mingling among bedraggled poets, flamboyant dancers, high-strung musicians, and who-knew-who-all. There were far more women than men, at least three for every one, but that was the case everywhere now that we'd entered the war.

Standing in that ballroom, I had a memory of my father. Once, to reward me for reciting a whole play from his huge, leatherbound book of Shakespeare, he'd hired a horse-drawn carriage to take us into the city for a performance of *A Midsummer Night's Dream*. I was young, not yet ten years old. When we got to the theater, there were no seats and for several minutes I saw nothing, only felt the heat of bodies and breathed the odor of cigars and sweat, but then my father hoisted me up onto his shoulders so that I had a clear view of the stage.

"This belongs to you as much as anyone," he'd told me. "Do you understand?"

Somehow I did.

"Now, you be my eyes, Dorothea," he said as the curtains parted. "Tell me everything you see."

It was hurtful to think of him, and mostly I forced myself not to, but he'd had such glamour to him, such gallantry, and I couldn't help but think he would've been fully in his element here.

I went back to studying the guests. I could've gone on listening and looking about for a long time, hours even, but I was conscious suddenly of the hard clap of heels against the parquet floor. I heard it even over all the noise in the room.

Looking over my shoulder, I saw a black cape, then a wide-brimmed black hat, then black cowboy boots and a silver-tipped cane. The figure wearing them streaked past me and across the room. His white shirt looked beautifully starched and crisp against all that black, as if he'd just stepped off a sunlit ranch or prairie, or else a movie screen.

My first thought was that it was a costume and he was an

actor. My second was that he was handsome, strikingly so. A John Barrymore type. Gorgeous. Tall and lean, with dark hair that fell into his eyes. I put him at about forty, though with the hat it was hard to tell.

Everyone at the party knew who he was—that was obvious. I watched him fall in with a group that had gathered just to the side of the balcony. He immediately became the center of attention, talking animatedly as the others, the women especially, looked on and listened and laughed.

I knew I was staring, but I couldn't seem to stop. There was a moment when he looked in my general direction and his eyes flicked up toward me. He'd seen me, or at least I imagined he had. The next instant he dipped back into the conversation. I had a sharp urge to get his attention somehow, or at least put myself in his line of sight, but I stopped. What could I possibly say to a man like that? And then the old familiar fear flashed over me. If I got closer, he'd see it. He'd see my crippled leg.

I picked my way through the room and found a pair of empty chairs. Soon Caroline reappeared with two cut-crystal cocktail glasses, each with a plump olive at the bottom. She touched her glass to mine.

"Is he part of the show?" I asked after we'd each taken a sip. "The man in the cowboy hat?"

"Oh," she said, tracing my gaze, "you mean Maynard Dixon." She was holding her glass cupped in both hands. She removed the olive and sucked on it meditatively. "He's a painter, but yes, he's always part of the show." She plucked the pit discreetly from her mouth, took a second then a third swallow of martini. Having drained her glass, she narrowed her eyes at me. "Hang on a minute. You haven't gone sweet on him, have you?"

There was a second's almost-awkward silence, and then we

were interrupted by the crash of cymbals. Someone had lifted the needle off the gramophone; the lights dimmed and flickered off; and people were suddenly streaming into the ballroom and scrambling into chairs. After another crash of cymbals, there was a long hush, and then everyone looked up toward the balcony.

The King of Bohemia stepped out from behind a pair of velvet curtains, his hair molded, his skin gleaning. He'd changed into some sort of long white robe. There were cheers and a burst of applause. In one hand he held a burning candle, which threw shadows on his face; in his other hand he held a large book bound in green cloth, from which he suddenly began to read.

Come, I will make the continent indissoluble;
I will make the most splendid race the sun ever yet shone
     upon;
I will make divine magnetic lands;
With the love of comrades,
With the life-long love of comrades.

Leaves of Grass. I recognized the lines from Whitman's "For You O Democracy," but the way he was reading the poem threw me off. He'd sing a few verses—actually sing them—then stop for several long moments, standing completely still. I tried to follow along, but the words began to meld and elongate so that I couldn't make sense of them.

He went on for an awfully long time. I wanted to like it, really I did, but after a few minutes I found myself fidgeting and peering around the dark room, trying to catch sight of the man in the cloak and cowboy hat. I couldn't find him, though, so I looked back toward the balcony and tried again to focus on what was happening there. A good deal of time went by—half an hour or more. When his words finally died away, the King of Bohemia brought the book to his heart and closed his eyes.

There was absolute silence. The lights were still low, the air was steamy. Then the lights flashed off, on again, and from somewhere behind him a clutch of doves broke loose and went soaring across the room.

Looking around, I saw the faces of people who'd witnessed a miracle. Everyone seemed to hold their breath until at last the king opened his eyes, gazed out at them, and bowed deeply. There was the sudden loud pop of a photographer's flash, followed by a long, raucous chorus of bravos as the crowd shot up for a standing ovation.

I got to my feet and was crushed, elbow to elbow, by people to either side of me.

I stood there for a long time, peering up at the now-empty balcony and trying to make sense of the performance. The doves had taken cover in the eaves, though one was circling the room in a clear but frenzied bid for freedom.

That was "theater"? Someone mangling *Leaves of Grass* in the dark and trapping birds in a ballroom?

With the lights back on, the gramophone had started up and people were milling about and talking loudly again. Somewhere, somehow, Caroline got lost in the shuffle. I was searching the room for her, when I realized with a jolt that he was right there, just a few feet across from me. Maynard Dixon. The man in cape and cowboy hat. He was gliding toward me with great loping strides.

"His real name's Sadakichi Hartmann," he said. No hello, no introduction or preliminaries of any kind. I was conscious of his height—he was six feet tall, at least—and I was so flustered it took me a moment to realize he was referring to the King of Bohemia. "I couldn't help but notice your confusion, miss," he went on. "He's a writer, art critic, actor, and a half dozen other things. I hear he and Walt Whitman used to discuss poetry over plates of fried eggs in Brooklyn. He drifted into town a few months ago from Paris, and he's been calling himself the King of Bohemia ever since."

"But he must have money. How else can he afford this place?"

Amusement creased the corners of his eyes. "You're new to San Francisco," he said pleasantly and by way of answer.

"Yes."

He smiled. A soft, slow smile. Now that he'd taken off his hat, I saw that his hair was tinged with silver at the temples but otherwise as dark and sleek as a blackbird's breast. Faint lines fanned out around his blue eyes, but there was something distinctly boyish about him. Also, I saw now that he wasn't wearing a costume, not really. His outfit was more than a little calculated, but he wore it well—as if he didn't take it at all seriously and he wanted you to enjoy it, too.

"See those ladies he's talking to?" He lifted his chin slightly in the direction of two women. I recognized the tall one with the two small dogs and ridiculous hat. She was the woman who'd been talking to the King of Bohemia when we first arrived, the one who'd gaped at Caroline. "That's Alma Spreckels. She's married to Adolph Spreckels, head of the Spreckels Sugar Company."

I turned. "I haven't heard of it."

"But you have heard the term 'sugar daddy'?"

I nodded.

"Well, that's her nickname for her husband. Adolph Spreck-

els is the bona fide original sugar daddy. At last count, their palace on Pacific Heights had twenty-five bathrooms and just as
many dogs. She wants to turn this city into Paris, to which I say
bonne chance, Madame. And over there, by the fireplace"—he
nodded toward a woman in a yellow dress—"is Mrs. M. H. de
Young. Mrs. Spreckels's husband shot Mrs. de Young's husband
sometime back in the last century. The two ladies are therefore
not on speaking terms. Some of the wealthiest women in San
Francisco are here tonight, and in a few minutes they'll be sitting on chairs borrowed from the mortuary down the street."

"You're joking."

He held my eyes, enjoying the moment. "I most certainly
am not, miss. This fine mansion was abandoned for months before our so-called king installed himself here. Now, for the tri-
fling sum of five dollars, these fine ladies have the privilege of
mingling with real live *artistes* and experiencing an avant-garde
recitation of *Leaves of Grass.* Some of them have already bought
season tickets, fifty dollars for the series."

"You mean it's a swindle?"

He laughed. "A magic show, more like. The audience knows
it's not real, the magician knows it's not real, but that doesn't
make it any less fun, does it?"

We stood next to each other for a few minutes, watching the
other guests. By then all the chairs had been pushed to the wall
to make room for dancing. Women were kicking off their shoes;
men were taking off their jackets and loosening their ties. Two
women whirled past us, laughing as they danced with their
arms wrapped round each other and the tune grew more fevered. Next I recognized Caroline, by the flash of her green
satin dress. She was dancing with a red-faced teenager in a bow
tie and fine-looking three-piece suit.

"Want to join them?" he asked.

That was something I couldn't do. Not with my drop foot. We'd been standing as we talked, so he couldn't have noticed my limp. At least I was pretty sure he hadn't. I couldn't let him see me stumbling and struggling.

"I'm not too good at dancing."

"You know, there's a secret to it." He leaned closer and dropped his voice. "A very secret secret," he said gravely.

I had to laugh. "Yes?"

"All it really takes is letting go."

"I'm not so good at that, either," I answered much too quickly, but he didn't hear me over the music, or else he was bent on proving me wrong, because the next thing he did was to take my hand and steer me toward the middle of the room.

I was terrified of embarrassing myself. Turns out, I didn't have to worry about that. We'd barely made it to the dance floor when I saw a flash of bright-yellow hair. A woman was thrusting herself through the crowd, pushing roughly and unevenly past one couple after another. A few times she stopped to yank a fallen strap from her bare shoulders. She was drunk, you could see that from twenty feet away, but it wasn't in her gait or her rumpled dress; it was in her eyes.

"You!" she shouted, and lurched to a stop a few feet short of us. My first thought was that she meant me. She didn't. She did no more than glance my way before focusing her attention on my companion. "You!" she screamed again, and caught him by the shoulder. Conversations faltered all around us. She was out of breath, cheeks streaked red from drink and exertion. Before I knew what was coming, she twisted toward me and slapped me very hard, so hard it set my ears ringing. I put a hand to my face, less in pain than in astonishment.

Maynard grabbed for her wrists, but he couldn't get hold of her. She was gripping a bottle of wine by the neck. When she raised it high over her head, there was a shriek, and all around us people stepped back and scattered. I saw a woman raise her hand to cover her open mouth. A few people fled.

"Now, Lillian, please be calm—" Maynard said, his eyes pleading and his voice pitched low in misery. He stepped toward her and reached for her arm.

I felt my shoulders tense up and I shrank back. I had no idea at all what to say or do.

"Don't you touch me!" she snarled, jerking herself free. "You think you can cast me off—is that what you think? Because if you do, you're a goddamn idiot!" There was more, a whole lot more, and much more swearing, too.

The next thing happened very fast. The woman came at Maynard with the bottle, swinging it up toward his head. This time he managed to grab her wrist, but she stumbled, took three reeling steps backward, tripped, and fell to the floor with a fleshy thump. When she landed, the straps of her dress had slipped off her shoulders, her skirt was hitched up to her thighs, and her legs were sprawled out in front of her. The bottle had flown from her hand, smashing into shards about thirty feet away. Amazingly, no one had been hurt.

All in an instant she was weeping, with her hands over her face. She seemed shrunken, deflated, and small. Her feet were bare, and for a moment I thought her shoes had slipped off, but then it occurred to me she hadn't been wearing any to begin with.

There was a moment when the whole room seemed to go quiet, which was impossible since the music was booming, loud as before. People stood stiff, as silent as mannequins.

He bent low and said something into the woman's ear, and it seemed to calm her slightly. She reached a hand out to him. With that, he lifted her off the ground and onto her feet, and people moved away to make room for them to pass.

I was confused. Until the woman appeared, he'd been fully focused on me, talking and laughing easily, but now he was stalking away, as heedless, or oblivious, to me as if I'd disappeared.

An effort was under way to clean up the glass. Gradually, people went back to whatever they'd been doing before—dancing, gossiping, flirting, arguing.

"Well," said Caroline.

I didn't know how long she'd been standing beside me, but she'd clearly seen the whole ugly scene unfold.

"Who was that?" I asked.

She took a moment to answer, and when she spoke, her voice was quiet and somber. "Lillian Dixon."

"His wife?"

"Ex-wife," she said, which only confused me more.

"But if they're divorced, why are they still so . . ."

"Tangled up with each other?"

I nodded.

"Well, I don't know the whole story—nobody ever does, I suppose—but it's been going on for years. She gets drunk, he starts drinking, and then they get in the most awful fights. He had her arrested once. To get back at him, she tried to shoot him with his own pistol. I think she would've killed him, but he managed to escape to the Bohemian Club—that's a very fancy gentleman's club downtown. Women are banned from the club, which is lucky for Maynard because it wound up saving his life. Another time she jumped off a boat during a party—a lark, supposedly, but everyone knows the bay's always freezing, and the currents can pull you right under. . . ." She gave a slow shake of her head. "Her mind's not altogether right."

"How do you mean?"

"Lillian drinks like a fish, always has, but there's more to it. No one knows what to call it, though. Episodes? Attacks? She makes a scene, then weeps and apologizes, and the next week it happens again. It's terrible. And very sad."

We could see them making their way toward the door, a tall figure all in black and a yellow-haired woman clinging to him hard.

Kind as Caroline was, I saw now that she was also the sort who always looked a thing straight in the eye. "You have to be careful there, Dorrie. He's a genius, and as charming as he's handsome, but he's trouble. You're more sensible not to give him a second thought, I know you are. Besides," she said when they'd disappeared from sight, "I've still got loads more people to introduce you to, so let's get to it."

It had been wonderful—so wonderful—talking with Maynard Dixon, but I didn't need to see anything more to know I should steer clear of him. By the time I put my hand in Caroline's and followed her from the room, I had the feeling I'd just dodged some very messy thing.

Of course, that wasn't how it turned out at all.

4.

So it began: my life in San Francisco.

When I first arrived in May of 1918, the city belonged to the bohemians, which is to say to the artists, poets, and writers—and the vast, varied company they attracted. You saw them everywhere, but the cafés, bakeries, restaurants, and pubs of North Beach, the small Italian village on Telegraph Hill, were bursting with them. They'd all come from somewhere else, and they all had a story to tell. That was another thing about San Francisco: Every time you met someone, it was like stepping into a story just as they were making it up. And now I was one of them. Or starting to be.

To hear Caroline tell it—which she did from a back booth at Coppa's during my first days in the city—San Francisco's best stories always started on Telegraph Hill.

"Close your eyes and picture it, Dorrie. Mark Twain sailing down Columbus Avenue. Wild red hair, scraggly beard . . ."

It was plain from the heaps of books in her room that she loved to read. Twain, I now learned, was a particular favorite.

"Fine," I said, shutting my eyes, "but where's he headed?"

"Fior d'Italia," she said without skipping a beat. "On his way to dine on oyster bisque and calamari and drink buckets of champagne with Ambrose Bierce."

I cracked an eye open. "Ambrose who?"

"Ambrose Bierce. Haven't you read *The Devil's Dictionary*?"

I shook my head.

"Remind me to lend it to you. It's wonderfully clever and more than a bit wicked."

"Is there anything you haven't read?"

"I just like stories," she said with a shrug. "Now, stop interrupting and listen, please."

Robert Louis Stevenson, Frank Norris, Bret Harte, Oscar Wilde, Ina Coolbirth, Mary Austin, Jack London. Once the Sierras had been stripped bare and the gold rush burned itself out, San Francisco drew hordes of people to its fog-soaked streets. For every journalist, novelist, sculptor, painter, or poet who'd made a name for himself (and occasionally herself) here, hundreds more came looking for anonymity or immortality—or some mix of the two. All day long, and for many years, they hustled up and down North Beach with their manuscripts, canvases, and political leaflets under one arm and their bottles of wine and loaves of sourdough under the other. At night they'd return to the large, squat building on Montgomery Street, where, after dining at Coppa's, they'd spill into the saloon at the other end of the building for a few rounds of Pisco Punch. Somewhere well past the edge of midnight, they'd hole up in the honeycomb of tiny rooms on the top three floors.

"Then came the earthquake."

This was the part of the story where Caroline's face fell and her voice softened.

In 1906, when the earth beneath San Francisco shuddered and cracked, barely a brick budged at the artists' colony on Montgomery Street, but with the rest of the city in ruins, the writers and artists fled to other places. Carmel. New York. Paris. Mexico City. One by one the rooms at Monkey Block emptied, and North Beach sank into a kind of sleep.

Now, a decade later, a new generation of bohemians had laid claim to the city. San Francisco was booming, even as the Great War was shattering an already broken world to bits. Up in city hall, a plump, silk-stockinged, mustachioed mayor named Sunny Rolph was shaking hands with a brash band of investors and an even brasher band of police, observing the city's oldest tradition: making money. Not that the war was far away. It wasn't. Large convoys of young men—such young men—shipped out from San Francisco each week in starched uniforms and gleaming boots. Tanker fumes tinged the air; pools of oil swirled on the shore. The news from Europe was worse and worse. The Germans were bearing down on Europe, advancing on almost every front. In the papers and in the streets, there was an ongoing litany against foreigners, anarchists, communists, and other subversives. In the cafés, studios, and saloons of North Beach, there was low, urgent talk of spies, enemy sweeps, arrests, and deportations. There was fear and uncertainty and dangers we couldn't even name.

Still, it was a new time. A time for fresh ideas and different possibilities. Mark Twain was long gone, but Frida Kahlo and Diego Rivera were on their way. In most ways San Francisco was still a small town, and the people were fascinating and the stories were glorious. There were men and women, women and women, and men and men. The city and the decade were positively made for each other. Everyone did whatever they wanted to do. When we gathered at Monkey Block to float above San Francisco Bay, there was a sweetness to it, a sense of possibility. Coppa's might've lost its luster a long time ago, but there was still a kind of gold to the place. In my memories I see the plush seats, the gilt-edged mirrors, the glittering chandelier. I see a place where the red velvet walls shimmered, the Victrola never stopped playing, and every hour of every day was shot through with laughter, secrets, and brilliant talk.

Most of all, though, I see Caroline.

A good night's sleep made it as clear as could be: I was never going to get a job by just wandering around the city. This was Monday, less than a week after I'd landed in San Francisco. Walking down Market, I happened on a Western Union office. I ducked inside and opened the city directory. The entry for PHOTOGRAPHY turned up a fair number of prospects. Well, that was it. I decided right then to take the very first job that got me back to making pictures, didn't matter what it was.

That's how I wound up working at Marsh & Company, a little five-and-dime shop on Market Street. In addition to selling luggage, umbrellas, and stationery, the owner ran a side business repairing cameras and printing photographs. My job there was a step down from my last one—several, actually. I was burning to make my own portraits. No chance of that. I was lucky to have the job, though. Very lucky. If it wasn't for the war, it would have gone to some young man. Working at Marsh & Company would at least keep me clothed and fed until I could find something better. Soon I might even be able to buy my camera back.

For now, though, I was stuck in the storeroom, a dank, dark place but one in which I was determined to make myself useful. I began by corralling the papers on Mr. Marsh's desk and filing them. When that was done, I separated the stacks of photographs I found heaped about and sorted them into a basic organizational scheme: still lifes in one set of files, portraits in the other, landscapes in a third.

Throughout the day, customers dropped in with their busted cameras and various other broken machines, but there were few of them, which made the store an unexpectedly peaceful place amid the hubbub of downtown. I'd spend my half-hour break at the Emporium lunch counter, where I'd eat a five-cent egg sandwich and stare out at a city that was not yet mine but that was looking less strange and forbidding all the time.

Since leaving home, I'd had precious little contact with my mother. Our estrangement started right away. The last thing I wanted was them thinking I'd made a mess of things. Mama would send me a letter care of the post office every few weeks, and I'd reply with the occasional postcard, filling her in on the most basic news—that I'd decided to stay in San Francisco, that I was working hard, that I'd found a place to live, that California was very nice.

A week into my job, Mr. Marsh gave me a spot behind the photography counter in the front of the store. It was still miles away from making portraits but an improvement all the same. In the afternoons, when business was the slowest, I worked on finishing photographs. That's what I was doing one day when I came across a picture that stopped me cold.

It was a portrait of a child, or rather of a child's hand. There

was a mossiness at the edges of the picture, as if the moment
had been softened by time, love, memory. I was mesmerized. A
hunger of the eye—that's what I felt when I saw a good picture,
and that's what I felt now. I went on wanting to keep looking; I
couldn't be satiated.

I peered at the signature. At the bottom right of the picture
I read: *I. Cunningham.*

How had I never come across his name? Where had he
studied? Did he show his pictures or only sell them privately?
And—the most burning question of all—might he need an
assistant?

I had to meet him, this I. Cunningham.

Fortunately, I didn't have to wait long. He appeared one Friday afternoon about a week later. A bespectacled man with a
mustache and a mass of thick, dark hair.

After he settled the bill, I screwed up the courage to compliment him on his photographs.

He stared at me for a moment, then smiled. "I'm afraid
you're mistaken, miss."

"I'm sorry?"

"Oh, they're fine photographs, very fine. What you're mistaken about is them being mine." He stuck out his hand. "I'm
Roi Partridge."

"Dorothea Lange," I said, and shook his hand. "But who—"

"These are Imogen's—Imogen Cunningham." After a pause
he added, "My wife."

Half-baked dilettantes. With the exception of one or two women
he himself had anointed, that's what Alfred Stieglitz called female photographers. In New York I'd come to espouse some of

that awful thinking, but here were some of the very best pictures I'd ever seen, and they were a woman's work.

That night I lay in bed, staring at the ceiling and thinking about Imogen Cunningham's pictures. It was a phenomenal stroke of luck to have printed those pictures in my first week in San Francisco, though it wasn't the first instance of great good fortune in the city and it wouldn't be the last.

But how had she done it? It took years to produce work of that caliber. I knew a bit about what made it possible for a woman to succeed, but I knew much more about what didn't. That was the whole miserable story of my years in Hoboken.

At night after we'd eaten and the dishes were washed and put away, I used to sit on the old sagging couch in the parlor and look at my mother and grandmother—my mother hunched over and squinting to thread a needle, a huge basket of mending at her feet, my grandmother's eyes purpled with fatigue, two deep furrows creasing her brow and a teacup of whiskey on the table beside her. The night would close around us, the room would grow smaller, the noises louder. There was the hiss of water coming to a boil, the ticking of a clock, voices from the street below. And there was something else, a sense of time standing still. Here I was and here I'd be next week, the week after that, and all the weeks to come.

I had to find a way out.

"I've been thinking about taking a photography course," I blurted one night. This was back when I wore black cotton stockings and still had my hair down to my waist.

I'd barely spoken the words when they started trying to talk me out of it, Grossmama with her taunts and Mama with her pleas. What was the point of that? Nobody wanted a lady photographer. A teacher or a typist maybe (but only maybe), but certainly not a photographer. *You're impractical,* they said. *Any extra money you come by should go toward the household,* they said. *Or do you think you have no responsibilities to anyone but yourself? Are you like those girls who cut off their hair one day and leave home the next? At the very least, you need something to fall back on,* they said.

That, I knew, would be a terrible mistake; once you fell back on something, you'd never stop falling. So I worked; I squirreled away my money; I took all the classes I could. Eventually I got a job as an assistant in a photography studio. I was good at it, better than I'd ever been at anything. Trouble was, I couldn't make it any further than somebody's assistant.

But things could be different for me here—maybe.

I'd met many photographers in New York, but very few were women. Now, suddenly, I was meeting one after another. First there'd been Consuelo, with her fiery talk of art and justice. She was devoted to her work, though often contemptuous of her profession, unyielding about her ideas of what mattered, and not the slightest bit concerned with what anybody made of her. No wonder Caroline loved her. Soon there'd be Imogen Cunningham, with her extreme close-ups of flowers and bodies and all manner of things, then Alma Lavenson and her magnificent landscapes. There'd be Tina Modotti, Louise Dahl, Margrethe Mather, and Hansel Mieth. There'd be the splendidly daring Anne Brigman, who trekked out to the Sierras to photograph herself nude and with that shocked a city you'd think had long since lost its ability to be shocked.

They hadn't just survived in San Francisco; they'd flourished.

It was no accident. Female photographers did well here for a reason. There was the war, of course, which had given them an opening, but they had other advantages. There'd never been an established set of photographers in San Francisco before the war—no Stieglitz to rule the profession as though it were his kingdom—and the ones who had settled here escaped after the 1906 earthquake and never returned. Arnold Genthe, my mentor, had been one of them. The sum of all this was that the absence of authority made it possible for women to develop their own methods and styles.

There were chances for me in California, many more than I'd had back east, but my real luck, I was starting to see, was that I'd landed in such excellent company. Caroline, Consuelo, Imogen, Alma, Anne—each of them was showing me something new. A future, a way forward, a sharper version of myself.

But to make the final, necessary leap, I'd need something besides inspiration. I'd need money. So it was money I began to think of now—how much it would take, how to get it, and what I'd do once I had it.

You wouldn't have guessed it from how she carried herself, but money was a constant source of worry for Caroline and had been for years. Monday to Friday she worked ten-hour days in the basement of the White House department store. Each morning she'd shrug off the pretty coat and dress in which she'd arrived and pull on the dull-black frock intended to make her invisible. All day long, under the tireless, merciless eye of her supervisor, she altered and mended and pressed dresses and readied them for display. The gloss and sparkle of the showrooms was off-limits to her, but she'd never pined for it anyway. What she loved was to create her own designs. To save some money for fabric and notions, but just as often to make ends meet, she took in mending, which paid a pittance. Three or four days a month she also modeled for some artist or another at Monkey Block, which paid even less.

The constant scrambling from one job to the next whittled down her days, but Caroline and I spent whatever free time we had together. From the beginning, poverty, as much as ambition, shaped our friendship. Our diversions were, of necessity, cheap. Caroline didn't care to come to my room at the Elizabeth, but I wouldn't have wanted her to, since I couldn't really stand it there myself, except as a place to sleep. Instead, we spent hours up in her apartment, surrounded by all that beautiful clutter. Sitting in the front room, with the shaded lamp casting a circle of light on the table and sofa and the rest of the room in pleasant dimness, we'd listen to a record on her third-hand gramophone as we played a little gin rummy, or we'd just sit and talk, drinking tea and eating toast and marmalade.

I loved her conversation, her splendid spirit, her magnificent, rambling stories. Her cheerfulness was infectious. Sometimes I'd wonder about her family and whether they lived in San Francisco, but she seemed free of all ties but the ones she'd forged at Monkey Block. One night during my first weeks in the city, she steered me around the building and introduced me to "everyone." There was her third-floor neighbor, George Sterling, who'd read his poems aloud to us in the robin's-egg-blue apartment where he displayed no fewer than twenty-three portraits of himself. There was Xavier Martínez, from Guadalajara, who painted moody nocturnes. There was Betty Haywood, a gorgeous and ferociously funny girl from Kansas who danced at the Hippodrome, the biggest dance hall up on Pacific Street.

There was plenty to keep us busy in Monkey Block, but we were young and hungry for what was "out there"—or as much of it as we could see. We were often barred from going where we wanted. It wasn't just a lack of money that did it. Fridays and Saturdays we tramped around the city and peeked into the dance halls. We got no farther than the door. We couldn't afford tickets, but half those places wouldn't have let us in anyway. An unwritten rule forbade Chinese from entering, much less patronizing, many establishments—and there were plenty of places where it was spelled right out: NO CHINESE. The closer you got to Chinatown, the worse it was. Up in North Beach I'd seen several businesses with large hand-lettered signs tacked onto their doors or placed among the items in their window displays. That stopped Caroline, but anything short of an outright ban and she'd just blaze right in wherever she pleased.

She knew what it was to be invisible, and she knew what it was to be too visible. She knew the places where she'd be turned away and where she was likeliest to move with ease, but she also knew where the hills had been hollowed out, where giant ships lay trapped underneath the bay, where a hundred thousand trees had once been planted to veil the shore from enemies. She showed me everything she loved and some of what she feared. Wherever we went, the trick, it seemed, was to feel joy and freedom despite, and sometimes because of, the ugliness around us.

If we had a scrap of money, we ducked into a nickelodeon or split a gelato at a café tucked back in a little North Beach alley or trawled for bargains in the basement of the Emporium (THE BIG E—YOU CAN ALWAYS FIND IT AT THE EMPORIUM!). We got cheap balcony seats at the California to see Charlie Chaplin or Douglas Fairbanks or Theda Bara. We ducked into Parentes for Pisco Punch, which, at two for a quarter, was the best deal outside of Coppa's. With the city ringed with green hills and wildflowers, we took many long walks, which didn't cost a thing. One of our favorite rambles took us across the sloping fields of

Golden Gate Park to the Japanese Tea Garden, where we'd wander for hours among the pines, cedars, and cypresses, the arched
drum bridge, pagodas, stone lanterns, and koi ponds. Thankfully I was back to walking more or less normally, with just the
usual hitch in my step, and Caroline had grown used to slowing
her pace to match mine.

For all our frank conversations, when it came to her par-
amours, Caroline kept her stories to herself. Of course she had
lovers—some part of me knew that's why she'd slip away some
nights—but she was very discreet. She had to be. Chinese men,
she said, kept their distance on account of her being a "half-
breed." Her suitors tended to be Latin American or European—
before the war she'd been in some complicated situation with a
devastatingly handsome Welsh poet—but that presented its
own considerable problems. An Oriental and white couple
could never be seen out in the streets together; it could get you
arrested, even in San Francisco. If it ever happened—and surely
it did, her own parentage proof of such mixing—it was not
something anyone admitted. You kept it a secret because that
was the only way you could grab at happiness without the world
snatching it away from you first.

Mostly it was the two of us, and that suited me just fine. We
wiled away one glorious Sunday at Sutro's, which we paid for by
going without a meal that day. It was a bright afternoon in June,
and Caroline was wearing a pair of round-rimmed sunglasses
that hid her eyes. The place was crawling with people, and that
was maybe why we didn't get turned away, though her nervi-
ness likely played the bigger part. The fashion for bathing costumes was still all the way to the ankles, though Caroline's suit
pushed it to the limit. She just sailed right in with her lavender
bathing costume and matching lavender bathing cap, found a

spot on the bleachers, and propped a book on her knees. Unless she was sewing, she didn't easily sit still, but books always held her in a state of silent enchantment. That day it was a dime-store novel.

While Caroline disappeared into her book, I swam in the heated pool. It was a delicious feeling, slipping into the water, feeling the warm silkiness of it against my bare skin. Water was the one place where I could forget my limp, where the weight and sense of being seen lifted, but I hadn't gone swimming in years. It was just one of those things I'd somehow lost or given up.

"You can't let any of it stop you," Caroline used to say. "You have to make your own rules."

"But what if they catch you?"

"You go someplace else. There's always someplace else."

What Caroline was teaching me was how to be free, which de-pended on knowing how to make yourself disappear.

It's no small trick to disappear as a woman, but I'd been prac-ticing for years. It started when I had polio, and it'd stuck. That's when I'd learned disappearing had as much to do with how you held your face and moved your body as what you looked like, but now I was discovering how to make use of my invisibility.

I took to wandering in the city on my own after work. I was determined to spend as little time as possible at the Elizabeth. Also, I loved the early-evening hours, loved the feel of the city shrugging off the day and easing into a looser version of itself. I'd set out from Market, starting from Marsh's, and drift up toward Van Ness before circling back to the boardinghouse.

Somehow I never felt tired on those walks, never felt more than a faint ache in my leg.

The tight, teeming streets and alleys of North Beach, the jazz dives and dance halls of Fillmore Street, the clamor of the shipyards at dawn—the city was strange and wonderful, and I was aching to see it, every slope, shoreline, street, and alley. You could walk ten minutes in any direction and find yourself in a new world. Trouble was, the only hours I had for myself were at night, and even in a city that didn't much care for propriety, a woman still didn't dare go out alone past dark.

Then one day everything changed. I was walking in my old mackintosh past the City of Paris after work, when I caught my reflection in the store window. There it was, plain as day: That coat made me invisible. I'd worn it for years on my walks through New York, walks on which I'd learned the pleasure of solitude and begun to shed my fear of being out alone in the city. A few weeks before, I'd nearly thrown it away outside the ferry building, but looking at myself now, I saw its power was undiminished; if anything, it was stronger.

What really struck me was that with my bobbed hair and my coat turned up at the collar, I looked almost like a boy. Something was missing, though, and all at once I knew what. I marched into the men's department and bought myself a hat. More specifically, a fedora. I worried for a moment about the expense—I was still saving to buy my camera back—but this, I reasoned, would be money well spent.

It was. That hat made the world suddenly much bigger. The streets were dark and mostly empty, but in my coat and new hat I felt safe, even strong. I wore it tilted forward, low over my eyes. It covered my eyebrows and half of my nose. I marveled at how

I could now walk in the streets without anyone looking at me. I threw my shoulders back, kept my gaze ahead. I walked for the sake of seeing. After leaving the City of Paris, I browsed the stacks at Paul Elder & Company bookstore for a while, then walked to the end of Market, all the way to Dolores Park, a part of the city I'd never been before, where I sat on a bench and stared at the palm trees and imagined the lives of the people who walked by. When I tired of that, I walked into a Mexican bodega and bought a pan dulce, which I ate while walking back toward the boardinghouse.

I stayed out much later than usual that night, timing things so that I got back to the Elizabeth five minutes before curfew. Mrs. Connors, the boardinghouse mistress, stood waiting in the foyer with her arms crossed over her chest, a heavy key around her neck and her eye on the tall grandfather clock. I sailed past her, my smile haloed with spun sugar from the pan dulce.

"It's brilliant," Caroline said when I showed her my hat and told her what it made possible, and it was, because that's the sort of thing San Francisco does: hands you a costume and sets you free.

It was on one of my walks that I saw Maynard Dixon again. I was wandering around North Beach on a Saturday afternoon after shopping for groceries—a clutch of eggs, a few apples, some cheese, and a small loaf of bread. I'd just stopped to arrange the basket under my arm, when I glimpsed something through the swarm of people: the flash of a familiar black hat. I tripped and nearly sent the basket flying. Two apples fell to the ground and rolled toward the gutter. I stumbled to my feet, jammed the now-bruised apples into the basket, and searched the street for him.

More than a few times I'd wondered where he might live, and when I heard he had a studio on Montgomery Street, just a few doors from Monkey Block, it seemed a matter of time before I'd run into him. Whenever I went to Coppa's or dropped in on Caroline, I'd glance around for that black hat and cape, but if he was there, I never saw him. It was as if he'd disappeared.

I wasn't sure what I wanted from him, but it was always there, just under the surface. The hope I'd see him again.

Back home, before the war, I'd had one or two of what my mother called "gentleman friends." Growing up I'd had the same crushes as other girls, the same awkward kisses and fumbling exchanges, but with my leg it was understood no one would want to marry me. At least it wasn't to be counted on, not for me. I never entirely shook loose the sense that I'd missed my chance, taking up all those years in one job or another, always working too much to be bothered to get myself sorted out, by which my mother and grandmother meant married. But I knew *not* getting married had made everything possible. Even the jobs, miserable and low-paying as they were, would have never been mine had I been married.

Mostly, though, romance struck me as not only pointless but dangerous. It'd pulled my mother right under, and I was determined never to let that happen to me. That I was afraid of being rejected and ridiculed was something I knew, but in a distant sort of way.

And yet. Somehow I couldn't shake off my preoccupation with Maynard Dixon. I started asking around about him, just a few questions here and there. As far as I could tell, no one had seen him since the party in Pacific Heights. Someone said he'd gone to Arizona. Carmel, said another person. Nearly everyone had an opinion of him, that was for sure, and I heard all sorts of stories: that he came from an extremely wealthy old southern family; that he had half the members of the Bohemian Club, an exclusive gentleman's club near Union Square, in his back pocket; that he had connections—close connections—as high up as the mayor's office.

The one thing everyone seemed to agree on was his brilliance. He was the best painter in San Francisco and had been for many years. No one else came close. He'd started out as an illustrator, working for newspapers, magazines, and publishing houses. He was excellent at it, but these days he worked mostly on paintings and murals. His landscapes were said to be incomparably beautiful.

All my poking around turned up plenty of gossip about his ex-wife. Lillian Dixon was also a painter, and for as long as anyone could remember she'd been "nervous." The word was always emphasized in a very particular way. Apparently, she'd embarrassed Maynard badly, and on many occasions. She had a habit of stalking him, and he hadn't been able to break free, not through half a dozen separations and not even through divorce. The party where I'd met him was just the most recent setting in what I now understood as a long, jumbled, and tragic play.

But just now all that had flown right out of my mind. Maynard Dixon was walking alone up Columbus, his hat rising far above the crowd and his cape billowing behind him as he went. He had a large portfolio under one arm, and it was tied with a ribbon to keep the papers in place.

I began to follow him, slowly at first, hanging back just enough not to be noticed, or so I hoped. Women (and more than a few men) were captivated by the sight of him, and several people turned their heads for a longer look as he passed.

I kept telling myself I'd shadow him for another block and then I'd turn around, but I kept going, street after street. When he got to the top of the hill, he ducked into a café. At first I walked right past, but then I circled back, stood at the edge of the window, and peered inside. He was sitting alone with his hat pushed off his forehead, a frown of concentration on his face. He had a notebook in front of him and was sketching. I watched his hands. They were broad hands, supple and capable.

It was silly to keep standing there. I should go inside, say hello. What stopped me was my fear, which was the fear of being seen. I was afraid of his attention but hungry for it, too—there it was. Maybe if I lingered awhile he'd look up and invite me to join him? It took me a few minutes to realize his concentration on the page was so intense—no, absolute—he wouldn't notice me from a foot away, much less twenty.

I didn't go inside. I told myself I couldn't get mixed up with him. So I took a long last look through the window, and then I turned and walked away.

5.

I tripped into Monkey Block twenty minutes late for my meeting with Consuelo Kanaga. By the time I got to Coppa's I expected to find her gone, but there she was, sitting at the bar, sharp and fresh in a frock coat and a pair of high-waisted, wide-legged trousers. I started to apologize, to explain I'd come from an errand across town, that I was still learning my way around and I'd lost my bearings.

Consuelo didn't let me finish. Only downed the last of her coffee, pushed herself up from the chair, and said, "Let's go."

The next instant we were out the door, on the street, and heading up Columbus, Consuelo taking the corners hard and fast, picking her unswerving way past one street after another with a camera around her neck and a tripod under her arm. The tripod was sheathed, somewhat shockingly, in red velvet.

"Can I help you with that?"

"Thank you," she said. "I manage just fine."

I was struck, again, by the dash of her, the air of unapologetic determination. She still hadn't told me where we were going. As we walked, I couldn't help but wonder what the whole thing was about, but it was Consuelo who began asking questions.

"Now, what's this new job?" she said after we'd been walking awhile.

"I'm working as a photo finisher at Marsh and Company."

"That's the five-and-dime shop on Market?"

"Yes. There's a photography counter there, a small one." After a pause, I added, "I'm only there until something better turns up."

She shot me a glance. "Nothing wrong with honest work."

"Actually, I've never had the choice not to work."

"Only makes you more interesting, is what I think."

I shrugged. "To hear some people tell it, a real photographer shouldn't bother with money."

She shot me another sidelong look. "Some people?"

I was hedging, and she wouldn't have it.

"Alfred Stieglitz, for one."

"I see." She stopped for a moment to adjust her hat. "I admire Stieglitz enormously. Reading *Camera Work* decided me on a career in photography, but from what I know, Stieglitz has the luxury of not making money from his pictures."

"Yes, I believe that's true."

"Well, the man can have his luxuries, but if you ask me, he'd be better off without them."

"How do you mean?"

"Working for money doesn't make you less worthy as an artist, less connected to some *wellspring of artistic truth*." There was no missing the sarcasm with which she emphasized these last words. "If a man wants to ignore the life right in front of his eyes and focus instead on some exalted idea of what art should be, well, to my mind that makes him less of an artist, not more."

I considered this. I'd never been idealistic about making pictures. I thought of it as work, plain and simple. I adored art, but I always considered it something wonderful and apart. I certainly never called myself an artist—that was a gentleman's profession, and I had to support myself and help my family out, as well. To me photography was a trade, and I was a tradeswoman. If my portraits were beautiful, well, so much the better. And yet, if I was being truthful, it wasn't only a trade. Everything I loved or wondered about or feared left a picture imprinted on me, always.

Consuelo stopped to switch her tripod to her other arm. "Recognize this?" she asked, nodding at the street in front of us.

The walk had taken us up Columbus, over the hill and to a place that smelled of wet gutters, seaweed, and gasoline fumes. The road ahead was thronged with people fanning out in both directions. Men with long black plaits, black tunics, and loose black pants walked among others in suits and Western-style hats. Sweet smoke wafted up from a window; vendors had set up baskets of writhing eels and barrels of live carp; and trussed-up pigs hung by the dozens in storefront windows.

"It's Chinatown."

She nodded. "I thought you'd want to see it, what with your working for Arnold Genthe."

So these were the streets where he had taken his famous portraits—the only surviving photographs of San Francisco's Chinatown before the earthquake and fires of 1906.

"I had no idea it was so close by. It looks different somehow."

"It *is* different. Genthe's pictures show what was strange and beautiful to him. A photograph's always a picture of who you are, after all. Besides, that old Chinatown is gone. The earthquake destroyed three-fourths of the city, but this part of town was hit the worst. All that cheap wood and shoddy construction. The place lit up like a tinderbox. Everything you see now was built after 1906. See that building?"

She gestured to what looked like a pagoda with massive curled eaves and bright red trim.

I nodded.

"Lots of people were glad to see Chinatown disappear, but in the end the city figured it could make money by turning it into a tourist destination. That's when all these faux-Oriental buildings went up. After the earthquake."

Genthe never spoke much about the earthquake, but I'd picked up bits and pieces of the story. When the earthquake hit, he didn't have his camera on him. He rushed to a shop that sold photography equipment and quickly borrowed one. To show the totality of the ruin, he climbed to the top of the hill and panned out as far as he could. The instinct to document what was happening—the toppled buildings, the crowds massing on the streets, the smoldering landscape—must have erased his fear.

"Without those pictures," Consuelo was saying now, "what happened would've been nothing but numbers. It's not always possible to tell a story with words, you know. But Arnold Genthe—well, he made people all over the country see it, and that made them care."

"Yes," I said slowly, "though in some ways I don't think he comprehended the extent of the devastation until much later. And then when he did absorb it, it was such a torment that he had to leave San Francisco."

Consuelo was silent for a moment. "Is it true that he's making portraits of celebrities now?"

"Mostly, yes. He lost everything in the earthquake. His studio was dynamited, along with all of his paintings. All of it disappeared, and afterward he couldn't afford to do that kind of work anymore."

"Maybe he *couldn't* do it. Maybe he'd lost too much, seen too much."

I'd never thought of this, but it struck me at once as true.

We continued walking. Windows festooned with laundry lines, dozens of chickens dangling in a shop window, a store devoted to selling only spices, another only tea—Consuelo strode past it all as though she'd been coming here every day of her life. Her eyes were alive to everything. That, I'd later understand, was the core of her genius: her curiosity.

After a while, she stopped to point out something on the side of a building. A handwritten calendar was fastened to the wall with a single nail, its leaves curling at the edges from the sun. I moved closer and squinted at the picture. Someone had drawn a black horse with its hooves reared up.

"You see," she said, "in the Chinese calendar, 1918 is the year of the horse. It cycles through twelve years, and now we're back at the year of the horse—same as 1906."

"That was the year of the earthquake."

"Yes," she said. Her face was grim. "People here knew something bad was coming, but no one believed it. Just like no one believed we'd be at war, or that the Spanish flu's going to reach us."

I turned to her, "But how could it? I read that's all over now. They've beat it on the East Coast."

"It's a long way from over, Dorrie." She suddenly looked very tired. "If there's one thing I've learned from working at a newspaper, it's not to confuse what you read with what's really going on. The truth of the matter is we're not supposed to report on the flu. Bad for morale, they say, what with the war."

A smokestack rose up from a factory in the near distance. In the alleyways, boys, some of them quite small, crouched on the cobblestones, laughing, smoking pipes, spitting on the ground. The sounds, more than anything, struck me—the shouts from one alley to the next, the eruptions of laughter, the music streaming through open windows. I could make out a few signs (BUTCHER SHOP, CHOP SUEY, LAUNDRY), but here English was one tongue among many, edged away from the center of things by the letters and rhythms and cadences of other languages.

"How do you know your way around here so well?"

"Oh, I come here a few times a week. I've been doing it for years."

"For your work at the newspaper?"

She laughed. "The last time this neighborhood was in the papers was when a Chinese butler was accused of killing his employer up on Nob Hill. People couldn't get enough of that story. Front-page news in all the city's papers. People love a seedy exposé, but try to cover the real crimes that happen here? Forget it. Vandalism, fire. Three men got roughed up on this very street last week. Broken ribs, busted legs. Nothing gets reported. Every time sickness tears through this part of town, the only thing you ever hear is 'Stay away.'" She shook her head. "No one can stop me from coming on my own time, though."

"And what do you do? When you come here, I mean?"

"Look around, take pictures. People here have a story—lots of stories." She stopped walking. "Here we are."

We'd come to a large brick building with a wide, steep staircase. A stiff, grim-faced guard of some kind stood barring the way. When he saw Consuelo, his expression softened. "Good afternoon, Miss Kanaga," he said, then turned and pulled on the large brass knocker behind him.

For a few minutes Consuelo and I waited in a spacious entrance hall, at the bottom of another wide staircase. The air was warm and scented with vanilla. A Chinese vase full of white-petaled lilies stood on an inlaid mother-of-pearl table and the green silk curtains were stamped with an Oriental pattern, but otherwise the intermingling of Eastern and Western styles left me with no notion of where we were.

"How wonderful to see you, Consuelo," said the petite young woman who greeted us at the door. She had a round face and full, pretty lips and was dressed in a tunic and matching pants.

"Likewise. Tien Wu, this is Dorothea Lange, a fellow photographer. I hope it's all right for her to accompany me?"

"Of course!" She smiled. "I'm glad you've come to visit us, Dorothea. Please come this way."

We followed her down a corridor of closed doors. When we reached one that was open, I spied a dozen small girls at rows of desks in a large room. They glanced up from their books and looked at us with curiosity as we passed.

"Is it a school?" I whispered to Consuelo.

"That, yes, and much more."

There were footsteps at the end of the hall and in the next moment a woman appeared with a welcoming smile on her face. Her dark hair was piled into a bun and puffed up in the front. She wore a high-collared white blouse and full black skirt that fell to her ankles, a somewhat austere ensemble, nearly Victorian. Her manner, though, was warm and inviting.

"Consuelo!" she called out, striding briskly through the door and into the hall, her skirt swinging. The thick stripe of white at the crown made her seem older than she was until you noticed that her face was young and unlined—girlish, even.

"Dorothea, this is Miss Donaldina Cameron."

There was a flash of dark eyes from behind round-rimmed silver spectacles. She offered her hand and I took it.

"Dorothea! I've been eager to meet you. Caroline tells me you've become such good friends."

How did she know? I was about to ask, but Consuelo broke in to say she had to get started.

Miss Cameron bustled me down another corridor and then out toward the back of the building. I was aware of activity behind me, women lining up the girls, shushing them, a burst of laughter.

"You cannot imagine how much she's helped us," Miss Cameron said as we watched Consuelo set up her camera and tripod. "You see, most of our board members and donors don't come out this way. It's too much of a bother, I suppose, for them to travel to this part of the city." She spoke with a faint accent, which I'd later learn was Scottish. "In any case, each year Consuelo photographs the girls for our annual letter, and we're very grateful for her work. Without her pictures, we wouldn't raise half the money for the home."

There was the sound of a bell, and then all at once dozens of girls spilled into the courtyard. The youngest looked to be about two years old; the oldest were young women in their twenties. They all wore long white tunics, white pants, and black lace-up boots.

"If you'll excuse me, Dorothea," said Miss Cameron. "Tien will need help settling the girls down."

I stood watching her as she ran back and forth, putting the finishing touches to the girls' outfits, straightening a collar here and tightening a bow there as they squirmed and chatted among themselves. The group lined up, youngest to oldest, with the littlest ones in the front and the babies in the arms of the young women. The light was soft, perfect for a portrait. Consuelo was quick and efficient with her work. Her flash popped once, then again, and she threw back the cloth. I could tell that if she moved the camera just two inches to the left, she'd catch the light better, but I held my tongue.

"Oh, I nearly forgot!" Miss Cameron said as she walked us to the front door half an hour later. She ducked into the corridor and returned after a few moments. "Plums," she said, handing Consuelo a basket covered with a red-and-white-checkered cloth. "They're Caroline's favorite." She turned to me. "You'll have to take a few for yourselves first, Dorothea," she said with a slight wink, "or else she'll eat them all."

"Miss Cameron seems awfully nice," I said when we were back outside.

"Nice? She's certainly *nice*. She's also the bravest woman in all of San Francisco."

Coming from Consuelo, this seemed an extraordinary compliment. "How so?" I said.

"You should ask Caroline. That's something she knows a lot about."

"Caroline knows Miss Cameron?"

"I should say so." She pulled back the cloth to reveal some two dozen purplish-black plums. She plucked one from the pile, handed it to me, then took one for herself, taking a hearty bite. The fruit felt warm and heavy in my hand. I was considering whether to save it or eat it now when Consuelo said, "Donaldina Cameron is Caroline's mother, after all."

When she answered the door, Caroline's hair was pinned back and she was wearing a dressing gown, a pair of wide-legged lounge pants, and low-heeled slippers. Even without a stitch of makeup she was impossibly pretty, though in her bare face she looked much younger.

"Are you busy?" I said, still a touch out of breath from hurrying up the stairs.

"Just finishing a dress. Come in, come in," she said, and waved me inside.

I walked into the flat, taking in its familiar messiness and comforting smell of oranges and bergamot. Caroline returned to the seat by the window, tucking her legs under her and resuming her work. Her Monkey Block neighbors were always knocking at the door, asking her to take in a dress or add a seam. If they had a bit of money, she'd sew them dresses. Today she was finishing the hem on a dress of raw silk for a girl down the hall.

Until Consuelo told me about Caroline and Miss Cameron, it hadn't occurred to me there was any relation between the two, much less that they were family. I was stunned, but Consuelo refused to elaborate. "It's not my story to tell," she'd said simply.

I'd have to ask Caroline myself. I cleared my throat. "I went to Chinatown with Consuelo today."

I drew the plums from my bag and held them out to her. She glanced at them, then said, "She took you to the Home."

"Yes. She had an assignment there. She introduced me to Donaldina Cameron."

"I see." She looked at me for some moments. "And now you want to hear my story?"

"If you want to tell it."

She drew in a deep breath, rolled up her sewing, and set it aside. "It's a pretty long story."

"I'm listening," I said, and leaned closer in my seat.

What Caroline told me that day was that she'd once had neither a mother nor a name.

Spring came early in 1906, chilly and damp. For months the Chinatown papers had been printing detailed predictions about the chaos and calamity to come. It would be a time of wild reversals, the likes of which descended on the world only every sixty years. The residents of Tangrenbu, San Francisco's Chinese quarter, did not doubt the dire predictions or the futility of preparing for what was to come.

One night in the second week of April, Donaldina Cameron—or Lo Mo, "Old Mother," as she was known to the girls of 920 Sacramento Street, or "the White Devil" to those irked or inconvenienced by her work—rescued five girls from a brothel on Jackson Street.

In her six years as head of the Occidental Mission Home for Girls, she'd already provided shelter to hundreds of babies, girls, and young women. Trafficking in girls was common and enforcement cursory. Most of her charges were Chinese, but over the years there'd also been many from other Asian countries as well as Latin America. No state-run institution would take them, and the city was glad, mostly, to have them off its hands.

Anything, Donaldina learned, could happen to girls in this city. They were bought with ease and sold with impunity. In narrow alleyways, in basements, and behind barred windows, girls as young as nine were drugged and dolled up and dressed in bits of cast-off silk. The unruly ones were burned with dripping hot wax, seared with metal tongs, chained to beds. From here few lived longer than four years. When they fell sick from syphilis or flu or mere exhaustion, they were locked into rooms where they either starved to death or died by their own hands—cut their throats with kitchen knives, slit their wrists with rusted nails, swallowed opium or coal or poison—only to disappear swiftly and without a trace.

That night Donaldina Cameron and her aide, Leung Yuen Qui, set out just past midnight. Flanked by two police officers from the city's Chinatown Squad, she charged through the brothel on Waverly Place and filed coolly past the myriad familiar horrors. She'd made this journey hundreds of times. The devil was here, in the dark, fetid basements below Chinatown, but she didn't fear it. This was her work and she did it well. But all at once she stumbled on a loose floorboard, and that's when it happened. When she found the girls penned under the floor.

Prying back the board to reveal a trapdoor, Donaldina found four little girls clinging to one another in a suspended box. They were huddled together, pale faces turned up toward her, their bodies naked except for the rags between their legs. They were so thin their ribs showed. One of them was gripping a broom in her small hand and had what looked like a month-old baby strapped to her back.

The sight broke Donaldina, put her beyond words. She wanted to hurt somebody.

"Bring them up!" she ordered the policemen as Leung reassured the girls in their native tongue. "Bring them up at once!"

She spirited them away to the Home on Sacramento Street,

where they were bathed and given dinner and put to bed. The next morning, after a lady doctor examined them and treated their bruises and burns, Donaldina drew a pair of wire-rimmed spectacles from her skirt pocket, hooked them on, and inspected the new girls at length. She hadn't noticed it before, but she now saw that one of them had bottle-green eyes. Leung had dressed her in the same white lace-trimmed frock as the others, then taken a brush to her long hair and plaited it into pigtails, with white satin ribbons at the ends. The only clue to her past was the tiny jade amulet strung around her neck. Donaldina thought she was maybe five years old, but it was hard to say for sure.

Donaldina stepped closer to the child. She was pale, thin, and sickly, with bruises, cuts, and lesions all over her body. What medicine couldn't cure, time could blur and sometimes even erase. What worried her was the girl's silence. At first Donaldina thought she might be deaf or perhaps slow, because when she asked the girl's name, the child only hung her head. Then she understood: She had no name. Either terror had scrubbed her mind clear of it or she'd never had one in the first place.

In the history of every tortured soul comes a moment when its mind parts from its body—pushes off like a boat without oars from the shore and gives itself up to the current. It had happened to this child, that was clear, but could it be undone?

"We'll call you Caroline," Donaldina said brightly. She spoke with a brogue handed down from her Scottish mother, who'd died when Donaldina was five. Caroline was the name of her childhood best friend.

No response. The girl only stared at her.

Donaldina crouched down, leveled her eyes to the child's, and smiled. She said the name again, more slowly. "Care-oh-line. It's a very pretty name, isn't it, love?"

It was no use. The girl said nothing. She didn't make even one sound. Not then, and not later, when the girls at the Mission House welcomed her with many names.

They waited until Donaldina retreated to her room for a nap, and then they marched the girl down to the basement, the dark, cramped, low-ceilinged space for which they reserved their cruelest games. "Fish Eyes," they called her on account of her green eyes, and "Dirty Face" on account of the smattering of freckles on her nose. Two of them held her, pinning her against a wall, as a third girl pressed a hand against her face as if to wipe away her freckles. The girl pressed harder and harder as the others laughed and pointed their fingers. She didn't belong here, they said. She wasn't one of them. She wasn't one of anything.

This went on for a long while, and it was only Donaldina's voice calling them that made them end their game that time.

Not a week later, a million-year-old seam in the earth cracked in two.

It started out as a lovely evening, the most perfect yet of the year, warm and very still—not a breath of wind anywhere in the city. A week had passed since the raid on Jackson Street, and the green-eyed girl was still refusing to speak.

The rains had been unusually strong that spring. The streets and alleys in Chinatown kept flooding, and for weeks people walked ankle-deep in squelching mud. The mud followed them from the streets and alleyways and into their clapboard shanties and one-room tenement apartments.

The rain had stopped right after Easter. Through the morning and into the afternoon of April 17, fog misted through the streets of San Francisco and clouds hung over the hills, but later in the day a strong wind cleared the skies, turning it a perfect eggshell blue. There was a joy-spangled quality to the city that night. The warm weather drew people out of their houses and shops and into the streets. Girls in their best dresses walked arm in arm. Boys and young men hung around the street corners, their pomaded heads shining in the gaslight. There was talk and laughter from the North Beach coffee shops to the Palace Hotel ballrooms to the Grand Opera House on Mission Street. All over the city, people said summer had come early that year.

Near dawn, San Francisco began rocking like a boat on a ruthless sea.

At the first tremors, Donaldina Cameron shot out of bed and made for the hallway. The ground tumbled and bucked and twisted. The roof of 920 heaved; the house swayed and groaned beneath the joists. She weaved down the stairwell, gripping the wall to steady herself, glass breaking under her feet, and she had not made it very far when a beam fell and knocked her backward. She lay with her legs pinned under bricks, howling in pain, and that was the last thing she knew for a while.

For the first several minutes after the earth stopped shaking, Leung and the girls of 920 Sacramento huddled under the great oak table in the dining room.

"Where's Lo Mo?" one of them cried out.

They found her trapped under a beam. She was still and silent. Again and again they called her name, but she didn't move. Her breathing was slow and heavy, and she might have drifted into unconsciousness and stayed there if the girls hadn't pulled her from the bricks and then prodded her and shouted her name until she came to.

Donaldina's eyes fluttered open. Above, where the ceiling

should be, there was a jagged slice of sky. She willed herself to stand. Eventually she massed the girls around her and told them to dress quickly and come down to the street.

Five minutes later she led them outside to see what could be seen. The sweep of destruction looked like the end of days. Up and down the streets, people were straggling out of buildings, women with hands to their faces, and men in their long johns, their faces covered in filth, eyes wild with fear or disbelief or some mixture of the two. People had fallen to their knees, praying, certain the world had come to an end.

The Occidental Mission Home for Girls stood at the farthest border of Chinatown, just across from North Beach, the Italian section of San Francisco. The girls gathered around Donaldina, and together they took in the full breadth of the thing. The building was still standing, but the chimney had fallen into a heap of rubble. The rest of Chinatown had fared far worse. Flimsy clapboard row houses slumped into the streets and crammed against one another. Up the street the façade had been ripped clear off a three-story building, and you could see straight through to the ruin inside, the toppled furniture, the shattered lamps, the cracked beams.

It was cold. The thick morning fog felt like a drizzle. For a few moments there was silence and stillness, but then the awful sounds began to emerge: cries and whimpers from within the collapsed buildings.

Donaldina stood stock-still. She was wearing a housecoat and her hair flowed loose and wild past her shoulders and down her back. She looked hard at her girls, counting them once and then a second time. They were all there, all sixty-one of them.

"Come here," she now told one of the younger girls. When the girl stepped forward, she loosened the sash around the child's waist. She did the same with a second girl, and then she bound the two girls together, wrist to wrist. When she'd repeated this thirty times, she tied the new green-eyed girl's sash to her own wrist. Then she stopped and considered what to do next.

Holding hands, bound together by their sashes, the group joined the crowds surging through the streets, moving up Broadway. The teenagers carried the babies, the younger girls led the toddlers. As they walked, Donaldina saw bodies slumped in the debris, and she quickened her step in the futile hope that the girls wouldn't see.

At the top of Nob Hill, she told them to rest as she surveyed the scene. Disaster, ruin, calamity. Hotels, libraries, houses, stores, brothels, theaters, dance halls, saloons, mansions—all had fallen in heaps of broken brick and shattered glass. Burned-out foundations rose from the ground like gnarled sculptures. Somewhere in the Tenderloin, a fire had sparked, then flared. In the distance, she could make out strands of smoke in the porcelain-blue sky.

As she crested the next hill, her eyes latched on to the bay, following the water to where it met the mountains of Marin County. Tomorrow they would walk west, she decided. Out toward Golden Gate Park, or as far as they could get in that direction.

That night sixty-one girls slept, head to foot, on the pews of a shuttered church. By then their faces and white pinafores had long-since turned black from the soot. The earth had more or less settled down, but what had started as a spark in the Tenderloin was now a wall of flames. A mile and a half long, it was advancing across the city. The girls slept with their shoes on their feet, because who knew what would come next?

Just as she started to nod off, Donaldina remembered: the papers. She'd managed to get her daughters this far, but without their immigration papers they were as good as missing. Or dead. She shook Leung awake and told her to keep watch over the girls, then she made her way back to Sacramento Street alone.

A solider was standing guard outside 920. He ordered her not to go into the building. She wouldn't have it. She climbed the stairs to the house and made her way to her office, where she grabbed the black metal box with the small handle in which she kept the girls' immigration documents as well as the register that held the names and stories of the 829 charges who'd so far passed through the Mission House.

By the time she returned to the church on Van Ness, fires were advancing from three directions. Her hair was matted with the dust of her vanquished city, and her housecoat was stiff with its ruin. Outside, San Francisco burned and burned.

In the morning they joined the thousands of people streaming out to the western and northern edges of the city, to the gentle slopes and open spaces of Golden Gate Park and the Presidio. By then the entire city—the trees, the birds, the parks, the buildings, the sun—had disappeared; there was nothing but a sky shrouded in black smoke.

The refugees—the quarter of a million people who'd been made suddenly homeless by the earthquake—beat a slow and wordless retreat. The roar of the flames was audible, but otherwise a deep and peculiar silence had descended on San Francisco. People carried what they could on their backs or in trunks, pushcarts, and wheelbarrows. Badly packed bundles of food and crockery. Mattresses and copper bathtubs. A shirtless man pushing a piano up the hill, an elderly woman in a dressing gown cradling a broken elbow, a businessman clutching a vast trove of papers to his chest, a bedraggled, dumbstruck family of ten—it was a vast but soundless exodus. No one screamed, no one wept.

Donaldina, Leung, and the girls continued on. They hadn't made it far when a soldier stopped them. One of General Funston's men. Earlier that morning the cavalry had burst through the ravaged streets to impose martial law.

"Pardon me, ma'am," said the soldier, raising his hand to halt them. He was young and rail thin, with a pimply face and a peaked hat and brass-buttoned uniform at least two sizes too big for him. "They're setting up a separate camp for the Orientals down there." He pointed in the direction of Fort Mason.

Donaldina straightened her spine. "These girls are my daughters," she told him.

"All of them?"

"All of them. I insist they accompany me to the Presidio."

The soldier stared at the girls for a few moments, then cleared his throat. "You're free to go to the Presidio, ma'am, but you'll have to take your . . ."

"Daughters."

"Yes . . . Your, ah . . . daughters. You'll have to take them to Fort Mason. That's where the Orientals go."

They stood there for a moment, staring at each other, until an understanding flashed between them. The disaster had leveled distinctions between rich and poor. At that moment, housekeepers and painted women were walking shoulder to shoulder with fine ladies; businessmen were marching alongside poets and bricklayers. Just a few feet away from where they were standing, a woman in sealskin, silk, and diamonds had camped out on the street corner and was sharing a loaf of bread and a tin of corned beef with a woman and two small children in bare feet and tattered calico.

For all that, certain barriers had survived. In fact, the chaos had rendered them more inflexible than they'd been before.

Donaldina readied herself for a fight, but then something stopped her. Her gaze swept over her girls. They hadn't eaten. They were weak and tired; several of them were also badly injured. It would take them hours to reach Golden Gate Park, if they managed to reach it at all today.

Without a word, she turned away and led the group down the hill and toward the bay. All along the way, trunks and baskets lay abandoned in the rubble. Paintings, silver trinkets, crystal vases, Persian rugs, gramophones—precious things saved, only to be abandoned. Then, halfway down the hill, they passed a large wrought-iron birdcage, and here Donaldina felt a hard tug on her sleeve.

It was the green-eyed girl. Since yesterday she'd stood by Donaldina's side, a small, silent shadow. "Caroline!" she said now, dragging Donaldina toward the cage with a power that belied her twig-like arms. Her voice was high but astonishingly loud. Donaldina bent down and looked to where the girl was pointing. Inside the birdcage, faint beneath a coat of dust, was a small green canary.

She tried to pull the child away, but her tiny body was suddenly so heavy and rigid that she couldn't move the girl even an inch. Donaldina locked eyes with Leung. The young woman nodded.

When Donaldina Cameron set off toward Fort Mason, she did so with all sixty-one of her daughters in tow, an iron safe tucked under the crook of one arm and a birdcage swinging under the other.

At the makeshift camp for Orientals, there were no tents or blankets and little to drink or eat. When the ferries finally started running again, Donaldina would take her girls across the bay to Marin County, to a theological seminary tucked in the skirts of Mount Tamalpais, but for now what mattered, the only thing that mattered, was that her daughters were safe.

That night, Donaldina closed her eyes and let sleep enfold her. All that night and the next one, the canary sang its wild, sweet song. On Saturday, the weather shrugged off its disguise of early spring and shrouded itself again in the cold and the damp. It began to rain. The fires had reduced San Francisco to ash; the rain now turned it to sludge. Still, there were blessings; there was grace. Summer that year hadn't come early after all, but the nameless girl with the broom and a baby on her back was Caroline now. She had a name, a pet bird, and a mother, the first and only one she'd ever know.

"That's how Lo Mo told the story, anyway. I can't remember much from those days. Mostly it's the feeling of them that's stayed with me."

Caroline had told me the story with the distant, haunted feeling of a person reliving it as it was spoken. As she fell into the story, her apartment—with all its messy loveliness—dissolved. The pretty, self-possessed young woman sitting in front of me also disappeared. What I saw instead was a child penned beneath a trapdoor, her small hands gripping a broom. A girl with green eyes and a tangle of hair down her bare back. A nameless, motherless girl in a quaking, burning city.

I shifted in my chair and pushed a tear away with the heel of my hand. The cup of tea Caroline had brought for me halfway through the story had cooled, forgotten on the table. I drank it now.

I couldn't think what to say, though there were things I could have said. Should have said, perhaps. But everything I could think of seemed trite and hollow, and I was grateful when, after a long, rending few minutes, Caroline began speaking again.

"The other girls were always speculating about where I'd come from. Why I had light eyes. They came up with all sorts of stories about who my parents could have been. All nonsense, of course."

"Did you ever . . ."

"Find out?"

I nodded.

She shook her head. "No. I was an orphan, that's all." Her hand went to the jade amulet nestled in the hollow of her throat. "This is the only thing I have from that other time. There's an inscription on the back with the surname Lee." She held it so I could see the writing, then let go of it. "I don't even know my birthday. I've always just used the date Lo Mo found me, April 11." She straightened herself in her chair and went on. "I never went back there. To Chinatown, I mean."

"But isn't the Mission Home in Chinatown?"

"Yes and no—it's on the border. It's hard to explain, but to me it seemed to sit at the very edge of the world. For some reason, I thought if I crossed that border, I'd never stop falling."

I turned this over in my mind. She'd spent eleven years of her life behind the walls of a missionary school, feeling not only friendless but alien. Small wonder that she fled that world.

"Yes," I heard myself say, "I think I can understand that."

It took a long moment, but then Caroline said, "Lo Mo took my side if any of the girls spoke out against me, and there was plenty of that. You see, the way they saw it, I was two things rather than one, two races rather than one, and because of that I wasn't less than them. I was nothing. After a while they learned to leave me alone. Well, most of the time." She drew in a long breath. "The thing that saved me was learning how to sew— that and learning to read. I was never lonely after that."

"But you wanted to leave?"

"I think I've always been looking out a window, even when I was a small child. Somehow I knew the world was so much bigger than what I could see. I left the day I turned sixteen."

"Lo Mo—I mean, Miss Cameron—didn't object?"

She shook her head. "She wanted me to stand on my own feet. She wanted that for all of us. The trouble was that unless you got married or went into service or moved to China, there wasn't really anyplace to go. No decent job, no place where they'd rent you a room . . ."

Her voice faded and for a moment I saw something in her, something of the person she might be when she was alone, not steeling herself against the world but not brightening herself for anyone's sake, either. Her transformation from a missionary girl into a Monkey Block bohemian, the way she carried herself and handled her life—I saw now how much it took to make it seem like you didn't care how people looked at you or what they said.

"That must have been very hard. To be so completely on your own."

Caroline started to answer, then stopped. Let her green eyes sweep the room, gaze out the window, and then come back again. She cleared her throat and then there was that sly look again, the look of a woman who'd tossed aside whatever didn't suit her.

The belief that you could create yourself—it was the most American part of us both, Caroline and me. Were we running from the past or toward the future? And what would it mean to arrive?

"You know," she said, "it wasn't all bad, not once some time passed and I got used to it. When you're on your own, there's no one to run to, but there's no one to run from, either. You go where you want or as far as you can. That's freedom, or a kind of it, don't you think, Dorrie?"

6.

Before heading out for my first meeting of the Camera Club, I stopped at Coppa's for two shots of espresso. I'd been up until two-thirty, finishing my photographs, trimming the edges, picking the right ones. My back was aching and my eyes were dry, but that didn't matter. If I was asked to join the Camera Club, I'd be displaying my pictures regularly, a chance I'd never had in New York and one I knew not to squander.

I arrived at the Palace Hotel early and alone. Consuelo and I had planned to meet at Monkey Block at half past ten and then walk to the meeting together, but at the last minute she'd been called to cover a strike by the shipyards. I'd never really thought of myself as the kind of person who walked into rooms full of strangers, but nothing seemed out of the question, not here, not anymore.

Enormous marble pillars, sparkling chandeliers, a stupendous glass-domed roof—every inch of the Palace Hotel was gilded and grand. I made my way up to the second floor and

toward the makeshift gallery, then for a moment I stood taking
in the scene. Dozens of framed photographs had been set onto
easels and propped against the walls. People were shuffling
around the room, nudging each other every so often over one
of the photographs. I passed a young woman in a velvet hat,
who was chatting with a lanky man in horn-rimmed eyeglasses
and an Eastern European accent—Russian, I thought, but I
wasn't sure. Were they collectors? Consuelo mentioned there'd
be many at the meeting. She also said there was a chance Imogen Cunningham might come, an even more thrilling prospect.

I found an empty spot along one of the walls, unsheathed
my portraits, and leaned them side by side against the wall. I
stepped back a few feet and considered them for a moment.

Not bad, I thought.

I'd managed to put down ten dollars toward the price of my
own camera, but I still didn't have enough money to buy it back.
In the meantime, I had use of an old Leica and a darkroom at
work. These two portraits weren't the best I could do, but they
weren't so far off, either. It was a solid start.

Once I finished setting up, I wandered about the gallery. The
room was full, and I weaved in and out of the crowd, sometimes
staring over someone's shoulder or stopping where a cluster of
people had gathered to admire a particular picture. I recognized
many of the places I'd seen in San Francisco: the enormous all-
white Victorian-style Conservatory of Flowers in Golden Gate
Park; the gold-domed Palace of Fine Arts, the last vestige of the
1915 Panama-Pacific Exposition; the ferry building, with its Italianate clock tower. Sharp images, the gleam of metal and
machines—that's what got you noticed nowadays. They were
fine, I supposed. A few were even quite accomplished. Trouble
was, most of them revealed nothing beyond what they showed,

nothing of the person who'd taken them and, in the case of the portraits, not much about the people in them.

Then, for the second time, I saw Imogen Cunningham's work.

It was a group of five portraits, likely part of the same series her husband Roi Partridge had picked up from the five-and-dime shop. I walked from one to the next, admiring the fleshy indent around a child's wrist, the dimples just above its hand. Each image reflected the photographer's tender, steady gaze.

"Imogen dear!" a voice called out.

So she *was* here. I swiveled around. The voice belonged to a woman in an ankle-length ivory dress and matching frock coat, the kind of woman who would've caused a stir on the fanciest street of the fanciest part of the city. I watched her open her arms to greet another woman—Imogen Cunningham.

Later, when I had time to think about the day, I was struck by how little she resembled any notion I had of what an artist looked like. She seemed a few years older than me—thirty or thirty-five. Her skin was fair and freckled, and she wore her hair parted in the middle and piled up in a bun. Her dress was simple and a bit creased. To complicate the picture, she was standing with a very young man with messy hair. They made an odd couple, and I couldn't make out the relationship between them.

Meanwhile, the woman in the stupendous ivory ensemble went on talking. "Everyone so admires the portraits you made of my daughters last year, Imogen. I've been desperate to have you up to do mine. Could you possibly make the time for a private sitting?"

When she at last drifted off, I stepped forward and introduced myself as a new friend of Consuelo Kanaga.

"Dear Connie," Imogen said with a smile. "Is she here?"

When I explained she'd been called away to cover a strike, Imogen said, "Of course she was! But I'm very pleased to meet you, Dorothea. This is my friend Ansel. Ansel Adams."

He was a young man—sixteen or seventeen years old, I guessed. A tousle of brown hair topped his head. His nose was crooked (I'd later find out the 1906 earthquake had sent him crashing against a wall, face-first, breaking his nose and setting it permanently to the left). It gave his face a mischievous look.

"Ansel thinks he's a pianist, but I'm helping him discover his true calling."

"Photography?"

"Exactly. But this"—here she gestured around the room—"isn't helping him take it seriously." She dropped her voice but only slightly. "He thinks it's all . . . How did you put it, Ansel?"

"Murderously dull."

"Yes, that's what it was." She turned back to me. "What do you think, Dorothea?"

"There are some very accomplished pictures."

"You don't sound impressed."

"Well, it seems to me there are other uses to a camera than showing off its technical powers."

That got the young man's attention. "Such as?"

"Well, what a photographer can do—what you do, Mrs. Cunningham—"

"Imogen, please."

"What you do, Imogen, which is to let people really see one another."

"Only one another?" Ansel asked.

I tilted my head toward him. "How do you mean?"

"What he means," said Imogen, "is could you use a camera

to make people 'really see' crickets and ponds and mountains? That's Ansel's notion of the world."

"Well, I make portraits, but it seems just as vital to show people what's around them. Everything's worth looking at, if only you can see it clearly enough."

Imogen smiled again. "I'm sure we'd both love to see your photographs. You did bring some, didn't you?"

For a few minutes after we reached my portraits, Imogen and Ansel stood looking at them without saying a word. There was a restlessness to Ansel, a barely contained energy, and it was focused now on my pictures. While Imogen narrowed her eyes and tilted her head this way and that, he stepped closer, then walked a few steps back to look at them from a distance.

The first was of my boss, Mr. Marsh. It was a picture I'd taken late in the day, just before we closed up. It had a blurriness I liked. It always took time before people showed who they really were. Some people never showed you at all, but I'd learned to be patient, to wait, to make conversation, to let time dissolve the mask they put up for the world. Mr. Marsh had a hardness to him, always, and it was only when I'd gotten him to tell me about his son, who'd fought in the war, that the mask began to fall. How extraordinary to see a face day after day, then one day find it strange and surprising. Mr. Marsh was that sort. His face gave nothing away, but it had some secret in it.

"And this one," Imogen said, nodding at the second picture. "Is it yours, too?"

"Yes."

This second portrait was of Caroline sitting in the window of her apartment in Monkey Block. She hated to sit still, and I'd just about given up trying to get a good shot, when I came up with the idea to shoot her while she worked on a dress. In the picture, she was looking down, but with the way I cropped it, you couldn't tell at what. The light from the window was strong. That kind of light usually washes people out, but not Caroline. It made her clear, fine features finer, her dark lashes darker, and her hair blacker and glossier.

It wasn't perfect—I wasn't entirely satisfied with the finish—but it was a picture that made you wonder about the woman in it. Who was she *really*? What sort of thoughts swelled through her mind?

"They're beautiful!" Ansel announced, clapping his hands together and smiling broadly at me.

I flinched. "Beautiful?"

He gave me a puzzled look. "Have I offended you, Miss Lange?"

"There's no quicker way to dismiss a woman's work than to call it beautiful."

His confusion seemed to deepen. "But what's wrong with beauty? Why is a picture only considered good or important if it's ugly?" He shook his head. "Surely you'd agree it's as necessary for an artist to show people the evidence of life's beauty as it is to give them a document of its ugliness and despair?"

"Well, for one thing I don't consider myself an artist."

"You should. You *must*."

"I agree, Ansel," Imogen said, and then turned to me. "Your pictures are the only ones that've interested him all day. I'm not at all surprised—it's excellent work, Dorothea. I imagine you've got plenty of clients already."

"Actually, it's been hard getting going."

She raised her brows. "Is that so? I can mention your name to some people looking to have their portraits done."

"That would be very generous of you, although . . ."

She lifted an eyebrow. "Yes?"

"I don't only want to make portraits. I want to open my own studio."

"I see. In that case what you really need is a business partner. Someone to front you the money, at least until you establish yourself."

"You think I could get someone to back me?"

She gave me a long, steady, curious look. "There's money in it. Why wouldn't they? In fact," she said, glancing over my shoulder, "opportunities are closer than you think."

She lifted her chin, just slightly, in the direction of a man standing to my right. I turned. He was squinting at one portrait, then the other. I'd been so absorbed in my conversation with Imogen and Ansel that I hadn't noticed him.

"Excuse me, miss," he said after a while. "I wonder if you might tell me the photographer's name?"

"Dorothea Lange," I said, and stepped forward to shake the man's hand.

From the corner of my eye, I caught Imogen's smile. The man turned to study the portrait of Caroline again, rubbing his chin and narrowing his eyes, and then he asked the one thing that most terrified me but that was also the thing I most needed to hear: "Do you have any more, Miss Lange?"

His name was Sidney Franklin. He was a well-dressed, square-shouldered man just shy of thirty, with a closely trimmed mustache and the beginnings of a paunch. When we met, I wouldn't have taken him for anything but what he seemed that day: a wealthy young gentleman with a fashionable interest in photography. Later I'd find out that his Irish grandfather had opened one of the first saloons in San Francisco—a place as old as you got here, anyway. He'd been brought up with the expectation that he'd help run it once he finished high school, but a year before what would have been his graduation, his father had died suddenly, dead at forty-one. The earthquake hit the next month.

His life started then—the life he made for himself. As one of the few saloons still standing in San Francisco after the earthquake, Franklin's suddenly swelled and heaved with patrons. In a fit of inspiration, seventeen-year-old Sidney Franklin set up dozens of stands in the Presidio, selling liquor and beer amid the vast encampments that had been created for the city's refugees. By the time San Francisco had gotten back on its feet two years later, he'd made a fortune.

From there he'd put his money in real estate, with spectacular success. But now he was hungry for something more than money, or perhaps in addition to money. Why else would he spend his weekends cruising through the Camera Club? Alcohol had made Sidney Franklin rich, but photography brought him pleasure. He'd found a way to link his money and his passion: He acquired photographs and photographers. What he didn't have was a portrait studio, and this is where I saw my opportunity.

I'd always worked best when I had something to prove and someone to prove it to. I had both now. For the next few weeks, I worked on building a portfolio. When I wasn't behind the counter at Marshs's, I was taking pictures or developing them. I photographed a waiter at Coppa's, a girl who sold flowers outside the church on Mission, and a sculptor friend of Caroline's. It was the first time since coming to San Francisco that I'd really given myself over to making portraits, and it was like falling back into a dream. I missed the way developing pictures focused my mind and let me drift at the same time.

A plan was taking shape, and it had as much to do with Imogen Cunningham as it did with Sidney Franklin. Portraits had been Imogen's bread and butter for years, first in Seattle, where she'd grown up and established herself as a photographer, and now, for the last decade, in Northern California. With two small children, she couldn't keep up with the requests for her time, and she had to turn down most of the work that came her way, but she still made good money visiting the homes of her established clientele and making portraits of them there.

Imogen was a natural teacher—generous, patient, unswervingly honest. That wonderfully strange boy, Ansel Adams, wasn't the only one lucky to learn from her. Some weekends I'd ride the ferry across the bay to visit her at her house in Oakland, and during those hours she taught me what I most needed to know, at the time I most needed to know it: Even if you were hemmed in by your circumstances, you could make something out of that. If nothing else, your frustration could fuel you. Imogen seemed like perfect proof of that. At the time, she was living in what I took to be a state of exile. She and Roi rented a little cottage in the Oakland hills, where you had to trudge up to a well for water and all the lights were fueled by kerosene. But from her tiny perch across the bay, she turned the lens onto her life and created pictures you wouldn't soon forget.

That humbled me and awed me and spurred me on. Six mornings a week I rose at six, scrubbed up, dressed, and ducked into the street. Every night, under the thin light of a single lamp, I spent hours in the darkroom at Marsh's, mixing chemicals and making prints. I stayed away from Monkey Block except to see Caroline. I worked for hours on end, keeping myself awake with a mix of cold coffee, ambition, and nerves.

7.

A week later I received a note on monogrammed stationery. For a long time, I stood staring at the words on the smooth creamy paper. On Imogen's recommendation, Mrs. Edythe Katten had invited me to her home to discuss the possibility of photographing her. I think I gave out a cry.

A few people had approached me at the Camera Club to inquire about hiring me to make their portraits, but if Mrs. Katten chose me, it would count as much as all those others put together, maybe even more. The Kattens lived on the grandest stretch of Pacific Heights. They had a reputation for eccentricity and stupendous generosity. Edythe Katten had studied economics at UC Berkeley and had established a charity to educate children from the city's poorest neighborhoods. She and her husband also financed theaters, art galleries, temples, hospitals, and newspapers.

On the day I first met her, I saw that Edythe Katten was exactly as Imogen had described her: warm, kind, vivacious. She was a small woman, no more than five feet tall, but there was an intensity about her. Later, when we knew each other well, she'd tell me that as a child she'd been picked on for her size. That was a while off, but our friendship began that first day.

"I hear you're from New York, Miss Lange," she said once we'd settled in the drawing room.

I hesitated. Ever since I'd come to San Francisco I'd been telling people I was from New York, not Hoboken. It was useful, particularly in certain circles. California, for all its enthusiasm for the new, still prized connections and credentials, as I'd found out when I met Consuelo. No one had less use for the pretense than Consuelo, and yet she'd taken note of my work with Arnold Genthe.

For some reason I found myself telling Edythe Katten about Hoboken and my years going to school on the Lower East Side.

Everything in her suddenly brightened when I mentioned the Lower East Side.

"Which school?"

"P.S. 62."

"P.S. 62? Why, I grew up on Hester Street!"

Hester Street. I blinked, trying to imagine this exquisite, cultured woman in a world of sweatshops, tenements, and push-carts, of women in kerchiefs and aprons, a world where the air was perpetually thick with the scent of cabbage, pickles, and corned beef.

It was the part of New York I knew and loved best. After my father abandoned us, my mother took a job on the Lower East Side. She found it easier to enroll me in school there, and so we took the ferry from New Jersey to the city every day. I was more a truant than a student in those days, and I spent much of my time walking up and down the streets, from the East Side to the

Hudson River, with my books pressed against my chest so no one would know I was bumming around. My only aim was to look at things. That's where I'd first stumbled on the idea of becoming a photographer, roaming that cramped, chaotic, beautiful world.

Now I watched Edythe Katten stir her tea with a small silver spoon and listened to her reminisce about those same streets. "I miss it terribly. My family, the neighborhood, the vitality, the closeness . . ." Her gaze drifted to the window and lingered there. "You'll perhaps find this strange, but sometimes I think if it weren't for my garden, I'd go back to my old neighborhood."

"I don't think it's strange, not at all, but will you show it to me? Your garden?"

She seemed surprised by the request, but she nodded and rose from her chair.

It was a rare day of sunshine. Along the side of the house was a terraced garden that reached to the bottom of the hill. We stood, looking down, admiring the path, the camellias and box-woods, the roses in full bloom. There were rows of citrus trees, thick with pale-green leaves and heavy with ripening fruit. All this was framed by an untrammeled view of the bay.

"How would you shoot me?" she said when we arrived at a lovely glass greenhouse.

On our way through the house earlier, I'd noticed a silver-framed studio portrait on the wall. It was a staid composition, rigid in the Victorian style. It showed a large extended family. The photographer had seated the women in chairs. Their starched white dresses fell to the floor; their hair rose up in complicated buns and braids. I recognized Edythe Katten by her diminutive frame. Above her stood a man who was clearly Mr. Katten.

Plenty of clients came with a fixed idea of the portrait they wanted made, and it wasn't possible to ignore them. With some, though, you felt an openness, which is what I perceived now in Edythe Katten. All the time we'd been together, I'd been asking her questions and listening carefully to her answers.

"I'd shoot you right here," I said.

She lifted her eyebrows. "Do you think?"

Despite all the hiding they did, people wanted to be known, to be understood. Even more than the desire to be admired, what they wanted, and so seldom got, was to be seen.

"Yes. It would make a beautiful portrait."

I was thinking fast, working out the details. She needed to be shot close up to show her exquisite profile. I hadn't taken many photographs outside the studio. It would be hard to pull it off, maybe even impossible. The spot was idyllic, but that didn't make it easy. In a studio, the light could be manufactured and manipulated. With the weather so changeable in San Francisco, I couldn't count on getting it right. But the idea had taken hold of me, and now it wouldn't let go.

"Mrs. Katten—"

"Edythe, please."

"Edythe. The light's perfect. We could start now if you like."

"Now?" The lines of her face softened, and her smile deepened. The afternoon sun had brought out the rich hazel of her eyes. "Why not?" she said gamely, and with that we began.

"I got it!" I said when I saw Caroline at Coppa's that night. I dove into the booth where she was sitting, tossing down my purse and fairly crashing against her in my excitement.

"What's that?"

I pulled Edythe Katten's quite generous check out of my bag

and handed it to her. I guessed Caroline would recognize the Katten name, and she did. She looked at the check, then at me, and then she let out a small yelp of surprise.

"But how is it that you met Edythe Katten?"

"Imogen put in a word for me, and I went to her house to see her today. I took some pictures of her in her garden, and now she wants me to make portraits of her daughters, as well."

"Well done!" she said, and threw her arm over my shoulder and gave me a squeeze. "With clients like Edythe Katten, you'll be opening up your own studio in no time! She's very well connected, I hear. All those ladies on Pacific Heights and Nob Hill and Russian Hill will want you to do their portraits soon."

On top of our usual plates of pasta, we celebrated with cannoli and champagne—my treat. I couldn't make a habit of it, but with the check in my pocket I was feeling flush.

Caroline wanted to know everything about the pictures I'd taken. She delighted in my story about Edythe Katten's having grown up on the Lower East Side. I went on talking for a while before it occurred me to ask her about her day.

All at once she looked uncomfortable. Her eyes dropped to the table. "They let me go today."

"What?"

"I was fired."

"But why?"

She folded her arms. Unfolded them. "You know that old bin?"

I nodded.

The bin was a large box full of White House castoffs. Remnants, old buttons, paper flowers from hats that couldn't be pinned back into place. Most of it was useless, but every once in a while Caroline would come across something that could be useful to her in some project.

"What about the bin?"

"Well, someone made up a story about some stolen fabric. When I was leaving, she came up with the boss, and he made me show what was in my purse. It was just a scrap of shantung I'd found buried at the bottom of the bin, but they said I stole it." She rubbed her temple. "All this time working for them and I've got nothing to show for it, not even a reference. They likely won't pay the wages they owe me. If you're fired for cause, you have no right to it."

"I'm sorry . . ." I started to say, and then I remembered the check in my purse. "I can lend you some money until you find something else."

"Oh, it'll sort itself out," she said, batting away the offer. "I'm so happy for you, Dorrie, I really am. Now that you have Edythe Katten on your side, there will be plenty of work for you. She's very well connected, I hear. Everyone will want you to make their portraits in no time. They'll be fighting over you soon. Just you wait!"

In the first week of July I knocked on the door of Sidney Franklin's downtown office with a sheaf of photographs under my arm. I'd dressed carefully, in a belted skirt suit and high-collared white blouse. For a second I was tempted to turn on my heel and flee down the stairs, but without an investor, my dream of opening a studio would remain a dream. If there was anyone who could help me, it was Sidney Franklin.

After riding up the little rattling box of an elevator, I walked down a corridor, where I found the door with a sign: S. FRANKLIN, INCORP. I took a deep breath and entered.

A wan-faced gentleman secretary was sitting behind a desk

when I walked inside. The reception room was full. Half a dozen men sat in chairs. He looked up and frowned. "You'll have to wait," he said. "He's in a conference." I had to give my name twice and wait close to an hour, but eventually he led me into Sidney Franklin's office.

When he saw it was me, he stood and shook my hand and gestured for me to sit.

"Have you brought me some pictures, Miss Lange?"

I pulled the prints and spread them over his desk one by one, aligning them neatly. He let his eyes wander over them. He lifted a few from the table, looking closely before he considered the rest.

"This is very good work. How much are you asking for them?"

My gaze drifted to the window. There was a view of the Mint, with its grand pillars and wide stone staircase. This was my chance. I cleared my throat. "Actually, they're not for sale."

"Not for sale? I'm afraid I don't understand, Miss Lange. Isn't it your intention to sell your photographs?"

I took a deep breath. "It's my intention to open a portrait studio, and I have a proposition for you, Mr. Franklin."

He lifted his brows and then shook his head. "Miss Lange. I don't quite know how to put this, so I'll say it as simply as I can. Women don't run studios."

"You said yourself at the Camera Club that some of the best photographers in the city are women."

"As they certainly are, but the simple fact is that none of them runs a studio."

"Surely someone has to be the first."

"And you think you're the one to do it?"

"I've had five years' experience in New York working with Clarence White and Arnold Genthe—"

"I'm sorry, Miss Lange," he cut me off. "But working for someone, however famous, however successful, is rather different from opening your own business. Anyway, that's not my usual line. I have no knowledge or experience of the commercial side of photography. I'm merely a collector."

I looked at his hands. On the fourth finger of his left hand was a thick gold ring. The gold was bright; he was newly married.

"May I ask you a question, Mr. Franklin?"

"Please."

"How do you feel about a man coming into your home to call on your wife?"

"A man? What sort of man?"

"A stranger, or near stranger. A man coming into your home and spending several hours alone with Mrs. Franklin. Would you care for such an arrangement?"

"I would not, but what is your point, Miss Lange?"

"In a word: access. Women can go places men aren't welcome."

I'd hoped for the full force of his attention. I had it now. I continued. "What man feels comfortable allowing another man into his home? There are exceptions, of course, but on the whole, how many men do you know who'd open their homes to another man?"

"Not many, it's true."

"With a female photographer, you don't have to worry about any of that. A woman gains the trust of both husbands and their wives. She can go anywhere."

"An interesting theory."

"It's more than a theory, Mr. Franklin. My clients the Kattens certainly appreciate the arrangement."

His eyes quickened with interest, as I knew they would. "Simon Katten?"

"And his wife, Edythe," I added. "Have you met them?"

"I haven't had the pleasure. But you said you had a proposition?"

"Yes, I do." I paused. "I'm looking for a business partner."

He regarded me calmly, but the flicker of interest in his eyes had turned into a steady flare. "And what do you propose to guarantee the loan?"

I glanced down at the ten portraits I'd set before him.

He unhooked his spectacles and took another long and careful look at each one. "They're terrific pictures," he said once he'd appraised them. "But with all due respect, as collateral they don't amount to much. You'd need, what, two thousand dollars just to get started?"

"Three thousand, actually." This was a sum I'd never seen in my life, but I kept my tone cool. "I'll pay it back. Down to the last dollar."

His brow furrowed, as if he'd made a swift calculation and found it coming up short. At last he said, "That's a large sum of money. Very large."

"Perhaps. Though in proportion to what you stand to make, Mr. Franklin, it's not so large at all."

He leaned forward and steepled his hands on the desk. "Let's imagine for a moment that I accept your proposition. I put up a large sum of money. What happens to my investment if you fail?"

It was a fair question, one I'd expected. "I'll pay you back in monthly installments. In no time at all, you'll have your money back with fifteen percent interest."

"Fifteen percent?" He seemed caught between interest and amusement. "To accomplish that, you'd have to charge twice what other photographers are asking. At least. Who'd pay those kinds of prices?"

I paused. "Think of the highest rate," Genthe used to say to me. I'd name it for him. "Now double it," he'd say. This was part of the nonchalant swagger he'd picked up from his years as a society photographer. He understood the logic of the wealthy. He knew that to please them, prices should be far out of reach of most people. He'd built his business on the theory, with great success.

Now I leveled my eyes at Sidney Franklin and repeated one of Genthe's guiding principles: "Nothing puts off wealthy clients like a bargain." After a moment I added, "The class of clients I'll be working with would insist on nothing less than the highest fees."

"You're clever, Miss Lange." He was smiling, but I could see he was thinking it over. "Let's make it twenty percent interest and a thirty percent share of the business."

I hesitated. Thirty percent seemed an awful lot, but then again without his support I'd own exactly one hundred percent of nothing.

"Fine," I said, "but I reserve the right to buy you out at any time."

Here he gave my photographs another quick, admiring look, then scraped back his chair and stood. "I accept," he said, and stuck out his hand. He gathered the pictures into a pile. "Until then," he said finally, "I'll take these off your hands."

When I told Caroline that I'd come to an agreement with Sidney Franklin and that I'd need to find a place for the new studio, she jumped up from her chair, threw her arms around me, and hugged me hard. Then, without missing a beat, she said, "Union Square. It has to be in Union Square!"

It had been a big leap, going to Sidney Franklin and getting him to back me, but it would take many more leaps to make the studio a success. To capture the clientele I wanted, I'd have to position myself just so. Imogen advised me that the very wealthiest clients would require that I come to their homes but that I'd still need a chic outpost to draw them in. Where I chose to set up shop mattered a great deal. Women were rarely seen in most streets of the city. The more prosperous the woman, the less she could be seen outside her home, though there was one important exception: The moneyed modern lady was permitted to spend money freely.

Union Square would be the perfect location for an upscale portrait studio. As soon as Caroline said it, I knew she was right. It was the fanciest shopping district in the city. With their department stores and hotels, the streets around the square were always dense with people, streetcars, and motorcars. Trouble was, the rents would be higher there than in almost any other neighborhood.

"Hang on a minute," she said when I brought up this last point. She bit her lip, narrowed her eyes in thought. "There's an empty storefront on Sutter. I've passed it a few times on my way downtown. It's been empty for months. It's not right on the square, but it could be close enough for your purposes. Want to go take a look?"

It turned out that 540 Sutter was a handsome old building, one of the very few that had survived the earthquake and fires. Like Monkey Block, something of the old Gold Rush days clung to it. Better yet, it was set on a busy street just a block from Union Square. You entered at the front through Hill Tollerton's swanky print gallery. Gump's was down the street, and right next door was the Elizabeth Arden salon, with its gleaming red door. It was all very promising, but only until we met the building manager.

"I don't rent to women," he said when I inquired after the empty rooms. He had no need whatsoever for subtlety, or apology, and stated his objection outright. What he didn't say, but his expression told me, was that there was only one possible business he could imagine two women running, and it was neither honest nor decent.

Caroline elbowed me.

"Actually, sir, it's my business partner, Mr. Sidney Franklin, who'd be renting the rooms."

"Sidney Franklin?" His brows sprang up. "That's the fellow who owns Franklin's department store."

"Yes, that's him. Mr. Sidney Franklin."

He remained watchful, but he warmed up considerably at this mention of Sidney Franklin. "What line of business did you say you were in?"

"Portrait photography." After a pause, I added, "For exclusive clientele."

"I see." His glance slid from me to Caroline and back. "And her?" he said, nodding to indicate Caroline. "What's she got to do with this?"

We'd prepared for this—actually, Caroline had prepared me for it. I looked at her now out of the corner of my eye. Her gaze was on the floor.

I felt the slight tug of her hand on my elbow. I cleared my throat and gave the answer we'd rehearsed: "Miss Lee is my assistant." He frowned.

"We haven't had any Orientals working in this building," he said, and rubbed his chin. "Plenty of them in the restaurants and hotels, though." I could sense the cogs of his mind turning over. The rooms had gone empty for a long time and could go empty for much longer. "I do hear they're hard workers. Can't hold it against them if they want to work, is what I think. Some may not agree, but me, I say you can't hold it against them, no."

He nodded as if we'd come to an agreement, then led us down a hallway and opened the door. For the space of two heartbeats Caroline and I locked eyes and smiled, but then the door creaked open and my spirits sank.

The rooms to which he led us were small, mean, and ruined. The walls needed paint. The large French doors opened onto a courtyard with a lovely little pool and fountain, but the windows were as cloudy and mottled as an old man's hands. That wasn't the worst of it. When we followed the man down a stairwell and into the basement, the sharp scent of mildew rose up to greet us, and I nearly gagged. Later we'd learn that many months earlier the water pipes had exploded, flooding the basement. The boards had swollen and the floors warped. There'd been some sort of dispute over who was at fault, and in the meantime the rooms had gone untenanted. By the time Caroline and I got there, mold was creeping up the walls and the grime was three inches deep.

"It's not *that* bad, Dorrie," Caroline said when we'd settled at a table in a pastry shop.

Our table had a clear view of Sutter Street. I glanced out the window and took in the details: the beautifully appointed buildings, the string of art galleries, the steady stream of well-dressed women. You would think it was a street in Paris—not that I'd seen Paris, but this was just how I pictured it.

And then my gaze landed on 540 Sutter and all I could see was ugliness.

"Are you kidding?" I said. "It's a mess. No, much worse than a mess. It's a disaster. No wonder the rent's so low."

"All right. It's awful, but it's not totally beyond hope. And you have to admit the location is perfect. You'd have to pay twice as much for a spot on the square."

"But did you see the floors in there? And that horrible wallpaper? It wouldn't be easy to fix all that."

"It doesn't have to be easy, Dorrie. It just has to be possible. The point is, that place has charm. The French doors are spectacular, and that fireplace is one of a kind. You could make it beautiful. You really could."

All at once I felt a flare of inspiration. I set down my tea. "I can't make that place beautiful, Caroline, but you can. In fact, I can't imagine anyone more capable of turning that place around. Why don't you come work with me?"

She lifted a brow. "As your assistant?"

"Assistant, partner—whatever you want. I'd just be so happy to have you with me."

Money was tight—likely even tighter than she'd told me.

She'd looked plenty of places, but since the war there'd been a steady uptick in the number of signs saying NO CHINESE and ORIENTALS NOT WANTED.

She wavered. "But I don't know anything about photography!"

"I could teach you as much as you want to know. And there'd be a lot to do besides taking the pictures. Keeping the books, scheduling sessions, greeting the clients. It's going to be much more than I can handle on my own."

I was thinking fast, picturing how it would happen, how we'd make it work, what it would mean.

"Just think, Caroline, you wouldn't be stuck in the basement of another department store. You need a job, so let's do this together. I'd pay you better than the White House did. You could make a break once and for all. And you could work less. During the slow hours—and there'd be some of those in the mornings—you'd have time to spend on your dressmaking."

"Caroline cocked her head slyly and her smile began to widen. "I see dark-green velvet curtains, maybe a chandelier or two . . ."

"Please say yes," I said, putting my hand on hers. "Say you'll do it."

I watched her very carefully then. For years now she'd worked ten hours a day, five days a week, in a place where the best you could hope for was not to be noticed. Those years in the basement of a department store had taught her something about what was possible for her and what was not.

"I guess we could make a go of it," she said at last, and that's how it happened, how the two of us became the "Lady Photographer and Oriental Girl" who'd soon, but only briefly, capture San Francisco's heart.

8.

The day we took possession of 540 Sutter, Caroline swept in smelling of lilac, her nails freshly lacquered, and her hair clipped shorter than ever in a pageboy complete with bangs. The new style suited her, not least for how it revealed the pair of drop earrings swinging from her ears. She'd recently had her ears pierced, a more than slightly shocking gesture, at least to anyone aiming at respectability. I thought she looked magnificent.

"Take a look at this!" she called out as she kicked open the door. Her eyes were shining with purpose and delight.

She'd brought two large leather chests and was heaving them into the front room. I sprang up and helped her carry them inside. There wasn't a stick of furniture in the place, so of course there was nowhere to sit. I watched as she sat cross-legged on the floor, unlatched the brass buckles on one of the chests, and began to unpack its contents.

Out came dresses in every color, faux fur coats and some

possibly real ones, along with a profusion of slips and chemises, scarves, and high-heeled shoes.

"Here it is!" she said after a few minutes of rooting around in the chest. She got to her feet and held up a garment. It was a loose-fitting embroidered gown in the Oriental style. The color was green, but a green so pale it edged into yellow. The sleeves were luxuriously wide, the cuffs embroidered in thin gold thread, and the fabric thickened toward the hem.

"Wow, that's really something. The fabric's stunning."

"Pongee silk," she said cheerfully, stripping down to her slip and pulling it on. "Bought it for a song at the flea market over in Alameda," she added, belting the gown tight at her waist.

I'd never seen her wear anything remotely like it. It looked truly spectacular on her, but, then, everything looked spectacular on Caroline.

She began rummaging through the pile of garments on the floor. I half-expected her to pull out the blue twin of what she was wearing, but it turned out to be some sort of tunic and a long, flounced skirt.

"I've got an idea, but first you have to put this on."

I figured she was working on some new design. She often asked me to model the pieces she sewed. It helped her see it, she always said. I pulled on the tunic, then the skirt. When I'd done that, she stepped back, narrowed her eyes, and considered the effect.

"Just a few finishing touches," she said. She looked through the trunk and came up with a long silk paisley scarf.

"Oh, I love that."

"It's gorgeous, isn't it? I bet you'd look stunning with it wrapped around your head."

"Let's try it, then."

"That's the spirit!" she said, fussing with the scarf a bit before knotting a large bow at the nape of my neck.

Next she made up my eyes with kohl, only a slightly less dramatic version of her own makeup. I let her work two circles of rouge into my cheeks, but I made her stop at the red lipstick. She herself was never without it (cherry-red during the day, black-red at night). I loved how it looked on Caroline, but I just didn't think I could carry it off.

"Take a look," she said, drawing a hand mirror from her bag and passing it to me.

I could only see myself in fragments, but it was far more dramatic than any outfit I'd put together for myself. I liked it, though. Loved it, actually.

"So," I said, passing the mirror back to her, "what's this new idea?"

She snapped the mirror closed. "There are already several portrait studios in San Francisco, right?"

"Twelve, and that's just the good ones."

"That's a fair amount of competition. More than fair, actually."

"By which you mean to say . . ."

"By which I want to remind you that you want to do something different from all those other studios. You've always said so. Well, that's got to do with talent, which you have, and so you will, but it seems to me that to get to that point you'll need to set yourself apart from the competition."

"Which I'd do how?"

"Remember how you once told me what clients really want when they come to you? That having a portrait done is an occasion for, how did you put it? 'Seeing yourself in a wonderful story'?"

This was one of Arnold Genthe's credos. I'd mentioned it to her a few times, but I was surprised to hear her repeat it to me now.

"Well, hiring Dorothea Lange shouldn't be about having your portrait made, or not entirely. It should be an *experience*. What better way to set the scene than a certain atmosphere?"

"Atmosphere?"

"You know, an aura, a mood."

"Like Sadakichi and his House of Grand Passion?"

"Now you're catching on! You saw how crazy all those society ladies are about him. People around here just love that sort of thing. They'll buy anything if you tell them it's new and exotic. Have you walked by Gump's lately?"

I shook my head.

"They've got antique kimonos in the windows this week. Last week it was third-century Chinese pottery. And all those showrooms inside! Oriental trinkets piled up to the ceiling all over the place . . . They're making a killing over there, and so's Sadakichi."

"But what he does is a performance, and before you tell me everything's a performance, do you really feel up to . . ." My eyes lingered on her silk gown. "Playing a part?"

"Look, Dorrie, you and I both know there's no point trying to hide that you've got a 'China girl' working for you, so why not make something of it? Use it to our advantage?" There was a glint in her eyes now. A flash of mischief and fun.

"Okay. I see your point, but what else goes into making up this 'atmosphere'?"

"Happy you asked," she said, and with that she popped open the second chest.

Caroline's idea, it turned out, was to turn the studio into a cross between an elegant English drawing room and a setting plucked from the pages of *One Thousand and One Nights*. The inspiration for the scheme lay swaddled in velvet and tucked beside her sewing machine: an antique samovar she'd scooped up at a flea market and polished to a high luster. I ran my fingers over the engraved silver, fascinated by its intricacy. The samovar was beautiful and grand and not entirely practical, which, of course, was exactly the point.

It would take some doing to decorate the studio with our limited funds, but this was San Francisco; according to Caroline, here everything could be scooped up cheaply. You just had to know where to look, which Caroline did. Together we went around secondhand shops and flea markets. She could see at once what was good and what wasn't. We began amassing a haul of furniture, decorations, and props. Soon we were the new owners of a button-back sofa in black velvet, which she picked up for next to nothing at the Alameda flea market, along with a few lovely if slightly threadbare Persian carpets. Getting it all across the bay by ferry had been no small feat, but she'd managed to hire two scrappy-looking young men for five cents each to help us.

While Caroline bent herself to the task of creating "atmosphere," I went about feeling dazed and anxious, half-believing we wouldn't be able to open the doors on the first of the month. As the days ticked past, I worried the repairs wouldn't be finished on time and that we'd have to put off opening. "It'll all work out," Caroline kept saying. I wasn't so sure. Aside from the repairs, there was a business permit to secure and contracts to be drawn up. Even after meeting with Franklin and securing a deposit, the building manager insinuated more than once that ours might not be the "right sort" of business for that part of town. Fortunately, Sidney Franklin stepped forward and lobbied on my behalf, an effort that may well have included some money under the table.

I hired workers to wrench out the ruined wooden floorboards and set down new ones. Plumbers replaced the busted pipes. When that was done, Caroline and I cleaned the place, top to bottom, front to back. We cranked open every window; swept the floors, the corners, the walls; polished the light fixtures; dusted the floorboards; rubbed the fireplace mantel with orange oil. The place brightened, then shone.

Slowly, miraculously, other things began to come together. I bought back my camera, which alone seemed a tremendous coup. Caroline and I trekked across the bay to the flea market a few more times, and while she scoured the stalls for furniture and decorations, I looked for photography equipment. It really was astonishing what you could find, but I was learning that in San Francisco fortunes disappeared just as often as they were made. An earthquake could twist you around twenty ways, a wildfire could torch everything you owned, or a flood could sweep you into the bay, but there was a sense your circumstances could change, soon and radically. The result of this was that just about everything you wanted could be had secondhand—if you knew where to look and how to refurbish it.

I'd told Caroline I would teach her as much about photography as she wanted to learn, and now was the time. We started with how to prepare a backdrop. Then I showed her how to hold the fabric to drape the clients. In the darkroom, I demonstrated how to prepare the baths, how to lay the pictures in the pans, how to know the image was ready to be plucked out and strung up on the line. It interested her well enough, but I could tell she was happiest upstairs, working at the small lacquered desk she'd set up in the front room or else thinking up new ways to decorate the studio.

I see now that it was a gamble but a gamble we took happily, because neither of us had ever had anything that really belonged to us, and because we both felt the promise and the rightness of working on something of our own.

On the last day of July, the workmen packed up and left. We'd open the next day, August 1, just as planned. To mark the occasion, we drank champagne. "A gift from Mr. Sidney Franklin, Esquire," Caroline announced, handing me a package wrapped in red tissue paper. With great ceremony, she uncorked the bottle and poured two glasses.

"To us," she said, and touched her glass to mine.

"To atmosphere," I added, which made her laugh.

"To atmosphere," she sang out.

It was as good and true a toast as any we might have made. The room had it in heaps now. The enormous brass samovar had been polished to a lustrous sheen and placed on a big round table in the center of the room. All month Caroline had kept adding things and fixing the place up. A phonograph with a huge fluted horn, little lacquered tables, silk rugs, plump cushions piled on the black velvet couch, bowls of oranges on all the tables, sprays of orchids on the mantel, windows swagged in velvet—every corner held something beautiful, intricate, dazzling. It was a room that made you want to linger or get lost in, which is to say it was perfect.

I loved it. Loved that it was beautiful, loved that it was ours, loved that we could share it with our friends. I hadn't been invited to many parties in New York—I wasn't rich or artsy enough. I was determined to throw parties in the studio as soon as we got going—big, glorious parties—to which no so-called notables would be invited. That is, of course, unless they also happened to be very nice and very, very fun.

That night we sat on our velvet couch, drinking wine and listening to records and talking until midnight, our joy the first flicker of a bulb before it settles into something steady and true. The next morning, I placed a hand-lettered welcome sign in the window, threw open the front door, and with that we declared ourselves open for business.

From *The San Francisco Call & Post*:

> Mere months since her arrival in San Francisco, Miss Dorothea Lange, a graduate of Columbia University, a protegee of the great Arnold Genthe, and herself a photographer of the crème de la crème of New York society, has made a great success in the West. Her new studio at 540 Sutter Street is fast becoming a magnet for the city's elite. To watch Miss Lange behind her camera is to find the New Woman in full command of her powers. We could all use some of the glamour bestowed by this lauded lady photographer and her lovely Oriental assistant on their exclusive clientele.

Most of it was lies; the other part was half lies. I'd sat in on a few classes at Columbia. I didn't have a degree from there—or any other university. I'd made up my own schooling as I went along, stumbling into most of it. As for my connection to New York society, that'd been confined to my time as Arnold Genthe's assistant, where my work never involved taking pictures—only helping him take his.

True, I wasn't the source of these distortions, but I didn't rush to correct them, either. On more than one occasion, Sidney Franklin had advised me to emphasize my New York connections, and so I did. I let the rumors spread, more or less unchecked, and now all sorts of stories were going around about Caroline and me.

We weren't an overnight success. A quick one maybe, but not instant. A dozen people walked through the studio the day we opened, but all of them were shopkeepers, managers, and saleswomen from close by. None of them came to have a portrait made, and we knew it. They were just curious for a look at the studio and the two women who'd taken it over. Still, we received them warmly, because you never knew where your clients could come from, and in the beginning so much depended on what people said about you.

That went on for a few weeks, which might not seem very long, but there's no time so nerve-racking as the first weeks of a new business. I'd seen it often enough. You could never get back that perception of freshness.

On Consuelo's advice, I took out ads in the papers. "Publicity," she'd said. "You've got to spread the word. People have to know you're here, or else they'll never come."

As the days went on, Caroline and I fell into a routine, meeting at eight each morning. She'd make coffee—she brewed it dark as mahogany and thick as syrup—and after we each drank two cups, I'd disappear into the basement, which I'd made over into a darkroom. Without any clients, Caroline was free to work on dressmaking, and I was glad for her, happy to see her busy with work she loved for a change and not only confined to helping me, though she never complained. Sometimes when the weather was good we'd walk down to Union Square for lunch, and in the afternoons we'd change into lovely things she sewed for us and wait for all the clients who'd surely turn up but rarely did.

By the second month we'd booked six sittings. I raised Caroline's salary, but it seemed we still needed something bigger. We got it: word of mouth. For weeks Edythe Katten hadn't just been talking me up herself but enlisting her husband, daughters, cousins, and friends to do the same. In the palaces on Pacific Heights and Russian Hill, over seventeen-course dinners on antique banquet tables, overtures were made and accepted. I could just hear it: *Have you met Dorothea Lange? She's the most wonderful photographer. She made the loveliest portraits of my family. I'd be most happy to make an introduction. She's frightfully in demand, you know. She's worked closely with the very best.*

And there I was, vouched for by a woman who had the ear of everyone who mattered in San Francisco. We became not just known but sought after.

In the large leather book in which Caroline kept a record of the names of our first clients, there were bankers and lawyers and politicians who came looking for portraits to announce their wealth and station. There were the wives who arrived brittle with resentment or limp with sadness and left splendid and bright and chattering. So many people showed up that we had to start turning them away. Caroline luckily could handle that with delicacy and grace.

The intricacies of San Francisco's upper echelon eluded me, but Caroline read the society pages, and she knew every twist and subtlety of this world. She made it part of her job to know. Most of her time now was taken up behind a desk, balancing the ledgers, scheduling sittings, collecting fees, and keeping the books for us, but it was also Caroline who received the clients and ushered them into the front room. She lit the samovar and served tea in small gold-rimmed Moroccan glasses. She put fancy cakes from Eppler's, with pastel-colored icing, on porcelain plates. Later, she was the one who escorted them to our clients before the camera and then flattered and charmed them while I did my work.

It wasn't easy work. I'd always thought portraits should be as unique as works of art, no less so than paintings. To do this, you had to really *see* the person first and let your idea of how to shoot them emerge slowly. It took extraordinary patience. Besides that, I was working with wealthy clients, which meant the portraits had to be both true and flattering. My clients could be infuriatingly demanding, but no one was ever harder on me than I was on myself.

Caroline spoke fluent Mandarin, having been tutored in the language for years at the Mission Home, and was keenly interested in the history of China and venerated its arts. Yet she had no qualms about improvising on the Oriental theme, not least in how she dressed and presented herself. There was the kimono, the jade amulet, the jeweled slippers, the way she lined her eyes with kohl and painted her lips red-black. She even made up a name for herself: Ah-yee. That's the one that got printed in the paper whenever reporters came around—at least when they thought to name her at all.

It was all far from authentic, as she herself well knew and anyone with more than a passing familiarity with the Far East would've told you, but our clients seemed untroubled or else oblivious to those sorts of details. They admired her gorgeous outfits, complimented her graciousness, swooned over her incomparably delicious cups of bergamot tea.

And Caroline played her part to the hilt. She could move in and out of character, right in front of you. She'd tip her chin down, clasp her hands in front of her, and still her face—and there she was, everyone's idea of a Chinese servant. Sometimes—just every so often and only with the people she liked—she'd drop the act. She'd start out quiet and demure, and then she'd say something in her perfectly accented English. What she seemed to most love was surprising people, playing up the contrast between the character they saw and the American girl she was, all insouciance and pluck. She must have felt some measure of power, calling out people's preconceived ideas of who she was, making a game of what had—and still sometimes did—hurt her. Out in the streets, she was only ever a foreigner, but here, she could trick you into seeing who she really was: a bit of everything.

There were plenty of people who'd come in and look at her sideways or refuse to talk with her and insist on talking to me instead, but for once—for the first time in her life, really—she didn't have to pretend they didn't exist. Now she could make them disappear. There was a look she'd sometimes give me when a certain kind of person came into the studio. I learned to recognize it immediately, and when I saw it I'd take up the large leather appointment book, pretend to study the page, and let them know that, unfortunately, we were booked solid, and we could not possibly lavish them with the care they deserved in the taking of their portraits. We were very sorry, but it was quite impossible just now.

We'd done it. We'd launched ourselves into the future. It was exhausting and thrilling and such incredible fun. Because it was our own, we loved it so. When we walked into those lovely lighted rooms, it felt like coming home. All we wanted to do now was spend our days in the studio. We worked so hard you'd think all the wolves of the world were at our door, which of course they were.

9.

One day I heard the beat of steel-tipped boots overhead.

These were the day's slow hours, and I counted on them to finish my work down in the darkroom. I was in the habit of leaving the front door to the studio open. That way if Caroline was out, which she often was in the mornings, and I didn't hear the bell ring, clients could let themselves in. Not that many clients came by at that time of day. Some unspoken rule commanded that a lady shouldn't circulate before noon, if that, and it was rare for anyone to turn up in the morning.

Now someone was pacing upstairs. I froze. I knew at once who it was. How many people went around in steel-tipped boots in San Francisco?

When I reached the top of the stairs, Maynard Dixon was standing in the front room with his hat in his hands, looking at everything with a kind of delighted attention.

"You've put on quite a magic show."

"How do you mean?"

"You've been here, what? A few months? I hear you've got all our merchant princes and princesses clamoring for your services." He paused and smiled. And there it was, if only faintly, all that charm, all that restless heat I'd felt the first time we met. "I'd say it's one of the most impressive magic shows I've seen in some time."

"I'd thank you, except it's more to do with work than magic."

He nodded, still smiling. "Well, I'd say whatever it is, it's wonderful." He took a step forward. "I'd also say San Francisco suits you."

The pull of his gaze made me blush. I was in my work clothes: sweater, overalls, boots. The sweater was new, a white that ran to cream, and so was the paisley-print scarf with which I'd pulled back my hair. Some curls had sprung loose from the scarf, and I pushed them off my face.

"Have a seat," I said, gesturing to the velvet sofa. I sat in a chair a few feet away, close enough to catch the smell of paint and turpentine that clung to his clothes.

As soon as he sat down, he drew a pouch from his jacket pocket. I watched as he rolled a cigarette with what I'd soon learn was the Indian herb kinnikinnick, a mix of tobacco, sagebrush, and manzanita.

"I wanted you to know I'm sorry for what happened," he said after he'd taken a long pull on the pipe. "My ex-wife. She . . . She isn't well. She's been ill for a long time. I've been in Arizona getting her settled. Anyway, it was rude to leave so suddenly. I'm sorry if you were hurt."

"I wasn't. And I'm happy you've come."

"It occurs to me I haven't properly introduced myself. Maynard Dixon," he said with the full glow of his charm.

"Dorrie—" I started to say, but then there was the sound of

voices from the window. I glanced at the clock. Ten past noon.
My first client, Mrs. Eustace Bennett, would be here soon, and
while my outfit hadn't put Maynard off, there was no chance of
charming Mrs. Bennett in my overalls and beat-up boots.

"I'd ask you to stay, but—"

"I wouldn't dream of interrupting a magic show," he said,
rising from the sofa. "I'm glad things are going so well for you.
I'd heard as much, but I'm pleased to see it with my own eyes."

How easy it was for him to get me to make up a story without
even asking me to.

I'd always tell people this was the first day we met, the day he
came to 540, and that I'd been completely surprised to see him.
It's true we hadn't introduced ourselves the first time we saw
each other—I didn't know his name until Caroline told me—so
I suppose it was our first real introduction. The truth, though, is
that this was where he wanted our story to begin and also where
I let it begin.

Back in my room at the boardinghouse, I pulled open the
door and found a piece of folded paper on the floor. I knew right
away it was from him, or maybe it was just the force of wanting
that made me think I knew. Still, I couldn't imagine how he'd
managed to get past the boardinghouse mistress, let alone up
the stairs and to my door. At the Elizabeth, men weren't allowed
an inch past the parlor.

Then it hit me: He'd slipped it to one of the girls. Yes, that
made sense. That I could picture perfectly: The smile he would
have smiled as he approached her outside the building. The
slow tip of his hat as he introduced himself. How he would've
made her feel he was doing her some delicious favor rather than

the other way around. With his charm turned full on, he could talk anybody, especially a woman, into anything.

I pulled the door closed, flicked on the light, and sank onto the bed. I tore open the envelope, unfolded the paper, and there, in his smooth, flowing hand that took up nearly all the page, was just one line:

Dorrie—Painting all day tomorrow. 728 Montgomery. Second floor, toward the back. Come by.

"Come by," I said aloud to the empty room. No question mark—of course not. No name, either. Instead, at the bottom, by way of a signature, he'd drawn some kind of bird, an eagle or a hawk. Its black-inked wings were spread wide across the page.

Even though I knew, with a certainty I'd only rarely felt in my life, that this was what I wanted—that he was what I wanted—I didn't go to Maynard's studio the next day or even the day after that.

For one thing, I knew what Caroline would say: Forget about him. She'd said it before and she would say it now. She'd known him for years, and she'd seen the worst of things between him and Lillian. She clearly thought he was a mess and too old for me, as well—forty-three years to my twenty-three.

Even though I knew she'd disapprove, I couldn't keep it a secret that he'd stopped by the studio.

"I know he can be very charming," she said when I told her. She spoke in a tight voice I rarely heard her use. "But what's the point?"

So. I should've folded up his note and tossed it into the trash. If I ran into him after that, there'd be some awkwardness, but that would pass. I could leave it at that. In fact, that was exactly what I would do—throw the note away and forget him. I didn't have time for his kind of complication when I'd been new to the city and I had even less time for it now.

But that night and the next I went to sleep thinking of him and woke up thinking of him. If there'd ever been any hope of forgetting him, I was beyond it. Even with all my insecurities and misgivings, I don't think anyone, not even Caroline, could've convinced me to stay away from Maynard. Of course, she had a point—more than one—but I could have laid out all the reasons why I should forget him, set them in front of me like playing cards, and it wouldn't have mattered at all.

Three days later I decided: I'd go to his studio the next day after work. Not because he wouldn't stop leaving notes for me at the Elizabeth, but because once I was finally done listing all the reasons why I shouldn't go, that left room for one reason I knew I should: I wanted to.

A "shrine"—that's the word that came to me when he held the door open. Walking into Maynard Dixon's studio on Montgomery Street was like walking into a shrine.

By then I'd dropped into many artists' studios in Monkey Block, and to call them eccentric would've been an understatement. You never knew who you'd meet or what you'd wind up seeing them do. There were dancers who threw the doors open and pranced around nude. A flamboyant gem cutter who crafted life-sized pheasants from jade. Rooms without a single piece of furniture except an easel. On the fourth floor, someone had set up a sort of mystic practice, with chanting and clapping and bells chiming late into the night.

Still, Maynard's studio was a revelation—strange, luminous, unearthly. Every surface in the room held some sculpture or ornament. My eyes danced over it all. One entire wall had been given over, top to bottom, to feathers, hatchets, rifles, amulets, turquoise beads. Ceremonial headdresses had been tacked up alongside paintings and prints. At the very top he'd mounted a bison skull. The slanting glass roof caught the light, illuminating each object, and with the tall arched windows thrown open, the scent of the bay mingled with the smell of paint, turpentine, and linseed oil.

And then there was his work, which, as far as I could tell, was the sky. He'd painted it with a low-slung winter sun, summer's pure blue, the glow of a luminous cloud. The paintings hung on walls, perched on easels, leaned in stacks on the floor. I took in the twisted tubes of paint, the primed, huge blank canvases stacked against the wall, the glass jars crammed with brushes. In one corner, there was an easel, and the canvas there was still slick with wet paint.

"What do you think?" he asked, lifting his chin toward the easel. He'd come to the door with a cigarette in the corner of his mouth and the cuffs of his white shirt rolled up to the elbows.

"It's astonishing. They're all astonishing."

I floated around for a while, taking time with each of his paintings. He told me he was moving away from Impressionism and Postimpressionism—"all that derivative European nonsense"—in favor of a modernist aesthetic of bold shapes, straight lines, and simple compositions. The painting that stood out to me most was a portrait, one of the few pieces in the room that included a human figure. It showed a young girl riding a horse, bareback and with a blaze of blond hair trailing behind her.

I crossed the room for a closer look. I felt him watching me as I studied the painting.

"That's my daughter," he said. "Her name's Constance, but we call her Consie." He cleared his throat. "I call her Consie."

I glanced over at him. He drew a cigarette from his breast pocket, struck the match with a precise beauty, and gave a thoughtful pull on the cigarette.

"I took her to Montana last year. A railroad commissioned me to do some paintings of Glacier National Park and the Black Feet Indians. That's where I painted that one. We stayed there two months, the two of us. She was born in New York, but you'd think she'd been born to that life. She took to it so quick. Like she'd always belonged there and it was her home." For a long minute he stood gazing at the painting, and then he said, "She misses it awfully."

"Is it the place she misses or is it you?"

He turned from the painting and smiled. "Some of both, I'd guess."

I nodded and went back to looking around the studio. After some time I noticed a set of drawings on the table. They were strikingly different from his paintings—precise and muted, where the paintings were looser and suffused with color and light.

"What are these?" I asked.

"This here," he said, lifting one, "is the rent money. And these"—he picked up two others—"are Consie's tuition for the month."

"I'm sorry, I don't understand."

"They're book jackets for *Harper's*. Commercial work."

"They're very good."

He frowned. "Good for what they are, maybe, but they're not art. Not the way my paintings are. Well, used to be. But enough of that," he said, and shuffled the illustrations under a pile of papers. "What do you think of San Francisco, Dorrie? Are you happy here?"

"I am. Very happy, actually."

He narrowed his eyes. "And why's that?"

"Oh, everything seems more . . ." All sorts of things flooded through my mind. I had to think for a moment about the best way to put it. "Possible."

When the *Chronicle* published a story about the studio, Caroline clipped the piece, pressed it with an iron, and kept it in a thick leather-bound album. She predicted others would follow, and soon they did.

In our first months at 540 Sutter Street, we made portraits for dozens of clients, many of them the result of private sittings, and several of these outside the city. In San Francisco, blending in depended on standing out. People here were tired of stuffy formal portraits, the whole family lined up, staunch patriarchs on chairs, unsmiling daughters with their crossed ankles, stuffed into crinoline and lace. No, they wanted something freer, more artistic, more singular. We were working all the time, all through summer and into fall, and there were always new clients and new commissions. We were making good money, too—not enough yet to pay back Franklin's investment, but enough to bring that goal within sight.

I was the photographer you went to only if you could afford

it. Not a single client balked at my prices. The lack of older hi-
erarchies in San Francisco made exclusivity more, not less, necessary, and soon we were booking sittings at three times the
already substantial rate we had when we opened.

Later, people would ask why it took me so long to quit the
studio, which just showed how little they knew about what it
took for a woman to build a business on her own. The truth
was, it was honest work, and work is never wasted if it's honest.
Caroline and I worked hard. "Atmosphere" helped, but that, finally, was the thing that mattered—what you put into your
work; how much of yourself you brought to it; what you gave.
At the end of each day, I was bone-tired, and yet I'd never felt
happier. I could've been back in Hoboken, trekking into the city
every day, stuck in the back room of some studio, working for
some boss or another. At the end of another hellish week I could
be handing over half my paycheck to Grossmama for rent. Now
that every dollar was a dollar toward independence, for me and
for Caroline, I worked harder than ever and didn't ever really
know it as work.

10.

"In our history one of the most thrilling episodes will be the story of how gallantly the city of Saint Francis behaved when the black wings of war-bred pestilence hovered over the city."
—*San Francisco Chronicle,* November 1918

And then everything—absolutely everything—ground to a halt.

Disasters can happen suddenly, but just as often they happen so slowly you don't notice they're happening at all. That's how it was when influenza descended on San Francisco in the autumn of 1918.

It'd torn through the East Coast earlier that year. Through Boston and then New York. Philadelphia was hit especially hard. Twenty thousand dead in a month. Mama sent terrified letters from back home. I followed the news closely and yet it all felt far away—farther away than even the war. Everyone, but most particularly Mayor Sunny Rolph, said the Spanish flu wouldn't come to California. That the weather out here was too mild. That it would burn itself out before it ever reached the West Coast. That we were safe.

And at first only a few people got sick. A waiter at Coppa's. A clerk at the post office. It was awful, but it didn't stop us going about our lives. There were no rules, then a great many, and they shifted continually. One day we'd be told to wear masks and avoid going out. The next day you'd open the paper and there was Mayor Rolph, presiding over some liberty loan parade and smiling broadly with the usual fresh flower in his lapel.

By October, fifteen thousand San Franciscans had fallen ill. Fear flew from person to person. A touch or a breath and you might die. Everywhere you looked, you saw a sea of white. It was suddenly illegal to go outside without a gauze mask. The one time I saw someone without one, a policeman hauled him off, but not without a sharp stab of the baton.

Schools, churches, movie palaces, saloons, theaters, parks— one after another they all shut down. I'd never forget the silence of those days. It was so quiet in the city you could hear the birds singing—which was beautiful but unsettling, too. But no part of it was so hard as the way a curtain was suddenly drawn between people. It reminded me, painfully, of polio, of the long months of isolation. You'd walk in the city and people would greet you with a nod, but no one stopped to ask you how you were, and with the masks only their eyes were visible, and even that told you nothing, because everyone looked away before you could meet their gaze.

With the city shut down, there was nowhere to go. Worse, we had no work. Half the people at Monkey Block were already scrambling to get by before the flu hit. Now it was everyone. Caroline and I were better off than some of our friends, but not by much and not for long. One client after another canceled, and by the end of October, we didn't have a single appointment left on the calendar.

"Everyone's gone," Caroline said.

"Gone where?"

She shrugged. "They've lit out to their country houses.

Napa, Lake Tahoe, Santa Barbara. I think the Claybornes sailed to Honolulu."

I was sure we'd lose everything. Sidney Franklin agreed to let me stop making payments on the loan, at least for a while, but there were still other bills to pay. After Caroline went through the books and came back with grim calculations, we went down to one meal a day to make sure the gas didn't get shut off.

The days bled into one another. It seemed best to keep busy however we could. Even though there was no work to do, Caroline and I continued to go to the studio every day. She cut up fabric remnants and sewed masks for the girls and women of the Mission Home. Every one of the aides, and many of the charges, had fallen sick.

We had a ritual, cemented over the months, of drinking coffee there together first thing in the morning. One rainy morning we were lingering longer than usual over coffee, when someone knocked on the door. It was a woman in a plain gray coat and gauze mask. I nearly turned her away, but Caroline, who'd met Edythe Katten only once before, recognized her at once.

"Mrs. Katten! Please come in."

The wind was so strong the rain was falling in slants, but Edythe shook her head. "I'm afraid I can't stay. Are you well, Caroline? Dorrie?"

"Yes."

"Good." She pulled her mask down slightly off her face. "I've come to ask you a favor, Dorrie. As you likely know, the neighborhoods south of Market Street have been devastated by the flu. The sick are dying unnoticed there. A group of us from Temple Emanu-El have been working to gather food and medicine, but it's been difficult to find people to go into the neighborhood and deliver provisions. I wonder if you could help us, Dorrie?"

"Of course."

"I'll come with you," Caroline said quickly. "When do you need us, Mrs. Katten?"

"Actually," she said, "I was hoping you might come now."

"You've never been South of the Slot, have you, Dorrie?"

Caroline and I were standing at the corner of Market and Third, pressed in close together under one umbrella. There were several butcher shops on that particular block, and with the odor of blood so thick in the air, I had to cover my nose. I glanced at the building in front of us. It was a wreck of a place—two stories of blackened brick with several missing windows. The boiler works on the next block had been boarded up, another casualty of the Spanish flu, but the saloon advertising ten-cent whiskeys had a line going out the door.

I shook my head. "No, I haven't."

"Lo Mo brought me down once. One of the girls from the home landed here. She was in a bad way, I think. . . . Men stay in the flophouses when they've got work and live in the streets when they don't." Her brows furrowed, then softened. "Shall we split up or go together?"

"Go together," I said.

A driver had taken us from the studio in a truck laden with clothes, masks, food, and medicine; it was idling on the street now. We loaded a dolly and headed toward the first rooming house. Inside, a feeling of fear, chaos, and decay hung in the air. Children jammed the halls. A man sat slumped in the stairwell, muttering in Russian between violent coughs. When we asked if he needed a doctor, he kicked at our shins. When we offered him medicine, he refused it with what were surely his choicest insults.

"Come," said Caroline, and pulled me gently away.

Initially it was Caroline who knocked on doors and did the talking. We were wearing masks, and the residents seemed leery of us. Many of them wouldn't, or perhaps couldn't, answer their doors, but when some saw that we'd come with food and medicine, they were astonished and grateful and kind.

After a few hours, I felt less nervous, and we began taking turns knocking on doors. We'd just entered our third building, a large rooming house and the roughest so far that day, when a woman came to the door and pointed a finger in Caroline's face.

"The girl's a Chink!" she called out. There were just a few people milling about the hallway, but she shouted as if there were a crowd to hear her. Then she stepped forward, and the next moment she'd torn Caroline's mask right off her face.

"You see! She tried to hide it, but I knew it from her Chink hair!"

For a moment the air felt tight. A small child with red hair appeared from inside the room and stood in the doorway. I was startled by the way she was watching Caroline. How quiet and still she was.

I lifted my head and stared the woman straight in the eye. My heart clenched and kicked, and then I balled up my fist and pitched myself forward. Before my arm could reach the woman, someone grabbed me around the waist from behind and pulled me away. It was a young man with longish hair and a shabby shirt we'd passed on the landing. He'd seen everything.

"Never mind her," he said to me. He turned to Caroline. "Are you all right, miss?"

"Is she all right?" the woman howled. "It's her kind that's spreading sickness, living like animals down in those filthy neighborhoods of theirs. Send her back where she came from, I say. Send the whole lot of them back!"

He ignored her. "You're not hurt, are you, miss?" he said, placing his hand on Caroline's arm.

Caroline straightened and lifted her chin.

To look at her then, you'd think she was brave and strong, and she was. She wasn't *only* those things, but in that moment she wouldn't let anyone see her as anything else.

"I'm perfectly fine," she said, removing the man's hand from her arm.

"Mama!" the redheaded child cried. She tugged on the woman's sleeve and was shoved away. "But her mask, Mama! You're holding her dirty mask!"

It was as if it were on fire—that's how quickly the woman flung Caroline's mask from herself. Horror-stricken, she began furiously wiping her hand on her skirt.

Caroline turned to leave. I followed her.

We'd nearly made it out of the building when we heard the woman calling out after us.

"That's right!" she shouted. "Out you go, you filthy Chink!"

Afterward, we walked for a while in silence. The rain had turned to a drizzle. Caroline didn't open her umbrella. When we came to a bench, she sat down and I sat beside her.

"I'm so sorry that happened."

"I know, Dorrie."

"I wish I could have done something."

She stared at me. "We're lucky someone stopped you before you tried to hit that woman. You do realize that, don't you?"

I said nothing. Studied my hands, then glanced back at Caroline. She was looking out at the city. I followed her gaze, but I couldn't make out what she was seeing.

I was cold and miserable and desperate to return to the studio. But not Caroline. After a few minutes, she got to her feet and said, "Let's go." She was proud and kind, but part of me always wondered if her strength came from fear, fear of what would happen if she didn't prove she belonged. Whatever the reason, we delivered more than a hundred boxes of food and medicine that day. The next morning, on Caroline's insistence, we did it again. And the day after that, as well.

When news of the armistice hit in November, people rushed out from every door on every street to watch the parade on Market Street. The crowds—masked but joy-blind, jostling, cheering—were so deep the cable-car lines shut down. The war to end all wars. We'd won it. The kaiser had abdicated. The world was safe for democracy. The doughboys were coming home. The flu was raging, cutting a deadly swath through the city, but there was no stopping people from celebrating. A group of men lit a massive bonfire at the corner of Market and Powell, in front of the Emporium Department Store, and everyone who walked by threw their masks into the flames.

That winter San Francisco was seized by the recklessness of a city sure it'd once again shaken off the worst. People said it was like the first days after the earthquake, when strangers wrapped their arms around you and hugged you and called you friend.

To celebrate, Caroline and I threw open the doors to 540 Sutter. We made the front room wonderful—lit up entirely with candles, with the furniture cleared away, leaving only the carpet to make a dance floor. Caroline piled coals under the samovar for the tea. Everyone brought something to share. There was champagne to drink, and homemade gin, and gallons of sweet Spanish wine. There was cracked crab, fresh from Fisherman's Wharf, sitting on a bed of ice, magnificent little mussels someone brought down from Tomales Bay, as well as banana fritters and chocolate cake. People kept arriving. Caroline met my eyes now and then from across the room, and we'd shake our heads happily. Through the smoke and laughter and shouting, there was the sound of Ansel beating out show tunes on the old upright piano Caroline had salvaged from someplace.

Not everyone was ready to dive into the celebrations. "Seventeen million dead," Consuelo reminded us, "a country's worth of people—and not an hour after the news comes crackling over the wires and the newspapers flash the first headlines, everybody's busy erasing the memory of war."

That's when I noticed a girl sitting by herself on the black velvet couch. She might have been nine, maybe ten. It gave me a start. You could see just about every kind of person among our friends, but a child was not one of them.

"Consie!"

It was Maynard's voice, coming from somewhere around me. He had to call the girl a second time before she trudged across the room.

"Consie, this is Miss Lange and her friend Miss Lee. Ladies, this is my daughter, Consie."

She was a wiry girl with sunburned skin and freckles. She wore a white dress, the kind of dress a girl might have worn to attend church, but it was wrinkled and soiled across the front. Her eyes I'd always remember particularly. They were the same bright blue as her father's, but there were two purplish half-moons under hers, as if she hadn't slept.

"Hello, Consie," said Caroline, smiling and shaking the child's hand.

I'd always remember my discomfort in that moment, how I'd felt her distance before either of us said a word. It settled something between us that time would never resolve.

"Pleased to meet you," I said, and stuck out my hand.

She didn't take it. Didn't even look at me. She just stood there staring at the floor, arms crossed in front of her, and looking as if she'd grown roots. She seemed not mean, really, but very angry.

"Shake the lady's hand, Consie," said Maynard.

"But she's just a kid. I don't have to shake a kid's hand," the girl replied.

I'd been working in the darkroom up to the minute our guests had arrived, still in my overalls and boots. Sure, I wasn't dressed for the occasion, but for a child to say I looked like a kid? I couldn't even think what to say.

"Don't be like this," Maynard told her in a loud whisper, and then for a moment she glared at him. I was struck again by what her eyes held—anger, but also pain—and I had to look away. Maynard felt it, too, because he gave up trying to make her act polite.

He turned to Caroline and me. "Her school shut down on account of the flu, so she's been staying with her aunt in Sausalito." He ran a hand through his thick black hair, and it fell immediately back into his eyes. "I thought it would do her good to bring her to the city for the day," he said, looking at her with a sad sort of bewilderment as she stood with her arms crossed over her chest and kicked at the floor with her scuffed-up shoes. "Nothing I do does any good."

"Consie," said Caroline, bending low and pointing toward the piano, where Ansel was taking a break. "Do you see that young man by the piano?"

She nodded.

"I bet he can play any tune you like. Shall we go ask him?"

At this her expression softened and her arms dropped to her sides. Holding Caroline's hand, she half-walked, half-skipped away. When they reached the piano, Caroline tapped Ansel on the shoulder, Consie whispered something in his ear, and the next minute Ansel's fingers were flying over the keys.

I'd have many reasons to remember that night, but the worst was this: it was the last time any of us would see Ansel for a long time.

We thought we'd beat the Spanish flu that fall. We hadn't. The deadliest wave came in winter. With the return of every large convoy of soldiers there was another occasion for people to gather in the streets and in the dance halls. Then, when bugles sounded in December and we were allowed to remove our masks, it unleashed a massive celebration. Offices and stores emptied. People went out in droves. Three weeks after the announcement that the Spanish Lady was gone for good, thousands more fell sick. Half the time you couldn't bring yourself to think what it meant, and the other half you couldn't think of anything else. That the masks were useless. That the vaccines were impotent. That so many more would die.

Then came the news that Ansel was terribly ill. Imogen took it hardest of anyone. The ferries had stopped going from Oakland to San Francisco, but she contrived some way to make it across the bay. I met her downtown and together we took a streetcar to Seacliff, where Ansel lived with his family on Twenty-Fourth Avenue.

As soon as I saw Ansel, my hand went to my mouth and I felt a hot rush of tears. I'd heard toward the end, people's skin turned so dark you couldn't tell one race from another. Ansel's skin had turned blue, and he was curled up in the corner of the bed, fevered and so terribly still. I hadn't considered for a minute that someone so vibrant could be laid so low. Ansel had always been so spirited and lively. I'd never once seen him quiet or at rest; he was positively catatonic now. But that's how the Spanish flu worked. It struck the young and healthy the hardest.

Imogen sat with him for a long time, holding his hand and talking to him in a soothing voice. He couldn't answer simple questions. His brain seemed broken somehow. I hated myself for it, but I couldn't stay in the room more than a minute. Instead, I went downstairs and sat in the parlor with Mrs. Adams.

"I think it's made him sick in the head." Her eyes stayed fixed on the table as she spoke. "He talks until he can't talk anymore, and then he lies still as a dog. Most of the time I can hardly make out a word he says, it's all such strange nonsense, but he's been begging his father to take him to Yosemite. He's convinced the only thing in the world that can cure him are the mountains and fresh air." Here she looked up at me. "Wouldn't you say that's madness, miss?" she said, her eyes brimming with tears. "Wouldn't you say my boy's not right anymore?"

Ansel spent three weeks in Yosemite, and whether it was the fresh air or his joy in returning to the place he most loved in the world, he came back cured. But illness changed him. We all saw it. There'd always been a mischievous glint in his brown eyes. It was gone now. He'd flinch if anyone came within two feet of him, which made it just about impossible for him to walk in the city. He was always looking around him, over his shoulder, skittering away. The one time he came to 540, he sprang up from his chair every five minutes to wash his hands, and when we asked him to play the piano, he held his palms up and shook his head. From fingertip to wrist, his hands were too blistered to play.

His energy eventually returned, along with all his strong opinions and his sweetness and his glorious piano playing, but for the rest of his life, Ansel didn't want to do anything but photograph mountains, rivers, and streams. Wherever the flu had taken him in the winter of 1919, he couldn't come back, and never wanted to.

11.

Live every day as if you might be struck blind—that was the rule I made for myself now. In those first few days after the second quarantine was lifted, we went around marveling at the smallest things, as if the Spanish flu had rendered us all blind and we'd suddenly gained our sight again. Every detail seemed suddenly as sharp as if seen for the first time. Life returned to San Francisco, and it had never been more precious. After weeks of uncertainty, friends began to find work again, and despite having contracted the flu, all the girls and women of the Mission Home recovered. Just to walk down the street or sit on a park bench became an exquisite luxury. Everybody smiled at you and said hello. One by one our clients came back to the city, and once again our calendar filled with appointments. We were back on our feet.

When the movie palaces reopened, Caroline and I each splurged ten cents for a Sunday afternoon matinee at the California. The main feature wasn't very good, but they'd shown a clip of Isadora Duncan dancing in her long white dress and bare feet. We'd both loved it so much we wound up staying in our seats and watching the whole show two more times through. We might even have stayed for a third screening except an usher kicked us out.

"I wish I were like Isadora," I said as we staggered out of the theater and into the bright streets. "Bold enough to . . ."

"To what?"

"To move so freely in the world."

"Aren't you, though?" she said. "I think you are."

I looked down at my brown boots.

"I wonder if learning to dance would help me. With my leg, I mean."

That's when Caroline stopped walking, put a hand on my arm, and told me I must learn to dance.

She looked so earnest that I had to laugh. "It's not exactly fatal, not knowing how to dance."

"Oh, but it is! It most truly is."

The cure to this dire condition was obvious, at least to Caroline: dancing lessons. Her friend Estrellita was a well-known dancer and occasionally taught at a place on Fillmore Street called the Majestic. Caroline was sure she'd cut me a deal.

In that moment, it seemed like a wonderful plan, but two weeks later, when we were getting ready to head out for my first lesson, it felt like the worst idea in the world. Caroline was putting on her stockings. She was taking her time, inching them up her legs with care. I found myself watching her and feeling uneasiness creep through me.

"I'm not sure I'm up for this."

She lifted her eyes and gave me a wry smile. "Of course you're not up for it, Dorrie. But you're the one who said it's what you need to do."

"Maybe you could just sew me a few more of these lovely long skirts. You can barely notice my limp when I wear them."

She'd finished putting on her stockings and was now fastening the buckles on her shoes. When she was done, she looked at me, not unkindly, but in a steady sort of way.

"I'll sew you ten more skirts if you like, but you'd still be stuck with your idea of yourself. That's what you've got to get rid of, wouldn't you say?"

It was true. Lodged deep in me, deep as muscle, bone, and blood, was my idea of myself as a cripple. I couldn't say the word aloud, but it was at the center of everything. Polio had plucked me out of an ordinary life, which gave me a sort of freedom. If I hadn't gotten sick, I might never have become a person who was happiest in a darkroom. And yet. Shame was in my drop foot. Loneliness was there. The constant fear of exposure and the burden of concealment—it was all there in the drag of my leg.

As generous and gentle as she could be, Caroline could also be stern, and just then sternness was what I most needed. A thing had to be dealt with. That's just how it was. If there was a way to get rid of my limp, I had to do it.

So out we went. Out of Monkey Block, into the city, and onto a streetcar. The narrow wooden buildings on Fillmore Street were smaller than those in other parts of the city. All sorts of people and businesses were crowded together here: Matsudo's candy shop was followed by a butcher storefront with Hebrew lettering stenciled on the window, which was followed by what looked like a Swedish bakery showing off abundant trays of pastries. In the space of five minutes I heard five different languages.

"It's got a bit of everything, hasn't it?"

"Yes," said Caroline. "Isn't it wonderful?"

At every corner, iron arches stretched from one side of the street to the other, each studded with small electric lights. Then, there it was: THE MAJESTIC spelled out in huge bright-blue letters. I stopped for a moment, dizzy in the glare of the lights, and then we stepped inside.

The Majestic interior was bigger than I would have guessed just looking at it from the street, and the rooms were crammed with people. I pulled my hat from my head and we thrust our way through the crowd. Music streamed from the back of the room, but I couldn't see the orchestra. The air was thick with smoke, and the music swelled all around us. Bass, drums, and some other instrument I couldn't place. We pressed on to the rear of the building, and at the end of the room we came to a door marked ACADEMY OF DANCE.

I was a truly awful student, worse than I'd even thought I would be, which was already really very bad. Estrellita was a raven-haired Spaniard beauty (born, I'd later find out, Stella Hurtig in Cincinnati to a Jewish theater family). She conducted the class entirely in her native tongue—not that understanding her would have helped me much anyway. She ran us through the basic positions, drumming out the beats with a cane. With my twisted foot, every bend and step was a challenge. I was the most hopeless one there that day, lurching, teetering, and scrabbling for balance, but Estrellita was a wonderfully patient teacher, and from across the room Caroline herself kept flashing me encouraging smiles.

It took a while, but toward the end of the hour, when the

accompanist played a slower tune, the music got into me and my hips started swaying of their own accord. I forgot my feet, forgot my counting, and then, somehow, for a few brief moments, I lifted right out of myself and began to dance.

Afterward, I felt wonderful. When Caroline and I stepped out of the hot, smoky, crowded rooms of the Majestic and into the chilly streets, we walked arm and arm, talking and laughing. Lights bloomed and flickered from the iron streetlamps above us, and the cold fresh air carried the scent of woodsmoke.

"Are you tired?" Caroline asked after we'd been walking awhile. Her cheeks were bright red from the cold, but her eyes were shining.

"Not at all."

"Then let's walk for a ways." She turned to look at me. "You were wonderful in there, Dorrie. I can already see a difference in how you're holding yourself."

"Do you really think so?"

"Absolutely. You must keep it up!"

"In that case we'll come next week and the week after that. Won't we? Caroline?"

But she wasn't listening. Her attention had been caught by something else.

Across the street and down another block, there was shouting and then the sight of a dozen men surging toward a larger group. Just beyond that I saw half a dozen policemen on horseback.

"It's a protest," Caroline said, spotting the slogans. She glanced over at me. "Consuelo says they're getting rowdy."

I'd heard there'd been a surge of protests and strikes in the last few weeks. With so many men back from war, and so many more on the way, there wasn't as much work as there used to be. The talk in Coppa's was sobering. There were at least three men for every job. Wages had gone down by a fourth, then by a half. On top of that, landlords were taking advantage of the sudden population boom, and it was getting harder and harder to find a decent, affordable place to rent.

All at once a large plate-glass window shattered. The policemen surged forward on their horses, whips cracking as they plowed into the crowd. A man climbed into the back of a truck filled with rocks and hurled one at the police captain. It caught the captain on the chest and he went over backward, tumbling to the ground and slamming against the front wheel of a parked car. A second man climbed into the truck and hefted a rock onto his shoulder, but by then the officers' long riot clubs were out and swinging.

"Come on," Caroline said, taking me by the elbow and steering us in another direction.

We turned the corner in tense silence. A few blocks were still and deserted—the mob had done its work and scattered. Then I saw them, two men slouching against the wall, faces canceled in shadow. I wondered if they'd been part of the crowd we'd just seen, but it was impossible to know.

We'd reached the corner when they shambled toward us. Up close, I noticed that one of the men had about two feet on us.

"Hello, hello."

At first they were all humor and flattery. How come two pretty girls were out on the town alone? Were we lost? Didn't we want to stop and make friends? Wouldn't we like to walk up to the saloon and have a round of drinks with them?

It was when we didn't answer that things turned ugly.

The taller one elbowed his friend. "The blonde's not bad," he said.

All the warmth I'd felt earlier, all the joy, was gone suddenly, and all I could think about was how to get away.

Tipping back a flask, his companion looked me up and down, then did the same with Caroline.

"The Chink will cost you less, or you'll get more for your money."

They laughed. They were staring at us openly now, and their stares were harder, hungrier. One of them, the taller one, stepped in front of us, blocking our way. Everything about him was pale: pale-blue eyes, barely visible eyebrows, white complexion, bald scalp slick and shining.

My arm was still in Caroline's, and I felt her go rigid. Something in her knew what was about to happen. Something in her readied itself. The man took another step toward us. He was so close now I could see the red cracks in his eyes, the white-blond stubble on his cheek. His jaw was working something. He spat it onto the street—a quid of tobacco mingled with saliva—and then, with a peculiar tenderness, he took Caroline's chin in his hand and lifted her face toward him.

"How much for the China girl?"

The question, I sensed, was meant for me.

Caroline went very still then, holding his eyes. A long time seemed to pass, and then there was the sound of voices, footsteps, and laughter. Two couples were making their way down the other side of the street. When the man turned his head in their direction, Caroline slipped out from his grip and clutched my arm, and then there was nothing to do but run.

Less than an hour later, we were back at Monkey Block, sitting at the table in Caroline's apartment. We'd run until our sides ached and our legs burned, until we saw the flash of a streetcar and shoved our way inside. When I stepped onto the curb, my foot seized up with pain, and I only just managed to hobble up the stairs. It was a Friday night, and Monkey Block was buzzing. Music and voices streamed from every direction, all of it now amplified by the silence in her apartment.

She moved about the kitchen breezily, her hands steady as she set the kettle on the gas ring, measured out tea leaves, and then poured the tea. She wasn't talking, though, which wasn't at all like her.

"Caroline?"

"Yes?"

"Won't you say anything?"

"You can't think that's the first time something like that's happened, Dorrie."

I shook my head. "No, but I really wish you'd say something."

"Say something," she echoed. For a moment she seemed to consider whether to answer or not, then she set down her cup and looked at me. "How about this: I was nine the first time something like that happened. At the Mission Home we learned some things much earlier than we should have. Other things we never learned at all. That first time I didn't have a name to put to it. All I felt was shame."

"I'm so sorry."

She shook her head. "Please don't, Dorrie. I've been propositioned, jeered at, told to go home. It's new to you, but it's not new to me. I've lived all my life with it. I've heard it all. But pity?" She shook her head. "Pity's just as bad as all that. Maybe worse."

The edge in her voice startled me. She'd never been angry or short with me, but now I heard what must have been there all along: the source of all that silence.

"You've got to walk with your head held up no matter what they throw at you," she was saying now, though it seemed she was talking as much to herself as to me. "You can't show them your fear. You can't show them anything. You don't answer, you pretend nothing's happening, you keep going."

She put a hand to her temple and closed her eyes for a long while. She seemed less angry than tired, and I could see the toll the night had taken on her.

"You wouldn't have noticed, Dorrie, but that's how it is. How it's always been. Just like how people see the two of us and think, *That's her servant, her 'Chinese girl.'*"

"My servant?"

"It's never occurred to you that's what people think?"

I felt a lump in my throat and looked away.

"You don't know what it's like. You can't."

What I thought, but didn't let myself say, was that on account of my leg I did know. All the times people saw my limp and edged away from me because they thought that to even breathe the same air would make them cripples, too—wasn't that the same or at least similar? But, then again, maybe it was different? I could hide my limp. Some of the time I could forget it. I could try to cure it through dancing, of all things.

I felt a hand on my shoulder.

"I'm sorry, Dorrie. It's only that I don't want to give those men a minute more of my time."

12.

I'd never gone so fast before. Actually, I'd never gone fast at all. Until Maynard took me out of the city, I'd never even driven in an automobile. That would've been enough of a jolt, riding in a car for the first time, but when I spotted him parked on the other side of Montgomery, I had to stop and compose myself for a moment before crossing the street.

He'd just gotten back from Arizona, where he'd been painting and waiting out the flu. The day he returned to San Francisco, he left a note for me at Coppa's, telling me to meet him outside Monkey Block at ten in the morning the next day. I didn't think about it long. I just showed up.

He was sitting behind the wheel of a yellow roadster, a thing of such sleek and singular beauty it made you ache to look at it.

"This is yours?" I asked when I'd climbed in.

"For the day," he said, and explained it belonged to a banker he'd known since his early days as a member of the Bohemian Club.

The sight of his tall frame folded into the car made it seem like a toy. He gripped the wheel and turned to me with his perfect blue eyes and his even more perfect smile.

"Ready to see the real California?"

I held tighter to the armrest, took a deep, steadying sort of breath, and told him I was.

He kicked the starter pedal. Once, twice, three times. Adjusted the valves and levers. Nothing.

"How long have you been driving?"

"Long enough," he said, which told me it hadn't been long at all, but on the fourth try the engine suddenly roared to life.

In those days, before there were bridges, you could take a car over the bay on a ferry. It was the strangest feeling, sitting in a car with the waves rolling under you, tipping you this way and that. I felt queasy and light-headed and was deeply grateful when it was over and he steered us back onto solid ground.

In the city, where the streets were thick with people, Maynard had driven slowly, nosing his way through the narrow lanes. On this side of the bay, where the roads were wide and empty, he soon had the car up to twenty, then thirty-five. Green hills flashed by, and west we flew, weaving through little towns until the buildings grew sparse and then seemed to disappear completely.

I watched him for the sadness I'd seen the night he'd come to the studio with Consie, but I didn't see a scrap of it. He was full of life and happy. He talked and talked. He told me about all the places he'd lived, about Fresno and his father's ranch and about Los Angeles, where he'd moved as a young man. He'd lived in New York for two years, in Greenwich Village. As he talked, the picture of his life there played liked a film in my mind. I saw him in Washington Square Park, threading through the backstreets,

ducking into the good cafés, taking in a play, stopping by a poetry reading.

It startled me to think we'd lived so close to each other. We
might have run into each other on the subway, in Central Park,
in a gallery—but no, for all that proximity, with the difference in
our ages it might as well have been the other side of the world.

Anyway, he hadn't stayed in New York very long. The apartments were small, the city a freezing hell in winter and a swel-
tering hell in summer, which said nothing of the chaos, noise,
and filth or the precious hothouse art scene or the millions of
souls ground down by the merciless, thoughtless, endless pur-
suit of money. It was all awful and he hated it and he couldn't
wait to get away.

After New York, he'd roamed all over the country. He kept
coming back to San Francisco, but again and again he traveled
east, to New Mexico, which he called the "true" West. It was
when he talked about the Southwest that everything in him became vivid and alive.

We'd been driving awhile when we plunged into a deeply
shaded grove of redwood trees. I was glad for my coat and glad
again when we hit the coast and cold blasted through the wind-
screen. I gripped the seat, basking in the view, the hood flashing
under a noonday sun. The smell of something foreign, which I
realized was eucalyptus, was heavy on the breeze, pungent and
sweet. This was open country, where snaky switchbacks led
onto the lush wilds of West Marin, where the houses fell away
and there was nothing but land and sky.

We sped along marshes tinged pink and orange and framed
by pines in the distance. Once, his eyes flicked toward me and he
called out something. I couldn't hear him over the noise. When
we reached the coast, he pulled onto a strip of turf and cut the

engine. The ocean spread out before us, close, immense, raw. An unbroken view of the Pacific Ocean was not something I knew. One glimpse of San Francisco from the train had entranced me, but now there was this. I felt my mouth open at the beauty of it.

"This is where the quake centered." He pointed off toward the towers of gnarled wood. "Hardly anything was left of the city, thousands of people died." He winced, as if ensnared in the memory of it. "It's all shiny and new now, but the land hasn't forgotten. Ten miles west that way there's a twenty-foot gash where the earth cracked in two. You can still see where it tossed redwoods in the air." He turned to me. "You know what I think about now?"

I shook my head.

"Islands." He narrowed his eyes and pointed at some spot in the distance. "That'll be an island someday."

I followed his gaze to where he was looking, but there was only land.

"If you look at a map," he explained, "the land out there seems to be tearing itself away from the continent. Every earthquake pushes it farther toward the ocean. That part of the coast over there will be an island someday. Most of the time you forget it's happening. That the earth's alive, that it does what it wants."

He was quiet for some time.

"When I first got to San Francisco, I used to come out here on the train to think and paint and eat mussels. I brought Constance once. She ate so many mussels she was sick for a week and swore she'd never set foot on a beach again." He shook his head and chuckled. "She's gone back to school. A convent boarding school in Arizona."

"You miss her."

"Very much."

"And Lillian?" I asked before I could stop myself. "Do you miss her, too?"

"That's not how it is between us. Not for me."

"How is it, then?"

"I worry about her. I've always worried about her. They said it might straighten her out, having a child." He looked out toward the ocean, eyes squinting in the sunlight. "Maybe it wrecked her. Maybe I wrecked her."

I tried to work out what he was thinking. There was a sadness to him, a sense that everything had gone wrong and he had no notion of how he could make it better. I had a hard time thinking what to say.

"I've scared you, haven't I, Dorrie?"

"You haven't."

He smiled and eased toward me. He smelled like sandalwood, tobacco, and soap. "You know," he said with such sudden sweetness, "you're really lovely."

He slung his crumpled leather knapsack up on one shoulder, and we made our way along the rocky edge of the land toward the breakwater. I had to keep my eyes down, watching for where the rocks were slippery and could send me flying. I held on to Maynard's arm as we walked, gripping hard when I slipped. From the breakwater we went carefully down to the shore, and all the way down he held my hand and let me keep the pace.

Pine trees leaned out over the water where the rocks met the beach. We sat down and he unpacked his knapsack. Cornbread, salt pork, a thick nub of chocolate, bunches of purple grapes.

He poured coffee from his flask into two small tin cups. I was hungry, which made everything taste delicious. He handed me a cup, drank his coffee in one gulp, then withdrew a stub of pencil and a notebook from his bag. We sat without speaking for a while, Maynard sketching and me watching him as the care in his face fell away and the pinched, haunted look of just minutes ago disappeared.

Watching the sky and the waves, I thought of home, of the Hudson, of the clamor by the docks and the shore. I thought of an afternoon in Cape May a long time ago, walking out to the pier with my parents, hand in hand in hand. I saw my father with his straw hat and blue necktie, how he always brightened everything. I saw the three of us walking along the shore, our feet bare, Father splashing us both, and Mama laughing, the sun so bright on her face, her hair flying free from its topknot, the feel of the tangled strands when she lifted me onto her lap and let me comb it with my fingers. This rare, happy time of my childhood strangely came back to me now.

"What do you think?" said Maynard, and held the notebook out to me.

How he could so quickly and effortlessly conjure the world with his pencils—I'd never seen anything like it, and I told him so.

Late in the afternoon, the winds came up over the ocean and riffled the water and tousled the trees. It was possible then to smell the night coming, to feel the press of the fog off the ocean. We talked and talked. We told each other about our work, what we'd done, and what we wanted to do. The drive, the easy talk, a day spent doing nothing—all of it softened me. We'd leave at the last of dusk, when the dark road was lit by spindly moonlight and the fog was fine-grained, but not yet. For a long time we sat looking out at the water, deep in conversation, and I thought I could go on talking with him until morning, but then his hands were in my hair and his mouth was on mine, and then for an exquisite while we were done talking about anything at all.

That's how it started. How it really began between us. It's hard to look back on my happiness in those days, after all that happened later, but it's rare to know such happiness. I think I knew it then, but I know it better now.

"What's going on between you two?" Caroline asked when she caught up with me a few days later.

I wavered. I was a bad liar, and besides, it wouldn't work on her. "Oh, he drove me out to this magnificent place by the water. We had a picnic and—"

"Oh, Dorrie, don't get mixed up with him. Just don't. He's a wreck. You saw it yourself." I could tell she had more to say—plenty more—but then all at once she stopped herself. "Too late for that sort of talk, isn't it?"

"Afraid so," I said, and smiled.

I thought she was going to tell me something else to discourage me. But no. Of course, I still got her message completely. It was far from a blessing. She knew him too well and for too long for that. The point was that I was too far gone but also that she was on my side, and from now on, that included Maynard.

"Promise me one thing. Don't let it stop you from doing your work, Dorrie."

I felt challenged, even a touch angry, at that. "It won't. It can't."

She nodded. "Glad to hear it. Now, tell me all about this magnificent place by the ocean."

Days would go by now without seeing Caroline. This was something she seemed to understand. Stepping back from our friendship was a kind of loyalty. She went about her life, which was plenty busy without me.

Every night after I finished with work, I'd throw on a pretty dress and head over to Maynard's studio, and from there we'd set out into the city together. Very quickly I got to know a different side of San Francisco, the swanky side. He took me to the Mark Hopkins Hotel to meet a client with a newly minted fortune he called "prime for plumbing." To a bar in the Sentinel Building, the Flatiron-style building with a copper-green dome. To the Fairmont, where the rail-thin waiter led us to the back table that always seemed to be available for him. There was the night he got us front-row tickets to see *Hedda Gabler* at the Curran. The night he introduced me to the mayor and a visiting French diplomat.

The best meal for under a dollar in the city was still a bowl of clam linguine and a cannoli at Coppa's, but now I acquired an appetite for the Salisbury steak and Oysters Rockefeller at Tadich's, the lobster at Alioto's, the chocolate soufflé for two at a six-story French restaurant called the Old Poodle Dog. Maynard was quick and irreverent, but more cultured and gentlemanly than any man I'd ever known. There always seemed to be some old friend willing to loan him a car, and so I got to see all sorts of places outside the city. We'd wake up at the crack of dawn, toss a basket and a blanket in the backseat, and set out in any direction we fancied, with no plan other than to follow whichever road pleased us. He'd sling his arm around my shoulder, I'd press in close to him, and we'd drive for a long time like that.

My shyness charmed him, but so did its defeat. The first time we went to bed together, I made him look away while I undressed, which he indulged with a nearly courtly graciousness, but once we were under the sheets, his hands were warm and lovely and everywhere. He named all the parts of me he loved, one by one: the hollow of my throat, the swell of my breasts, the soft flesh between my thighs. I didn't stand a chance against any of that. Who would want to?

Falling in love woke me up in a way that was jarring and marvelous. All my life there'd been what I wanted, which I'd rarely let myself have, and now there was Maynard. Who knew I had the power to make someone so happy? Or, just as astonishing, to be so happy myself? It was nothing I'd expected—but I had it now.

"Who's this new girl with Maynard Dixon?" I'd overhear people say. I could just imagine the rest: *She's got a limp. She takes pictures. She's half his age.* One night he and his friends smuggled me through the back door of the Bohemian Club. Women weren't allowed inside its scarlet-red rooms, but on occasion the staff could be made to look the other way. All night we drank Tom and Jerry cocktails and Maynard told long, richly detailed stories about his boyhood adventures in what he called "the country"—which I knew to be Fresno. He was making it up as he went along; he always did. Afterward he kissed me hard and said, "You passed." Turns out, the group always vetted new girlfriends. It was, he informed me, a difficult test to pass. That made me uneasy, but mostly I felt pleased because he'd been so pleased.

I think all that scrutiny and judgment and gossip would've bothered me more, but by the time we started going around together, I'd found my footing in the city. I'd built myself up. I wasn't anyone's "girl." That, I knew, was what'd drawn him to me in the first place. When he called me "clear-sighted," he said it like it was the most beautiful thing in the world. Lillian's glamour had been caught up in her chaos; I was a solid, steady sort of person. A constant person. He told me that before we met, he'd been falling, sinking, going under. Everything he tried failed. He was washed up. Finished. He couldn't paint. He couldn't draw. It was a curse, but now I'd come along and broken it with my clear-sightedness.

It was hard to pull him away from painting. I didn't even try. He was better company when he worked, and, if I was being honest with myself, without my own time to work I was restless and cranky. I spent fewer hours at the studio, but I worked with more focus than I had before.

I'd never studied anyone's life the way I studied his. I spent hours watching Maynard paint, which was an education of a kind. He could be silent for hours, peering at a painting as if mulling over some exquisitely complex puzzle. He'd spend days in his studio, so absorbed in the scars and marbles of the sky that he'd barely glance up at me. Usually when the light started to go he'd pull on a fresh shirt, steel-tipped boots, and cloak and head down to some old hideout for an inch or two or three of whiskey, but often he'd paint through the night, and there'd be times I'd find him in the morning, stubble-cheeked and bleary-eyed, still at work. That could go on for days. But there were times, too, when he'd finish a painting and he'd just know it was good. At times like that it was as if he'd discovered the secret to joy. And he had.

All through the gray winters and cold San Francisco summers, his studio stayed soaked in the orange light of the chiminea he'd brought back from the Southwest some years earlier. He surrounded himself with his paintings and the spoils of his travels, the sculptures, the Navajo blankets, the arrowheads, the textiles. His disillusionment with San Francisco was tied to his faith in the West's true potential: a world of raw possibility, free from the excesses and posturing of East Coast culture, which was itself still a prisoner to the Old World. He was out to make himself something rare and remarkable: a truly American artist.

He admired fine things, but he was the least materialistic person I'd ever met. He craved what was singular, loathed the mediocre, and shunned the middlebrow. He was friendly with a lot of very wealthy people and walked through the world like it was his, but he never forgave a person who put on airs. Nobody escaped his irreverence or his sharp tongue. I certainly didn't.

He'd tease me for working so many hours at the studio and for worrying so much about money. He said I ought to take pictures that pleased me instead of chasing clients all the time. "I'm a portrait photographer," I'd say, and he'd tell me I wasn't *only* a portrait photographer, that I had something you could study years and years for and never get. A gift. He said that all serious artists had a glorious gift that was also an obligation. He said I had it. I'd tell him I didn't have time for that kind of talk. I knew what it was to live at the edge of poverty's knife. So did he, he'd say, but he seemed untroubled by the prospect of poverty.

And there it was: the fundamental difference between us. He lived in a temple he called art; I could never live anywhere but the world.

Under all that talk about the evils of materialism, there was a steady faith that somehow he'd make good—he'd be chosen for an exhibition or secure a commission, and then the rent would be paid and everything would come out right in the end.

It was a kind of faith I'd only seen in people who'd come from money, and Maynard had plenty of that kind of faith.

You might've thought he had no cares at all, which was a big part of his charm. It didn't escape me that, in fact, he had plenty to worry about. There were the letters and cables from Lillian. She'd gone to some sort of clinic in Arizona. There was always a situation, it was always urgent, and it always involved money. Or it was something to do with Consie—a fight she'd had at her boarding school, a dress she'd pinched from a store, a string of days when she refused to eat.

It should've given me pause, his refusal to see anything but what he wanted to see, his complete, unwavering absorption in his work, but it didn't, not yet. For now it was enough to sit cross-legged on the floor of his studio in the evenings, talking and watching him paint. It was enough to see the sky emerge from under his hands. In a corner of the studio stood an iron-framed bed. In that bed, we'd make love, eat, drink, sleep, smoke, spend hours talking and listening to music. We made up a world of our own, and it was the only one I wanted. I'd study his paintings, the fierce and tender beauty of them, and I'd think, *There you are*.

13.

One night at the end of April 1919, I walked the whole way from the studio in the rain, so by the time I got to Monkey Block I was drenched and shivery. As soon as I shrugged off my coat and pulled the door to Coppa's open, I could tell that something was wrong. Every table was empty. Plates of food, glasses of wine, cups of espresso—all of it had been abandoned.

A large group had gathered by the bar, and people were talking in urgent hushed tones. I spotted Caroline and angled my way toward her. She was dressed in her raincoat and still wearing her hat and gloves.

"What's going on?" I said, and touched her shoulder.

"Haven't you heard?"

"Heard what?"

She took me by the elbow and pulled me aside. "A bomb went off at the district attorney's office today. And it wasn't the only one. Two others were sent by mail to the mayor's office in

Seattle and to the governor of Georgia. The one in Georgia blew a poor housekeeper's hands right off."

I couldn't make sense of it. I couldn't think at all. I shut my eyes against the image of a woman without hands, which did nothing to dispel it.

After an hour, a young man hurried inside, flushed and hatless, waving the late edition of the newspaper over his head.

"Another bomb went off in Washington State," he announced. "And one in New York."

He stood up on a chair and proceeded to read the story aloud to us. When he came to the end, Poppa Coppa walked to the back room without a word. It felt as if the very air in the room had changed. For a few minutes everyone was silent, and then Consuelo spoke, her words sure and hard.

"It's the anarchists. Half the places in North Beach will be shut down by tomorrow morning, you can be sure of it, and you can also be sure the police won't give up until they find someone—anyone—to pin this on."

We ended up staying at Coppa's for hours that night. It'd been like this during the war on the worst nights, when we'd wait for news and sit up late talking about it. It was past midnight when, at last, we peeled off to our own places.

The news the next day came through in fits and starts—two dead, then five, then seven. Slowly a bigger picture began to emerge. Dozens of bombs wrapped in brown-paper packages had been mailed to prominent judges, business owners, law enforcement officials, and politicians across the country. They went off at multiple locations: Seattle, New York, Boston. By the end of it there'd be thirty-six bombs. Not a single one of the bombs hit the intended target. Instead, those injured were servants or mail carriers or bystanders, who'd been struck and maimed or killed.

Retaliations were swift—and vicious. A few nights after the district attorney's office was bombed, vandals set fire to a theater on the corner of Columbus and Green. They tore down the marquee and took a torch to it, then set the whole building alight with petroleum. It was a Friday night and the theater was nearly full. People only just made it out and into the streets before the flames engulfed the building, the smoke twisting like a tornado against the dark sky. It burned with a ferocity no one expected or would ever forget. All that was left in the end was char.

Then came the news that Poppa Coppa's young cousin Dante had been beaten up and left for dead. He'd been dining at a little Italian place up the hill, and a group of men had been waiting there and followed him out. "Dirty socialist!" they called him, and then slammed him headfirst against the pavement. An acquaintance found him, quite by chance, and dragged him back to his house. He lay in a hospital now, alive but unconscious.

Suddenly all anyone could talk about was what would happen next. All Maynard could talk about was getting out of town. The night of the first bombings, he'd had too much to drink and wound up spending the night at the Bohemian Club. He only found out what happened the next day, but like everyone else, his nerves were shot.

I didn't need to ask where he wanted to go. New Mexico had been his escape for years, and he was eager to show it to me.

Trouble was, it would be difficult to get away, much as I wanted to. I had several sittings booked, and on top of that, Edythe wanted to introduce me to one of her friends, a certain Russian heiress with seven children, which would be work for days.

"Would it kill you to take some time off, Dorrie?" Maynard demanded.

I felt a pulse behind my eyes—the first sign of a headache. "Not that again."

"Sweetheart," he said, his voice softening. "I already got us two train tickets. We leave tomorrow for Santa Fe."

I blinked. "Tomorrow?"

"I thought you'd be pleased."

"I can't just abandon Caroline."

"She seems plenty capable of watching over things for a while."

"She is, but we've got so much work to do, and I'm counting on that money."

"There's work there, too. Mabel might want you to do some portraits."

"Mabel?"

"Mabel Dodge. She's invited us to stay with her in Taos and—"

"Hang on. Mabel Dodge. She's the woman who ran that salon in Greenwich Village."

"That's right."

I remembered seeing pictures of her in the paper, a woman with a turban on her head, diamonds at her throat, and poets and painters surrounding her. For years she'd been one of the most talked-about women in New York.

"She left the city?"

He shook his head and smiled. "Mabel hasn't just left. She's *exiled* herself. Hightailed it to the desert. She bought a dozen acres on the Taos pueblo and she's building a big house there. She's asked us to come see it." He laid a hand on my cheek. "I want us to be together, Dorrie. Don't you want that, too?"

"Of course I do, but—"

"So it's settled," he said, and pulled me closer.

14.

It was early in the morning when we reached the Santa Fe train depot. Maynard wanted to show me around before driving on to Taos. The town of Santa Fe, with its scent of piñon, sage, clementine, and dried leather, was wonderful, but even better was the feeling of having Maynard to myself. We wandered around and looked at everything. At a trading post I bought a wide-ribbed silver cuff bracelet, which I'd wear every day for the rest of my life. We ate far too much, and very well, and drank too many glasses of cold, tart tequila.

For the first time in months, I felt my body relax and my head clear, and as guilty as I felt about leaving Caroline, I quickly found I was happy to get away. I hadn't stopped working since I arrived in San Francisco, but it wasn't until now that I realized how drained and anxious I'd become. Maynard was right. I needed some time away.

By the time we rolled into Taos, it was past midnight and I'd slid into a state of happy exhaustion. Mabel had sent a driver. It was a long way from Santa Fe, and the road was dark and rough. When we arrived, the property was quiet and dark. We wouldn't meet Mabel and the other guests until the next morning. Until then, we'd rest.

Our cabin stood about a hundred feet from the main house. It had two rooms, each with a chiminea. That first night, we slept with the windows wide open and woke to a pair of blue quails trilling from the windowsill. When I went to the window, they fluttered away, and then I saw it: the sky Maynard had been painting over and over again. The riddle he couldn't quite solve, not without coming back here.

He came up behind me and rested his head on my shoulder. We looked out at the meadow and the mountains for a long while.

"It's too beautiful," I said.

"Nothing in this world's ever too beautiful, Dorrie. Too ugly, yes, but never too beautiful."

"Well now," said Mabel, smiling as she moved toward me and took my hands in her own.

She was a tall woman, and her hair was cut short with heavy bangs. She wasn't beautiful, not in a conventional sense, but her eyes were lovely—green, with flecks of gold—and she had a full, sensuous mouth.

She flicked her eyes up at Maynard and held them there. "I hope you're making good use of him, Dorothea."

"I'm not sure what you mean."

"Yes, what *do* you mean, Mabel?" said a woman with a strong

German accent. On her arm was a skinny, vaguely sickly-looking man. He had a long face, heavy eyebrows, and a dark beard.

Mabel looked at me. "What I mean, sweet girl, is that Maynard's a genius." She paused to adjust her shawl, a brightly colored garment I'd seen women wearing in the market in Santa Fe. "He's a complete and absolute genius, and you must always make very good use of a genius."

"And how do you make use of a genius, Mabel?"

"Come now, Frieda. Of all of us, you'd be the one to know."

"Perhaps," she said with a tilt of her head, "I'm only testing your knowledge, Mabel."

Mabel laughed, then turned to me again. "Dorothea, these are my friends David and Frieda Lawrence. I'm sure you're aware of the scandals David's writing has stirred up. I've just had a peek at his new manuscript and it's brilliant, absolutely brilliant." She cocked her head toward David. "How intimately you know the depths of a woman's soul! It's simply astonishing how authentically you reveal us to ourselves." After a pause, she directed her gaze back to me. "Dorothea, you mustn't say a word, but the Lawrences are on the run from the law just now."

"Actually," the man corrected her, "we're on a savage pilgrimage." No explanation followed. I wasn't sure I wanted one. "Are you an artist, too, Dorothea?" he asked.

"A photographer."

"Is that so?" said Frieda. She was a tall woman, taller than her husband, with fleshy arms and a round face. "Have we seen her work anywhere, Lorenzo?"

"Oh, I'm just a portrait photographer—" I started to say, but Maynard put his hand on my arm.

"Not just a portrait photographer," he told them. "Dorrie's the most sought-after portraitist in San Francisco."

There was a long pause. "How very . . . fascinating," Mabel finally said. "But, Maynard," she purred as she hooked her arm under his, "you haven't said a word about your paintings. You must tell me what you've been working on. I'm positively *aching* to know what glorious things you've been up to."

The day, said Mabel, was just right for a picnic by the river— a bright shimmering spring day, with the cicadas trilling in the sage bushes and the hawks wheeling lazily through the sky. Thick with orange wildflowers, the land seemed lit by fire.

We drove in a caravan, Mabel behind the wheel of a cream-colored convertible, Maynard chatting and laughing beside her in the passenger seat, and me wedged into the jump seat. Frieda and David—or was it Lorenzo?—took a separate car. I didn't much like Mabel, but I could see her charm and intelligence. The Lawrences I didn't like at all. What in the world was a "savage pilgrimage"? What were they actually doing here? Come to think of it, what was I doing here?

Taos was beautiful, there was no denying that. The light was dazzling. As dazzling as Maynard had promised it would be. So potent, so pure, I wanted to gather it to me. I let myself be distracted by the landscape, the rolling vistas, red mesas, sandstone, and shrubs. A chain of mountains rose up off the mesa, and the sky was streaked orange and red, and long violet shadows cut against the hills.

We crossed a hill dotted with sage, bumping along a dusty dirt road until we reached a magnificent gorge. Here Mabel pulled roughly off to the side of the road, kicking up a cloud of red dust. Maynard was still talking when we climbed from the car. He'd never needed coaxing to talk about his paintings, and he didn't need it now.

When we reached the riverbank, I saw that the servants had come ahead of us. A picnic had already been set in the shade of a tree: sandwiches on a pewter platter, a creamed confection in a glass bowl, a carafe of lemonade, and many bottles of what I knew was excellent wine. Just across the river, a young man had set up his fishing gear and was preparing his line. I watched him awhile, happy for a diversion.

Maynard started telling Mabel about plans for a major civic mural in San Francisco and how he was sure to clinch the commission. This was the first I'd heard of the project, and I was about to ask about it, but all at once came the sound of a car jolting down the rocky slope and screeching to a violent stop.

David and Frieda. David switched off the car. The engine sputtered and died, but I could see him sitting with his hands still gripping the wheel, staring ahead. Frieda had turned toward him and was waving her arms and shouting. I couldn't make out the words, but it wasn't hard to make out the sum of their exchange.

"Oh dear," said Mabel to no one in particular. "Here we go again."

"Seems they're having a bit of a row," Maynard said.

One car door slammed, then another. Frieda clambered down the rocky embankment, shoes in her hands. We watched her progress in silence. David called out to her with a kind of wounded fury. He'd nearly reached her when she pulled her dress up over her head.

She wasn't wearing a stitch of clothing underneath.

I heard Mabel laugh. Maynard coughed and looked away, but I couldn't stop staring. Not then, and not when Frieda marched into the river, where she stood waist-deep in the rushing water for a few moments with her face to the sun.

The young man had dropped his fishing line and was now watching Frieda, though he seemed to be doing so with more shock than lust. After a few moments, she crossed to the other side, took the boy's face in her hands, and kissed him deeply before throwing a look back over her shoulder. She held her husband's gaze for a long moment. Her mouth was open with delight. Then she turned and kissed the stranger again.

David climbed briskly back up to the road and toward the car. His face had gone bright red. In another minute, he started the engine and was gone.

I watched it all with a quivering sense of horror.

"Good God," said Mabel. "They can be so tiresome sometimes." She sighed and drew a Japanese-style fan from her purse. "You wouldn't know this, Dorrie, but she was married to some dumpy old professor when they met. Three children, and she just up and ran away. She's quite temperamental, you know. David's besotted with her, but between the two of us, I do sometimes wonder what he sees in her. . . ."

Mabel's voice trailed off and she began fanning herself. Frieda was now quite entwined with the young fisherman. I don't know if I looked confused or distraught, but after a few minutes Mabel reached out and patted my hand.

"Nothing to worry about, sweet girl. They'll sort it out soon enough. And now that they're gone, you can tell me about these lovely little pictures you take."

·   ·   ·

I didn't understand them. The preening, the cool detachment, the careless cruelty—it confused and irritated me.

Like Maynard, Mabel had built her own world, filling it only with things that pleased her and people who amused her. After a decade of championing modern art and running the most talked-about salon in New York City, she'd had the idea to start an artists' colony in Taos. At first people said no one, not even artists, would travel so far away from civilization, but Mabel wore them down with her charm and conviction and generosity. Then, when the war started and the Spanish flu jumped from continent to continent, then city to city, it took less and less convincing. By the time Maynard and I visited her in Taos, she was hosting a steady stream of artists and writers.

"None of this is real," I told Maynard, which was the closest I could come to expressing my uneasiness.

"Not real?" He stared at me. "Why is it any less real than the madhouse out there? Sure, Mabel's . . . Well, Mabel is Mabel, but she's devoted to this place. She's put everything she has into preserving it. She wants the world to know there are other ways of living. Saner ways of living. She wants them to see all this before it's paved and built up and destroyed. Can't you see what's at stake?"

I could, but the way he went on about it, you'd think she'd made some great contribution to humanity by transplanting her salon to the Southwest. Still, I did have to admit the place steadied Maynard. He drank less, just a glass or two of wine at dinner, and he looked healthier, his eyes brighter, the lines of his face softer. Best of all, he worked easily and well.

Each morning just before dawn, he gathered his satchel of brushes and leads and paints, a small collapsible chair with an easel attached, and we'd walk the quiet dirt road behind the house toward the mesa. He could glance at a tree and then draw it from memory, down to the patterns on the leaves and the texture of its trunk. He could capture the muscles of a horse in motion, the exact yellow of the cottonwoods, the dark folds between rocks in the far distance. I saw him now in a way I hadn't really seen him before, calm and happy. He'd learned everything he most wanted to know in the desert: how to sit still, how to wait for the light, how to look. At that hour, the mesa was perfectly quiet; there was only the call of birds, the rustling of leaves, the sound of our footsteps and our breath.

I'd been so in awe of him in the beginning, but by now that awe had softened to something else: love. I loved his humor, his spontaneity, his passion. I loved his intelligence and the tenderness that shone through all that brashness.

While he set up his easel, I'd make my way toward a stand of trees just beyond the property and watch the sun breach the horizon. Then I'd turn up the legs of my trousers and wander off in my simple white shirt, canvas slacks, boots. We'd left San Francisco in such a rush that I'd only packed my work clothes. Now I couldn't think why I'd ever bothered with anything else.

Some days, if I walked all the way out to the road, I'd see children on their way to a village school. I might continue into town to the market, where I'd watch native women weaving in their stalls, their hands flying over the looms. Then I would browse the other stalls, admiring the garlands of red peppers, the handcrafted pottery, the bright bolts of textiles. The jewelers had a courtyard of their own, and the turquoise was the purest blue. Another day I went into town to mail Caroline a letter, and outside the post office I saw a man with one of the most extraordinary faces I'd ever seen—eyes black as onyx, skin deeply bronzed and cut with a thousand lines. The next day, I went back with my camera and asked if I could photograph him. He said I could.

That was the first time I let myself take a picture without any thought of money. It was a joy and a revelation, and it wouldn't happen again for another ten years.

One afternoon near the end of our stay, Maynard and I followed a trail to the top of a hill that overlooked Taos Pueblo. He threw a blanket on the ground. His mood was good, as it was when his work was going well. We lay side by side on the blanket. Maynard watched the clouds coursing through the sky, and I watched him.

"You should see this place in the winter, Dorrie, when the pueblo's dusted in snow."

"It must be very peaceful."

"It is. It's the most peaceful, beautiful place in the world."

Suddenly he turned on his side, propped himself on one arm, and looked at me.

"We should stay here."

"What do you mean?"

"Just what I said. Stay out here. Forget San Francisco. Mabel's offered us the cottage for as long as we like."

What was he asking me? To move out here for good? My head pounded with a dull pressure. I half-longed to give him the answer he wanted, but I felt something in me tighten and then close. Part of me wanted to stay, but the other part, the part that made up the core of me, had to go back to the city, back to the studio and Caroline and to my own work. I couldn't jeopardize all that. Not now.

"But I'm so close to paying off Franklin, to owning the studio outright."

For a few minutes he said nothing, just looked up at the sky. When he started to speak again, it was to deliver one of his long speeches about life and art and the awful state of the world. How people distracted themselves with all sorts of stupidity, how they gave away their freedom for things, how in losing touch with the land, they'd lost an essential element of their humanity—he went on for a long time.

I was familiar with every complaint and argument. It wasn't that I disagreed with him—I didn't, not at all—but that I thought somehow you had to get on with things despite all that. Also, a true artist—and here I was thinking of Maynard, not myself— shouldn't cut himself off from life. Not completely, anyway.

And then he turned to the subject of commercial work. "I've spent the last two years drawing cowboys and Indians for some junk magazine or billboard or another. I'm sick of it. The materialism, the insincerity, the greed. It's killing me, Dorrie."

What I said then surprised us both.

"Why don't you quit?"

He went very still. "How do you mean?"

"Quit taking commercial jobs. Weren't you just telling Mabel about a big new commission?"

"Yes, but—"

"Listen. The studio's making plenty of money. I could lend you some to get you through the next few months. That way you can focus on this commission and your own paintings."

He was thrown, I could tell. He sat up and ran a hand through his hair. Looked out at the mesa for a long while, then turned back to me.

"You're sure about this?"

It wouldn't be easy, not if I aimed to buy back my share of the studio from Franklin anytime soon, but I thought if I took a few more private sittings each month, I could manage. If it could stem his frustration and convince him to go back to San Francisco, then it would be more than worth it.

I didn't say that, though. What I did was lean over and kiss him.

When he pulled back and looked at me, he laughed. "I love you, Dorothea Lange." He pushed away that one lock of hair that always fell into his eyes. It flopped right back down. "You're lovely and you're talented and I'm forever in your thrall."

15.

America for Americans. You heard it everywhere you went in 1919—in the newspapers, in people's conversations, in newsreels—and it was getting louder all the time. I'd been in San Francisco more than a year, and the sentiment was familiar to me, especially when it came to the Chinese, but never had it been expressed so loudly or with such vehemence.

"Ship them out or shoot them" was one politician's recommendation concerning "alien radicals."

This became a slogan for a new kind of war. We'd beaten the Germans, and now we would beat the socialists and pacifists, beat the wily Italians and the conniving Jews and long-haired radical Slavs. In California, it was said that the dark- and yellow-skinned races constituted a worse threat to the country than even the Germans or the communists; the infiltration of alien blood threatened nothing less than the end of Western civilization.

Those who'd never liked the Chinese, who believed that they

were a backward race, a menace to our public health as well as to our racial purity, were increasingly vocal. They should never have been admitted to the country, not even to work the mines or build the railways. Assimilation was an impossibility or else a horror. These arguments rang out loud and clear. "Even Mexicans, chronically indolent as they are, would be preferable for menial labor," asserted one editorial. There were others who were tired of competing with low-wage workers. They, too, began to speak out freely.

A flare of hate went up all over the state, north to south, Fort Bragg to San Diego. Twenty Chinese men were lynched on the streets of Los Angeles in one night. Farms and fields were torched all through the golden hills. It was a time when nativism wasn't just tolerated or sanctioned; it was law. It was a time when you didn't need to veil your ideas of racial superiority. You could let it loose into the bright light of day. You could arm it with bottles and sticks and pistols. You could watch it breed and spread and grow.

For me the night began with the crash and splinter of wood breaking beyond the door. A second wave of bombs had gone off in May, again the presumed handiwork of foreign-born radicals. Everyone I knew was on edge, but summer had passed and now it was fall.

The night of the raids, Maynard was dining with friends in the city. I'd gone to Caroline's. While I worked on some prints, she slipped down to Coppa's for a bite to eat. For a second I was startled, because the crash sounded so close, as if it was in the next room. I listened harder, frowning. Then I heard screams.

I sprang up and flung open the door. There were three policemen at the end of the hall and five in the stairwell. I couldn't count how many after that. All at once there was the sound of footsteps and yelling in the hallway. A woman—Lila, a painter I knew slightly—appeared at my side. She was pale and looked very grave.

"They're saying there are Bolshevists here and that they've come to make arrests."

I wasn't thinking properly, or else at that moment I would've gone down the back stairs to Coppa's to find Caroline. Instead, I followed Lila along the hall and leaned over the banister. Directly below us, two floors down, was a knot of writhing arms and shoulders. For a moment, I saw a man's face, and then it was gone, swallowed in the confusion of arms and legs.

"It's Josef Abramovic," Lila whispered.

He was a young man with a mass of dark curls, whom I remembered as having migrated from one of the Balkan states. He always dressed impeccably, in a suit, vest, and tie, but now his collar was torn and his hair disheveled. We watched as he stumbled a few feet, as if in some strange dance, then swayed and toppled to the ground. Three plainclothesmen encircled him and yanked him to his feet. One tore off his glasses, another punched him and then slammed him against the banister. It snapped. A fourth man, a uniformed police officer, appeared. He picked up a heavy wooden baluster. I shut my eyes, but I couldn't shut out the sound, over and over, of wood cracking against bone.

I was about to scream, when a hand reached around my waist and urged me forward with the butt of a rifle at my back.

Women were being herded together and led to the fourth floor, while the men were taken downstairs. I was led to the upper floors with the others—climbing the twisting staircase, around and around and up and up, and then down a long hallway to the battered old door that led to the attic.

"Inside," the officer shouted, pushing the door open with a rusty creak and shoving us in one by one.

There was darkness, the clamor of boots, the door slamming shut. Blinded for a moment, I stumbled against something cold and hard, some kind of metal table or machine. The attic was a graveyard for broken, cast-off things: three-legged tables, carpets with holes, busted chairs, old tins of paint. It was so dark I couldn't see any faces. Only the outlines of faces. I scanned every last one, searching for Caroline. There were so many women crammed into that tight, low-ceilinged place—at least fifty—but she wasn't among them. I could only hope she'd somehow found a place to hide.

For hours we waited for something else to happen, but nothing did, or nothing we could make out. In the morning the door creaked open, and just like that we were free to go.

My head was throbbing viciously. All I could think was that I had to find Caroline.

Monkey Block sat in utter dishevelment. Everywhere I looked I saw trampled canvases, overturned desks, and toppled bookshelves. People were slowly putting things back in order, righting the upended furniture, sweeping glass. I'd never heard the place so quiet. If there was one thing you could count on at Monkey Block, it was noise: heated political debates in the corridors, music streaming from the apartments, poets, playwrights, and singers rehearsing in the halls. It was as if the building had been stripped of an essential element.

The main stairwell was blocked, so I walked through the courtyard, thinking I'd go up the back stairs. That's where I found Caroline, in the empty courtyard.

"You're here," she said, and held out her hand.

In the center of the courtyard stood a massive old oak with great spreading branches. Who had thought to plant such a thing here, in the sea-sodden heart of the city? And how long had Caroline been sitting under it with her hands folded in her lap, looking up at the sky? She had no coat or shoes and there was a run in her stockings, but she was smiling. She was safe. She hadn't been hurt. It was the one thing that mattered. The only thing.

I hadn't let myself imagine the worst, and I wouldn't until much later. It was the same, I think, for Caroline. Only when we both knew the other was safe did we let ourselves feel the true force of our fear.

All night, soldiers, sailors, police, and a ragtag group of volunteers had torn through Monkey Block. They burst into apartments and dragged people into the hallways. They seized books, pictures, and papers. They opened window after window. Wastebaskets, chairs, ink bottles, paperweights, typewriters—anything and everything that came to hand was thrown out onto the street. Those who fought back or who couldn't speak English were dragged outside and thrown into police wagons, pushed up the ladders by men wielding rifles. We'd hear later that at least three people died in jail. Many were deported, never seen again.

The raid had gone on through the night and into the morning. As the night went on, it had taken on a festive quality. The men who came didn't just strip the studios and apartments of papers, typewriters, and cameras but also of jugs of wine and bottles of whiskey and vodka. Now and then they'd sit down and drink straight from champagne bottles they'd swiped from Coppa's bar, wiping their mouths on the backs of their hands, getting drunker as the hours passed. Another swig, a few laughs, and then they went back to work.

It was the time of the Palmer Raids, named after the attorney general who'd been targeted in the bombings. From November 1919 through January of 1920, thousands would be searched, harassed, and arrested; they'd be imprisoned and even shot for no reason, though reason wasn't required. Word was that the men who started appearing in North Beach—uniformed police officers, black-suited FBI agents, plainclothes detectives—were going after anarchists and communists. In San Francisco, the most frequent targets were Italians. Palmer's men came for them without announcement or warrants, opening drawers, rifling through cabinets, shining flashlights. Their methods followed a pattern, though knowing what they'd do only intensified people's fears. They came for papers, for arrests, for alibis, for bribes. On a single night in January, they'd arrest four thousand people in thirty-three different cities.

"I heard they're deporting American citizens," I overheard a woman at Coppa's say one day. "Do you think it's true?"

"No. Citizens can't be deported," her companion answered. "People are just scared. They'll believe anything they hear these days."

"But that's exactly why it can happen! Because everyone's so frightened now."

"I tell you it can't happen. This is America. They can't do things like that here."

They could and they did.

16.

BETROTHAL OF ARTISTS ANNOUNCED. MAYNARD DIXON WILL TAKE BRIDE.

—*San Francisco Chronicle*, January 22, 1920

When the terror from the raid lifted and the shock eased, it wasn't because the danger had passed but because we needed to believe it might. Soon, everyone was grabbing at anything that felt good and true. I certainly was.

We were in Maynard's studio one evening when all at once he laid down his paintbrush and spun around.

"Dorrie, I've been thinking . . ."

"About what?"

"That I'm going to ask you to marry me one day."

Now, that knocked the breath out of me.

I gazed at him. His expression was serious, but he was smiling.

"Well, what do you say? Would you say yes to me?"

"I . . . Well, yes, I would."

"In that case . . ." he said. He straightened his collar, walked toward me, and then got down on one knee.

Everybody but Caroline tried to talk me out of it.

In our crowd, the most conventional thing was not to be conventional. And what was more conventional than marriage? When a woman got married, she went home and shut the door. Once you were somebody's wife, people stopped asking about your work. They expected less, or nothing, from you afterward. Of course, we all imagined our stories would turn out differently. Very few of them did. It always came as a blow to learn that a friend had given up working altogether. It would happen to Alma Lavenson, to Margrethe Mather, even to Consuelo. Anne Brightman was as busy as ever, but, then, she'd always stood apart. She'd left her husband and was working alone up in the High Sierras. For months at a time, no one saw or heard from her, and that was a lesson, too, about what ambition cost a woman.

And then there was Imogen. She was the most brilliant woman I knew, a far more gifted photographer than I was. By the time we met, she'd been shut up in the house in Oakland with two small children for over a year. Roi's salary at Mills College couldn't have been very high, but a house that far out of the way, and with no running water or electricity, wasn't anything less than a choice—a choice he'd made to stop her going to the city and getting important. That she managed to work at all showed how much grit she had, but it'd worn her down awfully.

I'd never have said any of this to Imogen, of course. And yet it was Imogen who opposed my marriage the most. When I broke the news to her, she said nothing for a full ten minutes, and then she said, "If you do this, you can't undo it."

"I won't want to undo it. That's the whole point of getting married."

She shook her head. "You can't know what you'll want in ten years or even two, Dorrie. The only thing you can be sure of is what you already know you need—your work."

"But I'm not giving up my work! Can't you be just a little bit glad for me?"

She sighed, then smiled—but only for a moment and only slightly.

"'To hell with her and all of them'" was Maynard's response. Other people's judgments were meaningless, unless you let them mean something. I felt torn, but not for long. He was just so sure we should get married, so wholly bent on it, and with all the awful things that'd happened, the war and the Spanish flu and the raids, I was holding on hard to anything that felt like happiness.

We took our vows in my portrait studio on March 20, 1920, before a blazing fireplace, a few branches of flowering peach and hazel, and some glowing candles. Maynard wore his Stetson and carried his silver-tipped cane, and I wore my heavy silver bracelet and a long, flowy dress Caroline had sewn for me. She was the only one who hadn't tried to talk me out of getting married, yet despite all their objections, my other friends all came, Imogen and Consuelo and loads of people from Monkey Block. My mother came out from New Jersey, which meant more to me than I would've guessed, especially since I could tell there was a lot she wanted to say but she didn't allow herself to say any of it. No one stood in place of my father; nobody gave me away. If my mother had any doubt that I'd become a bohemian, it vanished now.

After a less than ceremonious ceremony, we trooped over to Coppa's for steaming-hot bowls of linguine and an enormous Italian rum cake. "This is their wedding banquet," Caroline had told Poppa Coppa, and he sent a bottle of very good, very old wine to the table. "To the talent in our midst!" Caroline sang out. "To the marriage of the Cowboy and the Lady Photographer!" someone else shouted. We drank a toast, Maynard and I kissed, and then Consuelo, on the arm of her new husband and in glowing good cheer, grabbed my camera, draped it in a black drop cloth, and nestled it in the crook of her arm. "And here's your baby!" she announced, and everyone burst out laughing. That was the happiest moment in my life, if you measured happiness in hope—cradling my camera, Maynard at my side.

I was proud of our wedding, its raucousness and its sweet simplicity. It was proof that Maynard and I would do everything on our own terms, that our marriage would be different. I'd run my studio and keep things smooth for him, all at once. BRIDE KEEPS IDENTITY was the headline that ran with our wedding announcement in the *Chronicle*. It says so much that it seemed funny to me then that this needed mentioning, and even more that I thought it would never be anything but true.

After our wedding, we moved into a house at the bottom of Broadway, a little one-room, windowless cottage with wide wooden steps and a tin roof. It was wedged between a cluster of shacks that'd gone up after the 1906 earthquake and fire. They were meant to be temporary, but people had just gone on living in them. Maynard and I couldn't afford anything bigger, but for as long as we could keep paying the thirty-dollars-a-month rent, it was ours.

I loved that little house on the hill. It was a just few blocks away from Montgomery Street and North Beach, home to the cafés and restaurants we loved, and down the street were a dance hall and a movie palace, where you could drop in and watch a film at any time of the day or night. True, a cable-car line ran right past the front door, so that at all hours there was the clang of the bells, and there were many nights when the rain pummeled the old tin roof so hard it seemed it'd pierce right through the metal, but if you walked up the hill to the corner, you came to a slight rise with a view of the bay, and if you walked in the other direction, the street went all the way to the waterfront.

We didn't have a stick of furniture when we first moved in, but with Caroline's help I found us a good cheap mattress and a lovely secondhand dining table and chairs. To ward off the city's dim gray fogs, Maynard painted the floors a deep indigo blue, and I dyed the curtains bright yellow. He cut a window on the side of the cottage so that light streamed in on sunny mornings. It was glorious. He planted poplars and bedded the soil in the backyard with flowers, and from then on, our view was of rioting glory marigolds, nasturtium, and Shasta daisies.

That house was proof of how far I'd come. When I thought of the stuffy old house where I'd grown up, or my cell-like room at the Elizabeth, I felt very grand in my new home. Not that my mother agreed. Before she left San Francisco, she dropped by to see it. I could tell by the way she looked around that she thought I hadn't made it far at all in life. But I'd made it further than she thought I would, and that, of course, meant everything.

The first days at the cottage on Broadway were our honeymoon. There were ten of them, and then Consie came to stay with us.

One day, I got back from the studio and there she was, playing jacks on the front steps. As far as I knew, she was in Arizona with her mother. Once I got over my surprise, I called out hello, which she answered with a sideways glance and a scowl.

"Lillian's been drinking again," Maynard said as soon as I walked through the front door. His voice was soft, his eyes creased with worry. "She left Consie alone in the house for three days. A neighbor found her scavenging for food in the trash."

"Is she all right now?"

He nodded. "Her aunt Mary brought her back to California two days ago. She's been staying with Mary in Sausalito, but . . ." He took a deep breath, looked at the ceiling, and then went on. "I didn't do right by her, Dorrie. I missed some important years in her life. All those times I was gone. All those terrible years with Lillian. I want to make it up to her. Can you understand that?"

I was silent, not knowing what to say.

"Would you mind if she stayed with us awhile? Just until I find a boarding school for her somewhere close by?"

"I'm . . . Well, I'm not sure I'd be good with her."

"You'll be perfect, Dorrie. I know you will. You're kind and generous and fun. It'd be a really wonderful thing for us, all of us, to be together."

"But where will she sleep?"

"I'll fix up a bed by the window. She's a tough little thing. Doesn't need much. You'll see."

I wasn't sure about any of it, which might have hurt him had I told him. But then he couldn't have ignored my doubts, which he was doing now.

We spent the afternoon in Golden Gate Park, where Consie re-fused to speak a word to me. Maynard invented games and dances on the lawn to make her laugh. His imitation of a ballet dancer was wonderful and had us both in stitches. He sketched cartoons for her, which was a kind of magic. In the evening, he made her a fort of blankets, told her stories, and sang her to sleep.

The next morning, Maynard was off early. Consie came thumping over to the little makeshift kitchen, where I was boiling water for coffee. She was wearing one of Maynard's white dress shirts, which I was fairly sure she'd taken from his closet. It was so big it billowed on her but came only to her knees, which were red and raw with cuts. She pulled a cake out of the icebox, sat at the table, and dug into it with a fork, working her way out from the middle.

"Daddy said I could eat it," she said, her face splotched with cream.

I doubted this was the case, but I said nothing.

The peculiar thing about Consie was how well she could read my moods. I'd never had any idea how to behave with children—except maybe how to coax them into a photograph. Some children, and Consie was surely one of these, could see right through you. Lay bare your insecurities. It was unnerving and even frightening, in a way. Also, there was a restlessness in her that nothing could cure. She'd stay outside for hours, but as soon as I got back from work, she'd charge through the house, making a racket. If she was drawing, there'd be ink all over the table. When she played with her dolls, they'd be scattered all over the house and in the garden. When Maynard was gone, it was much worse. Sardine cans and cracker boxes and candy wrappers strewn about the floor. Ransacked drawers and greasy fingerprints everywhere.

I tried to be patient, I really did. For one thing, I wanted to make everything easy and pleasant for Maynard. Although I wouldn't have said it was for him but for us, I suppose it was. And then there was Consie: always waiting on the front steps for him, scanning the streets for a glimpse of him, clinging to him when he finally appeared. As frustrated as I was by her sudden appearance, I wanted to make a place for her with us. I just didn't know how.

With just a few months left of the school year, Maynard said it didn't make sense to send Consie to a new boarding school until the fall. He'd find her a summer sleepaway camp, but for now he enrolled her in a public school down the street. It was a disaster—all around. One day he'd pick her up on time, and the next two days he'd forget to pick her up altogether. He'd promise to shop for food, and half the time he'd forget that, too, so when I got home from work, I'd have to put dinner together with whatever happened to be left over in the icebox. Every day, the house sank deeper into chaos, but he didn't seem to notice.

He was a marvelous father—when he wanted to be. He never felt guilty about leaving Consie; if anything, he seemed pleased that we'd taken her in. It occurred to me he'd never spent so much time with her and in such close quarters—even when he'd taken her to Montana for two months, there'd been a housekeeper to watch her all day, and he'd been free to roam and paint. He must have felt out of his depth when she came to live with us. Not as much as I did, but still.

He'd held on to his studio—I'd insisted on it—but now he was spending most of every day there. When I asked him to help out, he'd go on and on about his big commission—a mural for the city—and how much it would mean for his career when he finally got it. Didn't I love him for how hard he worked?

Didn't I know how important his painting was? Didn't I want him to succeed, not only for his sake but also for ours?

I was running 540, earning every penny that came into our lives, and now I was suddenly taking care of Consie, too. How had I let myself get into this situation, and how on earth could I get myself out of it? Mostly I tried to push my problems out of my mind. Time, it was just a matter of time. When the commission came through, everything would change. Maynard would take a break. Get Consie settled in a new boarding school. We'd be fine.

In the meantime, I didn't see the point of telling him I needed his help. We'd just get into another fight, he'd skulk out of the house, and then it'd be days before he came around again. I counted on him less and less, but I was hungry for some time to myself. One Saturday he and Consie visited Golden Gate Park, just the two of them. As soon as they left the house, I wanted to jump out of my skin for happiness. I poured myself a glass of wine and sat out in the garden. I paced around barefoot, making all sorts of plans. I had a second glass of wine and stretched out on the ground and looked at the clouds until I dozed off. When they returned just a few hours later, my smile came back easily and I could love them both so much better.

But he'd only taken her out that one time. So for me it was always the mad dash at the end of the day to get from downtown to home. Two days a week I hired a neighbor to pick Consie up and watch her for a few hours, and they'd paint together or walk down to the little park in the Marina. The other days, Consie had to walk home by herself. "She'll be fine," Maynard said, but I thought she was too young. Mostly, I'd make it back in time to pick her up from school, but there were days when I didn't, and she'd be waiting on the curb with her arms crossed and her face closed with anger.

What strikes me most about that time was how much I blamed myself for what was happening. I was boiling with resentment, half-crazy with rage, but I told myself I just had to try harder, wait a little longer, want less. You can strip the life right out of yourself like that. Women do. I did.

17.

No parties—it was one of my strictest rules for myself. True, I spent my days on Nob Hill and Pacific Heights, but I never hired myself out to take pictures at society parties. You could make loads of money that way, but I couldn't stand the idea of being the evening's entertainment.

The invitation that came that summer was written by a secretary on behalf of her employer, a man whose name she could not reveal, though he was, she noted, a man of *the utmost esteem.* Guests would be coming from as far as New York, and preparations had been under way for months. *Your presence will lend an essential element to the gathering, Miss Lange.*

I sent my regrets. The secretary's answer was to double my fee. When I refused again, she quadrupled the sum. Now, that got my attention. Every click of the shutter was a cut against the debt I owed and the chaos at home. The trip to New Mexico had cost me many hundreds of dollars in lost income. An evening's worth of portraits at this party would equal a month's commissions, which meant I'd be a month closer to buying Sidney Franklin out and owning the studio outright. Consie was in summer camp in Stern Grove, but I was still scrambling to mind her much of the time. When I owned the studio free and clear, I'd have enough money to hire someone to watch Consie full-time. I wouldn't have admitted it to anyone but Caroline, but the simple truth was that working made me happy and staying home with Consie did not.

So, money and freedom were what it came down to. The party, the portraits, and everything that happened afterward—in the end, it all came down to those two things.

"Hold this," said Caroline.

She'd picked out the drop cloth, so of course it wasn't just an ordinary piece of fabric. It was thick and silvery, and there were yards and yards of it.

I rubbed the material between my thumb and forefinger.

"Silk?" I asked.

"Of course."

"It'll give off a beautiful luster."

"Exactly. Now, help me pin it up."

She slipped out of her shoes and climbed up on a chair. She was wearing a sort of long, loose coat, with a lavender slip dress underneath that only just skimmed her knees. When she steadied herself on the chair, I handed her one end of the fabric. She pinned it up against the wall, climbed down from the chair, took a few steps back, and narrowed her eyes.

The mansion sat on ten acres in the skirts of the Santa Cruz Mountains, one of those elaborate Italianate villas that had sprung up on California's low golden hills. We'd arrived to a bustle of activity. Servants rushing from room to room, across the statue-laden grounds, past the pools and pergolas. We were assigned to stay in the carriage house at the foot of the property, which was easily ten times the size of Caroline's apartment and five times the size of my house. Our host—the esteemed gentleman whose identity still hadn't been revealed to us—was nowhere in sight.

It would be a long night. There'd be over two hundred guests, and while not all would want their photograph taken, most would. A room just off the entrance of the main house had been given over for a makeshift portrait studio. There was a long tufted couch in the center of the room and heavy drapes drawn against the light. All around the room were Greek bronzes set upon pedestals, and behind them stood rows of glass bookcases in which hundreds of leather-bound books had been encased. Caroline made a quick inventory of the gleaming spines: the speeches of Marcus Aurelius, the plays of Shakespeare, the novels of Joseph Conrad and Henry James.

When Caroline finished arranging the backdrop, we got to work moving the couch against the wall, where the light would be better. While she rigged up the additional lights we had brought, I placed my camera on its wooden tripod and gave the lens a final polish.

"Miss Lange!" a voice called out. "I'm delighted you've joined us this evening!"

I turned to find a woman approaching me. Her face had a thick coat of white powder and her hair had been cut in a very short bob, neither of which suited her. Her narrow drop-waist dress—Chanel, most likely, though Caroline could have told me in a flash—did her no favors, either, but it had the intended effect of broadcasting her wealth.

"Elizabeth Simmons," she said, and extended her hand.

"Pleased to meet you, Mrs. Simmons."

"The pleasure is mine entirely, Miss Lange! I'm a great admirer of your portraits, you know. As soon as I saw the pictures you did for the Kattens, I said to myself, if she can make a beauty of little Edythe Katten, she must be a magician."

She smiled. I didn't like that she'd taken a jab at Edythe, but I said nothing.

"Yes," she went on, "that's when I just knew I had to have you out for my brother's little fete." Her eyes slid toward Caroline. "I see you've brought your Chinese girl."

"This is Miss Lee, my assistant."

"Pleased to meet you, Mrs. Simmons," Caroline said primly.

Mrs. Simmons flashed what she must have believed was her most charming smile. "Your English is excellent," she said loudly, as if Caroline were hard of hearing. "Do keep it up."

The only question in these moments was how to maintain composure. I sent Caroline a weak smile, hoping she might meet my eyes.

She didn't. She kept her gaze on Mrs. Simmons. "I certainly will, madam," she said brightly, as if it were a marvelous plan.

Mrs. Simmons turned to me. "Where in the world did you find her, Miss Lange?"

"San Francisco."

She looked back at Caroline. "Did you, now."

There was a long beat of silence, and then a footman appeared with a tray of champagne.

"How glorious!" Mrs. Simmons sang out as the footman

bowed and presented her a glass. No offer was extended to me or Caroline.

"Does she have papers, your girl?" Mrs. Simmons asked after several sips of her drink.

I blinked. "Papers? She's American."

I glanced at Caroline, but she was fussing with the backdrop. Her back was to us, and if she'd heard anything, she gave no sign of it.

"And yet there's been such a great deal of fraud. What do they call them? Paper sons? One hears so many stories nowadays, you know."

"As I say, Miss Lee is American."

"Mmm . . . Are you quite sure about that?"

It took me a moment to realize she meant the backdrop.

"I promise you it will be very flattering."

She turned to me and her smiled snapped back on. "You're wonderfully clever, Miss Lange. *Everyone* says so. I will therefore defer to your expertise," she said, tilting her head slightly forward in a kind of mock bow. "Feel free to get yourself some food from the dining room later." Over her shoulder as she walked toward the door, she added, "You can fix a plate for your girl, too."

The first part of the night passed in a blur. Portraits of families, couples, elders, children. Eight-year-old triplets, dressed in identical white dresses and holding identical white pugs. A big-bellied gentleman in a tasseled fez and a velvet smoking jacket. The work got trickier as the night went on, what with the guests stumbling in drunk and chatting loudly and incapable of sitting still. These wouldn't be my best portraits, not by a long shot, but they didn't need to be, as Caroline reminded me several times.

We worked for five hours straight, until the stream of people stopped. I hadn't eaten since lunch, and by ten o'clock I was famished.

"Meet you back at the cottage?" said Caroline as she collected her coat.

"You don't want to get something to eat?"

She threw me a look. *Not a chance,* it said.

I wandered off in search of the dining room. Passing a long hallway, I took in the gold curtains, gold-leaf ceilings, gilded moldings, marble pillars, and bronze statues. Except for several white-frocked servants, the dining room was dim and deserted. The candles had burned down to oozing stumps and the table held the remnants of what appeared to have been a sumptuous spread. Cracked lobster shells on a glittering plate. The hollowed-out carcass of an enormous turkey lay splayed on a white marble slab. A raft of wineglasses, smeared napkins, and half-full plates—all of it had been left for the servants to clear, which they were doing now with lowered eyes and silent efficiency.

I heaped my plate with cheese and fruit and walked toward the French doors. In the center of the patio stood an enormous gilded cage filled with dozens of parakeets. I stepped outside. At first it was mild curiosity that kept me there. From where I was standing, I could see that the party had gathered at the far end of the lawn. There was a profusion of gauzy frocks and feathers among the women, immaculate white linen and carnation buttonholes among the men. Some of the people I knew by name and others by sight. The men were clumped together toward the front, while the women stood at the edges, grabbing hold of children and shushing them. In the distance was the valley, dotted with plum trees.

Then I saw a man standing on a raised dais, giving some sort of speech. I could only make out fragments of what he was saying: "true patriot," "peril," "generous support." I slipped among a clutch of women on the perimeter of the garden. There was a round of applause as a second person stepped onto the platform. He was a short, dapper man, with an impeccably trimmed beard and impeccable suit.

Senator John Pharrell.

A gentleman of utmost esteem. This was our patron. The esteemed gentleman whose name had been withheld from the invitation. I knew his name. I knew what it stood for. The knowledge spread through me like a sickness. I felt furious and light-headed and locked in place.

"In a few months," he was saying, "we'll once again have the chance to decide the course of our country's destiny. Once again, no issue weighs more heavily on my breast than the question of race and the absolute necessity of barring further immigration from undesirable lands. Throughout our nation's history, men of sturdy northern European stock have made up the lifeblood of our country, but now there come throngs of men of the lowest class from the furthest, most sordid, and most hapless corners of the earth, men possessed of neither skill nor initiative nor intelligence. As you well know, our southern cousins have long fought against the defilement of our race. Yet the threat to our nation is not theirs alone, nor is the fight. I speak, naturally, of the Yellow Peril.

"Of the myriad undesirable immigrants living among us now, none poses a threat so great as the Chinaman. Some say he comes here only to labor, to which I must ask, what of our own men, so many of them just returned from the war and so many without work? What of them?"

A buzz went through the crowd. Murmurs of recognition and angry assent.

"No matter how long he dwells here, the Chinaman is incapable of assimilating. His gaze, indeed his very soul and heart, are only ever cast backward, toward his true home. His fidelity to China is woven into his heart just as tightly as the braids are woven upon his head. Like the Negro and his cousins the Jap and the Hindu, he is an unassimilable body, a foreign substance.

"We are a good people, a decent, generous people. For generations, we have opened our arms to the world. The question we must now ask of ourselves is how long ought we keep them open? I will put it plainly: Will we cede our country to whoever comes to claim it? Will we threaten our own safety, plunder our riches, compromise our most cherished values, and destroy our civilization for the sake of these inconceivable aliens?"

His eyes swept around the crowd, as if to be certain he had every last person's attention. He did. His voice dropped a register and his face turned grave. "One final matter. I am loath, most genuinely loath, to expose the ladies here this evening to so indelicate a topic, and yet I feel it is my obligation to state that it is not only for our jobs that these strangers come. No. Gentlemen, as we are in the company of the fairer sex, I will only ask you this: Is there anything so dear to a man as the safety of his beloved wife and the virtue of his precious daughters?"

I never told Caroline about the senator's speech. Not a word. Only when he finished speaking, and people had fallen into knots of smaller groups, did I feel I could breathe again. I went around to the back of the house, along the high hedge of cypress and past the portico, where I cut across the grounds and the fountains and the pink cabbage roses. The air was thick with the scent of jasmine.

I let myself into the cottage, and there was Caroline, under the covers, breathing through parted lips, fully asleep. I undressed and slipped into the bed. The guests had cheered and clapped for several minutes after the senator ended his speech, and then the music had started up and everything became very pleasant and cheerful again. I could hear the thrum of music in the distance. I lay awake a long time, listening to Caroline breathing, smelling the perfume on her hair, and wondering how I'd tell her what I'd heard and what I'd seen. And then I decided: I wouldn't tell her anything at all. Whatever it took, I'd make sure we left early in the morning, before she could discover any of it.

How simple it seemed, how easy. How foolish I was, how blind.

18.

The day he got word he'd lost the commission, Maynard came home after midnight, rumpled and angry and drunk. The timing was awful. He wouldn't be able to pay Consie's boarding school fees in the fall; if he'd even started searching for a school, he gave it up now.

Most nights he couldn't get through without a whiskey or, more often, two. Now he started drinking during the day. Drinking made him mean, and part of me believed that he stayed away to protect me from seeing him at his worst. When he wasn't out, he'd hole up in bed with a bottle or two, drinking until he fell asleep.

He said he should've stayed in New Mexico, that he couldn't work in the city, the light here was wrong, it was too noisy, the place was bursting at the seams with hacks and dilettantes. He said his work was useless, that he was washed up, that he didn't have anything left, that he wouldn't finish another painting, that soon no one would remember his name, that you could lose the game as swiftly as you'd once won it, and he had. He was finished. Done.

I tried to hide the bottles from Consie. I tried to calm him when he went off on one of his rants. Of course, it was no use. She saw everything, heard everything. But wild as she was, that child knew how to make herself disappear. That told me none of this was new to her. As soon as she saw him coming, she'd steal away to the garden, to a spot under the house, where she'd hide for hours, talking to the flowers and trees and stones.

He didn't ask how the portrait studio was doing anymore or how my day had gone. Without my work, he wouldn't have been able to hold on to his studio or spend his days at home. Not that I could say that to him. All I'd get would be some cutting remark or, even worse, another night or two or three of him gone. Still, I didn't anticipate how much his indifference would hurt. Telling him to quit his commercial work had seemed like the most reasonable thing in the world. Now I saw the foolishness of thinking I could fix things, that all it would take was money and time and he'd be better, calmer, happier.

Where once he'd spent all his time at his studio, now he barely left the house. I'm not sure what he did when I was working at 540 during the day. When I was home, I'd watch him blunder from one end of the cottage to the other, cursing and complaining. A few times he set up his easel by the window and tried to paint. He'd pace the room, take up his paintbrush, work for a few minutes, and then toss the canvas aside. There were dozens of canvases lying around, most of which ended up in the rubbish bin.

There was no pleasing him anymore. Nothing was right. He'd snatch at anything and make an argument of it. Every word I said somehow landed wrong. So I waited. I stayed quiet.

It was all so typical, and wasn't that the one thing I thought I'd never be?

There was a glimmer of progress one morning. He'd managed to work steadily on a new painting, which lifted his spirits, but then Consie kicked a ball against the wall. It wasn't a hard kick, but it bumped his easel and almost tipped over the canvas.

He spun around. "Damn it, Consie, do you think you could go outside for ten minutes?"

Consie stood there, looking wretched.

"She can't go outside," I said.

"Why the hell not?"

"Have you looked out the window? The city's completely fogged in. It's freezing out there."

"Then maybe you could try spending some time with her. Have you considered that?"

"I have. I've offered to take her to the movies, but she won't come."

"Is that true, Consie?"

She nodded.

"And why won't you go to the movies with Dorrie?"

She looked down at her feet and then back up. "Because I hate her, Daddy," she said. "I hate her so much."

Well, that made everything so much worse. I managed to shrug off what Consie'd said—she was a child, after all—but Maynard seemed positively wrecked by it.

Seeing his friends could cheer him up. It'd worked in the past, and it could work now. I asked him to invite Ralph Stackpole and his wife, Adele, over for supper. He said it was a terrific idea. Ralph was one of the first people Maynard met when he came to San Francisco from Fresno. I liked them, Adele especially. Ralph had the name and the reputation, but Adele was a phenomenal artist and immensely kind, as well. I was always grateful when Maynard's old friends made an effort to draw me out, and Adele had done that, more than once.

I spent the morning scrubbing, dusting, and polishing. I bought everything fresh for dinner: meat from the butcher at the foot of Telegraph Hill, bread from Maynard's favorite bakery, flowers from the stand at the corner of Broadway and Polk. Consie, in a blessedly sunny mood, helped make the cottage pretty. When I finished up in the kitchen, I dusted, changed the bedsheets, put out clean towels and a fresh soap in the bathroom. I showered and washed my hair, changed into a new dress with a pretty lace collar and stockings and shoes.

At eight o'clock, when Maynard was due to arrive, I looked out the window, hoping to catch him coming up the street. Once, I thought I heard him coming up the front steps and nearly went to the door, but I stopped myself. He had a key; he'd let himself in.

When Ralph and Adele rang the bell at half past eight, he still hadn't shown up. I smiled, made an excuse for his tardiness. He'd been held up by some client, I said. They were kind. Wasn't that Maynard, always getting caught up in some conversation, as popular as he was? We agreed it was one of his charms, and we all laughed.

Somehow I made it through the meal, and I even managed, after a glass of wine, to put my mind off Maynard and ease into the conversation. He'd show up or he wouldn't. It didn't matter. He'd gotten held up somewhere, so what was the point of worrying?

It was close to ten when he finally stumbled home, reeking

of liquor, his hair falling over his eyes. After loudly greeting Ralph and Adele, he stood behind me and grabbed my shoulders. He pressed his mouth to my cheek, but missed, landing closer to my ear.

He'd been drinking. A lot.

Thankfully, Consie was asleep, tucked inside the small canvas tent Maynard had pitched for her in one corner of the room. Even if she was used to it, I always hated for her to see him in that state.

He sat, heavily, on a chair and looked at the table. The roast was still there with the fork stuck through it.

"Well, well, look at the girl from Hoboken. She's getting to be a gen-u-wine fixture of San Francisco society. Thick as thieves with Edythe Katten—did you know that, Ralph? Takes every client, chases those merchant princes up the hill, does what they want, same as any servant. And now"—here he picked up the serving fork—"she's done us the honor of cooking dinner." He turned to me. "I'd like a picture of this," he said, and gave the meat a stab. "You think if you took a picture, they'd run it in the papers, Dorrie?"

I stared down at my lap. My cheeks were burning. I couldn't speak. The pretty dress with the lace collar suddenly felt too tight at my throat. Ralph and Adele were looking away, smiling like anything, pretending they hadn't heard a word or seen a thing, but then Adele threw me a look and mouthed, *I'm so sorry.*

After Ralph and Adele left, I bashed about the kitchen doing the dishes while Maynard stumbled into bed and fell asleep immediately. Who was this man? It was a different man, an impostor, who would say what he said, but of course it wasn't. He'd proven himself capable of such cruelty. It broke my heart. That he resented my success even as he'd taken my money was already bad enough, but that he'd spoken so viciously about me to our friends—there was a real meanness to that.

He slept most of the next day and the day after that, and as usual it fell on me to take care of Consie. The rage and hurt kept building in me hour after hour until I thought I'd explode. When he finally dragged himself to the table for supper, I set a plate for him, but I didn't talk to him. Didn't even look at him. I just stared ahead and ate my food.

"I'm sorry, Dorrie. It was rotten of me. I was counting on that commission. I was sure I'd get it."

I glanced up. He looked haggard and sorry and absolutely miserable.

"I've got to get out of here," he muttered, and shook his head. "I swear this city's making me crazy."

"You'll be fine. Just let yourself rest awhile."

He didn't say anything for a long time, but then, in a tone so low and choked, he said, "What if your father lost his mind? What if you were always sure you'd lose yours? Would you tell someone like that all he needed was a bit of rest?"

I was too startled to speak. "Is this you?" I asked finally.

"I don't know." He lifted his eyes to the ceiling and kept them there. "My most vivid memory of my father is of the day he was taken away. That and his hands. His hands were my hands. *Are* my hands. I was afraid of him from the time I could walk, but, my God, I loved him." He took a long breath, then said, "He died at Agnews."

"Agnews?"

"Agnews State Hospital in Santa Clara. The 'Great Asylum

for the Insane.' There's a hell in this world, Dorrie, and that's it. It caught fire after the earthquake. A hundred and one inmates died." He buried his head in his hands. "It would've been better if the flames had taken him, but they didn't."

Until this moment, he'd told me exactly two things about his father: that he'd fought for the Confederacy and that he'd come west after the Civil War. Why was he telling me this story now? Did he mean to warn me? Explain himself? And then it was clear. He was scared. That was the only thing that needed understanding.

"I can help you," I said cautiously.

He lifted his eyes. "Yes. You can. You have."

"You can keep painting."

"Not here."

"You know I can't leave now, not with all I've got to do."

"I'll go alone, then. Mabel says she's got room for me in Taos."

"You've already talked to Mabel?"

He dropped his knife and fork onto his plate. They came down with a loud clatter and I jumped.

"I'll do what I damn please!"

"What about Consie?" I said, fighting to keep down my voice.

He didn't answer.

"You haven't thought of her at all, have you? You were just going to take off and leave her here. You didn't even think about your daughter."

There was a sound from somewhere behind me. I whipped around, and there was Consie in her nightdress and long tangled hair. Her cheeks were streaked with tears.

She went missing the next day.

I suppose Maynard felt badly that she'd overheard us. I did, too, but it didn't stop me from banging out of the cottage first thing in the morning. That things had been awful for a while was something I couldn't admit to myself, and what he'd told me about his father had me scared and confused. All I knew was that I had to get out of the house, so I grabbed my coat and left.

I walked around downtown for a long time before holing up at the studio for the rest of the day. When I returned home, it was close to six and Maynard was passed out with an empty bottle of liquor beside him in the bed. Consie wasn't in the house or in the backyard.

I closed my eyes, trying to think. She was in the habit of going out by herself. The nights I was working late there was no way to know really where she was. So I didn't worry, not at first. I went to the kitchen, warmed up a plate of leftovers, and ate while reading the paper.

A knock came at the door. I flung it open.

"Consie—" I started.

But it wasn't her. Just a salesman I managed to scare off with whatever look crossed my face when I swung the door open.

I went back to reading the newspaper. At some point, I looked up at the clock—five of seven. It was already dark out. Consie could be anywhere. Or nowhere. That thought hit me hard. I pulled on my coat and headed down the hill to the park. She wasn't there, and she wasn't in any of the other places she usually went—the five-and-dime shop down the corner or the penny arcade.

I felt my panic beginning to rise. What if I couldn't find her? What if she'd gotten lost or if some stranger had taken her home? She was ten—not so old that she couldn't be duped. My mind started reeling. Finally, I could focus on one thing: I needed Caroline. She could help me; she had to.

"Consie's missing," I told her as soon as she opened the door.

"What do you mean, 'missing'?"

"I mean she didn't come home from school today."

"Maybe Maynard took her out someplace?"

I shook my head. I couldn't bring myself to tell her why— that he was passed out drunk, dead to the world.

"Listen, Dorrie," she said, looking at me very calmly. "She's done it to get back at you. Children are very clever that way."

"I'm sure that's true, but that doesn't change the fact that she's gone and I have no idea where!"

"She's ten years old. She can't get far."

"Maybe not. But do you know how cold it is tonight? Between the fog and the wind?"

She squeezed my hand. "Let's go find her."

Caroline knew the city better than anyone. We went back to Broadway and searched the neighborhood near the house. All that time, Caroline was steady and determined, but after an hour I could see that worry started clutching at her. Every few minutes she'd offer a new suggestion of where Consie might be. "Maybe she's gone to see one of her friends," or "Maybe she's at the penny arcade," or "Maybe she's at the house?"

The last guess was right. When we returned to the cottage, there was Consie, fast asleep on the couch. "Oh, thank goodness!" said Caroline. As I stepped close to her, I saw that Consie's hair was tangled, with bits of branches and leaves, and her cheek was smudged with dirt. Maynard was snoring heavily. All that time I'd been out searching for his daughter, he hadn't even stirred.

I felt my eyes fill with hot, angry tears. I pushed them away. I pulled a blanket from the closet and tucked it over Consie. The thought that struck me in that moment—and that cut right through my anger and hurt—was how very small she was.

I turned around, and there was Caroline with an empty whiskey bottle in her hand.

"How long has this been going on, Dorrie?"

I couldn't answer—couldn't even meet her eyes. I covered my face with my hands.

She set down the bottle and walked toward me, and then she pulled my hands gently away from my face so that I had no choice but to look at her.

"He isn't well, Caroline."

She nodded slowly. "No more secrets," she said gently. "Not from me."

I took a deep breath, leaned against her shoulder, and then I just let myself cry.

He took Consie and left me his skies. When I got home the next day, the house was dark. I lit the lamp. Maynard's paintings weren't heaped up in a corner as usual but instead faced out, one next to the other, all around the room. I didn't think much of it, not at first, but then I saw that the shelf where he stored his paints and brushes was bare—that's when I knew he wasn't just out late. He was gone, and he'd taken Consie with him.

Of course, I knew where he was. I closed my eyes and I saw

him so clearly, stepping off the train in Santa Fe, blank canvases under each arm and a satchel of paints and brushes slung over his shoulder.

My gaze came to rest on the painting propped up on an easel. I stood in front of it and stared at it for a long while. It was exquisite. A desert sky flush with lavender, indigo, and eggshell blue. Beneath the sky he'd painted a wide stretch of unlit earth.

A few months ago I'd watched him lay down the first brush-stroke on this canvas. It was my favorite painting of his, but Maynard always told me he could do better, that he *would* do better for me, and he hadn't let me hang it in the house. Now he was gone and the painting, along with all the others he'd left behind, was mine.

19.

Except for one postcard he sent a week after he left San Francisco, I didn't hear from Maynard for weeks. No letters, no telegrams, no phone calls. Just that one postcard, telling me he'd sold a few paintings to his old patron, Anita Baldwin, and found a boarding school for Consie but that he still needed some time away to work. *Fine,* I thought. He'd taken up so much space, first with his ambition, then with his confusion and rage. I wouldn't have admitted it, but after the flare of hurt died down, it was a relief, in some ways, that he'd left. It made work easier, for one thing.

One morning before heading out for a private sitting I told Caroline I'd be back by three o'clock to help get the studio ready for our Thursday night gathering with our friends. But I was late. The client on Nob Hill insisted on changing outfits three times and by the time I returned to 540, it was half past four. I shrugged off my coat, hung it in the hall, and went straight to the front room. Everything looked perfect. The fire crackled gently and cast a soft glow; the brass samovar gleamed; the warm air was scented with black tea and bergamot. But no Caroline.

I wandered out to the hallway and checked for her coat. It was hanging on its peg. Where was she? Usually at this hour she'd be bustling about, putting a record on the gramophone, humming to herself, lighting candles, setting out flowers, roses in summer, camellias in winter. I ducked into the butler's pantry. Empty. Not a trace of her, no note scribbled for me on the table. She wasn't outside in the courtyard, either.

I figured she must have ducked around the corner on some last-minute errand. Any moment the door would fly open and she'd be sweeping through the rooms, asking me why I was late and telling me to change my clothes, put on a record, light the candles.

I heeled off my shoes, stretched out on the couch, and closed my eyes. I told myself I'd lie down for a few minutes, just until she got back, and I might not have gone downstairs except I heard the faintest sound, soft and strangled, coming from the darkroom.

I swung my legs off the couch and sat up. The fire snapped and crackled, but aside from this the room was silent. I slipped down the back stairs and yanked open the door, letting it slam behind me as I groped for the light.

For a moment, everything was quiet. Then I heard it again, softer than before, almost a murmur. I pulled the string, and white light flooded the room.

"Caroline?" I said, wincing at the glare. "Are you in here?"

I hovered in the doorway, taking in the darkroom. The first thing that came into my head was that we'd been robbed. My camera and tripod had been sent flying against a wall. A table lay belly-up.

My shock was so sudden, and so complete, that it took a while to notice the hunched figure toward the back of the room. It was Caroline, or some strange version of her. She was sitting on the floor, knees drawn up to her chin and her forehead dropped against her knees. The floor around her glinted with shattered glass.

"What's happened? Are you hurt?"

She didn't answer.

I sank to the floor and knelt beside her. Her usually sleek black bob was matted and in tangles. The collar of her dress was torn, leaving one shoulder bare and exposed.

"Caroline?"

When I touched her arm, she lifted her head and shoved away my hand. It was a visceral motion, a thing of muscle and blood and memory. And that's when I saw her face. Just below her left eye was a cut, and the skin underneath was stippled with blood. Worse, there was something in her eyes I'd never seen before. Fear.

"Leave me alone," she said. It wasn't her voice at all, just a brittle whisper.

Everything she couldn't say was there in that look, but only for an instant, because suddenly there was a ring, high and long, then a silence followed by two more quick rings.

It was our friends, ringing the bell, banging on the door.

She caught my wrist. "Don't go," she said. And then: "Please don't go, Dorrie."

I didn't leave her side. The ringing and knocking went on for a long time and then, finally, stopped. I draped a drop cloth over

Caroline and sat on the floor beside her. She leaned against me, her head against my shoulder. She seemed to be staring at some permanent distance, into another world or a time outside of time. I didn't understand then, but I've learned since that sometimes you need to lift right out of yourself to survive.

I didn't ask Caroline anything more about what happened. Even if I couldn't name it, I knew. I felt it in how she flinched when the bell rang, in how her teeth rattled against the glass when she raised a cup of water to her lips, in how she wouldn't let go of my hand.

I stayed calm, but the truth was I was panicked. I stayed awake by Caroline's side as the minutes passed, then hours. A few times I felt my eyes grow heavy, but I struggled upright and blinked them open. Eventually, Caroline fell asleep, slumped against my body, her hand still in mine. I stayed up and memorized that hand. The lattice of blue-green veins. The pale white of her skin.

"Wake up, Dorrie."

I woke to a nudge against my shoulder. I'd managed to stay awake almost until morning, but not quite. When I startled awake, Caroline was beside me. For a moment I didn't know where I was. Another nudge, and I remembered.

"We need to go," she said.

Her face was swollen, and there was a cut on her cheek. The bruises hadn't appeared, but they would.

"Of course. We'll go now."

She got to her feet without any trouble, but once she started to walk, she gave a soft moan. It hurt her to walk. Every step hurt. Was her leg broken? She was in pain, that's all I knew.

I put an arm around her and took her by the elbow. Her skin was cold. She sank into my side, and I held her tighter for fear she might slip. I went slowly, letting her set the pace. She stumbled along, with her body curved toward mine.

When we got to the door, I took her coat off the peg.

"Let me help you put it on," I said quietly.

"No."

"Shhh . . . You'll catch cold."

I held it up while she submitted one arm and then the other. That's when I saw that there were cuts on both her arms and also at her neck.

Outside, my eyes swept the streets. It wasn't yet six in the morning. The stores were all closed, and the streets were empty in all directions, no streetcars or carriages in sight. We shuffled down the block, past shuttered storefronts. The sun was slanting through the buildings; the air was crisp and cool. Caroline kept her head down and walked along with uneven, pained steps, clinging to my arm. I slowed my steps even more. Monkey Block was less than a mile away, but it might as well have been a hundred. My mind was skittering. We'd have to walk. No, it wouldn't come to that. It couldn't.

A cab turned from the left and made its way in our direction. I flagged it down.

We'd already settled in the back seat when the driver looked over his shoulder at us. I watched him take in Caroline's swollen face and the cut on her cheek.

His eyes went to me. "What happened to her?"

I felt a hot flush of panic. He saw that we were in trouble, or had been, and who wanted to get involved with that? He wasn't going to make us get out and walk, was he?

"She fell down the stairs."

I wasn't a liar, but the lie came easily.

He hesitated, but only for a moment. Either he believed me or he decided it didn't matter one way or another, because he gripped the wheel and pulled into the street without complaint or comment.

At Montgomery Street, a new wave of panic came over me. Very few people at Monkey Block kept anything approaching regular hours. Most everyone would be asleep at this hour, but some people worked through the night and would still be banging around at dawn. How would I explain Caroline's state if we ran into someone? It was one thing to make up a story for a stranger, but here there'd be friends, acquaintances, people who knew her well.

We'd have to take the back stairs.

How I eventually managed to get Caroline up to her apartment, I don't know, but we walked slowly up the narrow back stairs, her arm under mine. Once we were inside, I peeled her coat off her limp frame, then unlaced her boots. She sank under the sheets. There seemed to be less of her now.

I found a bottle of rubbing alcohol in a cupboard and doused a handkerchief with it. Her cheek was still bleeding.

"Hold still."

My hands were shaking. I took a deep breath and tried to still them, then pressed the cloth gently to her face. It must have stung terribly, but she didn't flinch. Didn't even stir.

When I'd finished cleaning the wound, I slipped down to Coppa's for ice. Back in the apartment, I wrapped it in a rag and touched it to her cheek to stop the swelling. I wanted to say something to comfort her, but nothing I could think of felt true, or right, and in the end all I said was her name.

Her eyes came up to meet mine.

"Promise me if you need anything, you'll ask."

She gave me a faint nod, then turned her face and looked, very carefully, at nothing.

She seemed worse than when I had first found her. Weaker. I did everything I could think to do. Covered her in blankets to warm her up. Found some cookies in a tin, set them on a plate, and took them to her with a cup of tea. She didn't touch any of it. Nothing to drink, not so much as a sip of water. No matter how many sweaters and shawls and blankets I brought her, she didn't stop shivering.

I went to the front room and sat on the couch, head in my hands. How many times had I climbed up the stairs and walked into this room? The secondhand antiques, the tables overflowing with stacks of books, the baskets of fabric and notions—all of it was as familiar as home to me—but I'd never sat here for so long without Caroline. What day was it anyway? Friday. In a few hours, the day's first clients would be arriving at the studio. I tried to think what to do. From the window came the sound of the streets, the clang of the streetcars, the high call of the gulls.

The question wasn't what had happened, it was who'd done it. I tried to think. I'd seen Caroline yesterday morning. We'd shared a cup of coffee in the studio. Had she seemed strange? Had she said anything? Men were always trying to get her attention, one way or another. Mostly she ignored them; sometimes she didn't. But she hadn't mentioned meeting anyone new, not in many weeks.

From the other room there was no sound from Caroline. I went to the door and looked in. She was still lying on her side, her legs curled up. I gently pulled the door closed to give her some privacy. I returned to the couch and collapsed. I was wrung out from lack of sleep, and my nerves were twisted and raw. Pressing the heels of my hands to my eyes, I dredged up every single thing I could remember about the last few weeks. I went through it over and over, the film unspooling frenetically in my mind, spinning backward and blurring to nothing before freezing at the moment I found her in the darkroom. Could I have stopped it? Yes, no, maybe. I went around and around. My head was throbbing, but eventually my eyes closed and I fell into a fitful sleep.

All that day I dozed, woke, dozed again. Every time I opened my eyes, the room was silent and full of shadows. I took Caroline a glass of water and some toast with marmalade. She took a sip of water but didn't touch the toast. Then, sometime late that afternoon, there was a knock at the door. I jumped. I hadn't counted on visitors, and I very nearly didn't open the door.

It was Consuelo.

I watched her take in my rumpled hair and creased dress.

"Are you ill?" she said.

I shook my head.

Her eyes swept over my shoulder to the room behind me. "Where were you two last night? I went down to Sutter twice, but no one was there."

I stepped into the hallway and pulled the door closed.

"Something's happened," I whispered.

How to start? What to say? I told her as much as I could. Or as much as I knew and could make sense of. That I'd found Caroline in the darkroom in her torn dress. That she had cuts on her cheek and her arms and her chest. That she'd been raped. That she was in shock, or something like it.

For a few moments Consuelo didn't speak, but her face had

gone tight. My own face felt very hot and I was choking back
tears.

"How is she now?"

I thought, hard, about how to answer this. "She won't say if
she's hurt."

"But you think she is?"

"Yes."

A door swung open down the hall. It was Caroline's neighbor Betty Haywood, who danced at the Hippodrome. Caroline
was mending one of Betty's costumes, and for a minute I
thought she'd come to ask after it. I didn't think I could face her,
or anyone, just then, and it was a relief when instead she waved
and then made her way down the stairs.

We waited until the footsteps receded down the stairwell.
"Tell me everything you know," Consuelo said once Betty was
out of sight.

I tried, but when I'd said what I could, the expression on her
face told me it wasn't enough to make a story. The parts didn't
fit together. It left out more than it told. But Consuelo was relentless. She'd get through one round of questions, stop for a
minute, then start in again with slightly varied questions. What
time had I'd gotten to the studio? How long had Caroline been
alone? Did she mention any names? Anything at all that might
tell us who it was? Had Caroline mentioned anyone bothering
her? Had she seemed uneasy or nervous lately? Was there anything else I saw or heard?

Somehow her questions pushed me deeper into not knowing. There was only one thing I was certain of: Caroline needed
a doctor.

"That's not possible" was Consuelo's response.

Not possible? I didn't understand. "Why on earth not?"

"It's past five. All the doctors' offices are closed."

"What about the hospital?"

"They don't admit Chinese patients, Dorrie."

"There has to be some clinic or nurse that could help her!"

"The only other place is the dispensary at the corner of Sutter and Grant."

Sutter and Grant—that was Chinatown. I glanced back toward Caroline's door. "She wouldn't want us to take her there."

"No."

"Just help her," I said. "Please."

She rummaged through her pockets and came up with a crumpled pack of cigarettes. I watched her strike a match and then light one. She drew on her cigarette—two quick, deep pulls—and then, without another word, she buttoned her coat, plunged her hands deep into her pockets, and was gone.

I never knew what Consuelo told her when she went to the Mission Home that evening, but whatever it was it had two effects on Donaldina Cameron. First, she must have immediately thrown on her cloak and flown down the hill, because she turned up at the apartment less than twenty minutes later. The second was that she never asked me a word about what had happened, not that day or any day afterward. She just greeted me with a quick nod and headed straight to Caroline's room.

When we entered, Caroline was lying on her side near the edge of the bed, facing away from us. I thought she was sleeping, but when we went around the bed, I saw she wasn't. Her eyes were open, but she wasn't looking at anything.

Donaldina took in the situation in one glance. She laid down her bag and then sat on the edge of the bed. "My darling girl," she whispered.

There was a faint flicker in Caroline's eyes then, a match flaring in the dark.

I felt my throat tighten. The only thing I could really see when I looked at her now was the bruise on her face. It had come in a pale lavender that would soon turn ink-blue, and though it wasn't bleeding anymore, there was now a raw and angry gash just underneath her left eye.

Miss Cameron laid her palm across Caroline's cheek, then pushed back a stray lock of hair. I expected her to pull away, but instead Caroline let herself be folded into an embrace.

I ducked out of the room and closed the door. I went to the window and drew the curtains closed, then opened them again. At one point I caught the sound of a chair scraping against the floor. I could hear a voice from behind the closed door—so muted I couldn't tell if it was Caroline's or Miss Cameron's—but then the voice stopped. Once I thought I heard the sound of crying, and once the sudden cry of Caroline's voice saying, "No!"

The minutes dragged miserably on until all at once the door opened and Miss Cameron stuck her head out. "Boil some water, please," she said in a low, steady voice. "And bring some towels, as many as you can find."

I darted down the hall to the small, cold kitchen. I caught a glimpse of my face in the old freckled mirror above the sink. My cheeks looked drawn and pale. I looked away quickly, filled the kettle, and lit the flame over the gas jet.

When I got back to Caroline's room, I saw that Miss Cameron had taken off her jacket, and the sleeves of her white blouse were turned up to her elbows. She'd opened the windows to the night air, and somehow she'd managed to switch out the sheets. Caroline was lying with a fresh blanket pulled up to her chin and her head resting against two pillows. Her hair was combed, though parted in a different way. Caroline, who never, in all the time I knew her, dressed in anything but one of her beautiful dresses, who took such care, who, when she saw me loping around in my overalls and a tattered shirt, told me it was bad for my spirits—and hers—was wearing a plain cotton shift. She hated that shift and only wore it to clean the apartment, but just now she seemed a world away from caring.

I watched as Miss Cameron folded the bed linens. Her efficiency was mesmerizing. "Throw these out, would you, dear?" she asked, handing me a bundle. She'd folded Caroline's clothes and tucked them into the sheets along with the towels. Carrying the bundle to the garbage chute was bad enough, but then came the mistake of looking. The towels, I now saw, had turned pink with blood.

Later, Miss Cameron and I sat over a plate of cookies and a pot of black tea. My head ached. It was nearly the middle of the night and I was exhausted, even though I'd slept through much of the day. I'd done a poor job steeping the tea—it was watery, with a scrim of loose leaves floating at the top—but she didn't seem to notice. She dropped two sugar cubes into her cup, drank it slowly, and when she finished, she set the empty cup down and looked at me.

"Dorothea," she said gently. "I'll look after her now. You can go home."

I didn't want to leave Caroline, but I knew that's what I had to do. The company of her mother was the only company she wanted—needed—now.

"Don't worry with that," she said when I rose and began clearing the table. "Go home and get some rest."

I started to protest, feeling instead just how exhausted I was.

She walked me out of the apartment and as far as the landing. The stark light of the hallway deepened the dark circles under her eyes and the creases in her face. "Dorothea," she said gently. She put a hand on my shoulder, leaned close. She smelled of vanilla and her hand was warm. "She'll come out of it. She will."

"But how can you know?"

She looked at me with extraordinary patience. There was, I understood then, no place for doubt or pessimism in her world. Those things could pull you right under, down to a place where you wouldn't be of use to anyone.

"It's my fault," I said. "What happened is my fault. If I hadn't come back to the studio so late—"

She took both my hands and squeezed them. "The only person at fault is the person who did this."

I nodded. Took a breath, then another. "What can I do to help her?"

She pressed her lips together. For a moment I saw the glitter of tears in her eyes, then she sighed and gave me a gentle smile. "Let her be awhile. The one thing she needs from us is to know she's safe now and that we'll stay with her for as long as she needs. Everything else . . . Well, everything else she has to do, she needs to do alone."

20.

Even though it was daytime, when I walked into 540 the first thing I did was light every last lamp. I hadn't been to the studio since I found Caroline in the darkroom. That was, what, three days ago? There was an edge to those first minutes in the studio, a steady thrum of anxiety. Walking inside, I tensed, waiting for what? I think I half-expected to find someone lurking there, to feel a sudden grip on my shoulder as soon as I entered, but of course no one was there. I was alone.

Everything was in the same place as when I'd last been in the studio. Flowers. Pastries. Candles. The room still held the scent of Caroline's cigarettes. I glanced at the velvet sofa and felt a wave of misery. All that time I'd been looking for her upstairs, she'd been in the darkroom, hurt and alone.

I hadn't wanted to go back, but I had no choice. There were pictures waiting to be developed. There were accounts to sort through. I spent the next hour at Caroline's desk, going through the calendar, canceling appointments for the next two weeks, trying to disentangle the snarl of our debts.

It calmed me to put things in order. When that was done, I lit the gas lamp and made my way down the hall. At the stairwell, I stopped on the landing, took a huge gulp of air, and forced myself to keep going.

The darkroom, too, was just as it had been when I'd last seen it. Upturned table. Broken glass on the floor. Graflex in the corner. I picked my way carefully across the room and lifted my camera from the floor. The lens stared back at me, a ravaged eye riddled with cracks.

I brought a dustpan and brush from the closet and began to sweep away the glass. I couldn't quite reach the corners, so I got down on the floor. I was hunched over, picking up the shards by hand, when I saw something lodged in an inch-deep groove between the wall and the last floorboard. An unusually large and utterly perfect pearl.

I carried the pearl in my fist. Carried it like a secret, or a key. I'd cleaned the darkroom floors countless times and I never had come across it before. It had to be from that night. All the way back to Monkey Block, I felt it in my hand, imagined it pulsing like a live thing.

Consuelo was sitting in the front room with several newspapers spread out before her, scribbling in a small black notebook. She must have arrived sometime that morning so that Miss Cameron could return to the Mission Home. That's how it would be from now on: the three of us working in shifts to care for Caroline.

"She sleeping?" I asked.

Consuelo nodded. "She hasn't come out of the room since morning."

I glanced at Caroline through the half-opened door. Her back was turned toward me. I took in the quiet of the room, the stillness, the curtains drawn tightly against the day.

I pulled the door to Caroline's room closed, then sat beside Consuelo on the sofa.

"I found something in the studio," I said, and took a steadying breath.

Her eyes went to my clenched fist. I unfurled my fingers. The pearl was as wide as a nickel. It was affixed to a silver fastener, which was about a finger's length.

She studied it for a moment. "A tie pin?"

I nodded. "Yes, I think so."

She took it from my palm and walked to the window, where she held it up to the light, twisted it one way, then around, narrowing her eyes and tilting her chin to study it from a different angle.

"There's no inscription," I said when she pried it open and looked between the clasps. "I've already checked."

She raised her eyes. "But you're sure it's from that night?"

I started to answer, but all at once the door flew open, and there was Caroline.

"What is it? What did you find, Dorrie?"

Seeing her there—her jutting elbows, pale skin, wild hair— was a shock, though still less surprising than the expression on her face, which was hard and fierce.

There was a moment after Consuelo handed her the tie pin when she looked as if she was about to speak, but something made her stop. Then she turned away. She went to the window and fell back into a silence thick with—with what? Fear? Rage? Sadness?

Minutes went by, and then she suddenly whipped around to look at me and then at Consuelo.

"You can't tell anyone you found this," she said, her voice measured, though firm and full of heat. Everything in her had sharpened to a point. "Do you understand, Dorrie?"

"No, I don't understand at all."

"I know you don't."

"Explain it to me, Caroline. Please. If you tell me what happened, I'm sure I can help you."

"You can't," she said firmly. She'd been holding the pearl in her fist, but now she stuffed it into the pocket of her robe. "And I don't want you going to the police, telling some story. Don't you dare."

"What if they could help? Wouldn't you want them to?"

"They wouldn't believe a word I say."

"You don't know that."

"But I *do*. No one will believe me. And even if they did, no one would do anything. Not for a 'China girl.'"

I felt my face flush. I had the sense then to say nothing. I glanced at Consuelo, but she avoided my eyes. I was sure she'd tell Caroline to reconsider, but Consuelo, ever fearless, ever decisive, said nothing.

I took a step toward Caroline, but already she'd made for her room, her thin frame twisting away, the door slamming behind her and the latch bolting shut.

Silence became the hard, burning core of our lives, radiating out in every direction, filling the air, flowing around me, swimming into my breath. It came at me in my sleep, wrenching me awake. Even as it bound me to Caroline, it lengthened the distance between us. The longer it lasted, the more it seemed it wouldn't ever end.

For days, I waited for her to leave the bedroom. She didn't, except to use the toilet. She needed to stay hidden for a while. I understood that. I learned to let her be. She'd tell me what she wanted, when she could.

More than anything, I wanted to go back in time and erase what had happened. I wanted to come to Caroline's apartment again, sit down with her and laugh until my sides hurt, or just sit quietly and talk over the next day's sittings and complain about all we had to do. Sometimes, a sort of dream would come over me, as if nothing had happened or had happened long ago or in some other place. That's how my mind tricked itself into a kind of peace. It never lasted. Inevitably, my thoughts kept looping back to that day in the darkroom. I kept thinking how it might not have happened if I hadn't come back to the studio so late.

Consuelo dropped by every day, though soundlessly and without warning. She worked long, irregular hours at the paper, so she came when she could. Sometimes I would wake to find she'd let herself in while I was asleep and left some offering on the table—a book, flowers, a cake—and set off again.

Caroline had left half a dozen sewing projects lying around the room. I folded them as carefully as I could and set them aside. To pass the time, I read whatever it was Caroline had been reading—*The Smart Set, Harper's Bazaar,* a five-hundred-page history of silk—but I couldn't concentrate for long. In the night, when I lay on Caroline's sofa and tried to sleep, I was restless. I missed Maynard. I hated him for leaving and for staying gone. He'd been away so long and I sometimes wondered if I had imagined him, too. Was he real? Was our marriage? There were times I'd wake up thinking he was there, and when I saw that he wasn't, I couldn't go back to sleep. I would lie awake, filled with both anger and worry, fearful for his well-being and unsure if he'd come back and what it would mean if he did.

Again and again, I went over the facts: Caroline did not want my help. *Don't you dare,* she'd said.

At the start of summer she'd set out pots of orchids in the front room. Sometime in the last weeks, they'd bloomed against the window, their velvety fuchsia petals pressing against the glass. I don't think Caroline noticed the blooming, nor did she seem to notice that the leaves were yellowing, that the stalks had gone dry and the flowers had started falling off. She did nothing all day but sleep, or pace her room, or stand by the window, gazing at the city. She seemed indifferent to everything. When I went out, she always looked surprised when I came back to the apartment, like she hadn't noticed I'd been staying there or why. She smoked endlessly, but she hardly ate at all. I'd bring her food from Coppa's, pasta and veal cutlets and all the foods she loved, and sweets from her favorite bakery up the street. She barely touched any of it. I brewed tea for her and sweetened it with tinned milk, just as Miss Cameron had. This she'd drink. As little as it was, it was something.

I became tired and suspicious. I avoided our friends. I took the back stairs to the third floor, and whenever I passed someone in the hall, I nodded and kept walking. Every time someone knocked on the door, I'd freeze. What would I say when someone asked what had happened to her? Why she'd disappeared? Only when I heard footsteps recede would I feel I could breathe again.

I didn't need to worry. Plenty of friends inquired after her in the days that followed, but I'd talk in a vague sort of way about a flu and no one asked much past that. Between fifty and a hundred million people in the world died from the Spanish flu between 1918 and 1920. In San Francisco there were thirty thousand cases and five thousand deaths in one year, and with so much death and sickness, it was easy to fold Caroline's absence into all that misery. By that time the flu had more or less disappeared, but people's fear of it hadn't. Our friends didn't come to visit, which was lucky in a way.

It's strange, what sometimes counts as mercy in this world. It can break your heart.

One night I woke to the sound of Caroline crying, her sobs so hard it sounded as though she was choking. I rose and went to her room. When I put a hand on her back, she didn't push me away.

We stayed together like that for a long time in the dark, and then, with her back still toward to me, she started to speak.

"I was alone, Dorrie. I was waiting for you. When the bell rang, I thought it was you, that you'd forgotten your key. Before I could say anything, he was . . . he was already inside, hat in his hand. Smiling and smiling. He said he'd come for some portraits you'd taken. I told him I had nothing to do with that end of things, that he'd have to ask you. I said you'd be back in a few hours but that I could take a look downstairs, in the cabinet where you keep your finished work."

There was a long pause, as if she was holding her breath, and then she began speaking again.

"He followed me to the darkroom. He . . . he watched me for a while. He put his hand over my mouth and pushed me against the table. I said no. I tried to get away. It made him angry. He made a fist and I fell to the floor and everything went black. When I opened my eyes, he was standing over me. He was standing over me and he kicked me. There was glass. Glass everywhere, and he . . . he was going to do what he wanted with me. I couldn't fight anymore. I couldn't breathe. I couldn't move. I think my heart stopped. But I could see him. I could see him so clearly. And all that time he didn't once look in my face, Dorrie. Like I was nothing. Like I was no one."

That, I think, would've been the end of it, except for the portrait. If it weren't for that, the whole story might have fallen away, sunk like a stone to the bottom of a distant lake. But then, not a week later, there it was. It would change everything.

I had a habit now of locking all the doors and of keeping the lights blazing whenever I was working at 540 alone—and I was always alone when I went there now. There was never a possibility that Caroline would come back, not soon, maybe not ever. The studio had been our home. It had been our life. All of that suddenly was over, as if it was only some part of a story we'd once told each other. Maybe I'd never have gone back to the studio, either, but I couldn't afford to keep it closed much longer. I'd just about drained our savings, and if we stayed out of business another few weeks, we'd lose everything.

From the moment I opened the door, I didn't let myself look back. I spent the first hour tackling the raft of mail that had accrued by the door. There was a letter from my mother. She and my brother missed me terribly. Why didn't I come home and spend some time with them, now that my work was going well? I set it aside and tore through the rest of the mail. Among the

bills, invitations, and notes of thanks there were two letters
with a South Bay address: the first was a polite request from
Mrs. Simmons. In the second envelope I found a sharply worded
demand, sent a week later, demanding I post the portraits immediately to Senator Pharrell in Saratoga.

Much as I tried, it had been impossible to put the senator out
of my mind. With elections coming up, the city was papered in
campaign posters. You saw them on church doors, in barber-
shops, at the post office. The one you saw most often showed a
man in profile with a puffed-up cravat and lavish mustache.
KEEP CALIFORNIA WHITE, it read. REELECT SENATOR JOHN
PHARRELL. The campaign's other poster showed a dark, long-
nailed, scrawny hand poised to grip a crude rendering of the
state. A man's white fist, presumably the senator's, clamped
over the dark one. This poster ordered you to STOP THE SILENT
INVASION.

I'd already shredded both letters into tiny pieces and tossed
them in the trash when I realized what it would cost me. The
thought of having put in all those hours only to come away
without getting paid made me furious. Besides, I hadn't worked
a single day since Caroline was assaulted. I needed money—we
needed money—and here I was staring at a hundred dollars
of it.

I wouldn't ignore them. Just the opposite. I'd finish the portraits today and send them off in the morning. I was determined to get through them as fast as I could. One hour passed,
two, three. Anger spurred me on. My fingers ached, my eyes
watered, my leg was twitching. I stepped away, stretched my
back, and got back to work. I worked briskly, taking much less
care with those photographs than I'd ever taken with anything.
Still, there were so many to get through that it was afternoon

when I came to the one that stilled my hands and stopped my breath.

The picture was of a man. I pulled it from the bath and pinned it up alongside the others. It was wet and out of focus. I frowned, stepped closer, and squinted. The image sharpened. I didn't see it, and then I did. Now I can see I should have made the connection at once, but it took me a few moments to understand what I was looking at. The knowledge settled on my chest, heavy as a stone. Under a handsome face with an ample mustache and easy smile and tucked through the man's topknot was an enormous pearl.

I spent the next several hours out walking in the city. I was shaken—very shaken. I'd stood for a long time gripping the picture, studying it until I felt dizzy. It couldn't be; it had to be. I didn't know what to do—or if I should do anything at all—but I knew I couldn't stay in the studio another minute.

I grabbed my hat and coat. I needed to be alone, and I needed to think. There was a little bodega near Dolores Park where I could sit with a cup of coffee in a dark back booth and think things through. Yes, that's where I'd go, but what should I do with the picture? I nearly left it in the room, but then I stuffed it into a bag I slung around my shoulders.

To my relief, the bodega was empty. I walked all the way to the back, found a table, and ordered a coffee. Now I took out the picture to study it again. Who was he? I'd assumed the man who attacked Caroline was a stranger. It had never occurred to me it was someone she knew or who knew her. How could I have missed it? Why didn't I make the connection to the party earlier?

I drained my coffee and set the cup down with a clatter.

It came to me then. Every minute that had led to that photo-graph. I played it out moment by moment. It was early in the evening. I'd only started taking photographs. The senator's speech was hours away. I'd just looked up from my camera when a tall man entered the room. He was handsome in the way that very wealthy men could be—three-piece suit, starched and pressed, hair and mustache just so. Everything about him had been perfect, including his smile.

I'd pulled the cloth over my head and watched him as he settled onto the chair. Caroline had come to stand beside me as I readied the camera. After adjusting his cravat, the man looked up and smiled. Many people don't know where to look when having their portrait taken. They need coaxing and guidance. But I could tell he was used to the camera, because when I leaned down and looked into the lens, I saw he was ready.

Because he was such an easy subject, it hadn't taken long to take his picture. Five minutes, maybe less. It was only later—after I'd pulled the cloth up over my head and straightened my back—that I realized his eyes hadn't been on the camera at all. They'd been on Caroline.

Now I brought my hands to my forehead, leaned my elbows against the table. I remembered very clearly the look and cut of his suit, the scent of his cologne, the ease of his smile, but if I'd ever known it, I'd forgotten his name.

I understood now why Caroline didn't want to make accusa-tions against her attacker. Whoever he was, he was wealthy, connected, powerful. I understood perfectly why she'd insisted on taking the pin the day I found it and showed it to Consuelo. She didn't want any of us going up against a man like him.

The pin. When had it come loose from his tie? Did it happen in a moment when Caroline had tried to save herself, or had he undone it himself and lost it later? Without that pin, there was no evidence, let alone proof. I'd tried, more than once, to find it. I searched the drawers, the cupboards, even under the carpets. Most likely Caroline had gotten rid of it days ago. But even if for some reason she'd kept it and I managed to find it, what could I do with it? I could still feel the weight of Caroline's stare when she'd snatched it and told me, "Don't you dare."

You couldn't put a man on trial with a photograph. I knew that. But what *could* you do with it?

For more than an hour, I sat at that back table in the bodega. I drank my coffee, drank two more, then headed out into the streets. I'd been walking for one, maybe two, hours by the time I got to Consuelo's rooming house, a run-down gray-shingled building up on Green Street. I'd met her here before but had only been as far as the front door. As far as I knew, she used the place only to sleep. Her husband had moved in with her, but things were going badly between them, and he'd left town.

The stairwell was narrow and shambling. I stood on the landing, peering down the shadowed hall, past the half dozen doors. Which one was Consuelo's?

A door opened, and a young man, thin and bowlegged, stepped into the hall. There was the smell of coffee and cigarette smoke from the room behind him. A flash of faces, men sitting at a table, a burst of music.

"Looking for Consuelo?" he said. When I nodded, he pointed to the end of the hall.

I wasn't sure she would be there, but when I knocked on the door, there was a scuffle of footsteps and then it cracked open, just an inch, and Consuelo peered out.

"Dorothea?"

She was dressed in a way I'd never seen her, shirtsleeves pushed up and her collar loosened. A disheveled version of her usual self. Books, papers, and newspapers were stacked all around the room, on the shelves, some like towers rising from the floor. Against one wall, a small table doubled as a desk. It held a chaos of newspapers and torn envelopes, a tray of half-finished coffee and toast. Consuelo cleared off a corner of the table and dragged up a spindly chair to the table, gesturing for me to sit. Then she sat back in her own chair. Behind her and out through the undraped windows I could see the streets of North Beach. They were hemmed in by shadows, the façade of the row houses dark and festooned with clotheslines.

"As you can guess, I don't entertain many visitors here." She smiled. "I can make you a coffee if you like."

I shook my head. "I need your help, Consuelo."

I placed the picture before her and her demeanor changed immediately.

"Dear God," she said. "Oh dear God."

"Do you know who it is?"

"That's Senator Pharrell's eldest son. John Pharrell Jr."

I felt my heart plunge. *That* senator. The one who was the main event at the party, with all his talk of the Yellow Peril and the necessity of exclusion. That horrible man. I remembered how he'd smiled and held his hands up to stem the cheers. And all those reelection posters. They'd been up for weeks. What had it felt like for Caroline to see that name and that face everywhere?

Consuelo was watching me very seriously. "When did you take this, Dorrie?"

"August twelfth."

"His fundraising party made the front page of the paper the next day, knocked down every other story, including mine." She glanced at the picture again. "He came to the studio?"

"No. We went down to the Santa Cruz Mountains—"

Her brows shot up. "To Villa Montebello?"

"Villa Montebello?"

"His estate in Saratoga. You took Caroline there?"

"It was a party. I was hired to shoot portraits. That's all I was told. If I'd known, I—"

She cut me off. "No wonder Caroline won't say anything."

There was silence for a while as we both took this in.

"You haven't shown this to her?"

"Of course not."

"Good," she said. "I don't want you to breathe a word about it to her."

"Of course, but . . ." I threw a look at the picture. "What should I do with this?"

She held it out to me. "Put it in the mail with whatever others you have. Make sure you get rid of all the plates. Do it today."

"Why?"

"No one can connect you with this, Dorrie."

"Fine, but tell me what you know about him."

She started to say something, then stopped herself. She stood and began pacing the room. She stopped a moment, then paced again. Her face had gone red. She took the portrait from me and looked at it again with great care, then handed it back.

"Please, just do what I say. Not just for your sake, but also for Caroline's."

I nodded, stuffed the picture into my bag, and rose from the chair.

21.

What was to follow I found out in bits and pieces, most of which I only put together much later. I'd assumed Consuelo's connection to Chinatown was limited to late-night rambles, an appetite for pork dumplings, and the odd favor for the head of the Occidental Mission Home for Girls. I was wrong. A decade of wandering its streets had yielded her a uniquely rich store of knowledge. She knew the neighborhood's secrets, what could be found there, where and from whom, and what purposes she could put it to. Also, she wrote everything down. Long past when she'd been made to understand no one cared about what happened in this part of the city, she kept coming back, walking for hours and making notes in a small black notebook she always carried in the inner pocket of her coat.

She had a name and she had her notebooks. That's where she started. There were a good many things Consuelo didn't know about the senator's son, which she now had a compelling reason to find out. Details. Particulars. To get them, she questioned everybody, starting with the boys who hung around the corners and moving on to street vendors and shopkeepers.

Most people didn't care to talk, but she knew who would. As for the others, her methods were more subtle; she was always watching and listening, especially when she least seemed to be. Consuelo Kanaga was not then and would never be a dispassionate observer, though you'd never have known it from the steady, quiet way she went about her work. With a story like this, she knew patience counted for everything; in your eagerness to break it, you could lose your one chance to tell it at all.

In the end, it took her eleven days to discover everything she needed to know. What days of the week John Pharrell Jr. visited Chinatown (Wednesdays and Sundays). Who accompanied him (no one). What he wore to disguise himself (a black bowler pulled low on his brow). How he traveled (by foot) and from where (Nob Hill). Which of the district's brothels he favored (Gold Mountain on Sacramento) and what time he left (between one and two A.M.).

They came from three directions, in the middle of the night. Setting out from an all-night dumpling shop at the corner of Columbus and Broadway, Consuelo walked with the long, quick, purposeful stride for which she was often mistaken as a man. Donaldina Cameron and her assistant, Tien Fuh Wu, traveled up Grant Avenue in practiced silence, their long tweed skirts swinging. Inspector Jack Manion and three members of his Chinatown Squad fanned out from Broadway. Manion and one officer were dressed in uniform, but the other two, both big men with barrel chests and thickly muscled arms, wore large, slouchy hats and loose tunics, the uniform of a criminal Tong, one of the many underground Chinatown brotherhoods.

At half past one in the morning, the group met at the corner of Sacramento Street and Brooklyn Place. It had been raining heavily that week, and the streets glistened in the feeble light. A lone pushcart clattered by somewhere in the distance. Horses neighed and whinnied in a nearby stable. Pigeons sang their warbled song.

After a brief final exchange, they split into two separate groups. The first, consisting of Inspector Manion and the two undercover officers, made their way down an alley to a building where a lantern swayed and creaked under a sign with GOLD MOUNTAIN written out in elaborate faux-Chinese letters. Manion rapped on the door. It opened a crack, revealing part of a man's face. He was plump and bespectacled. His eyes darted between Manion and the two other men.

The inspector reached into his breast pocket, producing a badge. "We've had complaints of people working here without papers." There was a flash of metal as one of the officers swung his club idly back and forth; a cluster of nails had been affixed to the head. This was meant to induce a particular fear and deaden inquiry.

It did. For a moment, the man stood as if paralyzed. If this was what they carried openly in the streets, what other torture devices did they carry beneath their tunics and in their pockets? He had the sense to step back and let the men enter.

On the first floor, a dozen men were playing fan-tan. Thick wreaths of smoke hung over their heads. Expressions of wariness and annoyance gave way to terror. A few men made for the door but were stopped with the deft swing of the club.

"Papers!" shouted Manion. "Show us your residency papers!"

While this scene played out in the parlor, Consuelo, Donaldina, Tien, and the uniformed officer went around to the back of the building, to the end of the alley, and stopped before a rickety door with a rusted hinge. Donaldina yanked it open. Here a steep, poorly lit stairwell led to the building's second story. They filed up the stairs. Thin bamboo partitions divided the rooms into small cells. "The True Gold Mountain," the employees called this floor and the next one. That the promised land of endless luck and boundless riches had been reduced to this evoked in them a bitter kind of relish.

Here, time seemed to speed up, spinning like the spokes of a wheel. A whistle sounded, followed by a chorus of shrieks and screams. Men sprang from pallets and rickety beds, pulled on their pants, and ran for the door. Women and girls rushed to hide or to cover themselves, scattering through the rooms, their voices calling to one another.

On the third floor, the visitors found a different, though familiar, world. Where the cells on the previous floor were scantly furnished, on this floor spacious suites were outfitted with flocked wallpaper, damask curtains, and carved wooden beds. It was a modest but unmistakable approximation of another San Francisco, a San Francisco of ballrooms and genteel drawing rooms and Sundays on the lawn.

This was the place.

Before the door swung wide, before the scream of a police whistle, before the sound of running and pistol shots, there was a moment of total stillness and quiet. And then Consuelo lifted her camera and a flash tore through the darkness, revealing what behind these walls was a familiar tableau. Two young girls and between them a half-dressed man.

They knocked the breath out of me, those pictures.

The girls were still dressed, or mostly dressed, but it didn't take any imagination to know what came next, or what would have come next but for the sudden intrusion. The girls' features were out of focus, expertly blurred, and yet you didn't have to work hard to make out the man's face.

The two pale white streaks to the left of the image were what I'd never forget. I picked up a second photograph, laid it down, make myself look at it again. What seemed at first like a dove in flight revealed itself on closer examination to be the ribbons of a child's pigtails.

For a very long time, all I could do was stare at those white streaks. "What will you do with them?" I said at last.

Consuelo poured herself a cup of coffee and swilled it. She held the cup in one hand and a cigarette in the other. "I'll tell you precisely what I plan to do with them, but first"—here she leveled her eyes at me—"let me tell you a story, Dorrie. That is, if you care to hear it."

I glanced up from the photographs. "I do."

"Good. Now, this story starts about seventy years ago. Let's say 1849. A fourteen-year-old Irish boy leaves the old country in steerage and lands in the Sierras. Instead of panning for gold, he opens a dry-goods store, selling basic supplies to the miners. He can't read past the third grade, but by the time he's thirty he's one of the richest men in California. His son, the first of the family born in America, is a real scholar. Well traveled, too. Spends months in Paris, Rome, and Athens. Fancies himself a patron of the arts. He's got no interest in the sordid messes of business and trade. No, his call is to politics. He runs for mayor of San Francisco, gets himself elected. As mayor he makes it his mission to beautify the city with fountains, monuments, and statues. The beautification campaign doesn't extend to certain parts of the city, which stay as squalid and segregated as ever. When the bubonic plague lands here in 1900, he quarantines Chinatown—that's thirty-five thousand people—in the name of guarding the city from 'Oriental pestilence.'

"Now. For all his gentlemanly airs, he's as shrewd as his father—maybe more. When the earthquake hits, he buys the only thing that's left in San Francisco: land. He buys it up, as much as he can, as fast as he can, and a few years later he sells it for a hundred times the price he'd purchased it for—every inch except his Chinatown holdings.

"In addition to the land, the family owns half the tenements in Chinatown. They don't put a penny into keeping them up. Let them fall to ruin. The Chinese are living like animals out there, people say. No one seems to think, *What choice have they got?* The city supervisors won't fix the sewers or pay for garbage collection. Men live twenty to a room in those ramshackle lodging houses. They sleep in shifts. And the Chinese can't buy those properties—there's already a law against that. Just to make sure they don't go anywhere else, the man proposes another law to make sure they can't live in any other part of the city. Stirs up all kinds of noise about disease and loose morals. The city's terrified. The law passes, no problem. Are you following me, Dorrie?"

I nodded, and she kept going.

"So. A few years later, he runs for federal office. Now that he's a senator of the United States, he's got to handle things a

little differently. He transfers the titles to all his Chinatown properties into a corporation, so there's no worry anyone will link his
name to any of that. Trouble is, he needs someone to go down
there to collect the rents, and for that he can't trust just anyone."

She paused to put out her cigarette and light a fresh one.

"Lucky for him, he's got a son. No, a perfect son—Stanford
graduate, summa cum laude, a real golden boy. The boy's two
generations away from a tenant farm in County Kerry, but if
you didn't know better, you'd take him for the son of an English
earl. You can bet that until his papa asked him to go down to
Chinatown, the boy hadn't set foot in that part of town—why
would he have? A young man of such manners and means?

"But here's the twist: The boy takes a liking to the place. Or
to certain corners of it." She leaned back in her chair. "Who's
the golden boy, Dorrie?"

My head was swimming. I felt sick. "John Pharrell Jr."

"Correct." She paused for a moment. "Now, would you say
this is a story I should keep to myself?"

"Of course not."

She nodded. "To answer your question of what I plan to do
with these pictures, I'm going to publish them, of course. This
is news, Dorrie. Big, big news. What's more, I got it fair and
square. Here's a senator who's built his campaign around keeping Orientals out of the country, and his son's caught in a Chinatown brothel with two girls, one of them fifteen and the other
one twelve years old? They're rotten, absolutely rotten, and
this"—here she stabbed a picture with her index finger—"is
proof. It can't be stopped from getting out and it shouldn't be.
And not just for Caroline's sake."

"But she doesn't want us to do anything, Consuelo. She
made us promise."

Consuelo shook her head. "She doesn't want us to do anything for *her*. This, Dorrie, has nothing to do with Caroline. No one will ever connect her to any of it."

"You're sure about that?"

"If there was a chance she'd be exposed, do you think I'd go public with any of this?"

"I know you wouldn't."

"Good. Not that it'll go down nicely. Not with what's at stake. There are very important implications, serious ones. Oh, it'll get very ugly, just wait."

The next morning, I slipped down to the corner to buy the paper. I hadn't slept and my head was thick with a headache. The story was on the front page of every one of the city's six broadsheets. SENATOR'S SON CAUGHT SLUMMING IN CHINA- TOWN BROTHEL, announced the *Examiner* in bold print and huge font. Consuelo had blurred the picture so that you couldn't make out the girls' faces, but John Pharrell's could be seen. It was him, clear as day, down to the curl of his lush mustache, against a background of flocked wallpaper, potted plants, and a wicker birdcage.

I paid for the paper, leaned against a wall, and read the rest right there on the street, a biting cold wind cutting through my bare legs.

Not since the Panama–Pacific Exposition and Grauman's sa- lacious, opium-infused exhibit has San Francisco glimpsed so shocking, grotesque, and revolting a spectacle.

Last night, the young Mr. John Pharrell Jr., son of Senator John Pharrell, was discovered *in flagrante delicto* in a Chinatown brothel with two females. Both females refused to give their names. One was later discovered to be twelve years old and the other fifteen.

The girls spent the night in the Occidental Mission Home for Girls. This morning the home's director, Miss Donaldina Cameron, appeared in court to secure guardianship for the youngest girl. The other girl has reportedly disappeared. Twenty-three other women were detained in the raid and await deportation.

It is a well-known fact that Senator Pharrell enjoys the president's ear on matters of immigration. For over a decade, the senator has been one of the most fervent and steadfast advocates of exclusion, and the gentleman has been a fervent proponent of the nationalist agenda for the upcoming elections.

Which leads us to ask: If the senator enjoys reelection and exclusion persists, what will it mean for his son's nighttime peccadilloes?

Consuelo said no one would ever link Caroline with the photographs or the raid on Gold Mountain. But she was wrong. There was one person who knew there was a connection, and she didn't waste any time letting me know. Caroline.

I'd been staying with her for weeks, and in all that time, she hadn't once left the apartment. Her hair, which she had always kept so trim and sleek, was long and straggly now, her lips bitten raw. She ate only what I brought her, though she didn't eat much of that. She rarely left her bed. But the morning the Pharrell story broke, I came back and found her sitting in an armchair in the front room. She was in her dressing gown, her naked feet tucked up under her, and the ashtray was overflowing. The latest edition of the paper sat, neatly folded, on the table in front of her. So far as I knew, she never left the apartment. How in the world had she gotten a copy of the paper?

"You did this," she said. "You and Consuelo."

I dropped my bag. For a moment I was too stunned to say anything. "How did you know?"

"Oh, I guessed you'd put it together. What I didn't know is what you'd do once you knew."

"Are you angry?"

She shook her head. "I'm not the least bit sorry to see it happening."

I hadn't expected this. But, then, I'd given up believing I knew what she might think or do—or feel—about anything.

"The thing is, Dorrie, it doesn't satisfy me, not the way it seems to satisfy you."

"What do you mean?"

"You're laboring under a huge misconception. Do you want me to tell you what it is?"

"What?"

"That people actually care about those girls. Oh, some people care—Lo Mo more than anyone—but for most people, it's just a story. Believe me, you'd never have heard a thing if it wasn't in someone's interest for all this to come out now."

"You mean Senator Pharrell's opponent?"

She shrugged. "Who knows? If not him, then someone else is making sure the story doesn't disappear. All I know is, there's a reason it's come out now, and it's got nothing to do with what happened to those two girls. Besides—" Here her eyes glistened and she smiled strangely. "This'll be news for a while, and then there will be other stories. There are *always* other stories. Give it a month. No one will remember any of this by then."

"But it's exposed him—both him *and* his father."

"That," she said, "doesn't matter. It doesn't matter at all."

She was both right and not right. By the next day, all the San Francisco newspapers, including the Spanish-, Italian-, and Chinese-language ones, were carrying the Pharrell story on the front page. The national press picked it up, as well. It seemed for a while that no one talked about anything else. Everyone had an opinion, and no one held back from sharing it. The drift of it was that it just went to show you, yet again, how you could never trust politicians.

But that was an old story; it would hold people's attention only so long. As the days went on, there was a hunger for more-salacious renditions of the Pharrell affair. The papers fed it. In some versions, there were up to a dozen girls in the room with the senator's son that night. In others, the brothel had been turned into an opium den. Not for the first time in the annals of San Francisco history, there wasn't any telling what was true and what wasn't. The more unbelievable something seemed, actually, the more possible it had some basis in fact. One account intimated that the Pharrells owned the brothel in which John Pharrell Jr. had been apprehended, which was less outlandish than you might have thought, given that the city's last mayor had known stakes in what had been widely dubbed "the municipal crib."

For the next weeks, not a day would pass without the story appearing in the newspapers. Both the *Chronicle* and the *Examiner* ran a series of exposés on the plight of prostitutes in Chinatown. More outrage, more editorials, more letters to the press. Among a cascade of donations, an anonymous gift in the sum of a thousand dollars was received by the Mission Home. Enterprising individuals began advertising slumming tours. For a dollar you could get an hour-long tour of *a genuine Oriental opium den;* for two dollars you could partake of the wares. One night Inspector Manion and his squad led a massive raid in Chinatown. More than one hundred women were rounded up and deported. It was one of the biggest sweeps in the city's history, and it wouldn't be the last.

Then the story took a tantalizing new turn. To the delight of the city's many papers—and readers—a Chinese housemaid came forward and claimed to have had a child by the senator's son. A scrum of reporters descended on the boardinghouse where the woman lived in a room with five other people. There was a much-reproduced photograph of the woman holding an infant on her lap. The child's hair was so blond it looked white in the picture, but then there were the eyes: black as olives, with an unmistakably Asian shape.

John Pharrell Jr. denied it up and down. He'd been set up; it was a plot by his father's political enemies; every word of it was a lie. Anyway, it wasn't a crime to visit a brothel or to father a child. He'd done nothing for which a man could be jailed or put on trial. In fact, was it not he who'd suffered a grievous wrong? Hadn't the *American Journal of Jurisprudence*, the country's most venerable legal publication, recently warned of "the great danger that men are often in from false accusations by female children and women"?

It was exhausting to follow the news. When it didn't turn your stomach, the exaggeration and misinformation drove you crazy. One day, the Chinese woman and her towheaded baby disappeared just as suddenly as they'd come on the scene. Nothing made sense. More and more, you heard that the whole story had been fabricated. Weren't reporters always making up stories? Weren't newspapers always staging pictures and doctoring images to show what they wanted to show?

But the senator had more enemies than anyone—maybe even Consuelo—realized. The scandal never fully died down. Senator Pharrell lost the reelection campaign.

That's when the enormity of what Consuelo and I had done really hit me. I was terrified there would be some connection to Caroline, that there'd be an eyewitness to what had happened, some neighbor eager to gain fame or to make some money by going to the press. I had many hard nights, lying in bed, thinking about what Consuelo and I had done, what I'd gotten us in for, trying to remember why I thought the portrait would help anything. I was sure somehow Caroline's name would come up, but it never did.

After John Pharrell Sr. lost his Senate seat, he came back to California and seemed to settle into a quiet life on his estate in the Santa Cruz Mountains. We later learned that this feigned retirement had been a ruse, that the bitterness of defeat only emboldened him. The ferocious eloquence that had made him San Francisco's mayor and then a U.S. senator was directed now to raising funds to completely end immigration from Asia. Turns out, John Pharrell could do far more to advance the cause from outside the circle of politics. As an ordinary citizen, he was unimpeded by the press and untethered from accountability. What it took was money, of which he had vast sums and could raise much more. By 1924, the National Origins Act was signed into law.

·   ·   ·

It didn't take even the month Caroline had predicted for the story to disappear.

One night, a jazz-crazy sixteen-year-old San Francisco girl put a pistol to her sleeping mother's head and pulled the trigger. With the woman's instant and gruesome death, the Pharrell scandal slid right off the page and into memory, and then right out of memory.

John Pharrell Jr. disappeared. For a while there were rumors he'd gone to Europe, or to the Far East, but then he turned up in Los Angeles. No longer a front-page fixture, he popped up regularly in the tabloids and society pages. There he was, at the Beverly Hills Speedway in a white linen suit. There he was, laughing with a dark-haired starlet at the grand opening of the Cocoanut Grove at the Ambassador Hotel. And there he was, at a fundraiser for his father's longtime business-associate-turned-political-ally.

A decade later, he'd be living somewhere down in Orange County. He'd be married to a different actress, a willowy blonde famous for her turquoise eyes and charming lisp. He'd make his own Hollywood debut, acting in the role of a millionaire's son. Everybody would say he was marvelous—a real natural. It was one of those California stories, outrageous and true. But all that was many years later. Within a year, the senator's son was back in San Francisco, and Caroline was gone.

22.

By the end of November, Caroline seemed, if not quite herself, then at least oriented in that direction. She still didn't want much company, and she avoided places where she'd run into people she knew. That mostly meant Coppa's but also our old North Beach haunts. There were times, long stretches of them, when she pulled away from everything. She was quiet, and some mornings she'd wake up with purplish rings under her eyes from lack of sleep, but slowly she seemed to be coming back to herself, waking up early each day, bathing, making up her face, dressing nicely again.

One day she went down to the corner to a salon and had her hair cut. A few days after that I let myself into her apartment and was greeted by the whir and clatter of her Singer. For the longest time, I'd seen only her huddled shape in a dark room, and here, suddenly, was a sight that just about made my heart burst with joy: Caroline behind her sewing machine, a length of tulle spread before her, her fingers working the fabric with deft grace.

And then one evening in the middle of the week, I came back from the studio and found her waiting for me on the sofa with her hat on her head and her purse in her lap.

"I'd like to go out, Dorrie." I watched her tighten her grip on her purse handle. "Will you come with me?"

"Out? Where?"

"Somewhere by the water. How about the wharf?"

It was past five. I was exhausted. I didn't at all feel like going out, but this was the first time in months she'd asked me to go anywhere. If she wanted to go out, we'd go.

Autumn in San Francisco was warm and sunny. No fog, no wind. Mostly the days were pleasant, but we'd had a stretch of particularly warm days, and you could walk by the salt-fresh, sun-baked shore without clenching at the cold. Caroline stopped at one of the little open-fronted cafés by the wharf, where a man stood cooking seafood in a steaming cauldron, and she ate a cone of fresh shrimp as we walked out on the pier. We started talking again then. Not about what had happened but about other things. It was a relief just to hear her voice after such a long period of silence. She was naming the world again: the sweet, briny taste of the shrimp, the gulls wheeling overhead, the thin silvery swath of fog on the horizon. She was letting herself be part of life again.

What happened wasn't over, and it never would be. It had rooted deeply within her; it was growing and entwining itself with who she was and who she'd become, but for the moment it seemed to have lessened its grip. Or so it seemed, until she told me she was going away.

We were sitting on a bench, side by side, looking out at the water, when she said she'd decided to leave San Francisco.

"But where will you go?"

"Somewhere. I don't know yet."

"You'll come back, though?"

She shook her head. Looked out toward the water. Said nothing.

A ferry lumbered up to the dock, unsettling the gulls and shorebirds, disgorging plumes of black smoke, and churning up the dark-green water. Passengers bumped along the ramp and onto the pier, then disappeared slowly into the streets. The waterfront settled back into silence.

"All your friends are here. Consuelo, me, everyone . . . And Miss Cameron. Won't she be upset if you leave?"

"I need you to promise you won't say anything to them. Not yet."

"But—"

She put a hand on my shoulder so that I had no choice but to look at her. "Dorrie, I need your word on this."

"But the whole awful story. It's dying down."

She shook her head. "Not for me. It can't. It won't."

For a long time neither of us said anything. Then she tilted her head and squinted her eyes. "Do you want to come with me, Dorrie?"

I had no idea where she wanted to go, but my first instinct was to say yes. Maynard was gone, so why not? But then it hit me: I couldn't give up my studio.

"Caroline—" I started.

"Never mind, it was a silly idea. Of course you have to stay here. You're a brilliant photographer. Everyone knows it now. You've built a business and a life. And then there's Maynard."

"Maynard," I said, and let out a long breath. "I don't know if he's coming back."

"Do you want him to?"

"I don't know. Isn't that ridiculous? That I could be unsure about a thing like that?"

"With how he's acted, it's no wonder you're confused." She reached out and grabbed my hand. "But if one thing's clear, it's that *you* belong here."

"So do you! You belong here as much as anyone."

"I don't," she said. "I never have."

I thought we had time. The way she talked about leaving, it seemed days, even weeks, away. But when I went down to Coppa's for coffee the next morning and the waiter placed an envelope on the table, my heart leapt up.

I need a change, please understand.

I sprang from my chair, not bothering to finish her note or even pay for my coffee, taking the stairs two at a time until I reached her apartment. My hands were shaking as I worked the key into the lock and pushed open the door.

Her apartment was pristine. No books scattered about, no toiletries on the table, not a thing out of place. That's when it hit me: She was gone. She'd tidied up and she'd left behind everything but her clothes and her sewing machine. The mirrored dresser, the folding screen, the lamps, her books, the sateen quilt on her bed. The sight of her dressing gown—the one garment she hadn't taken with her—hanging from her bedroom door broke my heart.

For a long time, I walked slowly from the front room to her bedroom and back again, touching everything, as if in a trance. I wondered where Caroline was and if she'd ever come back. And how long had she been planning this?

I went to the window, pressed my forehead to the glass. Outside, the city moved on, resplendent and oblivious. I turned away, walked out of the apartment, down the back stairs, and out of the building. I walked up Columbus, toward the piers, and stopped at a bench. I didn't feel well. I got up again and turned back, and then I don't know where I went. Eventually I found myself climbing up Telegraph Hill. I didn't stop, not until I'd reached the top, where I wandered among the eucalyptus trees and wept.

There were days—many of them—that I thought there'd be a knock on the door and I'd open it to find Caroline. Even if I couldn't see her or speak to her, I saw her everywhere. I could feel her whenever I went down to Coppa's or into the studio or a hundred other places in the city, Caroline and the sweet shimmer that seemed to follow her everywhere. Her laughter echoed through my head like a bell.

When I asked around, neither Donaldina Cameron nor Consuelo had any idea where Caroline might have gone. And yet neither was surprised by her departure. I was the last one to see her, it seemed.

For a while I pitched between despair and denial. Imogen was stuck in Oakland, and things were going badly between Consuelo and her husband. I rarely saw either of them anymore. I worked all the time. I didn't sleep. I wrecked my health. I was thin as a rail. A cold I ignored for too long suddenly worsened. Then I started having trouble walking. Going up and down the stairs became a challenge, and one day when I was out in the city, my knee buckled under me.

I was taken to the hospital, where the doctors told me my

polio had come back. It could happen sometimes, and it had happened to me. If I didn't rest, I might not be able to walk again.

One day I woke up and there was Maynard, sitting at the foot of my hospital bed with his hat in his hands.

"What are you doing here?"

"Imogen told me you were here. That you were sick. I had to come, Dorrie."

I shook my head. "You left."

"Yes." A long moment passed in silence. He looked down at his hat, squeezed the brim. Folded it, unfolded it, refolded it. "It was a hard time—for Consie. For all of us."

"Are you . . . Are you all right?"

"Do you mean have I cracked up?" He flashed a smile, though there was a trace of pain in it. His skin was sunburned, which sharpened the blue of his eyes. He pulled his chair closer and placed his hand on my cheek. "You were right. I needed some rest, but once I got it, what I needed was you."

And there it was: all that gorgeous, infuriating charm. I sighed and looked away. After a while I asked, "How's Consie?"

"Better. I found her a new school. So far she's only tried to run away twice."

He smiled, and I found myself smiling, too.

"Come on, then, Dorrie," he said with such tenderness it was impossible not to soften toward him, at least a little. "I'm back. I love you and this is where I want to be."

There was a string of days when I barely talked to him. He seemed to understand, but he kept coming back anyway. Each day he brought me a gift, placed it on my lap, and waited for my reaction. A bouquet, a pretty shawl, the new book of poems by

Edna St. Vincent Millay. Peace offerings. He took my clothes to be washed and brought them back in tidy bundles. He'd ask me to name something I loved, and then he'd draw it for me, beautifully.

For as long as I'd known him, he'd always been leaving, or thinking of leaving, but here he was, day after day, present and devoted in a way I'd given up thinking he could ever be. The worst things he'd done I'd never forget, but this—the way he stayed when I was sick, the way he loved me, really—in the end, that defined him in my eyes. Each day, I let myself love him a little more.

It was Maynard who helped me clear out Caroline's apartment when I left the hospital. For a long time, I just sat on the edge of her bed and cried. That's when, for the first time, I told him everything that had happened with Caroline. He listened quietly. He was steady and so kind.

There was so much to go through in the apartment—cabinets, books, photographs. We had to give away most of Caroline's possessions, but the things that reminded me of her the most—her green velvet sofa, her beautiful silk screen—Maynard hauled to his studio and kept there for me. I found a scrapbook she'd made with all the newspaper stories and notices about the studio. I sank onto the sofa, in the same spot I always had, Caroline's place empty beside me. I handled everything delicately, as if it were already a relic of a lost time. There was one with a picture of us together, and that's the one I took and kept.

I didn't work well or very much, but Maynard encouraged me to keep at it, no matter how hard it felt. "You can't lose everything you've built, Dorrie," he said. It was something Caroline would have said, and he said it many times. I lost a month grieving Caroline's disappearance, but eventually I got on with things, the way I'd always had to and I'd always done. Sometimes I'd walk up to her old apartment. I'd stop and gaze at the door, let myself feel the pain of never being able to go back, and I'd think how it takes one kind of bravery to leave a place, and another kind to stay.

23.

Strange how long you can stand a thing, only to reach a point where you know it has to end. I'd done good work, work I was proud of, work that showed me who I was and what I could do. For years I told myself I wasn't an artist, and I never called myself one, but as time went on I started longing, against reason, for something else. For something out there—out in the world. I wanted to see other faces. I wanted to take different pictures. I wanted a different kind of life.

In the end, I gave up portrait work for one reason: The world changed and I chose to change with it. One day I looked out the window and onto the alley. It was the spring of 1932. The Depression was beginning to cut very deep, but it hadn't happened overnight. How did Ernest Hemingway describe going bankrupt—"gradually and then suddenly"? The Depression was like that. It started out slow and quiet, and then one day there was nothing but chaos and need. All around the country, people were without work. Everyone was shocked and in a panic. No one knew what was ahead. San Francisco was a different place—serious and brooding and bleak in a way it hadn't been since the war, and maybe not even then. The drifting homeless were everywhere—hollow-eyed, disheveled, hungry, and afraid. Across the bay in Oakland, where huge encampments had sprung up along the waterfront and railroad tracks, hundreds of people were living in sections of old pipe that'd never been laid because funding had dried up.

I was making solar proofs of some portraits one morning, when I glanced up from my work, looked out the window, and spotted a young man standing on the sidewalk. It was a particularly sunny day and I could see him clearly. He was shirtless and bareheaded. He walked up to the corner and stood there a little while. Behind him was the waterfront; the wholesale district to his left; the financial district ahead; and the Hall of Justice and the flophouses of the old Barbary Coast to the right. He didn't seem to know where he was or maybe even who he was.

The distance between what I was working on and the image of that young man was more than I could reconcile. I'd never gone into the streets with the aim of taking a picture, but on an impulse, I slung my camera around my neck and walked outside with it. I didn't wear my fedora; I went out just as I was. I took nothing else with me. No bag, no money. And that was how I began.

That year I saw the face of want. I saw that it was a merciless and ugly face. Day after day I'd head to the Mission District, where the city was billeting the homeless. I'd pick my way through crowds of bedraggled souls, zigzag my way past teeming garbage barrels and heaped-up trash and makeshift tents. There were whole families sleeping on the sidewalks. Men in once-fine suits selling apples on street corners. Women walking in ripped stockings and no shoes. Small children roaming the city, begging for food.

I had to show the truth of it somehow. I had to make myself useful. Somehow, I had to get people to see.

Each time I went out, I had no idea what was going to happen. Taking pictures on the street was different from working in the studio. But I knew to trust my eye.

One day, when I was walking down Third Street, I happened on a breadline. I edged past dozens of men, men who coughed and scratched, men who smelled of need and misery, men slumping against walls and sitting on sidewalks as if they'd been shipwrecked there. I couldn't hide what I was doing; my Graflex was too big and it always took a few minutes to set up a shot. Nobody paid me any mind. I wandered around for a few minutes and then my eyes seized on a particular figure in the breadline. A man in a ragged coat and hat. He was alone, facing away from the large group of men. His stubbled cheeks were hollow and his hands folded before him as if in prayer. Something in me wanted him to look up, but he didn't. Or maybe he did see me, but he was long past caring who looked at him and why.

I'd never forget the bend of his shoulders or the angle of his head, but it was his hands, most of all, that drew me to him. To understand people at all, sometimes you have to focus on one feature, to look very hard at it and let it reveal the rest. How a person held their body, the way they looked at you or looked away—any of that could tell you a story. Even when people were hiding, their bodies were always telling you their secrets.

I lifted my camera and did the one thing I could always do. I took my shot.

Stories are everywhere, Consuelo had once told me. *Wherever there are people, there are stories to tell and pictures to make.*

Here suddenly was a story I knew I had to tell, in the one way I knew how to tell it. I stayed in the streets for hours, and when I came back, I developed the pictures and hung that print on the wall. *White Angel Breadline*, I called it later. I put it up right next to my portraits of the Levi Strausses, the Freudenthals, the Fleishhackers, the Haases, the de Youngs. When people saw the picture—my clients, but also many of my good friends—they told me not to go to those sorts of rough places. Or else they looked at it and asked, "What are you going to do with that?" I didn't have the slightest idea. I only knew that I would go out again tomorrow and the day after that.

Every day that I walked out of the studio and into the street, I felt humbled, frightened, and energized. I counted on Consuelo's and Imogen's encouragement and got it, but Maynard surprised me. He told me I had to keep going out. The suffering in the streets had lit a fire under him, too, and he was roaming about just as much as I was. He'd introduced me to the natural beauty of California and the Southwest, but now we were bent toward the same vision: the necessity of documenting what we were seeing in the city. He started working on a large painting, a portrait he titled *Forgotten Man*. I thought it was the best work he'd ever done. After looking at it for a long time, I understood something I'd never really seen: how he'd been withholding some vital part of himself as an artist, that as much as he'd given to his paintings, he'd erased himself from them, too.

I'd always been a steady sort of person, and I might have stayed in the studio and held on to the life I'd built for myself, but over the course of those days and weeks, some version of me faded, then disappeared. That was the end of my portrait work. Well, not right away. I didn't shutter the studio until 1935, but that's when I began to let it go.

·   ·   ·

A portrait is many things: a document, a moment in time, a refuge for memory. But above all, it is the meeting of two people, the seer and the seen.

When I was younger, I wanted to walk in the world as if I were invisible, but slowly I came to realize you couldn't really see people if you're bent on hiding all the time. You had to show people who you were if you hoped they'd show you something of themselves. You had to let yourself be seen. If you gave a person that as well as your deepest attention and then waited, sometimes you could capture their secret stories. People are grateful for genuine attention; they reward you by looking back.

I'd been exploring San Francisco for years. I knew its every corner. There wasn't a street I hadn't walked. But all that time I'd been hiding. I was done with that now. I was doing different work, I told anyone who asked. And then it became true. I took a job with the Farm Security Administration, documenting the Dust Bowl and the migrant crisis. In most ways I was starting over completely, but I didn't mind. I was eager for the change and grateful for the chance when it came.

It was during the Depression that I learned how to go everywhere on my own. I bought myself a Model T from a painter I knew who'd moved to Mexico. I learned how to drive. If a project included money for an assistant, I'd sometimes hire Imogen's son, Rondal Partridge, to accompany me, but I liked to know I could get in a car and take myself wherever I needed to go without waiting for anyone. I'd wake up early, before the sunrise, and I'd climb into my car. I didn't know a mule from a tractor when I started out, but now I traveled through all the state's rural areas—out on the fields and orchards, where out-houses were hung with blankets and clothes and signs marked WHITES ONLY; past tin shanties and mud huts where Mexican laborers and their children lived beside ditches and overgrown lots; along the sun-soaked roads of the Central Valley, where the land had been farmed so hard it finally refused to yield.

Everywhere I went, I heard, "Who is this *woman*?" "Why is she here?" "What is she doing with a camera?" I learned to an-swer when I had to and keep quiet when I could. Once I got the hang of it, I found that walking into a new place as a woman had its advantages, as it had with my portrait work. People didn't hide from you as much. I'd wander about with a handheld Graflex and a small notebook, just taking everything in. Usually I didn't bother hiding my limp—it made people kinder to me somehow. If someone seemed uncomfortable or closed off, I'd move away, but otherwise we'd get to talking and they'd tell me their stories. Many times it seemed they'd been waiting for years to tell them.

One afternoon in 1936, I was driving home, when I saw a hand-written sign by the side of the freeway that read PEA PICKERS. I'd been on the road for weeks, and I was eager to get home to my sons. It was always the same story. Maynard disappearing to the desert for months at a time, leaving me to both take care of the boys and work to support them. Whenever I left on a long assignment, I'd have to board them with friends or rela-tives. Sometimes I had no choice but to board them with strang-ers. I'd work too much, then I'd hurry home to try to make it up to them. I never did, not really. When I got back, I couldn't even get them to look me in the eye, and just when they'd soften toward me, I'd get called away on a new project and they'd pull away again.

The day that I saw the PEA PICKERS sign, I drove another twenty miles, but then something, some instinct, told me to turn around. At the camp, the earth looked parched despite the recent rains. Heat had splintered the trees in two, and vultures perched on leafless branches. Ahead and all around me there were men, women, children, and infants, a miasma of suffering and endurance. I walked around for a while, and then I saw her: a woman under a faded canvas tent with several children huddled around her.

I waited for her to notice me before approaching. When she finally looked up, a line of confusion appeared on her forehead, but then her face opened.

We see not only with our eyes but with everything we are. Everything that'd happened had brought me to this place and to this time. So many other moments filled that one, so many stories, so many ghosts. I somehow saw them all when I met this woman's gaze.

What seized my attention, what held me there, was the sense of a whole life, a whole story, in the woman's expression.

I walked toward her and said hello. She told me her age—thirty-two—and that she and her seven children had been living off frozen vegetables from the surrounding fields, as well as birds that the children killed. She'd just sold the tires from her car to buy food; she and the children were now marooned in the camp. She seemed to know that my pictures might help her. When I knew she was ready, I tightened my camera strap, checked the lens, then moved closer. I made five exposures, working closer and closer from the same direction.

A photograph is only a piece of paper with a silver image burned onto it, but there's something about some of them—the rare few—that you can't call anything but an act of love. And you give it—not to only one person; you give it to the world.

I always felt lucky to have landed in San Francisco. Despite everything that happened with Caroline and the complicated guilt I carried as a result of it, my life there had brought many gifts. I found friendship like I'd never known, I found love, I found my work and, finally, a life worth living.

After I closed my portrait studio, I worked in a darkroom in the shed next to my house. I kept it very spare. It suited me. It suited the kind of pictures I was taking. I'd been living in the Bay Area for years at that point, but I hadn't exhausted my love for it, and I never would. For years Maynard kept disappearing and coming back, but the absences grew longer and longer, and by the end I barely saw him at all. I suppose it was easier, losing him gradually over so many years, but it gutted me. After the divorce, I stayed in California but not in the city. I moved across the bay, to Berkeley. I married Paul Taylor, a professor at the university. Maynard left for Arizona and never came back. From the hillside, between the redwoods and eucalyptus, San Francisco flashed and beckoned me, like the memory of someone I'd once loved but had lost.

I drove all up and down the state and then across the country. I can't remember ever taking a day off. More than once, I pulled over by the side of the road to sleep and woke up in the car, stiff, bone-tired, and weary-eyed, and yet not since the first days of 540 had I felt so alive and so certain I'd found my true path.

Each photograph I took was a fragment of time, standing for

the whole. Together they made up a map of my journeys, which is to say a map of my life.

Over the years, I'd watch San Francisco change. I'd see wrecking balls swing through its foggy sky, sheets of dust gust through the streets, bulldozers vanquish whole blocks. The entire Fillmore was destroyed and its Black residents exiled. At first you wondered when it would end, and then you knew it never would.

So many of the old places in North Beach disappeared. At the top of Telegraph Hill, where children and lovers once met among eucalyptus trees, there was now a massive white tower and an endless stream of tourists. It was awful and infuriating, but none of it prepared me for the day I'd stand on the corner of Columbus and watch Monkey Block come down. This was in 1959. The Second World War had come and gone, and after that, whole swaths of the city were blasted and razed and turned into money.

It was Imogen who told me Monkey Block was slated for demolition. We'd stayed friends over the years. When Roi divorced her, she'd plunged back into photography. Time makes many people bitter, but it only made Imogen more herself, more generous, more hardworking, more original. When she found out about Monkey Block, she telephoned and we agreed to go see it one last time together.

I hadn't been back in years, and yet it was as if I had never really left the place—or some part of it had never left me. There were just a handful of us from the old days. One by one our friends had dropped out, gotten married, taken jobs, wandered away, but the building was still full of writers and artists, young people who'd come to San Francisco in search of their own bohemia.

I'd never forget that first deep, booming blast. A few people stopped to watch, then walked on. When it was done, when the beautiful, old, sumptuous building was razed and gutted, it felt like the very earth had been cut away from under my feet. I sat down on the ground, in the middle of the sidewalk, with my legs crossed and my eyes shut, memories swelling to the surface.

There was the very first time I walked into Monkey Block with Caroline in 1918. I felt as if I'd fallen into another world, and all I wanted was to keep falling. I was never the same after I saw the warmth and grace and light of that place, though later I knew so much of that feeling had to do with Caroline. After she left San Francisco, I could never go inside without thinking of her. Of how much fun we'd had together. Of how we'd watched over each other and kept each other safe, as long as we could, anyway.

There was the night Maynard and I went up to Tosca's with Ralph Stackpole to listen to Ansel play the piano in the back room. After a few minutes, an extraordinary woman asked if the seat beside me was taken. She wore a long, embroidered dress, and her black hair was braided with flowers and crimson ribbons. In one hand she held a cigar and in the other she held a glass of cognac. Ansel asked what she'd like to hear, and she replied, "Habanera." And then from Ansel's fingers came a perfect rendition of the aria from Bizet's *Carmen*, and from the heavily bejeweled throat of Frida Kahlo came a perfect rendition of *"L'amour est un oiseau rebelle."* I nearly fell off my stool. Afterward, everyone laughed because I hadn't heard of Diego Rivera and his young wife, Frida.

There was the time everyone came to the cottage to see our

firstborn, Daniel. Someone had the idea to paint a mural for him, and one by one, anyone who could paint, and plenty of people who couldn't, took turns with a paintbrush. By the time the party was over, and our friends had wandered tipsy and laughing into the streets, they'd left a wild rendition of the city, populated entirely by circus animals.

And then there was the day the Golden Gate Bridge opened, in 1937. People said it was madness to build a bridge across the bay, what with earthquakes forever tearing through the area. It was Maynard who'd recommended his friend Irving Morrow, the architect, to design it. Irving got the job. Just before it was set to be painted gray, we went out to see the bridge with him. The orange-red primer looked so splendid that I joked to Irving that he ought to keep it that way. By the time the Golden Gate was finished, Maynard and I had split up, but there it was and there it would stay: a glorious blaze of copper against green hills and a pure blue sky.

It was all such a long time ago, and now there was nothing left of Monkey Block but a few blackened beams and a massive, smoking gash at the bottom of the Hill. All that glorious, messy life had been destroyed, the whole era coming to an abrupt end within the span of a few agonizing hours. There'd be ten years when there was nothing but a parking lot where Monkey Block had once stood. Some of the younger artists and writers drifted up to Haight-Ashbury and settled in the neighborhood's ramshackle Victorians. By the time the Transamerica Pyramid went up, few people remembered Monkey Block. It was lost and gone, as if it'd never been there at all.

After the last blast, there was a long, terrible silence, and then someone began to recite George Sterling's ode to San Francisco, "The Cool, Grey City of Love."

Tho the dark be cold and blind
Yet her sea-fog's touch is kind,
And her mightier caress
Is joy and the pain thereof;
And great is thy tenderness,
O cool, grey city of love!

George Sterling—he'd been Caroline's friend. I closed my eyes and there he was, walking the halls in his ridiculous silk robes, reciting poems at the top of his voice.

"Did you know he killed himself, Dorrie?"

I opened my eyes. "No."

"Cyanide. Poor, sweet, mad George."

After that a small group of us, the ones who were left, went up to the Black Cat and drank until we laughed, and then until we cried.

Amazing how deeply we can love a place, how that love makes us hold it within ourselves until it becomes a part of us, as real as skin or blood or bone. Though so much had changed, and would still change, there'd never be a more magnificent time than those early years in San Francisco. I'd landed there by chance, alone and lost, but in the end, there was no place I'd ever love as much or miss more. The city was my home, my own good great place, and it would always be.

Epilogue

CAROLINE DE MODES. The words were engraved on a small brass plaque.

One year passed without my seeing Caroline, then many. Year after year of scattered letters and untold stories and thinking I wouldn't see her again. Now here I was, standing before her door.

Her address on the Rue du Faubourg Saint-Honoré in the Eighth Arrondissement was grander than I'd imagined— a lovely dove-gray Haussmann-style building with pale-blue shutters and a pale-blue door. Lush green plane trees lined the sidewalk, and the wrought-iron fence opened onto a garden. It was early spring; there was a chill in the air. I angled my hat, took a breath, then raised the brass knocker and let it fall.

It was a young woman, a blond slip of a girl, who greeted me. She was, she told me, Mademoiselle Lee's assistant. I followed her through the foyer and down a long hallway lined with paintings, the thick pile of Persian carpets muting my footsteps.

We walked past the salon and through a door to reach the second floor, where, her assistant told me, Caroline had her office and her private rooms. Here there was a tall, carved door. The woman knocked softly, then pushed it slightly open.

"Excuse me, Mademoiselle Lee? The lady is here. Your friend."

A fire was going in the grate, and there, in a chair beside the fireplace, was Caroline.

"Dorrie," she said, and rose from her seat.

She was wearing a tomato-red dress with a cinched-in waist and wide skirt. She looked, at a glance, just as she had in San Francisco, as if no time had passed. Her small jade amulet still hung around her neck. But then I saw that her hair was longer now and that it fell in waves. Faint lines fanned out from her beautiful eyes.

For a moment we simply stood there, facing each other with the distance of years between us, and then she stepped closer and drew her arms around me.

"Now, let me get a good look at you!" she said.

She stepped back and narrowed her eyes. I watched as she appraised my heavy silver bracelets, my black beret, my gray gabardine slacks.

I smiled. "And?"

"You look positively splendid, Dorrie. You've become the woman you always wanted to be!"

That she greeted me warmly made me so happy. As if I wasn't only welcome, but I'd been missed. I thought that to see her again would open a deep wrenching hurt. It didn't. I hadn't been in the room but two minutes and here were all the things I'd missed so much and for so many years: her generosity, her vitality, her charm. The way she seemed to be in motion, even when she was sitting down. Her gift for making a place wonderful.

I'd thought about her so many times over the years. I knew she was in Paris, that she'd worked as a seamstress for a while and that she'd eventually opened her own salon. Those were the rough outlines, but to see her now told me she'd done better than survive—much better. Her apartment was a stunning, light-filled jewel box of a place. I took it all in—the velvet curtains, the glass tables, the lacquered screen. A trio of enormous bright windows framed the view of the street. When I'd first entered the room, it seemed as if I was in 540 Sutter again, but now, as I looked more closely at everything, I saw that nothing here was shabby or secondhand.

"It's got such . . . atmosphere."

We both laughed. Then it really was all right. We were becoming real to each other again.

The young blond woman returned with a tray, which she placed on the mother-of-pearl table. She reached for the silver teapot, but Caroline said she'd pour the tea herself.

It had taken a long time to answer her letter, the one she sent about a year after she went away. She'd written that she'd left the States and was living in France. I was so startled that for a long time I just stood gripping the letter in two hands. When I sat down to write her back, I thought I wouldn't get it right. In a way, I never did. There was so much I couldn't put down in a letter. Every year or so I'd slip a picture of the boys into an envelope along with a note, but I couldn't bring myself to tell her the messy parts of motherhood and marriage, which was most of it, really. It wasn't that I wanted to hide the truth from her but that I'd gotten so good at hiding it from myself.

Caroline's letters tended to be brief as well, relaying news

about her work, a recent holiday, a bit of gossip about a mutual
friend who'd turned up in Paris.

I told myself that someday I'd visit her in Paris, and then
we'd really catch up, but it wasn't ever the right time. The boys,
Maynard, the studio. It was impossible to get away. Then, when
I finally got a chance to do the work I wanted, I ran toward it. I
hadn't stopped running for years.

But after Monkey Block came down in 1959, I couldn't stop
thinking of Caroline. I'd taken pictures all through the Depression and World War II, but by the fifties I was working less.
Mostly freelance assignments for magazines. I'd had a slew of
surgeries, and I was in constant pain, always unsure how much
longer I'd be able to work or travel. Time seemed to be running
out, and it was.

One morning I stood in my kitchen in Berkeley and dialed
her number. We talked for an hour and by the time we hung up,
I'd arranged to meet her the following month.

Now we sat opposite each other, taking tea on a small round
table by the fireplace, and began trading stories—about life and
love and work. She asked one question after another about my
pictures. She seemed to have kept up with everything I'd done.

"That portrait you did of the migrant woman and her children. It's extraordinary."

"You've seen it?"

"It would be hard not to, Dorrie. It's been printed everywhere. Didn't you know?"

I did, but to hear Caroline praise the picture—well, that was
something else.

"People were hurting so much, and for so long. Many of
them have never stopped hurting. . . . Anyway, I was lucky to get
that photograph."

"Perhaps, but I doubt it was only luck, Dorrie."

"Thank you."

"I don't think I ever told you how sorry I was to hear about Maynard's passing."

I nodded. He'd died of cancer. He'd been gone thirteen years, but it still hurt to think of it. I drew a deep breath.

"You're the only one who didn't try to talk me out of marrying him. Why?"

"I knew it wouldn't have mattered. You'd only have resented me if I'd said anything. Besides, your mistakes were yours to make."

I had to smile. "I'm glad I made them. Well, mostly. Whatever else, Maynard was never boring. Up to the very end he could still make everything seem marvelous." I paused. "After the divorce he moved to Arizona. He went back to painting the desert, but it was different. He found a new way to see it. It was beautiful work—it *is* beautiful work."

"He was an extraordinary artist—"

"And an extraordinarily bad husband. I should have given him a harder time. Goodness knows he deserved it. I was never brave enough for that."

"But you were. In the end, I mean."

"Yes."

We were quiet for a few moments.

"Paul sounds wonderful," she said. "And of course he loves you madly."

I remembered the picture I'd sent her of me and Paul at Stinson Beach last summer. "You can tell just from a photograph?"

"Of course I can."

I laughed. "Nobody's been more supportive of my work than Paul—nobody since you."

"I'm so happy you found that kind of love, Dorrie. I just wish I'd been there to see it."

I didn't quite know how to answer this, but I smiled and thanked her.

"Caroline," I said after a while. "Do you wish sometimes you hadn't left San Francisco?"

A faint line creased between her eyes. She stared down at the table, fiddling with the plate of macarons. Her nails were clipped short and painted the same deep red as her lips, and stacks of rings flashed on both her hands.

I almost gave up thinking she'd answer. And then she did.

"San Francisco," she began. "What happened there changed things for me in a way I knew would never be undone. I spent weeks working out how to leave. I shouldn't have waited so long, but I didn't want to go without you. Then, suddenly, and very clearly, I knew I just couldn't walk anymore on the same streets as the senator and his son, not even for one day. I had to get away, from the Pharrells, from Monkey Block, from everything I knew and everyone who knew me.

"Once I made up my mind to leave, it didn't take long to decide where to go: Paris. Everyone seemed to already be there—or on their way. Paris was cheap, but it was also glamorous and fun. You could do what you wanted and live as you pleased. That's what I'd heard, anyway.

"What I needed was a passport. One day I went to city hall to apply for one, only to be told I didn't exist. 'We have no record of a Caroline Lee,' the clerk said. And you know what I thought? It was a mistake. It had to be. I looked at that clerk, at her beigey-green jacket, her stern updo, her mouth stretched in a thin line. 'Are you certain you have the correct spelling?' I asked. I spelled it out for her. 'C-a-r-o-l-i-n-e L-e-e.' The face behind the counter stayed rigid, frozen in a blank stare, full of mistrust and hate. Oh, I knew the look. I'd seen it all my life. The woman didn't believe me and never would. I told her I was born in San Francisco. 'Have you brought your birth certificate?' she asked. I hadn't, for the simple reason that I didn't have one. It'd been lost in the fire in 1906. That's what Lo Mo had told me when I asked.

"But there had to be some kind of record. I asked for the supervisor and was told he was out. I asked for the supervisor's supervisor. This gentleman was also away. I was so angry I was shaking, but I wouldn't make a scene. I'd wait, if that's what it would take. I watched the clerk look after a whole line of people who'd come in after me. Two hours later, I was still waiting. This was a Friday. I'd come before noon and it was afternoon by then. The building wouldn't open again until Monday. At a quarter of five, the clerk and I were the only ones left. Our dislike for each other was thicker—so much thicker—than the glass partition separating us. It was nearly five o'clock when something tugged at me, an intuition that sparked across my memories, and I walked outside the building and headed up Sacramento Street."

"To the Mission Home."

She nodded. "Poor Lo Mo. It was an awful shock to her when I showed up that day. I had to wrench it out of her, but I finally got her to tell me the story—the *whole* story."

She took a deep breath and went on.

"In the spring of 1906, on the morning after she found me in Chinatown, she went to the courthouse near city hall. On each form, under the entry for place of birth, she wrote *unknown*.

Under the entry for *legal guardian,* she signed her own name. She was as knowledgeable as any lawyer in the city, and twice as fierce. In all the years she'd been at the Mission House, she hadn't once failed to get papers for her daughters—signed, stamped proof that we'd been born, had names of our own, a claim to legal residence, and therefore some foothold in this world.

"After the earthquake, she managed to save the metal box with the girls' papers—but the five of us who'd just come to the home didn't have any papers yet; our paperwork was still being processed. With no courthouse, there were no hearings and therefore no petitions and no papers. There were many Chinese in this situation. Hundreds, thousands. People started saying there were too many of us, that the Chinese ought to be expelled, or at the least those without papers should be made to leave. For many weeks there was nothing, not a thing, to do for it, but then Lo Mo had the idea to write to the Chinese Embassy, which was known to be helpful in such cases, and they were helpful—in all but my case. That this was on account of my mixed blood was something she guessed but didn't know for sure."

"She never told you any of this?"

"She had no reason to. She figured I'd get on fine, and I did. One year slipped past and then another and another. You didn't need papers to get hired as a servant in a house on Russian Hill or work sixteen hours each day in a laundry or spend years in the basement of a department store. You didn't need papers to be invisible, which is all anyone ever expected me to be."

Her gaze went to the window and lingered there for a moment before she continued.

"For a long time after I left the Mission Home, I was blind to the world. Something twisted inside me—anger and loss and the thin sharp blade of fear. I'd lived all my life in San Francisco. It was my only home. To discover, almost by chance, not only that I'd never been American but that I never could be, that my future there was as unknowable as my origins—it broke something in me. Of course, Lo Mo was bent on fighting it, but if I'd had even the smallest bit of faith that things could be different, the senator and his son had done away with it. You see, I knew all I needed to know about justice. The impossibility of it for someone like me.

"I remember walking through San Francisco that day, crossing the French Quarter, along the border of Chinatown, and up into North Beach. For once, I had nowhere to be. I could look at everything closely, and I did. I thought about the Mission Home and the basement of the White House. I thought of the studio and how hard we'd worked there together, the wonderfulness of that time, and the waste of it.

"All at once, it was as if a switch had been thrown in my mind. There were other cities. There were other countries. Why should I stay there? No one could stop me from leaving, which in and of itself seemed a reason to go."

"But you didn't have much money. How did you get all the way to France?"

"The pearl," she said, tilting her chin and smiling. "I paid for my passage with John Pharrell Jr.'s pearl."

"But I thought . . ."

"That I'd thrown it away? Come now, Dorrie. I was a wreck, but I was never a fool. Of course, I'd never have taken it to a pawn merchant myself. Instead of going, I sent someone else, someone who didn't even know my name. It fetched a very large sum, which was lucky. Without that pearl, I couldn't have gone as far as France. I wouldn't have been able to leave the country at all."

"But you still didn't have a passport."

She shook her head. "I didn't need one. You see, among the luxuries afforded by a first-class suite on a fancy ocean liner, there was one of incomparable value: It did away with the need to present passports or visas. Oh, you should've seen me the day I left San Francisco, tricked out like a rich gentleman's exotic mistress embarking on a pleasure voyage—cream cloche pulled low over my brow, cream stole, cream suit with a peplum waist, cream ankle-strapped heels. I *was* first class. The second I slipped out of the hired car, a porter took charge of my suitcases and led me right past the other passengers and up to my suite.

"For days, all I did was stare out at the sea from a small, salt-splattered rectangle of a window. I'd packed all my most beautiful clothes in one of those suitcases. The other one was full of fabric, bobs of thread, a pair of dressmaking shears, and my sewing machine. I didn't bother to unpack any of it. I didn't talk to anyone. I slept and slept. It was a rough passage, and many weeks long, but one morning toward the end I woke up to a blue sky and a smooth sea. I dressed and went to the upper deck and into the sunlight. I took a deep breath of fresh air, and I swear in that moment it was like a stone lifted off my heart.

"From Calais, I took a slow train to Paris. As you know, the world in 1920 was not a tender place for a woman to make her way in. It was one thing if you had a man's arm to hold or the kind of money that bought you a limousine and a driver and first-class suites on luxury ocean liners. I had none of those things—after paying for my ticket, I had just a few hundred francs left—but the farther I traveled, the more American I seemed to become in others' eyes. To the French, America's a half-civilized land—if that—populated by bizarre but occasion-ally charming 'mongrels.' They'd look at me and they wouldn't bat an eye. If anyone asked what I was doing in France, I'd tell them I was traveling around the world—me, who'd never left San Francisco before!

"I remember staring out of the train window. In every direction—on the railway platforms, out in the villages, on the streets of the towns we passed—I saw pretty girls and elegant women, and as I looked at them I thought of all my dresses and blouses and skirts, all the lovely things I'd made in San Fran-cisco, all the ones I knew I could make again.

"What I wanted more than anything, what I'd always wanted, was a life filled with beauty. That, to me, was freedom. The day I got to Paris, I took a car from the Gare Saint-Lazare straight to a little hair salon, where I splurged on a trim, a tin of talc, and a bullet of red lipstick. I stepped out of that salon an hour later dressed in my lilac-colored skirt suit, and, oh, I felt wonderful.

"From there I headed to Montparnasse, to one of the new *revues*. In a back room of the theater, I met Madame Moreau, the theater's owner. She spoke no English, and I of course spoke no French, but what happened next didn't depend on words. You see, we liked each other. Understood each other. She hired me on the spot. I worked in that theater for five years. The *revue* became an absolute sensation, and I was the in-house seam-stress, the one tasked with keeping the dancers' seams, sequins, beads, and feathers in top form. With my first week's wages, I rented a tiny room on the fourth floor of an old building on the Rue des Martyrs, and that's where I finally unpacked my Singer and started a new life."

. . .

Was this what we called fate? As I listened to Caroline's story, I thought of the long, tangled chain of cause and effect that makes up our lives. For years I'd thought if I hadn't found the pearl and then the portrait, everything would've happened a different way. We would have stayed together, Caroline and I, working in 540, making our way together. Only now, all these years later, did the story truly come into focus. She'd chosen to leave. She'd chosen to make a new life for herself.

Still, I couldn't help but ask why she hadn't told me where she was going.

Her answer came easily. "You would've tried to make me stay. I know you wanted me to. And that was the last thing I wanted. To be forever in need of favors. To have people's eyes on me, judging, looking down, never really seeing me. I had to get away from all that. You do understand now, don't you?"

I nodded and looked around the room. My gaze stopped at the pictures above the fireplace mantel.

"May I—"

"Of course."

She lifted the frames one by one and showed them to me. A group of friends sitting on a beach, their faces bright in the sun of a long-ago summer. Caroline—there she was, on the left—in a white drop-waist dress. Caroline standing alone in a fur cap in some snow-swept place. Caroline encircled by a dozen gorgeous sequin-clad showgirls.

Those pictures spoke of a life that had been lovely, but looking at them then, I felt such sadness. The people in them were strangers. The life in them was strange to me. How could we make up for so much lost time?

That's what I thought as I studied her photographs, but what

I said was this: "You've made a beautiful home for yourself here."

She thought for a moment before answering. "No. A life, I suppose, but not a home."

I shook my head. "I don't understand."

"That I don't belong here, well, it was never a surprise. I didn't expect to belong here. I think it was a year before anyone ever called me by my first name. I'll always be a stranger in this country, no matter how long I live here, but somehow it bothers you less when you don't expect to belong to a place."

"But have you been happy?"

"Oh yes. I have, Dorrie. Very much so."

For a few moments we were both quiet, pulled into our thoughts and memories.

"Caroline," I said slowly, "do you remember I wanted to go to Paris but I couldn't on account of the war, so I went west instead?"

"But then you got to San Francisco and you were robbed. I remember everything about those days. You were always watching the world so intently as you made your way through it. It was a wonderful thing to see."

I nodded, trying to imagine myself as she remembered me.

"It's strange," I said.

"What?"

"I don't think I would have stayed in San Francisco if I hadn't met you, and now, after all this time, here you are. In Paris."

"Here *we* are," she corrected.

"Yes, here we are."

"You were born to see the world, Dorrie. And so," she said with a smile, "was I."

She held my eyes for a moment, and then she asked if I'd seen much of Paris yet.

I shook my head.

"Oh, I'd love to show it to you! Shall we go out now? We'll walk around, find a café, eat too much delicious food, and catch up. What do you think?"

"I'd love that."

She stood up and smoothed the front of her dress. I followed her down the hall and then to the bottom of the stairs, where I watched her pull on her coat and her hat. While she drew a tube of lipstick from her purse and painted her lips, I stood in front of the large foyer mirror, angling my beret. She snapped her lipstick shut, stepped beside me, and there she was in the reflection, as radiant, fierce, and free as the day we'd found each other on a cable car in San Francisco so many years ago. It was that Caroline I saw standing next to me. Caroline with her sleek black hair and her blood-red lips, walking through the city that first day we met. Caroline in the back booth of Coppa's, leaning close to tell me some marvelous story she'd just heard.

"Ready?" she said now as she pulled the door open.

It was the loveliest time of the day, the lavender hour, when the sky gathers up all the day's beauty before letting it go. A crowd of gray pigeons erupted from a window and scattered into the sky. A group of schoolgirls went past, elbowing one another and giggling. The windows across the street shone yellow, and there was music playing somewhere down by the Seine.

For a minute, we stood on the threshold, and then Caroline took my hand.

There are moments in life when time seems to stand still. This was one. All you can do is hold your breath and hope it will wait for you. All I had that day was my memory, but I caught that moment. I kept it with me always. Whenever I stepped forward and lifted my camera, it was just like that. Like reaching into the sky and grabbing a hunk of lightning. Every time, I thought, *It's impossible, it can't be done, you'd be foolish to try,* but then the picture came into focus and the shutter closed and clicked.

Author's Note

There's no Montgomery Block anymore, no bohemian haven called Monkey Block. Instead, where it once stood, you'll find the Transamerica Building, a pyramid-topped skyscraper in the dead center of San Francisco's financial district. Beyond that, you'll see a concrete curtain and, if you're lucky, a sliver of fog-drenched sky.

Looking now at its newer, sleeker neighbors, it's hard to imagine that the Transamerica Pyramid was once the tallest building in the city, much less the site of a four-story artists' colony that housed some eight hundred writers, performers, and artists over the course of nearly a century.

But wait. If you walk up Columbus Avenue toward Telegraph Hill, you'll discover the survivors of an older, scruffier, artsier city. The Sentinel Building. City Lights Booksellers & Publishers. Vesuvio Cafe. Take a left and you'll find a Chinatown much like the one of a hundred years ago; take a right and you'll happen upon the seedy remnants of the Barbary Coast.

On a good day and in a certain kind of mood you might pass the ghosts of Mark Twain and Jack Kerouac.

It's nobody's bohemia anymore, but duck into any of the little side streets of North Beach, linger awhile, and you'll find it: the past.

The Bohemians is a novel about a lost time and a hidden history, subjects of enduring fascination sparked, as most obsessions are, by the circumstances of my own life, in this case my family's arrival in San Francisco in the late 1970s.

The first thing my parents did when they came to America was to buy a Buick and set out on a cross-country road trip from New York to California. Thousands of miles away, on another continent, there was an apartment whose rooms still housed most everything we owned. There was a revolution; soon there'd be a war. Every mile my father drove took us farther from that place and from the possibility of ever turning back.

The long, hot days of our journey have dimmed into a single indistinguishable blur, but even now I remember vividly the sudden, electrifying sight of the Golden Gate Bridge. My mother, whose heart that year was full of grief and fear, would later tell me she was searching for the most beautiful place in America. One look at San Francisco and she knew she'd found it, the city that might assuage the loss of one home and inspire her to make a new one.

Her love for it became mine. I grew up calling San Francisco "the city," as if it were the only city in the world. We lived ten miles away in the suburbs, where my parents owned and managed a run-down twenty-room motel by the side of the highway. Our trips across the Golden Gate, rare and therefore thrilling, usually took us to the dazzle and bustle of Union Square and ended with a spin down the wild curlicues of Lombard Street, but the most special occasions were punctuated by dinner at the spinning restaurant atop the Hyatt Regency, from which you could see the city in all its 360-degree glory.

At sixteen, newly licensed to drive and in possession of a secondhand cherry-red Chrysler LeBaron, I took my first solo drive across the Golden Gate. After cruising the city, I stopped at North Beach. It was a trip I'd make many times. I used to love drifting through the streets, squares, and alleyways of Telegraph Hill. I spent hours in the basement of City Lights bookstore, nursed a thousand and one espressos at the Steps of Rome. North Beach was the closest place to the Left Bank that a sixteen-year-old immigrant girl from the suburbs was likely to find. It was a place in which I could get lost. It was my own bohemia.

At sixteen I'd never heard of Monkey Block or Dorothea Lange, but this book began on those delicious, solitary rambles.

Years went by. I left the Bay Area and came back. I did all that a second and then a third time. When I moved back for good in 2014, I could barely recognize whole swaths of San Francisco, but North Beach was almost exactly the same. More than ever, spending time there had the feeling of a pilgrimage—a pilgrimage to the city's past and my own.

The moment I heard about Monkey Block I fell deeply in love with it—or rather, the idea of it, and it wasn't long before I started to consider writing about it. Because I am a novelist and because novels need more than a setting (however atmospheric a setting may be) I began casting around for people who'd been part of the world for which Monkey Block had served as a wild but steady heart. I landed eventually on the documentary photographer Dorothea Lange.

There are places that happen to you and places you choose. For Dorothea Lange, San Francisco was both. She was twenty-three years old when she arrived in May 1918. She thought she was just passing through; instead, she stayed for the rest of her life.

The city she found was just a decade old, having been almost totally destroyed in the earthquake and fires of 1906. Then, as now, it was a city on the edge of the continent, a place of beauty, promise, and tragedy. Then, as now, it had little use for memory.

In Lange's time Telegraph Hill was still populated by Italian families who'd come over in the nineteenth century to work as fishermen on the nearby waterfronts. Mexican and Irish enclaves still existed, though their populations were far less robust than in the nineteenth century. The residents of North Beach were laborers, artisans, farmers, mechanics, shopkeepers—working-class people living in humble cottages, some dating to the 1850s. And then, of course, there were the Chinese, who could trace their roots in the city back to the Gold Rush, when they came by the thousands to build California's railroads, only to be confined to a segregated ghetto once the state was stripped of its silver and gold.

When Lange arrived in San Francisco in 1918, World War I was raging and the Spanish flu was closing in. The bright mon-eyed days of the twenties glimmered in the far distance, but the New Woman had already stepped onto the scene. In the first decades of the twentieth century, women were in open rebellion against the past. They fought to escape the strictures and prohibitions that had for long sought to keep women quiet and small. It was a battle Lange first joined in her native New Jersey and would continue to fight the rest of her life, but its most delightfully raucous interludes took place in those first years in San Francisco.

"I found myself in San Francisco," she would later say. Her coming-of-age spoke of a city innocent of Silicon Valley, the locus of California's twenty-first-century Gold Rush, a city where artists and writers could still arrive with nothing and make a home, where a young woman with no connections or money but heaps of grit might encounter a new version of herself.

A new city can change you, in the way a friend can change you, and there are moments in life where both happen at once. San Francisco was such a point of intersection for Dorothea Lange.

The Bohemians focuses on a time when she wasn't yet an icon, but rather a young woman finding her way forward through life. In writing it, I wanted to think about what had made her who she became. I wanted to explore the beginnings of her career, her start as a photographer at a time when photography wasn't commonly thought of as art or documentary. I wanted to trace how her training as a high-society portrait photographer prepared her for what came next: her life's work documenting ordinary and often unseen people. And I wanted to explore the ways that San Francisco, and California more broadly, transformed her sense of herself as both a woman and a photographer.

One of our most abiding myths about creativity is that of the solitary genius. We can admire the relentless drive it took for a young woman like Dorothea Lange to build a business a hundred years ago and still acknowledge the fact that she did not do it alone. By settling in Northern California, she was entering a community of skilled and innovative photographers, many of them women. Imogen Cunningham and Consuelo Kanaga were real women, women she deeply admired, women far more fascinating than I could've made up. Lange would likely have accomplished great work anywhere, but the work she did was shaped by the mentors she found and the friends she made.

The relationship that most captured my imagination, however, was between Lange and her Chinese American assistant. Her name was Ah-yee, but she was literally without a name in most accounts, referred to only as the "Chinese girl." The details about their collaboration were scant but compelling. Together they had transformed Lange's first studio at 540 Sutter Street into a place of bohemian splendor. I felt, but I could not prove, that the experience of working together must have changed them both.

But who was she? Apart from her beauty and vivaciousness, the one detail attached to her—that she'd attended a mission school—suggested a past she'd outrun, an identity she'd shed even before she showed up at Lange's studio. She likely would have been young and unmarried. On California's color line, she would've been consigned to the lowest rungs. She would have had far fewer choices than Lange, but her talent and ambition might have been equal.

As a writer of historical fiction, I have a peculiar relationship to history. Whenever I look back in time, I find myself drawn to unknown persons and nameless figures. I find myself looking not solely for what's there, but for what's missing, what hasn't yet been written, what can't ever be known, except, possibly, partially, through invention. Caroline Lee comes from my imagination, not from the historical record—it couldn't be otherwise. What I wanted to know about her didn't exist in historical and sociological records, most of which would have seen her as someone undeserving of a story.

One of the joys of writing fiction is that you can interrupt history and insert your own tale. The rebellions of my own generation had their roots in the erasure of women like Dorothea Lange's assistant. I imagined her as mixed-race, an outsider, a child of immigrants or perhaps an immigrant herself— experiences I knew well. Almost immediately I decided to bring her into the picture, and with top billing. In tandem with exploring Dorothea Lange's artistic coming-of-age, I wanted to question and explore the kind of life this young woman, and more generally, girls and young Asian and immigrant women in cities of the West Coast, led in the early twentieth century. In a place and a time when you couldn't count on anyone setting down your name, much less your story, what was possible and what was beyond imagining?

"The past," wrote William Faulkner, "is never dead. It's not even past." In much the same way that every portrait is a self-portrait, every historical novel is to some degree a contemporary novel. What I saw when looking back at San Francisco in 1920 was necessarily shaped by my sensibility and interests as a woman writing in 2020, and yet there were many moments when the continuities between Lange's world and mine felt uncannily, even uncomfortably, close.

The hours I spent with Lange transported me to another San Francisco. She brought into focus a city that had lived on in the strange and wonderful magnetic force that lured my parents from halfway around the world, both a ravishingly beautiful place and a frame of mind. To her, as to me, San Francisco was freedom, yet the longer I spent looking at Lange's early years in the city, the more I understood how little I knew about its history—and how much of that history had survived.

One morning I decided to take a break from writing the scene in which two characters lead a raid on a brothel. It was a difficult scene to write and for some reason I thought I'd find respite by checking the news. What I found on the home page of *The New York Times* was a detailed account of an FBI raid that had taken place just that morning at an Upper East Side mansion. Like the scene I'd written, the story involved an extremely wealthy and well-connected man, a large number of teenaged girls, and a raft of crimes that captivated the public, but that would go wholly unpunished.

Again and again I'd sink into my research into the past, only to be confronted by the present. In the speeches of James Duval Phelan, the California governor who'd run on the platform "Keep California White," I heard the ever-louder rhetoric of nativism and white nationalism. In Lange's Dust Bowl pictures, I saw the horrors of homelessness as well as the international refugee crisis. In her pictures of the Japanese internment, I saw borders, prisons, and cages of "alien" children. In her pictures documenting the flooding of a small Northern California town, I saw the flaming hills and valleys of nearby Sonoma and Napa. In her pictures of the American South, I saw the relentless brutalities of racism.

I realize now these weren't coincidences, or even synchronicities. Violence against women and people of color are not subjects easily or rightly relegated to the history books; they persist in our common reality. As Dorothea Lange's biographer, the historian Linda Gordon notes the gradual disappearance of white nationalism from public view didn't mark its defeat but the country's adoption of many of its ideals into law. To give one example, the anti-Asian sentiment dramatized in *The Bohemians* became enshrined in the 1924 National Origins Act, which established immigration quotas based on race and effectively halted all immigration from Asia, Africa, and the Middle East. In 1965, a coalition of activists and reformers succeeded in abolishing that law. Had they failed, I would have been just one of the millions barred from the United States.

Lange's America and mine were intimately connected, but to what use, if any, should I put the connection? I didn't know, not for a long time. I kept writing, one eye on my characters, the other on the times in which they lived. The character of Senator Pharrell in the novel draws purposely on the real-life Senator James Duval Phelan's stance toward the "Yellow Peril," a stance in which he was far from alone. Invention in this instance would have been a betrayal; it would have erased the very real cruelties engendered by such a world view as his. Instead I had to push deeper into the truth, and that's where I found the story I needed to tell.

What do we owe our fellow humans? That's the question Lange always seems to be asking with her camera. All her life she resisted the title of artist, though she did eventually come to embrace the term "documentary photographer." She knew that photography couldn't solve the problems and prejudices of her times, but she believed it could make them known to a wider swath of the country, and that change couldn't come without such knowing. Her pictures were meant to show America to itself, and they did. The photographs she took of the Japanese

Internment did this so well they were suppressed for nearly fifty years, but censorship only sharpened her resolve.

What Dorothea Lange discovered through photography was a more expansive point of view, one suited to not only the places she traveled but also to the multiplicity of perspectives and people she encountered through her work. Frame by frame she honed her extraordinary ability to see people as individuals, no matter their external circumstances. Truth, pain, beauty, dignity: these are what she saw, and what she makes us see still. She looked at America, at all of its present and all of its past, and she found the churn of history in a woman's furrowed brow, in a man's clasped hands, in a plowed-out, forgotten field, and again and again she asked us to imagine a different ending to the story.

Historical Notes

DOROTHEA LANGE

One of the most noted documentary photographers of the last century, Lange is known primarily for her searing images of the Depression. In 1941 she gave up a Guggenheim award to record the forced evacuation and illegal incarceration of Japanese Americans during World War II. The photographs were suppressed for nearly fifty years. She also produced powerful documents of environmental destruction and its ravages, including a series about Monticello, a Napa County farming community where five hundred people lived before it was drowned in 1957. She died in San Francisco in October 1965 at the age of seventy.

MAYNARD DIXON

Maynard Dixon left San Francisco not long after his divorce from Dorothea Lange in 1935. He settled permanently in the Southwest, where he married the muralist Edith Hamlin and continued to paint. They split their time between Utah and

Arizona, where he died in 1946. Today he's acknowledged as one of the greatest painters of the American West.

CONSUELO KANAGA

A renegade photographer and journalist, Consuelo Kanaga got her start in San Francisco but ventured far and wide over the course of her career. Like Lange, she showed a lifelong devotion to documenting the lives of the disenfranchised and the poor. Her portraits of African Americans differ dramatically from the frequently condescending and impersonal photographs taken by photographers of her generation. She died in February 1978 in New York, where she'd lived for several decades after leaving California.

IMOGEN CUNNINGHAM

Cunningham and Lange remained close friends all their lives. In the 1930s she joined with like-minded photographers, including Ansel Adams, to form Group f/64, a group of photographers committed to a new modernist aesthetic based on precisely exposed images of natural forms and found objects. Cunningham, like Lange, eventually turned to documentary street photography, supporting herself with her commercial and studio work. She continued to take photographs until just before her death at age ninety-three in June 1976, in San Francisco, California.

DONALDINA CAMERON

In her forty-seven years at San Francisco's Occidental Mission Home for Girls, Cameron rescued nearly three thousand women and girls forced to work as prostitutes and household servants. Working with lawmakers and other civic groups, she helped eradicate the slave trade that flourished into the 1930s in San Francisco and also helped enact state and federal laws for Chinese people across the United States. She died in 1968 at the age of ninety-eight and is buried in Northern California alongside her onetime charge and eventual colleague, Tien Fuh Wu.

GIUSEPPE COPPA

Giuseppe Coppa, an Italian immigrant who'd come to California in the 1890s, opened "Original Coppa's Restaurant" in 1904. At first, it catered primarily to local Italian fishermen, but it soon became the favorite watering hole of the city's artists and writers, who decorated its walls with spectacular murals. Coppa's survived the 1906 earthquake, though in later years it moved to various other locations. *The Bohemians* situates it within its original Monkey Block home.

SADAKICHI HARTMANN, "THE KING OF BOHEMIA"

Born to a German father and Japanese mother, Sadakichi Hartmann was a noted photography critic and multifaceted artist. After leaving San Francisco, he did a stint in Hollywood, appearing as a magician in *The Thief of Bagdad*. He later retreated to a cabin in Banning, California, mostly living a hermit's life with the exception of visits from his friend, the actor John Barrymore. He died in Florida in 1944.

ANSEL ADAMS

Adams's photographs of Yosemite are among the most popular and enduring of all time. Both longtime residents of the Bay Area, Adams and Lange collaborated on several occasions. Their radically different treatments of the Japanese Internment

in 1942 foregrounded their temperamental and artistic differ-
ences, yet they were good friends and faithful champions of
each other's work. A passionate environmentalist, Adams died
in Monterey, California, in 1984.

MABEL DODGE (LUHAN)

After presiding over one of the most famous salons in American
history, Mabel moved to Taos, New Mexico, in 1918, where she
established an artists' colony, put on some of the first exhibi-
tions of Pueblo and Hispano art, and advocated for the rights of
the Taos Pueblo Indians. In 1923, she married her fourth husband, Tony Luhan, a Native American to whom she remained
married for the rest of her life. Mabel and Tony's guests also
included Georgia O'Keeffe, Martha Graham, Ansel Adams, and
Willa Cather. The novel puts D. H. and Frieda Lawrence in Taos
in 1919; in fact, they first visited Mabel there in 1923. Dorothea
Lange and Maynard Dixon visited the Southwest more than
once, with their longest stay at a cottage lent to them by Mabel
and her husband in 1931 to 1932. Mabel Dodge Luhan died in
Taos in August 1962.

JOHN PHARRELL

While John Pharrell and his son are fictional creations, they are
inspired by the real-life John Phelan (1861–1930), who served as
mayor of San Francisco from 1897 to 1902 and California's rep-
resentative in the U.S. Senate from 1915 to 1921. Phelan was
stridently opposed to Japanese and Chinese immigration to the
United States. His 1920 campaign slogan was "Keep California
White." In 2018 San Francisco's Phelan Avenue was renamed
Frida Kahlo Way.

CONSTANCE ("CONSIE") DIXON

Consie lived with her father and stepmother on and off for years. At age nineteen, she was hired as a reporter for the *San Francisco Examiner*. She lost her job in the Depression and worked for a time as a secretary to Mabel Dodge Luhan. She married and had a daughter, who lived with her until she was eight and was later formally adopted by her father's second wife. Consie refused to attend Lange's memorial, but would always be troubled by the decision. She herself died having experienced long periods of poverty and mental instability.

CAROLINE LEE

After working with Dorothea Lange to establish a thriving portrait studio at 540 Sutter Street in San Francisco, the woman referred to in most accounts as "Ah-yee" or the "Chinese Mission Girl" disappeared from Lange's story and into her own. This book is in part my imagining of her story.

Acknowledgments

In writing this story, I am indebted to a number of sources, including Linda Gordon's *Dorothea Lange: A Life Beyond Limits* and Milton Meltzer's *Dorothea Lange: A Photographer's Life*. Linda Gordon and Gary Y. Okihiro's *Impounded: Dorothea Lange and the Censored Images of the Japanese American Internment*, the Museum of Modern Art's *Dorothea Lange's Words & Pictures* and *Dorothea Lange: Politics of Seeing* helped me to better appreciate Lange's work. Maynard Dixon's work is beautifully showcased in Donald J. Hagerty's *The Art of Maynard Dixon*. *Imogen Cunningham: Ideas Without End* and *Consuelo Kanaga: An American Photographer* brought the lives and work of these two extraordinary women into focus. Enormously useful to my understanding of the experiences of Chinese Americans in the first decades of San Francisco's history were *Chinese San Francisco 1850–1943: A Trans-Pacific Community* by Yong Chen, *The Chinese in America: A Narrative History* by Iris Chang, *Unbound Feet: A Social History of Chinese Women in San Francisco* by Judy Yung, and *White Devil's*

Daughters: The Women Who Fought Slavery in San Francisco's Chinatown by Julia Flynn Siler.

Andra Miller helped guide this project in crucial ways and with such kindness and generosity. I am thankful to my agent, Sandra Dijkstra, as well as to Elise Capron, Andrea Cavallaro, and everyone on the Dijkstra team. I gratefully acknowledge the insights of Lydia Morrey and the work of Salt & Sage Books. Many thanks to my colleagues at California College of the Arts, particularly Leslie Carol Roberts and Tina Takemoto. Hiya Swanhuyser, who has written incisively about Monkey Block, introduced me to this extraordinary part of San Francisco history. Toni Piccinini is the steadiest, most generous friend I could wish for. Endless thanks go out to my family, Heshmat Darznik, Kiyan Darznik Banaee, and Sean Reiter. With love, gratitude, and admiration I dedicate this book to my friend Rebecca Foust.

ABOUT THE AUTHOR

JASMIN DARZNIK's debut novel, *Song of a Captive Bird*, was a *New York Times Book Review* "Editors' Choice," a *Los Angeles Times* bestseller, longlisted for the Center for Fiction Prize, and awarded the Writer's Center's First Novel Prize. Jasmin is also the author of the *New York Times* bestseller *The Good Daughter: A Memoir of My Mother's Hidden Life*. Her books have been published in seventeen countries. She was born in Tehran, Iran, and came to America when she was five years old. She holds an MFA in fiction from Bennington College, a JD from the University of California, Hastings, and a PhD in English from Princeton University. Now a professor of English and creative writing at California College of the Arts, she lives in the San Francisco Bay Area with her family.

jasmindarznik.com
facebook.com/jasmindarznikauthor
@jasmindarznik
Instagram: @jdarznik

ABOUT THE TYPE

This book was set in Dante, a typeface designed by Giovanni Mardersteig (1892–1977). Conceived as a private type for the Officina Bodoni in Verona, Italy, Dante was originally cut only for hand composition by Charles Malin, the famous Parisian punch cutter, between 1946 and 1952. Its first use was in an edition of Boccaccio's *Trattatello in laude di Dante* that appeared in 1954. The Monotype Corporation's version of Dante followed in 1957. Though modeled on the Aldine type used for Pietro Cardinal Bembo's treatise *De Aetna* in 1495, Dante is a thoroughly modern interpretation of that venerable face.